Penny

Penny Ingham has a degree
archaeology; she is often to l
trench with a trowel in her hand. After a career in newspapers
and the BBC, Penny now lives with her family in rural
Hampshire and writes full time. You can find out more by
visiting Penny's Facebook page, The Saxon Wolves, and by
following her on Twitter @pennyingham.

Praise for Penny's previous novels

'A pacy, engaging, enlightening and hugely enjoyable novel.'
The Historical Novel Society

'An exciting best seller bringing history alive, featuring
forbidden love, jealousy and betrayal and based, to a large
extent on fact.'
The Basingstoke Gazette

'For history and archaeology buffs, this novel is a treat.'
Book Bag

The Saxon Plague

PENNY INGHAM

To Joan,

Best wishes,

Penny Ingham

NERTHUS

First published in Great Britain in 2018 by Nerthus

A CIP catalogue record for this title is available from the British Library.

ISBN 978-0-9955034-1-0

Cover design by S. Hunt

Printed and bound by print2demand

Published by Nerthus

For Steve, James and Louise

Britain in 456 AD

ONE

The kingdom of the Dobunni, 456 AD

Snow was falling heavily and the freezing air was beginning to seep into Anya's bones. She pulled the hood of her cloak more tightly about her face, but the wool was wet and cold against her skin and she shivered violently. She had been heading west all day. There had been no sun to guide her, but she had felt the pull of her mother's homeland drawing her closer, like a beacon fire on a winter's night.

She had reached the pasturelands of Vortigern's kingdom now, a tree-less landscape on the top of the world, swept clean of all features by the rapidly settling snow. She shivered again. Fear was prowling at the edges of her mind, slinking closer to torment her with dark imaginings. She knew she had shamed Vortigern by running away from their marriage bed, just as she knew he would never abandon his search for her. If he found her, if he carried her back to Aquae Sulis like booty from a battlefield, what terrible punishment would he inflict upon her?

Certain she could hear the thundering hoof beats of his warband bearing down upon her, she glanced over her shoulder for the hundredth time, but all was silence. The

1

uplands of Vortigern's kingdom were utterly deserted; she could see neither village, nor farm, nor barn. Fear crept ever closer. This was the time of year when the days were at their shortest, when men looked back with nostalgia to the great fires of Samhain, and forward with hope to the spring festival of Imbolc, when the ewes would come into milk once again. This was not the time of year to spend a night outdoors, alone, with only a small, blunt dagger for protection.

Her footsteps faltered and she looked about, confused. She did not know how long she had been walking but darkness was falling. She was vaguely aware that she had stopped shivering and could no longer feel her fingers or toes, or the icy air biting at her cheeks. She took a few more steps but a deep sense of drowsiness was enveloping her. She wanted to sleep; she needed to sleep, just for a little while, just until she felt better.

'No! Keep walking!'

Anya opened her eyes and wondered if she had wandered into Nifheim, the underworld of ice and rime, final resting place to all those who die of illness or old age. It was several moments before she noticed the outline of a shepherd's hut against the darkening sky. Rubbing her eyes, she looked again. She had not imagined it. The shepherd's hut was still there.

Her legs felt like marrow jelly and she feared they might no longer support her weight. It took all of her willpower to put one foot in front of the other and her progress was painfully slow. With her last shred of strength, Anya pushed open the door of the hut, too exhausted even to utter a prayer of thanks to the goddess.

The small shelter was simply built, with walls and roof of coarsely hewn planking. As she had expected, it was deserted. In Germania, shepherds spent summer in huts such as these, guarding their flocks until it was time to herd them back to the villages for the winter months. The air smelled musty, with traces of rotting wood and unwashed men. There was an empty hearth in the centre of the earth floor, and a low rope-pallet bed, with neither mattress nor bedding, in the corner. Cooking pots and wooden platters were piled haphazardly on a rickety shelf.

Anya barred the door but cold air still crept between the gaps in the wall planking. The small leather pouch containing her fire-steel, flint and touchwood had been snatched from her belt by the storm off Tintagel all those months ago. She had little hope of lighting a fire now and besides, she had no firewood. But she needed to find a way to keep warm.

Her gaze settled on the small bale of straw propped against the wall. Crouching down, her numb fingers struggled to untie the twine that bound it. The straw fell to the floor, its brittle stalks releasing a sweet, fresh scent, redolent with memories of summer. She grabbed a handful and pushed it inside her cloak, continuing until she had built up a thick, prickly layer of insulation. Glancing down at the yellow stalks peeking from the edges of her cloak, she smiled ruefully. She looked like one of those sad, forgotten scarecrows, flung to the field edge after harvest. They too were cast out and all alone in the world.

The night wore on and the cold bore down. Hunger growled in her stomach and her thoughts turned maudlin and wretched. As the months had passed, each new blow had become harder to bear, stripping away her strength. She felt painfully vulnerable now, like the stalks of long summer grass she had played with as a child, peeling away the layers of stalk to expose the fragile green stem beneath.

At last, she fell into a fitful sleep. Her dreams were of her wedding night. Vortigern had failed to consummate their marriage but his brutality had left her feeling humiliated, abused and defiled. The dream shifted until it was no longer Vortigern looming over her, but high mountains. Britannia was drowning in blood, a deluge to end the age of men. And then she saw the sword, its ancient blade nicked by centuries of battle. It was held aloof and the blood could not reach it, as if it alone had the power to turn back the tide. Where was it? And why did she dream of it, night after night?

Her dreams repeatedly jolted her into wakefulness. Each time she stared fearfully into the blackness, fully expecting to feel the cold touch of a dagger at her throat. When dawn finally broke, she was chilled to the bone, her cloak pin-pricked with tiny drops of dew. They brought back memories of her mother's stories of the black-haired goddess Natt who rode the night skies upon her moon-silver mare, the foam upon its bridle falling as morning dew.

Anya stood up, straw tumbling from beneath her cloak. Tentatively, she opened the door. There was no sign of Vortigern or his warband; there was not another living soul in sight. It had stopped snowing but a heavy mist had settled and the air was oppressively still. Crouching down, she ate a handful of snow. It was a curious meal, neither solid nor liquid and although it did nothing to mask her hunger, her throat no longer felt so dry.

She began to turn slowly on her heel. There was no sun but she knew when she was facing north. Hengist and Horsa were in the north, holding back the painted Picts for Vortigern. Horsa, her kind and honourable brother, would willingly offer her sanctuary, but Hengist, the half-brother who had always hated her, was in command of the Saxon warband, and he would simply send her back to Vortigern.

4

No, she could not go north. She spun on her heel again. Now she was facing east, facing Germania. The pull, the yearning for her home, for her kin, was as fierce as fire. But she was exiled from her homeland. She could never return.

She made another quarter turn. Now she was facing south, facing Silvanus, and the pull was stronger still, like the moon pulling the oceans across the earth. Her heart ached for him, but she could not return to Dumnonia. According to the Christian church, she belonged to Vortigern now and he would kill any man who dared to presume otherwise.

She made a final quarter turn. Now she was facing west, facing Siluria. Her mother's homeland, the village she had been dreaming about for so long, a huddle of stone and slate in the shadow of high mountains. Her resolve hardened. This was the path she must take. This was what the goddess wanted.

And besides, there was nowhere else to go.

Tugging her damp cloak tightly about herself, she set a straight course across the snow covered fields, trying hard not to dwell on the fact that Vortigern's men knew every inch of his kingdom, whilst she was walking blind through an unfamiliar land.

The day wore on and the uplands began to fall away. If Taliesin's map was accurate, she was not far from the great tidal river now, and a ferry boat operated in the next village. She paused, torn with indecision.

She was a woman travelling alone with only a blunt dagger for protection, an easy target for thieves, or worse. But the road to Siluria lay across the river. If she did not take the ferry boat, she would have to walk inland, adding many miles to her journey. Whispering a potent charm of protection, she hurried on. The air was full of the sea now, salt and fish and the distant crying of gulls. Her eyes widened in awe at her first glimpse of the great river. It was wide and fast flowing, borne along by a fierce, incoming tide. She guessed the village was close now, for the river-bank was crowded with small coracles of wicker and hide, and brightly coloured clinker-built boats, eel traps and hemp nets.

The village was little more than a haphazard huddle of round-houses, clinging like limpets to the river's muddy bank as if afraid they might be swept along in its wake. Melting snow dripped from thatched roofs and ran in streams along the track. Herb and vegetable plots rested beneath the frost, and tethered goats bleated mournfully.

Anya walked into the centre of the village, looking about nervously. After the silence and solitude of the snow-swept uplands, the place was alive with noise and activity. The stench of fish filled the air, reminding her poignantly of the villages around Tintagel, but these women were not gutting herring or mackerel. Their baskets were filled with salmon the size of cats, and shiny eels, as broad as a man's wrist.

Her presence did not go unnoticed. One by one the villagers stopped what they were doing and turned in her direction. An ominous silence descended. Anya came to a sudden halt.

She had no horse and no visible sign of wealth, the gold torque about her neck hidden beneath her cloak. She was painfully aware of how wretched she must look: hollow cheeked with exhaustion, soaked to the skin and covered in the dirt of the road.

'I am looking for the ferry,' she said loudly.

The villagers stared at her, their expressions wary.

She tried again. 'Do you speak Latin?'

And still, they stared at her. A cold chill ran through her.

She wondered if this would always be her fate. The fate of the exile - the stranger who could not be trusted, the outsider who posed a threat. From the corner of her eye she saw a flash of movement. A man was bearing down upon her, moving fast. There was a long knife in his hand, and a jolt of terror shot through her. She spun on her heel and began to run, splashing through the puddles. She glanced over her shoulder. The man was gaining on her. She quickened her pace, vaguely aware that the villagers were closing in around her, creating a human barrier against her escape.

She hurtled towards them, her mind racing in panic. What should she do? Attempt to barge straight through them? Her pursuer was almost upon her; she could hear the sound of mud sucking at the soles of his boots. She felt his hand graze her shoulder. She changed direction, her boots skidding across the mud. This time he grabbed her long plaited hair, yanking it violently, as if she were a disobedient hound. She jerked to an agonising standstill, and pain exploded in her scalp.

She couldn't move, held fast by his tortuous grasp. He was going to knife her in the back. If the blade found her spine, she would never walk again. She would die slowly, a broken thing. But if the blade found its way to her heart, it would be quick, and these would be her last moments on earth.

Anya's terror gave way to a sense of fatalistic determination. She had come this far. She would not die in this forsaken village without putting up a fight. Slipping her hand beneath her cloak, she withdrew her dagger from her belt. Then she wrenched herself from his grasp and spun around to face him.

'Keep away from me!'

She saw the look of surprise upon his face, watched it quickly shift to anger. Without warning, he grabbed her wrist, twisting her arm forcefully behind her back. Anya gasped with pain and her dagger fell harmlessly into the mud. He was behind her now, holding her fast, his fish gutting knife across her throat. Anya froze. She knew that if she tried to move even a hair's breadth, her arm would break.

'Shall I kill her?' her captor shouted to the crowd, in the language of the Dobunni.

A man replied: 'I'd wager she's one of Tewdric's whores, sent to spy on us!'

Another voice: 'Aye, we can't let her report back to him, or he'll come for us next!'

And then another: 'We've no choice. We have to kill her!'

And now a woman: 'Yes, for our children's sake!'

Anya's fear intensified. She did not need to speak their language to understand the crowd were baying for her blood. The glistening fish guts smeared along the dagger blade smelled rank, and she fought down a wave of nausea. She had to do something. But what?

'I am a priestess, a healer,' she said loudly, in Latin. 'I mean you no harm.'

It was a futile gesture. She knew they did not understand her, but she could think of nothing else.

'Hold your tongue!' her captor snarled.

The knife pressed harder against her throat. The blade cut her skin, each shallow breath she took edging it deeper into the wound. Terror consumed her. She didn't want to die, not here, not like this.

'Rhodri? What is happening here?'

A wiry man of advanced years stepped out from the largest round-house, and the crowd parted to let him pass. He wore breeches, ankle-high boots and a simple homespun tunic that hung loosely from his thin frame. A lifetime lived outdoors upon the water had cured his skin the colour of smoked ham. He strode up to Anya. 'Who are you?' he asked, in the tongue of the Dobunni.

'She tried to kill me. She's a dangerous bitch,' Anya's captor complained.

'Let her speak, Rhodri.'

Rhodri muttered something under his breath then fell silent.

'You would be wise to tell me who you are,' the elderly man said, 'for my people wish you dead.'

Anya's mind was spinning. Unlike the villagers, this man's tone was calm, measured. And her captor appeared to have deferred to him, albeit unwillingly. Was it possible he was the village elder?

'Do you speak Latin?' she asked, more in desperation than hope.

'Only if I must,' the man replied in perfect Latin. 'So tell me, are you in Tewdric's pay?'

Anya felt a flood of relief. She could communicate with this man, perhaps even reason with him.

'I do not know this Tewdric,' she replied carefully. 'I am a priestess and a healer. And I am no threat to your village.'

The old man eyed her appraisingly then leant forward and tugged the edges of her cloak apart. Anya started in surprise. Rhodri's knife cut deeper into her skin, and she winced with pain. The village elder was staring fixedly at her gold torque.

'Who are your people?' he asked, his voice laden with mistrust.

Anya hesitated. If she admitted she was a Saxon, this man would most likely give the villagers their wish. Rhodri would slit her throat and her last memory on this earth would be the stink of three day old fish guts. 'I am of the Dumnonii,' she replied. It was only half a lie, for in her heart, she felt she belonged in Silvanus's kingdom.

'Dumnonia?' He sounded sceptical. 'I would have said your accent is Saxon.'

Anya's fleeting sense of hope quickly faded.

'No, you are mistaken.' She began to shake her head, but quickly realised her mistake as the knife edged ever deeper.

'Tell me about Dumnonia. Tell me about your people.'

She knew he was testing her. If she did not answer correctly, she would die. Pain, exhaustion and terror were making her head swim, and it was not easy to focus her thoughts.

'King Etar rules Dumnonia,' she began. 'He has two sons. Silvanus is the eldest and his heir. His youngest son, Lucan, is lately accused of treason for attempted patricide. I do not know his fate.'

The village elder raised his eyebrows, and Anya realised he had not heard this news.

'Etar's stronghold is Tintagel. I serve Taliesin, his high priest,' she went on, her heart hammering. 'I am not a spy. I'm a traveller, headed into the mountains.' She came to a breathless halt. Blood was flowing freely from the wound at her neck now, trickling over her collar bone. It felt warm against her cold skin.

'You travel into the mountains of Siluria?' the village elder asked incredulously. 'Why?'

How could she explain to him that a recurring dream was drawing her to Siluria, to a village in an isolated valley, surrounded by black, louring mountains?

'My father was of the Dumnonii, but my mother was of the Silures. I am going to find my kin.'

'How is it you speak Latin?'

10

'Perhaps for the same reason you do?' she replied evasively.

Their eyes met and Anya forced herself to match his gaze. She knew he was deciding if he should trust her. A heavy silence descended. After what seemed an age, he stepped back and addressed the crowd, first in his own tongue and then in Latin.

'This girl is not a spy for Tewdric, or for anyone else. She is no threat to us.'

Anya's sense of relief was short lived, for his gaze had settled on her gold torque again.

'But I must presume you are high-born?'

Anya hesitated again. If he believed her to be of value, would her life be in less danger, or more? Would he hold her captive and attempt to ransom her? When she did not reply, he looked searchingly into her eyes, as if hoping he might find the answer written there. And then he flicked his hand, a small impatient gesture.

'Let her go.'

'What? No?' Rhodri sounded angry.

'Don't argue with me. Do not forget I am the elder here.'

Anya could hear furtive mutterings from the crowd. Rhodri didn't move, his fury palpable. She sensed her life was literally in his hands now. If he chose to disobey the village elder, he could slit her throat in a heartbeat.

The two men were glaring fixedly at each other, their eyes locked in some kind of silent battle. Blood was still trickling down Anya's neck, and the pain in her pinioned arm was increasing.

And then, suddenly, Rhodri released her, pushing her roughly towards the village leader.

'If you're wrong about her, then you've just killed us all.'

Released from his grasp, Anya swayed dizzily. Taking a

11

deep, ragged breath, she glanced about warily. All eyes were upon her. It appeared the village elder had not convinced his people of her innocence. Her gaze fell upon her dagger and she stepped forward to pick it up. From the corner of her eye, she saw Rhodri match her step and she came to an abrupt standstill.

'Let me offer you some advice,' the village elder said curtly. 'You should turn back now. The Silures are barbarian savages, little better than beasts.'

'My mother was no savage,' Anya retorted.

The man shrugged. 'I tell it as I see it. And their king is no better. Tewdric's people starve because his rents are so severe, and when they can no longer pay him, he sells them as slaves to the highest bidder.'

Anya lowered her gaze and said nothing, thinking of her mother, torn from her kin and sold into slavery, long ago.

The village elder shook his head impatiently. 'You are insane, girl. Either the Silures will steal your gold and leave you dead in a ditch. Or Tewdric's men will take you, and you will spend the rest of your life as a slave.'

'I will take my chances. I need to cross the river. That is the way my path lies,' Anya replied, her confident air masking her deep unease. Was the man right? Was it utter madness to journey into Siluria alone?

He bent down to retrieve her dagger and placed it in her hand. 'It seems I cannot change your mind, so I will say no more about it.' His tone was milder now. 'I apologise for the inhospitable reception, but these are uncertain times. We have grown wary of strangers. Please, let us make amends. Eat with us tonight.'

Anya replaced the dagger at her belt with trembling fingers. On the one hand, his offer was tempting. A mouth-watering aroma of frying fish was drifting from the largest round-house. She needed to tend to her wound. She also yearned for sleep, for food, and for warm, dry clothes. On the other hand, she was no longer so naive to trust men who, only moments earlier, had held a fish gutting knife to her throat and called for her blood.

'Thank you, but no,' she said stiffly. 'Is there someone who can take me across the river?'

He nodded. 'I will arrange it.'

As Anya stepped onto the wide flat-bottomed ferry, a little girl with long, plaited hair thrust a parcel into her hand. Wrapped inside the cloth was a slice of fried fish wedged between two slabs of bread. Anya ate it quickly. It tasted wonderful, like nectar from the world tree of Yggdrasil.

The current was strong and it took four men to row the ferry across the river. The far bank was swathed in mist and its eerie silence seemed somehow ominous and threatening. Each soft plash of the oars took her closer to the village in the shadow of the mountain, closer to Tewdric's lawless kingdom. Daylight was fading as the ferry reached the wooden jetty on the opposite shore.

'Go to the temple. The old priests will look to your wound and give you shelter for the night,' the nearest oarsman said in the clipped, nasal language of the Dobunni, his face red with exertion. 'And you should make an offering to the old god, because I'll wager you'll need good fortune in the kingdom of Siluria.'

'I don't understand you,' Anya said apologetically.

The man pointed up the hill, and made a series of hand gestures to get his message across. She nodded and offered them one of Taliesin's gold coins as payment, but they refused to take it. 'Worthless Roman coins are no use to us.'

'It's solid gold. It was minted long before Britannia bowed to Rome. Here, see for yourself.' She thrust the coin into the nearest man's hand.

They bit the coin and scratched it with broken fingernails. Eventually, still shaking their heads suspiciously, they accepted it, and rowed back the way they had come.

Anya watched them until they disappeared into the low lying fog. Her boots were sinking into the mud but she waited until she could no longer hear the sound of their oars through the water. Only then did she turn and look up at the temple of Nodens, perched on a steep spur of land, high above the river. Her gaze settled on the winding track that led up the hillside. It ran through a dense, dark forest of oak and ash and elm. Images of bears, wolves and outlaws darted across her mind and she swallowed nervously.

Beyond the river, Taliesin's map bore a single annotation, a faded image of a snow capped mountain range. It was useless now. It could not guide her to her mother's home. What chance did she have in a dangerous, unfamiliar land with only a dagger for protection? And even if the merciful goddess led her to the village of slate and stone, would anyone there remember Eown? What kind of welcome could she hope to receive?

TWO

The kingdom of the Atrebates

The snow had melted and the pot-holed road was awash with water. Vortigern was cold and saddle sore and the piece of dried beef he had been chewing for the last two hours had the taste and consistency of old leather. He turned in his saddle to face Rufus. He thought his tax-collector looked ridiculous on a horse. With his scrawny body, nervy demeanour and black beady eyes, he resembled an emaciated pigeon perched on a roof-top.

'So, Marcus has broken the terms of the treaty?' Vortigern asked bluntly.

'Yes, lord,' Rufus replied.

Vortigern belched loudly. He watched Rufus's face wrinkle in distaste and decided to rile him further by spitting the dried beef into the nearest puddle. Rufus closed his eyes in disgust, his already pale face turning an unhealthy shade of green.

'Journey sick, are we?' Vortigern taunted, enjoying himself now.

'No, lord,' Rufus replied dully, his lips compressing into a thin, hard line. He shifted awkwardly and then, as if abandoning all hope of comfort, his shoulders sagged and he slumped forward in the saddle like a deflating pig's bladder. Vortigern had seen sacks of turnips with more finesse in the saddle. The man was an embarrassment, feeble both in mind and body, and without any discernible masculine virtues. Vortigern loathed effeminate men; they were an abhorrence of nature. Rufus was utterly useless but for his uncanny ability to tax people until they bled.

Vortigern glanced over his shoulder. His household guards were on horseback and they put Rufus to shame. Straight-backed, heads held high, they rode under the command of Julianus. Vortigern had always found him to be a distractingly ugly man, with his overly large forehead, jumble of uneven teeth and abnormally pronounced jaw. But for all his unsightliness, Julianus was a brave, steady and loyal soldier.

The rest of Vortigern's warband were on foot, a cohort of three hundred shield-warriors bristling with iron-tipped, ash-wood spears. Vortigern pushed another piece of dried beef into his mouth and began to chew it loudly. He did not enjoy being beholden to anyone, but three hundred spears spoke louder than any words. He needed these men. Men willing to die defending the banner of the black boar, but it was a constant thorn in his arse that they expected land, gold and interminable feasting in return.

His gaze fell on his son and his sense of irritation increased. Many people told him Ronan was his spitting image, but he couldn't see it. Ronan was pale and listless, no doubt exhausted from yet another night of drinking, whoring and generally avoiding responsibility of any kind. Vortigern had begun to suspect his son was a changeling child, until he had redeemed himself on the battlefield last autumn, making light work of separating the old king of the Coritani's head from his shoulders, thus annexing yet another powerful kingdom. But

16

he had no intention of lavishing his son with praise, for in all other matters, Ronan was a wastrel and as useless as a puppy. And puppies needed slapping down, not spoiling with tasty treats. He turned back to Rufus. 'So, why didn't the garrison commander kill Marcus and be done with it?'

'I believe it was out of deference for your friendship, lord.' Rufus sneezed, his eyes red-rimmed and streaming. 'Forgive me but I have developed horse-fever again.'

Vortigern rolled his eyes impatiently. 'Give me strength.'

Rufus looked away. There was a shard of resentment in his gut. It had been festering for a long, long time, and each snide comment, each sarcastic eye roll, wormed the shard a little deeper. Removing the cloth from his purse again, he dabbed his watering eyes. They itched mercilessly, but he dared not rub them for it would only make the condition worse. When he spoke again, his voice had a curiously nasal quality.

'Calleva contributes fifty percent of its harvest in return for a garrison to guard the city -' he began but Vortigern shouted over him.

'I remember the terms of the treaty!'

Rufus pulled a sour face. 'The sacks were loaded on the carts and all appeared to be in order until Plautius led my agent to another granary on the edge of the city. It was found to be full of grain.'

'Why would Plautius betray Marcus like that?' Vortigern interrupted again.

'Perhaps he fears you more than he fears Marcus,' Rufus replied through gritted teeth. 'But whatever the reason, Marcus is now refusing to hand over the surplus grain. He demands to speak to you.'

Vortigern grimaced. Over the last few years, he had picked off the towns of the Atrebates one by one, forcing them to agree to brutally harsh terms. It was a system that had worked remarkably smoothly, until Marcus had dared to defy him. He had known the man all his life. They had played together as children whilst their fathers had spent their days hunting wild boar in the forests around Calleva - in the days when the Dobunni and the Atrebates had been allies, in the days when there had been time for sport, and life had been so much simpler.

The town of Calleva came into view on the horizon. It sat on a spur of land, its high flint walls dominating the rolling fields of the Atrebates. An image of Anya darted across Vortigern's mind. He had first laid eyes on her in Calleva. From the moment she had walked into Marcus's dining hall he had been captivated.

She did not look like a typical Saxon; her eyes were an extraordinary green and her hair was the colour of fire. She was feisty and headstrong, but she belonged to him and he wanted her back. He had sent riders into the winter storms. His arm was long and she would not be able to hide from him forever. He would find her and bring her home.

And those who had given her shelter would be punished severely. Just as Anya would be punished for running away, and for unmanning him with her witchcraft on their wedding night. He had told no-one of his failure in the marital bed, but there were times when he felt the shame was burning a hole in his gut. The girl was a pagan witch and he wanted to beat her until the rugs on his bed were stained with her blood, and just the thought of it made him hard.

He gave the signal to halt, and the command was passed down the line. Through the open gates of the town, he could see Marcus and his fellow council members, huddled together like cowering children. Surrounding them in a loose semi-

18

circle stood the massed ranks of Vortigern's garrison, a hundred strong, their hands on the hilts of their swords. Charged by Vortigern to keep martial law, their eyes were cold and battle-hardened. The silence was absolute.

Vortigern dismounted, wincing as his feet hit the ground. He was forty years of age but on days such as these, when every battle wound ached, he felt much older. He straightened up and turned to face his men.

'Ronan, Julianus, with me. The rest, wait here – battle ready.'

Thrusting the reins of his stallion at the nearest soldier, Vortigern entered a town that seemed to be holding its breath. With Ronan and Julianus at his heels, he walked straight up to Marcus. The leader of the council of Calleva always reminded him of the ancient statues that filled the niches in the basilica of Aquae Sulis, for Marcus still clung to the old Roman ways with his freshly laundered toga, clean shaven face and neatly cut hair. But Marcus appeared to have aged considerably since they last met. His face was now gaunt and deeply lined, his hair flecked with grey.

Vortigern quickly assessed his surroundings with a soldier's eye. They were standing at a crossroads. The ranks of his garrison were blocking the road that led into the centre of the city. To his left and right, two muddy roads ran parallel to the city walls. They were lined with houses, taverns and workshops, all falling into ruin, melting snow dripping from their broken roof tiles. They looked deserted although he suspected many eyes were watching him through the cracks between barred doors and shuttered windows.

He turned back to Marcus. 'You wanted to see me?'

Marcus took so long to reply that Vortigern began to wonder if the man had lost his tongue. A muscle was working furiously in Marcus's jaw. Finally, he said, 'I did not expect you to come.'

'We were friends once,' Vortigern replied carelessly.

'Then let us talk as we once did, without all these,' Marcus glanced towards Vortigern's men, 'distractions.'

'We can talk here.'

A look of alarm flashed briefly across Marcus's face.

'Very well. I am willing to give you a generous share of our harvest -'

But Vortigern cut him off. 'The terms of the treaty we signed were simple, and yet you chose to betray me.'

Marcus's hands were clenched into fists at his sides and he sounded breathless now, as if he had run a great distance. 'When I was elected leader of the council of Calleva, I swore an oath to serve and protect its citizens. If I give you the disputed grain, they will starve before the winter is out. I cannot allow it to happen. My conscience will not allow it happen.'

Vortigern let out a sigh of exasperation and ran a hand over the bristly stubble on his shaved head. He stepped closer to Marcus, towering menacingly over the smaller man.

'I don't give a fuck about the oaths you made to the people of Calleva. We signed a treaty, before witnesses. You agreed to give me half your harvest.'

Marcus held his ground but his face was utterly drained of colour now. 'You are a man of honour, Vortigern. I cannot believe you would want women and children to starve.'

'You are wrong on both counts, old friend. I have never been a man of honour and it is no concern of mine whether the women and children of Calleva starve this winter.'

Cries of outrage erupted from the councillors, but Vortigern silenced them by raising a hand. 'I need your grain

20

to feed my army. It can't fight without bread in its belly. And if it can't fight then Britannia will fall to the Saxons, the Picts and the Irish. Is that what you want?'

'You are being unreasonable.' There was an unmistakeable tremor in Marcus's voice now.

'No. It is you who is being unreasonable, Marcus. But this can still be resolved amicably. Give me what I am owed, and I will forget this unfortunate incident ever happened.'

'I cannot give you the grain,' Marcus replied quietly.

Vortigern sighed. He had come here out of deference for their friendship, but he had always known it would be a waste of time. It had been inevitable that Marcus would not capitulate, and equally inevitable that he would have to die.

'Kill them all!' he commanded. 'But Marcus is mine.'

The crossroads erupted into chaos. His garrison drew their swords, closing in. Some of the councillors were whimpering like children whilst others began to scream, but they were as trapped as wild boar in a thicket. One councillor produced a short-sword from beneath his cloak, only for it to be flung from his grasp by the brutal thrust of a shield. Another stabbed a knife towards a soldier's belly and was repaid in kind with a spear plunged into his gut. The rest of the councillors were unarmed, and they fell where they stood. The butchery was a short, sharp and brutal.

Vortigern was pleased to see Marcus scramble to pick up his fellow councillor's fallen sword, for there was no sport in killing an unarmed man. Marcus's anger was twisting his features into an inhuman snarl. He swung the blade awkwardly, missing Vortigern's torso by several feet.

'*The man is no soldier. No doubt grown weak from interminable council meetings,*' Vortigern mused, drawing his own sword.

Marcus lunged again, and Vortigern neatly sidestepped

from the path of his blade. In the split heartbeat before Marcus regained his footing, Vortigern stepped forward. With a precise, controlled flick of his sword, a long gash appeared above Marcus's right elbow. Marcus gasped as blood began to seep through his woollen toga. He gritted his teeth and lunged at Vortigern again, but Vortigern parried with ease.

And then, with a second delicate flick of the wrist, Vortigern's blade sliced another deep cut across Marcus's right forearm, this time below the elbow. Marcus staggered, his face contorted with pain. He swung his sword again but the grip was slick with his blood now and his fingers were losing their grasp.

Vortigern parried the blow as easily as if he were swotting away a fly. Marcus stumbled backwards but managed to right himself, and then he charged forward again. Vortigern waited until Marcus was almost upon him and then he thrust his sword deep into the muscle of the man's right thigh. Marcus went rigid for a heartbeat and then collapsed to his knees.

'Please, I beg you,' he whimpered in agony.

Vortigern stepped closer. At times like this he felt strangely separate. Deep inside, he knew it was dark and shameful to take such pleasure in inflicting pain, and one small part of him felt saddened by his friend's suffering. But a much larger part felt exhilarated beyond measure. To hold a man's life in the palm of your hand was more intoxicating, more arousing than anything on earth.

'Father,' Ronan said under his breath. 'He has suffered enough.'

Vortigern spun around and grabbed a handful of Ronan's leather cuirass, wrenching his son towards him until their noses were almost touching.

'Don't question me boy, or I'll have you whipped.'

Ronan tore himself from his father's grasp, his eyes blazing with anger and humiliation.

Vortigern turned back to Marcus. It appeared his last sword cut had severed an artery for the man was losing a lot of blood. The sword had slipped from his grasp and he was barely conscious. Vortigern kicked him in the chest and Marcus fell onto his back like a toppled toy soldier. Taking a step closer, Vortigern nudged him with his boot.

'Your city will return to the earth, and you only have yourself to blame. I am your high king, and I will be obeyed.'

Marcus's eyelids flickered open. 'May God forgive you.'

'Oh, he will,' Vortigern replied and then he sheathed his sword and took his dagger from his belt. He was not a barbarian; it was time to put the man out of his misery. Crouching down, he slit Marcus's throat and watched his old friend gasp and choke as the life faded from his eyes.

Vortigern straightened up. His back was aching and he longed for a hot bath, but his veins were still charged with battle fever.

'Let it be known throughout Britannia,' he roared, addressing the citizens of Calleva cowering behind their locked doors, 'that this is the fate of all those who defy me.'

Julianus came to stand at his side. There was blood on his leather cuirass, on his hands and face.

'Your orders, lord?'

'Put Marcus's head on the north gate. Burn the rest. And hang any trouble-makers on the street corners.'

'Yes, lord.'

Rufus was scuttling towards them, shoulders hunched, hands clasped to his chest. He had all the traits of a wood louse: small, insignificant and pitifully easy to squash. His eyes were darting from one heap of corpses to the next.

23

'You've killed them all...' he began, his face pale with shock.

'Marcus and his council rebelled against my authority. What did you think I was going to do? Dine with them?' Vortigern asked, exasperated.

Rufus was still gazing about the crossroads, his expression one of appalled disbelief. Vortigern grabbed hold of his shoulders.

'Listen to me, you imbecile. Get the grain on the carts and get it out of the city. Now!' Vortigern enunciated every word as if talking to a half-wit. 'Do you understand?'

The rebuke felt like a slap and Rufus tensed against the blow. He nodded mutely, his entire body taut with suppressed rage.

Vortigern released him, pushing him away as carelessly as if he were a stray dog. But he saw the look of loathing in Rufus's eyes, for the scribe was making no attempt to disguise it. If Rufus had not been as ineffectual as a twig, he might have felt a twinge of alarm at such blatant animosity, but as it was, he found the man's impotent rage faintly amusing.

Ronan was yawning loudly, and Vortigern felt his patience snap. 'Where's your stamina?' he railed. 'I didn't raise a son of mine to be tired all the time. What's the matter with you for God's sake?'

'I need to eat,' Ronan replied dully. 'Killing is hungry work.'

'*I need to eat.*' Vortigern's imitation of Ronan's sulky tone was cruelly accurate. 'You sound like a mewling girl. Has the snow shrivelled your balls?'

When Ronan did not reply, Vortigern glanced sharply at his son. Ronan's expression was infuriatingly familiar. It was utterly blank, as if a shutter had fallen behind his eyes.

Father and son stood side by side in stony silence and

24

watched Vortigern's men throwing the corpses onto the pyre. Rain then sleet began to fall, the fire-wood was damp, and the corpses were drenched. Their clothes steamed like suet puddings over a kitchen fire before more kindling was brought, and the slaughtered council members of Calleva finally began to burn.

'The job is done,' Vortigern said abruptly. 'We have Calleva's grain. Enough to see our army through this damned winter. We got what we came for. Come on, let's find some food.'

The main street of Calleva ran north towards the centre of the town. Vortigern's men were looting enthusiastically, breaking down the hastily-barricaded doors of the finest homes and carrying away their treasures like a line of ants from a honey cake. Vortigern and Ronan kept to the middle of the road and neither made any comment on the terrible screams drifting from within.

Vortigern's thoughts had already left Calleva far behind. Britannia was like a game of chess and for as long as he could remember he had battled to control all the pieces. But it was a never-ending game, and like a battlefield carrion crow hopping from corpse to corpse, his mind was darting from one problem to the next.

Ronan had slaughtered Pascent of the Coritani but his young son, Aquila, had survived the battle. For the time being, the Coritani were paying their tribute on time, but Aquila had watched his father die, and what was the purpose of sons if not to avenge their fathers? It was only a matter of time before the Coritani marched upon the Dobunni again.

Vortigern quickened his pace, his thoughts tumbling over themselves like butter in a churn. There was a particular piece on the board he had coveted for a very long time. Dumnonia lay at the very edge of Britannia, a wild and isolated kingdom that no-one would remember were it not for the gold, silver, copper and tin that lay beneath its soil. With the coming of spring, he intended to slaughter the entire in-bred house of Etar and claim the throne for himself.

Vortigern allowed himself a brief moment of satisfaction. His father and grandfather before him had governed with distinction. Every decision he made, every action he took, was in honour of their memory. But with kingship came heavy responsibility, the responsibility to mete out justice, to maintain order. He felt his forebears would have been proud of him today.

'If your soldiers kill any more of Calleva's citizens, there'll be no-one left to harvest the fields, except perhaps the Saxons, of course,' Ronan said slyly.

'So you do have a tongue after all?'

Ronan ignored his father's jibe. 'The Saxons are like rats. The south coast is over-run with them. They are pillaging and slaughtering and taking farmland for themselves. Hengist has broken the terms of the treaty a hundred times over, and yet you do nothing!'

'It's not his warband pillaging the coast,' Vortigern replied testily. 'He is in the north, fighting the Picts, just as we agreed. Any man can be bought, as long as you are willing to pay the price. And I have bought Hengist's loyalty with a few hundred acres of farmland by Corinium, although I doubt he will find much pleasure in it. Borderlands are notoriously difficult to control. I fully expect the Catuvellauni and Coritani to come in the night and burn their barns and take their women and children for slaves.'

'It will be no more than they deserve. But in the meantime, Hengist's banner flies over the fort of Andereida, and it is at

Andereida that the Saxon boats land,' Ronan retorted angrily.

'What would you have me do?' Vortigern rounded on his son. 'I do not have enough warriors to patrol every border. I need his warband.'

'But you can't trust him -'

Vortigern raised a hand to silence him.

'I trust no-one. It's the first rule of kingship and you would do well to remember it.'

'But you trusted Anya, didn't you? And yet she ran away,' Ronan needled.

'Shut your mouth, boy!'

Vortigern's battle fever was abating rapidly. As usual, it had left behind a feeling of irritability and emptiness that only the thrill of more killing could slake. Unless he wanted outright civil war, there had been enough death today, but there was one other option that might improve his mood.

The inn was down a narrow side street. Its regulars had fled, but the prettiest girls of Calleva had been wrenched from their distraught families and barricaded into a back room as reward for Vortigern's soldiers. An officer was attempting to bring some kind of order, but Vortigern cleared a path through the crowd like an enraged bull in a potter's shop.

He flung open the door and chose quickly. She was perhaps fourteen years old. She lay on the filthy floor, spread-eagled beneath a young soldier whose bare buttocks were pumping up and down vigorously. The girl's eyes were dead, as if she had no more tears to spill.

Vortigern punched the soldier viciously in the left kidney. He cried out in pain and Vortigern plucked him off the girl as if he was removing a sated leech.

'Get out! All of you! Out!'

The boy, doubled up in agony, grabbed his clothes and fled.

Unfastening his breeches, Vortigern straddled the young girl then bellowed at the officer in the doorway. 'Bring me some food! I'm starving.'

He had bedded many women since his disastrous wedding night with Anya, each nameless girl an attempt to rid himself of his mortification. Each time his seed flowed, he felt as if a tiny shard of shame had been chipped from the block of humiliation he carried like a quern stone around his neck. The girl turned her face from him as he thrust repeatedly into her young flesh. His moment of release came quickly. His body relaxed, spent, and he felt a fleeting sense of blissful absolution.

THREE

Tintagel, kingdom of Dumnonia

They laid Etar to rest in the burial mound overlooking the sea, where countless generations of kings had lain before him. They buried him with gold and silver, so he would be wealthy in the world beyond, with fine platters for feasting and an amphora of Lucius's best wine because Etar had been most partial to its fine flavour.

Silvanus stood beside his father's shrouded body in the fetid gloom of the chamber. The wicks of the tallow candles hissed in the draughts and cast flickering shadows down the narrow entrance passageway. His gaze drifted to the neat piles of bones lying in the dark recesses of the chamber. Taliesin had told him stories of the ancient, half-forgotten rituals of Samhain Eve, how the ancient Dumnonii had shared their homes with the bones of their ancestors, before returning them to their final resting place the following day.

One part of him found the idea so morbid, so alien and so far removed from acceptable behaviour. And yet, as he stood in the musty darkness another part of him could still feel a lingering sense of connection to the spirits of his forebears. They had built this ancient tomb; they had understood the movements of the sun and moon. Each year at dawn on the mid-winter solstice, a shaft of sunlight flooded down the long passageway. It illuminated the ancient carving of the ship that would carry Etar on his final voyage. Its high bows faced east, its decks filled with stick figures of departed souls. And above the ship, Lugh, the circular sun, guided them on their journey to the golden land of the gods.

Silvanus knelt and touched his father's face. The shroud was cold and damp and he withdrew his hand abruptly. A thousand memories flooded his mind but one image rose to the surface.

A *bright summer's day, a deserted beach. A father and son were running across the sand, laughing, with seemingly not a care in the world. The father was fit and strong and powerful and the small boy wanted nothing more than to keep up with him, and to grow up to be just like him.*

Silvanus stood up again. He cast one final look at his father's body then turned and walked back down the dark passageway, taking care not to crack his head on the low granite roof slabs. After the darkness of the burial chamber, the bright daylight made him blink and the fierce, gusting wind took his breath away. He stood for a long time on the cliff-top, staring out to sea, angry with the gods for taking his father, and bitter with grief, for the world felt empty without him.

He was the new king of Dumnonia now. The years of his life stretched bleakly before him, endless responsibility and decision making, until his strength was spent and he too was laid to rest in the burial chamber on the cliff top. Etar had been a great king, and he was very afraid he would never live up to his father's high ideals. What if he made the wrong decisions? What if his people suffered because of his incompetence? It would all be so much easier to bear if Anya was by his side. When she was with him, the world had not seemed so overwhelming.

But she was not here. She was far away. She was Vortigern's wife, sharing Vortigern's bed. Silvanus put a hand to his temple, forcing the unwelcome images from his mind. He was king now but he didn't know what to do. He didn't even know where to start. What had Anya said in that cold watchtower room?

Just start at the beginning and the rest will follow.'

Squaring his shoulders, he turned around. The crowd of mourners were waiting in respectful silence, their cloaks billowing in the wind. They would have waited until the sun set then rose again if necessary. From this day on, Dumnonia would move at his pace, guided by his hand. It was a terrifying thought.

Anya's words echoed around his head. And so he took a deep breath and said, 'my father was the greatest of men and I am humbled he chose me to be his successor, just as I am honoured that the council chose unanimously to endorse his decision. I pledge to serve the kingdom of Dumnonia with my heart, my body and my soul. I swear by Epona to put my duty to you, my people, above all else, each and every day, from this day forward, until such time as I am laid to rest beside Etar in the burial chamber of our ancestors.'

Silvanus bowed his head. In a time-honoured gesture of unity and support, the assembled crowd placed their right hands over the cartwheel shaped clasps that held their cloaks in place, the symbol of Lugh, the sun god, who even now was guiding Etar on his final journey. No-one spoke, but the noise on the cliff top was deafening. The ever-present, howling wind; the cries of gulls circling overhead; the shrieks of

31

guillemots diving for fish from the stacks below. Silvanus did not hear any of it. He was thinking of his treacherous half-brother, imprisoned in the watch-tower of Tintagel. And he was thinking of Vortigern. It was surely only a matter of time before the army of the Dobunni marched on Tintagel.

For centuries, large scale conflict had mercifully passed Dumnonia by, and Etar had seen no reason to change the status quo, preferring to place his faith in the gods to keep his kingdom safe. But Silvanus did not plan to put his father's unyielding faith to the test.

He had a warband, fifty men, tried and proven, but what he needed was an army. He had horses aplenty. Dumnonia was famous for them, traded across the world. He would train cavalry, and he would train infantrymen. He would teach fisher-folk and farmers to ride, to wield a spear, a shield, a sword.

One by one, Silvanus's men offered their condolences. Evric, his oldest friend, stepped forward to embrace him. He was handsome and charming but there was no sign of his infectious grin today. Instead, his eyes were full of compassion for his king.

'I am here for you, just as I have always been,' he said quietly.

'I know it, and I am always grateful for it,' Silvanus replied as they drew apart.

Boult, Gorran and Jago, resplendent in their warriors' garb, gathered around him, a shield in human form, as if their imposing presence might somehow protect their king from his grief. Gorran was tall and wiry, with all the nervous energy of an unbroken colt. Jago was a calmer soul, impossibly handsome with dark eyes and black hair, like so many of the Dumnonii. He had been married for just over a year, and

32

adored his beautiful wife, Eloise. Boult was built like an ox, solid in both body and mind, steadfast, dependable and loyal.

Taliesin approached, leaning heavily on a walking stick, his thin frame buffeted by the strong wind. The old priest looked emaciated and fragile and Silvanus's jaw clenched. He had just lost his father and it was unthinkable he might soon lose Taliesin as well.

'My lord,' Taliesin bowed low, white faced and clearly in pain.

Silvanus placed a hand on the old man's elbow. 'There's no need for that.'

The priest straightened up. 'Thank you, lord,' he said gratefully. 'I wonder if I may say a few words.'

'Of course,' Silvanus nodded and stepped aside.

The old priest took a deep, laboured breath. His chest rattled like rustling leaves and when he spoke, the wind carried his words away.

'Let us now prepare for the funeral feast. Let us sit down and eat together, as is our ancient tradition. Let us give praise to Epona, our goddess, the protector of our land, our people and our herds. Let us share the flesh of the sacrificed mare, and so bind the new king to his people, to his land and to his gods.'

Taliesin dropped his hands to his sides. His shoulders sagged and he closed his eyes. Alarmed, Silvanus stepped forward and took the old man's arm. Taliesin gave a start and Silvanus wondered if the old priest had actually fallen asleep standing up.

'Here, let me escort you.'

Silvanus helped the old man into the covered wagon and drew the drapes to give him some privacy.

'Take it slowly,' he told the wagon master.

A stable boy approached. 'Shall I bring your horse, lord?'

But Silvanus shook his head. 'No, I'll walk.'

Jago rode back to ensure all was ready for the feast, leaving Evric, Boult and Gorran to accompany Silvanus on foot. They kept a respectful distance and made no attempt at conversation, as if sensing he needed some time alone.

Silvanus strode on ahead, quickly putting more distance between them. At twenty five years of age, he was a strikingly handsome man, with a honed, warrior's physique. He exuded a commanding presence but outward appearances are often deceptive. Inside, like hot fat spitting in a pan, his emotions were spiking dangerously out of control.

Ever since Anya had ridden away with Rufus, Silvanus had fought against a compelling desire to march on the kingdom of the Dobunni, slaughter Vortigern and carry her back to Tintagel. But then a voice inside his head would remind him of their last moments together in the cold watch-tower room. They had talked about duty and sacrifice.

'My best interests?' he had asked bitterly. 'Don't you mean Dumnonia's best interests?'

'They are one and the same. At least, they should be,' Anya had replied.

Silvanus reached the courtyard of Tintagel burdened with self-loathing. Anya didn't want him to ride to her rescue. Above all else, she wanted to protect the people of Dumnonia. Anya was a truly good person. A better person than he would ever be.

Evric was waiting for him. 'How do you feel about eating horse flesh, then?' he asked, placing a hand on Silvanus's shoulder.

'Uncomfortable.' Silvanus grimaced. 'Apart from anything else, our horses are sacred to Epona.'

'Our goddess will forgive you,' Evric replied lightly. 'Just be grateful you're no longer expected to mate with the mare first.'

Silvanus shuddered and grinned simultaneously.

Bolt had caught up with them. 'I heard that in the old days, once you'd mated with the mare, you had to sleep with a virgin - something about binding you to your land and to your people?'

'That's more like it,' Evric mused. 'But whether we could find a virgin willing to share Silvanus's bed is another matter!'

Silvanus rolled his eyes. 'Very funny.'

He stopped for a moment in the doorway of the great hall, taking in its familiar sights, sounds and scents. Fine tapestries of hunting scenes hung from the walls, and intricate carvings of horse races spiralled up the wooden aisle posts towards the roof joists.

No raised dais separated the high king of Dumnonia from his people. Instead, there was one long, oak table, laid with fine silver and glass ware, decorated with winter greenery and lit with hundreds of sweet smelling beeswax candles.

The guests were already seated, talking in subdued tones as befitted the sombre occasion. Huge joints of mare's flesh were roasting on spits over the central hearth, droplets of fat hissing into the flames.

'*It smells like beef,*' Silvanus thought vaguely and then his gaze drifted to the table.

There was no place set for Etar. No place for Anya. There was no place set for Lucan either. Silvanus ran a hand through his hair, an unconscious gesture of frustration.

Lucan and Mairi were under house arrest but it was not a permanent solution. Lucan's crime carried a sentence of death, but Lucan was his own flesh and blood. He remembered the day he had been born, a mewling babe with a shock of shiny jet curls and blackcurrant eyes. He had loved him then...

'Time to eat horse flesh,' Evric said lightly, jolting him from his dark thoughts.

Silvanus smiled grimly. 'Let's pray I don't vomit at my own initiation ceremony.'

And then, with his oldest friend at his side, he entered the great hall of Tintagel, and his people rose from their benches to greet their new king.

This is it', Silvanus thought. *'And so it begins.'*

FOUR

The kingdom of Siluria

Anya knew she was close to her mother's village now, even though Eown had rarely spoken of her homeland. It was not so much a sense of familiarity or recognition, but more a fierce, persistent tugging at the edge of her mind, guiding her and giving her the strength to continue, to put one foot in front of the other, mile after aching mile.

At night she had sheltered in empty shepherds' huts, and once in the hollow trunk of an oak. She had heard wolves howling in the forest, and watched a great brown bear devour a salmon struggling to leap a waterfall. But, despite the village elder's dire warnings, she had seen no sign of Tewdric or his slave traders - thus far.

She had been following the stream for several days as it wound its way through a bleak, treeless landscape. But now the louring mountains were all around her, sheer precipices and soaring crags that towered above her like the crests of waves about to break. Anya shivered. She was a child of the flat lands of Saxony, where all the world was sky. It was hard to believe this intimidating, alien landscape had been her mother's home. She passed ancient burial cairns, many reduced to mere tumbles of slate, and in the distance a circle of standing stones, black silhouettes against the wide expanse of snow. The path climbed higher and the towering mountains closed in, crowding out the grey sky. The stream was tumbling over vertical waterfalls now, crashing into deep pools encircled with moss and ferns.

Stones, carved with curious swirling symbols, marked the path. She stared at them as she passed by, wondering if they were markers, or an ancient curse on anyone who did not belong here. The path continued to climb, steeper than before. Finally, when she feared her lungs might burst, the incline lessened, the track wending its way up a gentle slope of scattered boulders and scree. And still the stream hurried from the mountains, gurgling noisily over its rocky bed. She followed it, picking her way between landslides of fallen rocks until at last she came to the crest of the slope.

The view was spectacular. The stream was calmer now, meandering gently along the bottom of a steep sided valley. The snow covered mountains were catching the last rays of the setting sun, and they glinted as if inlaid with garnets and gold.

And there, in the distance, was the village of slate and stone. It lay nestled beneath the mountains, a handful of round-houses squatted behind a rampart and ditch enclosure. Dusk was falling and only the bleating of sheep disturbed the tranquil silence. It was all just as she had seen it in her dreams. It was almost impossible to comprehend but, against all the odds, she had found her mother's home.

Lifting her face to the sky, she offered a prayer of thanks to the goddess. She realised she was trembling, every nerve and sinew taut with feverish anticipation and at the same time, pure terror. Had she been foolish to come here? What kind of welcome could she hope to receive? Summoning her last dregs of courage, she walked on.

The stream passed close by the village and she tried not to dwell on how, in her dreams, its torrent always turned to blood. A child was fishing. He dropped his line, and ran back to the village, shouting an alarm. Within moments, a large crowd of men, women, and children had gathered at the entrance of the enclosure. Shoulder to shoulder, they formed a defensive barrier that bristled with sticks, rakes and shovels. Wielded with enough force, any one of them could crack open her skull.

Anya stared at the villagers incredulously. It was hard to believe these people were her kin. They shared her red hair and pale skin, but the similarity ended there. In some primeval way, the black mountains had claimed these people as their own and moulded them in their likeness. Their hard eyes were the colour of the soaring crags, and their chequer pattern cloaks were the muted tones of the high moors. They were staring back at her and it was not curiosity she could see on their faces, but open hostility.

Anya was engulfed by despair. She had foolishly believed that she might find a welcome, a home, in this bleak valley. But these people were inhospitable strangers with weapons in their hands and hatred in their eyes. She had come so far and it had all been for nothing. With a deep shuddering breath, she turned and began to walk away.

A sudden image of her mother sprang into her mind, half-forgotten memories of kind words and warm embraces. This was her mother's village. These people were her mother's kin. Emboldened, she turned back to the silent crowd.

'I mean you no harm,' she called out, in Latin. 'My name is Anya, daughter of Eown. She was taken from this village by slave traders some twenty years since. Do any of you remember her?'

The villagers stared at her blankly.

'Eown,' she repeated loudly, but there was no flicker of recognition in their eyes. The ominous silence stretched on, and she realised with dismay that these isolated people, like the fisher folk on the great river, had little use for the language of the Romans. Her courage was hanging by a thread now and tears of bitter disappointment stung her eyes. She was about to turn away again when one man pushed his way to the front of the crowd. He was no longer young, and his red beard was speckled with grey, but he carried himself with immense dignity and bearing. He looked her up and down. And then he said just one word.

'Eown.'

Her heart leapt. 'Yes. She was my mother.'

Taking her right hand, the man unfurled her fingers, and touched her mother's ring. To her astonishment, his expression was full of tenderness and loss. And then he said, in broken Latin, 'Eown is daughter of,' he jabbed his chest, 'Llewelyn ap Mawr.'

Anya stared at the stranger who was not a stranger, but her own flesh and blood. It was too much to comprehend.

'My mother is dead,' she said, and her voice wavered with emotion.

'I know this,' her grandfather replied. 'I know this, here,' and he touched his heart.

Anya knew what he was trying to say, for she had often felt the same coldness when a soul passed through the veil. This man had felt his daughter's death. Without thinking, she stepped forward, put her arms around him, and drew him into an embrace. He smelled of fire-smoke and his beard felt

40

bristly against her face. He did not return her embrace. Instead, he stood awkwardly in her arms, like a statue made of stone. She released him hurriedly, presuming she had caused offence.

His eyes were glistening with tears. 'You are,' he began hesitantly, searching for the correct Latin words. 'You are her very image.'

She nodded. 'So I have been told.'

'Come,' he said, and the crowds parted in stunned silence to let them pass. He led her to the largest round-house. Inside it was hot and dark and smoky, the air pungent with the stale smell of many people living together in a confined space, the dirty, oily tang of sheep's wool, and the lingering traces of a thousand bean and mutton stews. Closer to the fire, the air was not so sour, tempered by the sweet scent of smoking peat.

She looked about curiously. The round-house had a high conical roof that tapered to waist height at the walls, where wattle partitions created storage space and privacy for sleeping. The large, central, living space was dominated by a stone bordered hearth, ringed by an untidy circle of cushions, woven in the same pattern as the villagers' cloaks.

Anya realised she was trembling. This was Eown's home. The mother she had lost when she was just eight years old, the mother whose passing had left such an aching void in her life. Eown had been born here, grown up here. At that loom, she had learnt to sew and weave. Beside that hearth, she had memorised the wonderful stories of gods and heroes she had subsequently told to her own children.

Llewellyn gestured to the fireside.

'Sit. Eat.'

A cold, black night fell upon the valley. Wolves howled on the high moor, but inside the round-house, all was warmth

41

and hospitality. They had not expected visitors, and had no meat prepared. Embarrassed and apologetic, they fed her wild mushroom and barley broth instead. It had an earthy taste, but she was so hungry she ate one bowlful after another, gulping it down so quickly she burnt her mouth.

And when she had taken her fill, uncles, aunts, cousins and distant cousins came forward and swept her up in warm embraces. There was little sign of their initial hostility. None of them knew a word of Latin, save for Llewellyn, but she was amazed by how much could be communicated with laughter and smiles.

Anya put down her empty bowl. It was hot and airless and her head was throbbing with fatigue. These people were Horsa's kin too and she wished he was here, not far away in the north. A feeling of 'hiraeth' settled upon her, the yearning for days passed and people lost. She forced her maudlin thoughts aside. Stifling a yawn, she realised there was one more relative she had yet to meet.

The old woman was seated on the cushions beside the fire, her huge body swathed in enormous rolls of fat. She was eating a bread cake and crumbs were tumbling onto her large bosom. She snapped her fingers and two young men hurried to her side. Together, they manhandled her to her feet and a shower of crumbs fell to the floor like blossom on a windy day.

'Thank you, my dears. This is always the high point of my day!' the old woman chortled in the Silurian tongue, her dark eyes glinting with delight.

A few people laughed but many more shook their heads in wry amusement and Anya suspected she said the same thing every night. The old woman waddled towards her like a grain-fed duck. Her plump face was completely unlined, her skin as soft as a new-born baby. Anya stood up to greet her, bowing her head in respect for the woman's advanced years.

'I am Ceinwin,' the old woman jabbed her ample bosom then clasped Anya's hands in hers. 'We have been waiting for you for a long time. I am so glad you are here at last.'

Anya smiled and nodded uncomprehendingly but she noticed several of her kinsmen were eyeing each other with wary, guarded expressions. What had the old woman just said? There was kindness in Ceinwin's eyes, but something else too, something difficult to read – anticipation, excitement, relief?

Ceinwin sat down beside Anya with assistance from the two young men. They showed her considerable respect, giving no indication they resented their role as nursemaids to an old woman. Ceinwin settled herself amidst the cushions and then tapped Anya on the arm, her eyes sparkling merrily.

'They all get their turn, a different pair every day. But I have my favourites, of course!'

Anya had no idea what Ceinwin had just said but, caught up by the old woman's infectious good humour, she laughed out loud. She had not laughed for such a long time and it felt good; as if a dam had burst, releasing a torrent of happiness.

She was aware that Llewellyn had been watching her all night, and she turned to face him, smiling shyly. She could see much of her mother in him. His eyes were Eown's eyes, as green as the sea after a storm. But they were full of ancient hurt, and questions, so many questions. Tentatively, she put her hand on his arm.

Instantly, her vision blurred, her surroundings fading to mist. She gave a sharp intake of breath as the tortured strands of Llewellyn's memories whipped across her mind: the agony of losing his only daughter to slave-traders; the daily torment of not knowing her fate; the unbearable sorrow that had

43

carried his wife to an early grave. She withdrew her hand, and the images faded.

The colour had drained from Llewellyn's face. He looked bewildered, and Anya felt a stab of guilt for raking through his private grief. He was fingering his temple gingerly as if expecting to find a wound. When he realised there was no external damage, he stared long and hard at her, his expression both appraising and wary.

Desperate to distract him, she said, 'I have so much to tell you about Eown.'

Llewellyn took a long draught of ale as if to steady himself and then he nodded sadly.

'I have waited... I have waited too long.'

'Then let this be an end to it.'

And so Anya told him of Saxony, a kingdom of flat lands and wide skies, far away across the cold northern sea. She told him of Eown, bought in a slave market by a high king who, despite the odds and against the counsel of his priests, married her and loved her unconditionally until her dying day.

At this, Llewellyn began to cry. Anya glanced about anxiously but, unlike the men of Saxony who would have taken this as a shameful sign of weakness, no-one looked embarrassed by the sight of her grandfather sobbing quietly. Instead, they simply bowed their heads in respect for his grief.

She clasped Llewellyn's hands in hers. 'Eown bore three children, all red haired, just like you.' She broke off for a moment. It was too soon to speak of Emma. Instead she said, 'you have a fine grandson. He is called Horsa. I hope you can meet him once day. You would be so proud of him.'

FIVE

Eboracum, territory of the Brigantes

The amphitheatre at Eboracum lay just outside the walls. Horsa sat alone on the very highest tier of seats. It gave him a bird's eye view of the old Roman city, and of the two rivers it lay between. One was wide and as impressive as a king, the other was as small and apologetic as a slave.

Shielding his eyes from the weak winter sun, he stared across the plains of Eboracum and homesickness squeezed his heart. The huge skies in the territory of the Brigantes reminded him of Saxony, of home. His thoughts turned to Elsbet, his betrothed. She was clever, and kind and beautiful, and she reminded him of Sif, wife of the warrior god Taranis, for she too had hair the colour of gold. There had been no word from Elsbet since he had crossed the northern sea almost a year since, and he was distraught with worry.

He had not sought a warrior's life. All he had ever truly wanted was to farm the land, to build a hall, to marry Elsbet, raise a family, and grow old together. But he understood why he had been sent to serve as mercenary to Vortigern. Land was scarce in Saxony, and Athelwald had his three elder sons to consider. He had done what he thought was best for his two youngest sons. He had given them the opportunity to make their own way in life, to find fame and fortune through loyal service to a high king.

But Horsa yearned for Elsbet. He loved her so much and his life felt empty without her. His thoughts turned to Anya and his sense of homesickness quickly shifted to anger. He could not bear to think of her at Vortigern's side, sharing his life and sharing his bed. Hengist had surely offended the goddess in choosing such a fate for his beloved sister.

He lifted his gaze. Further north, where the horizon faded to blue, was Hadrian's wall and beyond that, the tribes he and his brother were being paid to subdue. He smiled sadly to himself, remembering his last conversation with Anya. She had assured him the Picts were mere men, not blue-skinned demons of the underworld and she had been right. Their skin was blue, but stained by tattoos and they had died screaming upon his sword just like any other man.

A robin swooped past his head and landed nearby. Seemingly oblivious to his presence, it hopped a little closer then lowered its head to peck for grubs in the rotten wooden planking. Horsa watched it absently, but his mind was far away. Vortigern had sent them to guard the wall, but it had quickly become apparent it was a thankless task. They simply did not have enough troops, and the northern tribes regularly over-ran the wall, burning and looting the civilian settlements in its shadow.

He had watched his brother's anger and frustration increasing by the day, until Hengist had finally sent word to Saxony, demanding reinforcements. But then winter had closed in and Hengist's frustration had exploded like badly fermented ale. Leaving a small contingent of men on the wall, he had led his warband south through drifting snow and freezing fog until they had reached the city of Eboracum.

Huddled around their firesides until the coming of spring, the Brigantes had not expected a Saxon warband to march out of the snowstorm. Hengist had slaughtered many of them, and sent many more to the coast, destined for the slave markets of Germania and Gaul. But like any shrewd farmer, he had not disposed of all his livestock. Strong young men were needed to dig latrine pits and repair the walls, and strong young women to cook and clean and sew.

Horsa had seen so much death and suffering over the last few months he was now weary, melancholy and on-edge. His gaze slid to Hengist's banner of the white wolf, flying proudly over the battlements of the city, and his anxiety intensified. Eboracum belonged to Vortigern, but Hengist had claimed it for his own. Winter was beginning to lessen its hold on Britannia, the snows were melting and the roads were passable again. Soon, they would have to face Vortigern's fury.

Hengist was beckoning him. 'Come down from there!'

Three men were being dragged into the arena, their hands tied behind their backs. From their appearance, Horsa guessed they were of the Votadini tribe. Their hair was pulled into a knot resembling a shiny black shield boss on the crown of their head. Their black woollen cloaks were ribbed like the clinker planking of a long boat and fringed with row upon row of black feathers. The Votadini reminded Horsa of carrion crows on the battlefield, the faithful scouts of the Valkyries.

'Are you deaf?' Hengist yelled up at him.

'I can hear you,' Horsa replied.

The acoustics of the old amphitheatre were superb. Even on the top tier, he suspected he could have heard a bone needle drop in the arena. He walked slowly down the steps. If there was one thing he had learnt these last few months, it was that nothing was ever as simple as you expected. Beyond the wall, there were many tribes, not only the Picts but also the Caledonians, the Attacottii, the Scottii and the Votadini, whose lands lay just beyond the wall. The tribes fought amongst themselves, thieving cattle and stealing grain but, when the fancy took them, they would happily unite and ride south, breach the wall, and raid and plunder at will.

It had been Vortigern's suggestion to employ the Votadini, for they had been loyal to Rome in times past, acting as a buffer between the hostile tribes further north. And so Hengist had offered them silver and watched them scurry back and forth across the wall, covering great distances at impossible speed, giving warning of any imminent threats of invasion. In a word, they were his spies.

Horsa went to stand beside his brother. Hengist was bedecked with garnets and gold, from the pommel of his sword, to the brooch at his shoulder and the intricately carved rings adorning his plaited beard. But despite all his grandeur and opulence, Horsa thought his brother looked unwell. There were black smudges beneath his cold blue eyes and his skin was as grey as a wolf's pelt, as if the harsh northern winter had sucked the life from his flesh.

Horsa shifted his gaze to the three Votadini. They had been badly beaten, their faces smashed to bloodied pulp.

'When I asked you to supply information,' Hengist said calmly, in Latin, 'I meant you to supply it to me, not to your comrades in the north. Every advance unit I send out is attacked. Every fort I leave temporarily unmanned is overrun. I don't believe in co-incidences.' He looked at each man in turn. 'Do you have anything to say?'

The three men remained silent. Horsa suspected they knew full well that nothing they said would change their fate.

Hengist nodded to the ring of soldiers surrounding them. 'Deal with these traitors.'

The Votadini did not struggle. Horsa had always found them to be a proud people and he was not surprised they went to meet their gods with dignity. One by one they were taken to the centre of the arena, forced onto their knees and their heads were severed in a swift, clean arc of a sharp Saxon blade.

Horsa watched the executions in silence. He understood why the Votadini had betrayed Hengist, even if he could not condone it. They lived north of the wall. It was obvious where their loyalties would lie, just as it was obvious where Hengist's loyalties would ultimately lie, no matter how much land or gold Vortigern threw at him. Horsa let out a deep sigh. Yet more death, yet more suffering. There were days when he felt he might drown in other men's blood.

Hengist turned to Aelfric, the commander of his household guard. 'Clean up this mess.'

'Yes, lord.' Aelfric clicked his fingers and soldiers came at a run.

Aelfric was never far from Hengist's side. Whereas many of Hengist's warriors were surly brutes, skilled with a blade but little else, Aelfric was a shrewd and intelligent man. Strong and tall with fair hair and blue eyes, he was also the living embodiment of Taranis, god of thunder and war - no doubt a pleasing reminder for Hengist that the lineage of the Saxon race could be traced back to Odin, father of the gods.

Hengist turned to Horsa again. 'I intend to ride south. I've had word from Corinium - our reinforcements have made camp.'

Horsa was taken aback. 'When did the messenger arrive?'

'This morning. It's not surprising you didn't know. You

49

spend most of your days up there,' Hengist gestured to the top tier of steps, 'where you daydream like a love-sick girl. You shame me, brother. Father appointed you as my second in command, but Aelfric is far more use to me.'

Hengist's words cut Horsa like a blade. He shot a sideways glance at Aelfric, who lowered his eyes and looked deeply uncomfortable. If he was honest, Horsa did not blame Aelfric for usurping his position at Hengist's side. He had allowed it to happen, for he neither enjoyed his brother's company, nor agreed with his methods.

And yet, he could not disregard his father's command. It was his duty to obey the brother he had never loved, the brother who had smiled triumphantly as dear, innocent Emma was sacrificed to the gods, the brother who had given Anya to Vortigern, against her wishes, against the goddess's wishes.

'I am loyal to you brother, to the death,' Horsa replied although the words on his lips felt as bitter as rue.

'Anything less would only add to your shame,' Hengist retorted maliciously. 'Make ready. We leave for Corinium tomorrow.'

Hengist's men were dragging the corpses from the arena, leaving a trail of blood and gore across the churned gravel. One soldier picked up a severed head but it slipped from his hands. Swearing loudly, he bent down and picked it up again by its top knot. Horsa grimaced and walked away. It would be good to ride south. He had had his fill of the bitter cold and the wind so raw it seemed to strip the flesh from your bones. Everything had seemed softer in the south - the air, the rain, even the light.

'Oh, and one other thing,' Hengist said casually, as if it were an afterthought.

Horsa turned. 'Yes?'

'Your betrothed is in Britannia. She has arrived at Corinium.'

Horsa stared at his brother in stunned disbelief.

'What did you say?'

'It seems her weeping and wailing was driving her family to distraction. They literally begged father to send her here.'

'Is this your idea of a joke?' Horsa studied Hengist warily, although his half-brother was not renowned for his sense of humour.

'Do I look like I jest? She is in Corinium.'

Horsa's doubt gave way to a tentative spark of happiness, which rapidly flared to a feeling of immense joy. Tears pricked his eyes and he quickly wiped them away. His face broke into a broad smile. He had forgotten how it felt to be happy. It felt like the heat of the sun after a hard, brutal winter.

'Are you a man or a eunuch, brother?' Hengist sneered. 'Shed tears in front of the men again and I'll gouge out your eyes myself.'

SIX

Tintagel, kingdom of Dumnonia

From the window of her bedchamber, Mairi watched Silvanus's warband return to Tintagel. She had counted them out, and now she counted them in. None had been lost. For some inexplicable reason, the goddess had smiled upon Silvanus yet again. If there was any justice in the world, it would be Lucan riding at the head of the warband. And it would be Lucan revelling in glory for driving the Irish raiders back to the sea, and slaughtering them in the shallows until the tide ran red.

Mairi turned away from the window and paced up and down her bed chamber. Breathless and uncomfortable, every step was a huge effort. The child moved inside her. She felt him turn, felt his tiny foot press hard against her ribs, and she inhaled sharply. She wanted the pregnancy to be over now. Even though her belly was so huge she couldn't sleep, she felt somehow diminished. As her precious child had grown, his needs, his will, had devoured her own, as if she was the smallest minnow and he was the largest monster of the deep.

She stopped for a moment, gripping the back of the chair until she caught her breath. She had naively supposed that marriage to the king's son would bring wealth and privilege. Instead, her husband's unceasing bitterness and cruelty had worn her down until she had agreed to drip poison into Etar's drinking cup, and stood by as Lucan threw an innocent child from a clifftop in order to ensure the boy's silence.

And now, she hated her husband, for he had brought darkness into her life, when she had dreamed of beautiful gowns and music and dancing. But she hated Anya more. If the Saxon witch had not come to Tintagel and ensnared Silvanus with her dark magic, Lucan's plan would surely have come to pass. He would be high king now, and she would be sitting beside him in the great hall. And the child in her belly, her precious, golden boy, would be heir to the throne of Dumnonia.

Instead, Lucan was locked away at the top of the watchtower, and she was confined to her chamber. And there were days when she felt as if the walls were closing in on her, suffocating her with boredom and frustration and rage. There was just one small crumb of comfort. One of Etar's final acts as king had been to send Anya back to Aquae Sulis, to spend the rest of her wretched days sharing Vortigern's bed.

Mairi gasped as another severe pain tightened its grip about her abdomen. Bending double, she clasped both hands to her belly and felt a rush of warm liquid between her thighs. It soaked through her gown, a dark patch spreading upon the fine damask. Appalled, she ran to the door and yelled at the top of her voice. 'The baby's coming!'

Her head was spinning with fear. She had seen women screaming with the agony of childbirth, just as she had watched them die in delirium from the fever that so often followed. But then, this was no ordinary baby. The wise woman who lived on the moors had looked into the flames and told them their son would be king. Mairi would never forget her words.

'Many will bow down before him, just as many will remember him in the years to come.'

And now it was his time to come into the light. She must not let him down; she must be brave and strong for him. But she couldn't do it alone. She banged on the door with her fists.

'Help me! It's Garth out there, isn't it? I know you can hear me! My baby's coming! You must find the midwife!'

Mairi put her ear to the door, and listened to the guard's footsteps retreating down the corridor. Over the last few months, she had worked hard to charm the men who guarded her door, dazzling them with winsome smiles. She had not sought to illicit their pity, but rather their admiration for the brave, wronged woman so cruelly imprisoned in the watchtower. Consequently, she felt certain they had all fallen hopelessly in love with her.

Time passed, but how much she could not say, for her mind and her body were utterly consumed with agony. Why had no-one come to help her? Silvanus must have decreed she should give birth unaided. He was a heartless bastard; he didn't care whether she lived or died. As each pain peaked, she bent double and howled, and cursed Silvanus that he might die without issue, in agony and alone.

The door of her chamber opened and the midwife hurried inside. Mairi's initial sense of relief was quickly tempered with suspicion. She had never seen this woman before. She was a tiny scrap of a thing, as scrawny as a fledgling. Grey hair, as soft as sparrows' feathers, peeked from beneath the unflattering cloth wound about her head.

'Who are you?' Mairi demanded, on her guard.

54

'Sirona, my lady.'

'Why did you take so long?'

'I'm here now,' the midwife replied briskly.

Putting her arm around Mairi's shoulders, she manhandled her onto the bed. The old woman's sleeves were rolled up to her elbows and Mairi could smell the sharp tang of juniper oil on her skin.

'Silvanus forbade you to come, didn't he?' Mairi hissed as another pain tore through her.

'What? No. They couldn't find me. I was tendin' out by Dynant Cove. It's been a hard winter, there's many folk dyin' with lung fever.'

Mairi didn't care about the coughs of a few fisher folk. She was on fire, burning up inside. Instinctively, she heaved herself onto all fours. The baby was coming fast, wrenching and tearing his way out of her. All dignity stripped away, she began to pant like a bitch on heat, sweat pooling at her collar bone and running between her breasts. This was all Lucan's fault. As long as she lived, she swore no man would ever touch her again.

She felt curiously invisible now, as if she was vanishing into the ether, absorbed by the pain and the child's unyielding will. And suddenly she was filled with an irresistible desire to push. She screamed and pushed, again and again and again. And it came to her then, in a storm of agony, exhaustion and terror that she was going to die on these fouled linen sheets, without ever seeing her unborn child.

And into that blood-soaked storm, a child was born. The son of Lucan, and the grandson of Etar, slithered onto the sodden rugs, a scrap of life with a shock of jet black hair. Mairi's eyes focussed upon her son's face and in that instant she forgot all the indignity and all the pain.

'You can't be keepin' it,' Sirona said gently. 'Look at its foot, lady.'

'What do you mean?' Exhausted and overwhelmed, Mairi followed the old woman's gaze. The heel of the baby's left foot was pointing downward, while his toes turned inward. How had that happened? Why was her son not perfect?

'The child's marked by the devil,' the midwife began, but Mairi cut her off. She was shaken to the core, but she was determined not to show it.

'How dare you say such a thing? I will have you whipped for such insolence! His foot is nothing to worry about. It will right itself, in time.'

She took her son in her arms and sank back onto the cushions. He was covered in blood and mucus but she didn't care. She revelled in the smell of him and the warmth of him against her skin.

'This is hard for you,' the old woman said firmly. 'But I knows 'bout these things. It's better for the babe to go to the gods now, than suffer life as an outcast. Believe me, it's for the best.'

The midwife attempted to take the child from her but Mairi slapped her away. One small, rational part of her brain knew the old woman was right. No kingdom would crown a crippled king. There was still time to have another son. A strong, perfect son, to wear the crown of Dumnonia.

But she had felt this child's strength and power growing inside her for nine long months, obliterating her own needs, her own will. No matter how improbable it seemed, *this* was the child who would be king. And she knew she would do anything to keep him safe.

Mairi heaved herself up the pillows, and looked Sirona firmly in the eye. 'This is a child of royal blood. You will never, ever try to take him from me.' She stroked the baby's twisted foot with a tender hand. 'This will be our secret, and if you speak of it to anyone, I will see you are burnt as a witch.'

The midwife flinched. 'As you wish, lady,' she replied, all meekness now.

The baby began to cry loudly. Mairi unfastened the ties on her gown and manoeuvred him to her breast. She winced as he began to suckle, shocked by how much it hurt. Bitterness and self-pity welled up inside her. She didn't want to be locked away in her chamber like a common criminal. She wanted to be at the fireside in the great hall, showing off her new born son.

The baby had begun to suckle vigorously, his pink lips working, his chubby little hand resting against her swollen breast. It didn't hurt so much now. In fact, the curious, dragging sensation felt strangely exhilarating. The baby was feeding from her. He needed her and no-one else, and the realisation made her feel powerful, invincible.

She would hide her son's spoiled foot from the world, for he was meant to live. He had been chosen by the gods, chosen to rule the kingdom of Dumnonia. Only Silvanus stood in her way but when the time came, he would be easy to sweep aside. Poison had worked for Etar. It would work just as well for Silvanus too.

She kissed the top of her baby's head. He smelled warm and new and intoxicating and her love for him unfurled, reaching towards the light. She felt as if her heart might burst.

Her boy. Her precious, golden boy.

SEVEN

The kingdom of Siluria

Snow continued to fall on the valley beneath the black mountains and the villagers' lives shrank to the confines of the smoky round-houses. Anya knelt by the hearth, turning the handle that rotated the heavy quern stones. It was hard, back breaking work, and every muscle in her body ached. She stopped for a moment, and watched her cousins transferring the freshly milled barley flour to mixing bowls for the next stage in the daily task of bread making.

Her cousins never stopped talking. They chattered and giggled, and their dark eyes sparkled in the fire light. She envied them in many ways. They were happy with their lives; they knew nothing else. And she envied them their warm friendship. It reminded her of the laughter she had shared with her best friend, Elsbet. When Anya had been chosen to train as a priestess, some of the girls in the village had been jealous of her new status but Elsbet had beamed with pride and delight.

Anya had spent long hours in the priests' school learning the ancient and secret skills of the priesthood, but when her work was done, she would always seek Elsbet out. In the winter they would sit at the fireside, laughing and gossiping. In the summer they would walk along the river-bank to the big meadow. Elsbet did not enjoy quietly sewing at her mother's side in the women's chamber. She much preferred to be outdoors, helping Anya to collect the healing plants for her remedies.

Anya had watched Elsbet and Horsa fall in love and their joy had seemed as natural as breathing. She ached to think of them so far apart, and she missed them both so much. She brushed a stray hair away from her face, her flour-dusted fingers smearing a white trail across her cheek. She had quickly learnt that there was little privacy, and constant noise in the round-house. There was wool to spin and weave, animals to feed, logs to chop, and peat to cut. There was water to be drawn, and food to be prepared and cooked. It was a never ending routine, a rhythm that had become as familiar as a heart-beat.

She smiled to herself. In Germania, she was the daughter of a king. In Siluria, she was the grand-daughter of a sheep farmer, occupied with tasks that just a few months previously would have been work for the slaves.

She caught Llewellyn's eye but he quickly looked away again. Her smile faded to a frown of disappointment. She had hoped that once he learnt Eown had found happiness as the wife of a king, the sadness might lift from his eyes. But her grandfather reminded her of a furled parchment, closed up and impossible to read. In such close confines, their paths crossed every day, but he avoided her now and she felt hurt by his rejection.

Her cousins prodded her playfully, dragging her back from her musings. Rolling their pretty eyes at her laziness, they pointed at her, and then they pointed at the quern stones. She laughed and began to turn the handle again, concentrating on keeping a steady pace. After a while, she paused, aware she was being watched.

Some distance away, two little girls were whispering behind their hands. They were perhaps five summers old and she wondered if they might be twins. Their hair was neatly braided into two long plaits and they wore identical dresses in the same chequer pattern as the cushions about the hearth. Hanging from woven belts at their waists were beautifully crafted wooden miniatures of keys, spoons, knives and spindle whorls.

The girls were kneeling beside a circular, wicker container with a tall, conical lid. Anya let go of the handle, rubbed her aching back and pointed at the container.

'beth yw bod?' she asked. What is that?

The little girls giggled in unison. Anya was beginning to pick up a few phrases, but she guessed her accent was appalling. She raised her eyebrows apologetically. The nearest child grinned then picked up the wicker basket and placed it proudly before Anya. The other little girl quickly followed.

The basket had been woven to resemble a miniature round-house, its lid a conical roof. Anya lifted the lid and peered inside. The hearth was made of pebbles. Two tiny corn dollies were asleep beside it, beneath a small piece of cloth. The girls were eyeing Anya expectantly, as if seeking her approval. She bit her lip, trying hard to remember the correct phrase.

'Da iawn!' she said at last. Very good!

The girls collapsed into another fit of giggles.

Admitting defeat, Anya lapsed into the Saxon tongue. 'Wait! I have something for you.'

Her cloak was neatly folded at the end of her makeshift bed. She knelt down and reached inside its deep inner pocket.

The ancient parchment of Taliesin's map felt dry against her skin. She closed her eyes for a moment, her thoughts drifting to Dumnonia, and Taliesin's parting words.

'A map, so you can find your way back to us.'

Anya sighed. She felt content in this hot and noisy round-house, but Silvanus had made her feel happy, brighter, as if the world was full of suns. But she could not go back to him. As long as she lived, she would do anything to keep his kingdom safe from the vengeful fury of Vortigern. With a heavy heart, she dug her fingers deeper into the pocket until she found what she was searching for, and went back to the girls.

'Here we are!' She held out her hand. In her palm were four acorn cups. 'For your dolls.'

The children looked blankly at her, and Anya realised she had spoken in the Saxon tongue again. Taking a tiny cup between finger and thumb, she lifted it to her mouth and mimicked taking a sip. The girls' eyes lit up and they snatched the acorn cups from her hand. Laughing delightedly, they too pretended to drink and she noticed with a stab of concern that their arms were painfully thin.

'Where are your manners?'

Anya jumped, startled. A young man was glaring crossly at the girls. She guessed he was about her age, but unlike the strong, virile, young warriors of her father's hall in Saxony, he was as thin as a silver birch sapling, with an open, guileless face. If she had not known him to be a sheep farmer, she would have taken him for a bard. His long autumn-red hair was held at the nape of his neck with twine.

'Diolch,' the little girls muttered sheepishly. Thank you.

The young man's frown subsided to a lop-sided grin.

'Please forgive Rhiannon and Olwen. My sisters may be

61

pretty but sadly, their manners leave a lot to be desired.'

Anya did not understand a word he had said, but she returned his smile anyway. She thought he had kind eyes.

'I am Rhys ap Dafydd.'

She nodded, fairly certain he had just introduced himself.

'Rhys,' she repeated.

'For the love of Brigid, wait 'til you are wed!' Ceinwin's voice boomed out.

Her kin erupted into gales of laughter. Only Rhys did not find Ceinwin's comment amusing. His cheeks turned bright red and he hurried away.

Anya looked about her, utterly bemused. It appeared understanding the occasional phrase of Eown's language was not going to be enough after all.

Weeks passed, and the winter dragged on relentlessly. Anya plunged the pails into the icy waters of the stream then drew them out again. She straightened up and stretched her sore back. Her fingers were red-raw and swollen with chilblains, and she struggled to attach the heavy pails of water to the yoke. Heaving it onto her shoulders, she walked slowly back to the village, taking care not to spill a single drop.

Outside, icicles hung from the roofs and snow lay deep on the ground but inside the safe confines of the round-houses, the villagers cheerfully and doggedly went on with the rituals of their daily life. But it had not taken Anya long to realise that appearances were cruelly deceptive.

In this isolated valley, starvation was just a late spring away. The haunches of meat that had hung from the rafters, preserved by the fire smoke as it filtered through the turf roof, had all been eaten long ago. Grain levels in the storage pits had dropped alarmingly. And she had begun to notice how sparingly food bowls were filled, how mothers quietly gave their own share to their children. There were the first signs of illness, of fevers and racking coughs.

How different life had been in her father's hall. There, her family had feasted throughout the winter. She had never once stopped to wonder if the people of Saxony had suffered to ensure the king's table was always full.

Anya closed the door of the round-house behind her. Lifting the yoke from her shoulders, she stamped her feet to dislodge the impacted snow, hung her cloak on the hook then carried the pails to the hearth. Ceinwin was seated beside a large cooking pot, chopping dried thyme leaves on a battered wooden board.

'Pour it in, *bach*,' she said, without looking up.

Anya poured some water into the pot. As the weeks had passed, she had slowly mastered the language of Siluria, her every waking moment filled with its gently lilting rhythms.

'Tonight, we celebrate Imbolc. Do you have such a festival in Saxony?' Ceinwin asked, dropping the herbs into the water.

'Yes,' Anya nodded. 'It coincides with when the ewes come into milk again.'

Imbolc fell half way between the winter solstice and the spring equinox, a celebration of the lengthening days. It was a festival of hearth and home, of candlelight, feasting and song, and the memory of it made her yearn for Saxony.

She glanced across at her grandfather. He was sitting beside the fire, sharpening a pair of shears with a whet stone. As usual, he was ignoring her as if she were invisible, as if she had never come to the village in the shadow of the mountain. In profile, Llewellyn reminded her very strongly of Horsa, and a sudden, cold feeling of hurt settled in her stomach. What had she done to offend her grandfather? Why would he not even look at her, let alone speak to her? Did he want her to leave? Was she not welcome here, after all?

There was only one way to find out. Pulling Eown's ring from her finger, she walked over to him and tapped him on the arm. 'You should take this.'

Llewellyn stared at Eown's ring in her outstretched palm.

'No. It is yours.'

And then he looked up. It was the first time he had made eye contact with her since the day she arrived.

'I am glad you are here,' he said.

Anya had not expected that. 'And I am glad to be here,' she replied, a bright smile spreading across her face.

'I am sorry...' Llewellyn's brow furrowed. 'I am sorry I have not spoken with you. I lost Eown. I was afraid... when you came... I was afraid I would lose you too.' A tear rolled down his cheek. 'I am a coward, forgive me...'

Filled with compassion for her grandfather, Anya knelt down and put her arms around him. 'There's nothing to forgive, and you are not a coward.'

His body tensed and, sensing his awkwardness, she quickly released him. Llewellyn's expression was far away, remembering.

'Eown was such a beautiful child. She was fearless and headstrong...' he swallowed hard. 'But she lives on in you.'

Gently, he drew back her sleeve and eyed her cartwheel tattoo. Anya's heart sank. She had said nothing about her life as a priestess, or about Emma's death, or her banishment, because she had not wanted to set herself apart from Llewellyn and his kin, because she had wanted to belong here.

In truth, she had yearned to belong here.

'Why did you hide this?' he pointed at her tattoo. 'It is nothing to be ashamed of. My wife and my daughter both had the sight. And it seems they passed their gifts to you.'

Anya's eyes widened in astonishment. 'I never knew my mother had the sight! I don't think any-one in Saxony knew.'

She had often wondered why the goddess had chosen her for the sacred grove, and now, at last, she understood. So often she had felt as if her life was a broken necklace, its beads scattered to the far corners of the world, but with Llewellyn's revelation, it was as if another long lost bead had been unearthed and re-strung.

'She was taken in summer,' Llewellyn said, his eyes full of remembered sorrow. 'I had gone with the men, herding our sheep to the high pastures. We prepared the shelters where the shepherd boys would spend the summer and then we returned to the village. Tewdric and his warband had taken five young men, and five young women.' His eyes hardened. 'Tewdric does not see slaves as human beings. They mean only wealth to him. But he is not stupid. He knows that a tree stripped of its leaves will bear no more fruit, just as a village stripped off its youth, will bear no more slaves. So he picks the best of the crop, and leaves the rest of us to mourn.'

Tears were brimming in Llewellyn's eyes again. 'I was not there to save her. And so I live with my guilt and my shame.'

'She found happiness,' Anya said softly. 'She loved, and was loved in return.'

Llewellyn nodded. 'I wish my wife was here now, to hear you say it. She died not knowing what happened to our daughter.'

'I would have liked to meet my grandmother very much,' Anya said sadly.

Her gaze settled on Olwen and Rhiannon, cuddled up to Rhys, like fledglings beneath protective wings. Earlier in the evening, she had watched Rhys give them his share of bread, just as he always did, but they were still losing weight. Their faces were gaunt, their limbs stick thin.

Rhys's expression was one of intense concentration. He had a small knife in his hand and was carving something, but she could not see what it was. Llewellyn followed her gaze.

'Rhys is a good man,' he said quietly. 'His parents died two winters since, and now he takes care of his sisters. He is an excellent wood carver. All those little trinkets at their belts – he made them all.'

'What's he carving now?' Anya asked curiously. It looked like a spoon.

'He will show you, in time,' Llewellyn replied and smiled cryptically.

Distracted by an unfamiliar sound, Anya glanced over her shoulder. Two men were sitting on the floor, drums between their knees, thumping out a fast repetitive rhythm. Women were standing up to dance, their home-spun dresses swirling about their ankles, their feet stamping in time to the drums. From their belts hung small, brightly painted, wooden bells. Anya guessed they must have pebbles inside, for they rattled as the women danced.

The sound of the drums pulsed around the round-house. It seemed the festival of Imbolc had begun. More people were on their feet now. Some clapped their hands, others joined the long line of dancers snaking their way across the floor. A man produced a wooden lyre but its gentle notes were lost in the clamour. Children were scrabbling inside wicker baskets for pan-pipes and tiny whistles made of bone.

'Our grain pits are empty, but there is no harm in forgetting it for one night,' Llewellyn said grimly. 'They will remember it soon enough in the morning.'

The rhythm of the music was hypnotic and soon Anya's

66

toes began to tap. When she could resist no longer, she stood up.

'Will you dance with me, grandfather?'

He shook his head but gestured for her to join in. Within a heartbeat, someone had grasped her hand, sweeping her along in their wake. She caught a glimpse of Olwen and Rhiannon tugging Rhys to his feet. He made a show of resisting, but quickly gave up the struggle. She watched him tuck his knife into his belt and pocket the piece of wood as the two little girls pulled him towards the fast moving line of revellers.

He was a surprisingly good dancer. Caught up by the music, he was no longer shy or awkward, his long limbs lithe and graceful. Suddenly, he picked Olwen up by her waist, and began to twirl her above his head like a battle banner, turning faster and faster on his heel, until the little girl's laughter rose to warm the cold spirits of long dead ancestors still lingering beneath the blackened roof.

EIGHT

The journey from Eboracum to their lands at Corinium felt interminable for Horsa; long, cold nights in a tent huddled beneath his cloak, followed by long, cold days in the saddle. Crossing the desolate flat lands of the Brigantes, they reached the old Roman town of Lindum on the second day. The air was harsh, a biting north wind with a tang of the distant sea.

At Lindum, they turned south-west, taking the spear-straight Roman road that cut across Britannia through fallow fields and villages with no obvious sign of life, save for rooks clamouring in the bare treetops. Hengist's warband was grimly silent. The far horizon had disappeared into a wall of low-lying fog and visibility was poor. They were close to Vortigern's kingdom now but they were still vulnerable, their safety not guaranteed.

Several months after the signing of the treaty, Hengist and Horsa had discovered why Vortigern had been so willing to grant them the land at Corinium: it sat on the borderlands, a lawless zone of barn-burning, raids and slaughter. Horsa felt a stab of unease. How safe was Elsbet in Corinium? Perhaps he should insist she return with them to the wall?

His thoughts turned to Vortigern and his feeling of unease intensified. Vortigern might appear uncouth, but he had a mind as sharp as flint. Horsa felt certain he knew the exact number of Saxon long-boats beached at the fort of Andereida, and the exact number of men making camp at Corinium, and the exact day Hengist had hoisted the white wolf banner above the battlements of Eboracum.

Digging in his heels, he trotted to his brother's side. Hengist rode dressed for war, his helmet gilded with gold to emulate Odin's battle helm, the image of a wolf standing proud at each cheek piece.

'All he needs now is a grey, eight-legged horse called Sleipne,' Horsa thought drily.

Out loud, he asked, 'why are you openly defying Vortigern? Why are you risking all our lives?'

'What choice do I have? I need more men. I have barely two hundred on the wall, less than fifty in Eboracum. And you know as well as I that fighting men will not remain satisfied with a weekly quota of a grain, pork and wine. If they are to remain loyal, they will expect silver, and eventually they will expect their own plot of land.'

'But you must realise you are putting Anya in an extremely vulnerable position!' Horsa persisted.

'And you must realise that Anya is no longer my concern,' Hengist replied sarcastically.

'You've always hated her,' Horsa said wearily.

'I don't hate her. But it defies the natural order to elevate women to the priesthood, to put them in positions of authority over men. I gave her to Vortigern because women should marry and bear sons.'

Horsa frowned. The truth was, Hengist had always felt threatened by Anya's power and authority as a priestess. But Anya no longer held power of any kind. The high priest had cast her out of the sacred grove, her father had exiled her from Germania, and Hengist had given her away as a chattel to a Christian king.

'Father told you to keep Anya by our side,' he went on accusingly. 'She speaks with the gods. She would have been a great asset to us.'

Hengist laughed humourlessly. 'Father made a fool of himself where Anya was concerned. She is the daughter of a whore, yet he seated her at his right hand as if she were his queen.'

'My mother was no whore!' Horsa exclaimed furiously, but Hengist cut in.

'She was a slave, and all slaves are whores. Our bloodline is pure, but our father chose to sully it by mating with a Silurian slave. Athelwald was a fool - a fool to marry a slave, and a fool to send us away. Forcing us to serve as common mercenaries in a foreign kingdom! He didn't even attempt to find us land in Saxony! But I tell you, I will take Britannia, and I will be more powerful than our father could ever imagine, and then he will see how wrong he was to cast us aside.'

Horsa sighed inwardly. Hengist's call to arms had become as familiar to him as the heroic tale of Beowulf. The conquest of Britannia was his brother's sole purpose in life, a quest which drew the breath into his lungs and caused his heart to beat. Horsa did not share his brother's burning ambition. He wanted wealth, and land, but only enough to build a home and a future for Elsbet. It was hard to believe, but soon he would see her again, hold her in his arms.

He glanced over his shoulder at Hengist's warband. Many were riding stallions acquired from Vortigern's stables in Eboracum. Hengist had acquired slaves from Eboracum too; farmers, shop-keepers, blacksmiths and potters who now trudged alongside their wives and children through a quagmire

70

of mud, their faces sullen and grey with despair. When they made camp at the end of each day, the male slaves erected tents, cleaned armour, dug latrine pits. The female slaves cooked the evening meal, using rations from the supply wagons supplemented by whatever could be scavenged from the surrounding fields. On Hengist's orders, they were brutally beaten if his army went hungry.

Horsa did not enjoy watching women whipped until they bled, but he kept his silence. His mother had been a former slave and risen to become a queen, but she had never once spoken out against the indignity of her former state. Slaves were a part of life, a part of the natural order, ordained by the gods. But they were slowing the warband down. So too were the cart horses, struggling to pull the supply wagons through the deep, cloying mud. Horsa kicked his stallion's flanks, urging it on, frustrated by the lack of progress. Elsbet was waiting for him in Corinium, so close now.

'You will keep pace with me, brother!' Hengist snarled.

Horsa turned in his saddle. 'I want to ride on.'

'Oh, I know you do,' Hengist mocked. 'I know you're desperate to bed that simpering girl of yours.'

'She does not simper, and - not that it's any of your business - I do not intend to bed her until we are wed,' Horsa replied.

Hengist laughed. 'Well, let's hope the girl has brought a priest with her, for all our sakes.'

At dusk they came upon a small farmstead sheltered by a densely wooded ridge of high ground. The farmhouse had a pillared corridor running along the front of the building, a modest emulation of Roman style. At first glance, the settlement appeared deserted but on closer inspection, Horsa

71

noticed the surrounding fields had been ploughed in readiness for spring planting, the herb patch by the house was freshly raked, and the barn was in a good state of repair.

He turned to his brother. 'We might find supplies here.'

'I can see that. I'm not blind!' Hengist snapped irritably.

They found the farmer and his two young sons in the dining room of the main house. The farmer was a big man with a shock of wiry hair and a profusion of warts upon his coarse-featured face. His initial impression of brute strength was tempered by the spines of straw sticking to his tunic, which gave him the appearance of a giant yellow hedgehog. He was brandishing an axe but, confronted by a Saxon warband of heavily armed warriors, his courage failed him. Flinging the weapon aside, he fell to his knees. His sons cowered behind him.

Horsa looked around the chamber. It might once have been pleasant, but the painted walls were mottled with mould now, and the room smelled damp. In places, the *tesserae* of the crudely executed, geometric mosaic had worked loose and rattled beneath his boots.

'Where are your womenfolk?' Hengist demanded, towering intimidatingly over the farmer.

The man said nothing, eyeing the Saxon with an expression of mute defiance.

'What are you? A scarecrow, or a man? Answer me!' Hengist roared.

The man remained silent. Infuriated by his insolence, Hengist punched him in the face. The farmer's head jerked sideways, blood spraying from his split lip. He righted himself, wiped his mouth on his sleeve and promptly spat a broken tooth at Hengist's feet. Hengist's expression hardened. He was already on edge, irritated Vortigern had played him for a fool

72

by gifting him land in a lawless border zone. Bending down, he punched the man in the kidneys, hard. A rasping grunt escaped the farmer's throat before he toppled sideways onto the mosaic floor.

The acrid scent of urine filled the air. The youngest boy, no more than seven years old, had pissed himself.

Hengist turned to Aelfric. 'We will make camp here. Strip this place, take everything. Grain, livestock, tools, buckets, blankets, cooking pots. We leave at first light.'

Yes, sir. And what shall we do with them?' Aelfric nodded at the farmer and his sons.

Hengist shot them a withering glance. 'Kill them. They'll be more trouble than they're worth.'

Horsa lay beneath his cloak on the hard mosaic floor, listening to the snores of Hengist's household guards, interspersed with the steady drip of rainwater from the leaking roof. On the wall of Hadrian, he thought he had grown accustomed to his half-brother's casual cruelties. But Hengist still had the power to shock him, even now. The farmer's sons were children, but he had ordered their deaths without hesitation. The farmer had died cursing the Saxons in his native tongue, but his sons had died crying out for their mother.

Close by, someone farted in their sleep. Horsa was about to turn over when he heard the sound of screaming. He shot upright. Were they under attack? All about him, Hengist's household guards were already on their feet.

Horsa fastened his sword belt and quickly followed his brother outside. The moonlit farmyard was full of Hengist's men, stumbling half-asleep from their tents and milling about in confusion. More ear-splitting screams came from the direction of the barn. High pitched women's voices. Without waiting for his brother's command, Horsa ran across the yard, dragged back the barn doors and stepped inside. He blinked, momentarily blinded by the bright light of a flaming torch, held aloft.

A middle aged woman was on her knees, barely conscious, blood pouring from a gash on her cheek. Six of Hengist's men formed a loose ring about one of their comrades, who was straddling a naked girl. The men were shouting encouragement, the bright torchlight casting their gurning faces into sharp relief. They were hungry for their turn, and Horsa felt sickened at the sight of them. In his mind, rape was abhorrent, an evil violation. For him, there were no exceptions, whether the woman was royalty, nobility, freeborn or slave. Horsa pulled the soldier off the girl.

The man grunted with frustration, clenched his fist and clumsily attempted to take a swing at him, but Horsa dodged him easily.

'S'my turn, you bastard, s'my turn.' The soldier's words were slurred, and Horsa realised the man was so inebriated he had no idea who he was berating.

The young girl had curled herself into a ball, whimpering like a wounded animal. There were bruises on her pale skin and blood was running down her thighs.

'I hadn't finished, you fuckin' bastard!' The soldier lashed out again. He swung his fist into thin air, swaying on his feet.

Rage boiled in Horsa. In one swift movement, he threw his cloak over the girl and punched the soldier in the face. He heard cartilage crack and felt flesh explode like an over-ripe plum.

The man teetered for a moment, blood pouring from his shattered nose and then he fell backwards, his breeches about his ankles, out cold.

Horsa took a deep breath and looked about. The soldiers in the barn were no longer grinning with sadistic delight. Instead, they looked uncertain and afraid. The older woman was keening, a strange, haunting sound which reminded him of the cries of seabirds on the crossing to Britannia. She crawled on her hands and knees to the young girl's side. Beneath the outline of Horsa's cloak, the girl was trembling and moaning as if racked with fever. The older woman drew back the cloak a little, laid her hand tenderly on the top of the girl's head, and began to gently stroke her hair.

'Who are these women?'

Horsa spun around. He had not noticed his brother enter the barn. Aelfric was at his side, as usual.

The soldiers were looking at one another, as if hoping someone else might reply.

'You will answer me!' Hengist bellowed.

One man stepped forward, contrite. 'We found them hiding up there, lord.' He pointed to the loft space above his head.

'And did you rape both of them?'

The soldier glanced at his companions, but they simply bowed their heads and stared at the straw strewn floor.

'Yes, lord. We drank too much,' the soldier replied, his voice wavering. 'It will not happen again.'

Hengist glared at each man in turn. The tension in the barn was palpable, the only sound the young girl's moans and her mother's unearthly keening. And then, finally, Hengist turned to Aelfric.

'Kill them.'

There was a heartbeat's pause, as if the world had stopped, and then the barn erupted into panic. The farmer's wife must have guessed the meaning of Hengist's words, for she let out an anguished cry. Clutching her daughter to her breast, she began to rock her back and forth like a babe in arms.

The soldiers in the barn were unarmed, their weapons stacked against their tents. They glanced desperately at one another and then they scattered, frantically weaving between barrows and barrels, hay bales and sacks of grain, searching in vain for another way out of the barn. In the confusion, the torchbearer dropped the brand, and flames began to lick across the straw strewn floor.

Led by Aelfric, Hengist's household guards pursued the soldiers, swords raised ready for the kill. But then Aelfric hesitated, glancing back at Hengist for clarification.

'You mean the men, lord?'

'No, the women.'

'What?' Horsa breathed, horrified, but Aelfric did not question his lord's command. He simply turned around, grabbed the naked girl by the hair, and wrenched her from her mother's arms. Wrenching her head back to expose her neck, he drew his dagger across her throat. Then, in an obscene parody of solicitude, he carefully laid her back down again. He turned next to the mother, dispatching her with the same cold efficiency. As the light went from her eyes, she was still trying to reach out for her daughter.

The dropped torch was still ablaze and the fire was taking hold now, dense black smoke and burning straw swirling about the barn. The heat was intense but Horsa barely noticed. He just stood and stared, horror-struck, at the women's corpses. His father would never have ordered the killing of women. How could Hengist do such a thing? Surely the goddess would curse him for this atrocity?

'What's the matter with you, brother? Do you want to be burned alive?' Grabbing Horsa's shoulders, Hengist forcibly manhandled him out of the barn.

76

Horsa fell to his knees and coughed and retched. He felt as if his lungs were on fire.

'Why did you do that?' he asked at last. 'Why did you kill the women? It wasn't necessary!'

'It was entirely necessary. The Saxon race is pure. We cannot mate with these filthy Britons. We cannot risk diluting our bloodline.'

Horsa pulled a face. 'The blood of this island flows through my veins. My mother was a Briton, and you insult her memory with your ignorant, bigoted words. Time and time again, you defy the goddess, Hengist. And one day you will pay.'

'No, brother, it is you who defies the goddess, by failing to fulfil your oaths of allegiance,' Hengist replied contemptuously. 'You question my every order. I cannot rely on you. I cannot trust you.'

Horsa opened his mouth to reply but succumbed to another violent coughing fit. Hengist eyed him disdainfully then strode back towards the blazing barn.

'If you don't get the fire under control,' he yelled at his men, 'I'll throw you all in the barn, barricade the doors and listen to your screams as you burn. And mark me well – Nifheim awaits you, for the Valkyries will not carry charred and useless corpses through the golden gates of Valhalla!'

And then, seemingly as an afterthought, he barked:

'Hang the rapists from the nearest tree. Let it be known that any man who ruts with a British woman will share the same fate.'

The following morning, the barn still smouldered, a skeleton of blackened timbers against the pale pink dawn. Horsa did not want to leave the farmer and his family for the wolves and so, in defiance of his brother, he ordered a burial pit to be dug so the family might be reunited in death. He rode away from the farmstead in morose silence, Hengist's callous brutality casting a pall over the prospect of being reunited with Elsbet.

He had hoped they would reach Corinium by nightfall, but herding the farmer's sheep and cattle was drastically slowing their progress. And the supply wagons were even heavier now, laden with grain, fowl cages, farm implements and kitchen pots.

Horsa knew the fledgling settlement at Corinium was in desperate need of these supplies, and they would make Elsbet's life far more comfortable. But the further delay was agonising. She was so close now and yet still so far.

They finally reached Corinium two days later. Horsa looked up at the high walls of the Roman city, his exhilaration at the thought of seeing Elsbet tempered with a creeping sense of unease. Shaven headed warriors were watching them from the battlements, the emblem of the black boar prominent on their leather cuirasses.

What were Vortigern's men doing here?

Hengist had ordered his hall to be built in the amphitheatre which lay just outside the walls of Corinium. Like so many of his kin, he loathed stone-built Roman cities, preferring to rest his head beneath wood and thatch.

The amphitheatre reminded Horsa of a huge, high sided bowl, the ancient wooden tiers of seating now smothered beneath tall grasses and saplings of alder, ash and birch. With its steep banks and single entrance, it was an easily defended, ready-made fortress.

Hengist's carpenters had been busy. The air was sweet with the scent of freshly hewn timber, the earth speckled with sawdust like blossom in springtime. A newly-fashioned palisade circled the top of the bank and sturdy gates guarded the entrance. Inside the arena, stables, kitchens, workshops, and a smithy were under construction. At its centre, stood a large wood-framed hall, thickly thatched with reeds from the river-bank. The hall reminded Horsa of home, its design identical to his father's hall in Saxony.

The settlement was full of life and noise. Scores of fighting men sat at trestle tables, eating and drinking in the late afternoon sunshine, their spears and shields stacked under the eaves of the hall. Axes chopped, hammers clashed, dogs barked and women chatted as they carried water from the river, small children at their heels.

At the sight of the warband approaching, one of the fighting men stood up and approached Hengist.

'Lord, my name is Sigbert, late come from Saxony to offer you my spear, my allegiance and my oath.'

Hengist inclined his head in acknowledgement but his gaze flickered over Sigbert's head towards the men at the trestle tables. Horsa wondered if he was disappointed, if he had hoped for greater numbers.

'Lord,' Sigbert went on. 'Vortigern has summoned you. There is a warband, two hundred strong, waiting to escort you to Aquae Sulis. They are billeted in the city of stone.'

Hengist nodded again then curtly dismissed Sigbert, his expression impenetrable.

'Will you go to Aquae Sulis?' Horsa asked under his breath, fear snaking about his heart.

'Of course I will go.'

'Is that wise, brother?'

'He sends two hundred warriors. What choice do I have? And besides, if Vortigern had wanted us dead, he would have ambushed us on the road.'

Horsa had expected nothing less from his brother. It

seemed Hengist intended to walk into the monster's lair with his head held high, as if he were Beowulf reborn. But then he pushed all thoughts of Vortigern and his reckless brother from his mind. Dismounting, he thrust the reins towards the nearest soldier and broke into a run, searching the camp for Elsbet.

Three seasons had passed since he had last held her in his arms, and every day without her had felt colourless and empty. His heart was pounding, his head a storm of clashing emotions: excitement and anticipation, nervousness and prickly apprehension. His love for her had not diminished, if anything, it had grown stronger in her absence. But would she still feel the same way about him?

He came to an abrupt halt. She was walking towards the great hall, her arms full of logs. She was moving quickly, her face set in concentration, and he guessed the logs were too heavy for her. For a moment, he just stood and stared, drinking her in. Sunlight was catching her long, flowing hair and it shone like spun gold. She had not changed; she was just as he remembered her.

She turned then, perhaps sensing his gaze upon her, and he saw her eyes widen with surprise then delight. She dropped the logs, stumbling over them in her haste. He laughed out loud and then they were running, and suddenly they were in each other's arms. He clung to her, revelling in her softness and warmth. He didn't want to let her go, as if this perfect moment might somehow obliterate all those long, cold, miserable months on the wall of Hadrian. As if she alone had the power to absolve him of all the blood he had spilled, all the suffering he had caused, all the lives he had failed to save.

'I've missed you so much,' Elsbet breathed.

Her hands were sliding down his back, pressing him closer

still. He let out a groan of desire and bent to kiss her eyes, her nose, her cheeks, her lips. 'I've missed you too,' he said, and then he laughed because the phrase was utterly inadequate to describe how wretched he had felt without her. 'I love you! I love you so much!' he shouted at the top of his voice.

He held her tightly about the waist and lifted her, turning round and round until the world blurred and the only sound he could hear was her laughter ringing in his ears. When he finally lowered her back to the ground, they fell into each other's arms once again.

'Is there somewhere we can go to be alone?' he asked.

She nodded, her eyes alight with anticipation. Taking him by the hand, she led him out of the amphitheatre. Many trees had been felled for Hengist's hall, but a wide tract of forest remained untouched. Brambles tugged at their cloaks as they picked their way through the dense undergrowth. Finally, Elsbet came to a halt beneath an ancient oak. There were tight lipped buds on the branches, the promise of spring.

She turned to face him. Her expression, so full of love and longing, was Horsa's undoing. His lips found hers again and their kisses were no longer tentative but urgent and full of need. He felt her fingers at his belt, fumbling to unfasten the buckle. Through a haze of longing, he remembered they were still unwed. With his last shred of will-power, he pushed her hands away.

'No, Elsbet. We must not.'

'But I want you, please, Horsa, please don't stop!'

'I must stop. I love you too much to dishonour you.' Horsa's voice was strained, desire and frustration coursing through his veins.

'But we're far from home. No-one cares what we do here. No rules, no parents, no priests!' she pleaded.

'Elsbet,' Horsa cupped her face in his hands. 'Your parents allowed you to come here because they trusted me.'

Tears of frustration were running down Elsbet's cheeks and he wiped them away with his thumbs.

'Let's find a priest to marry us, right now,' he said gently.

'You weren't listening. There isn't one. He died of a fever before I arrived.'

Horsa felt a flicker of alarm. It was surely bad luck to build a hall without a priest to bestow the blessings of the gods upon it, or to carve the sacred runes about the door. But he did not voice his misgivings.

'The spring tides will bring many more boats from Saxony,' he said reassuringly. 'A priest will come - I am certain of it. We will not have to wait much longer.'

'But I don't want to wait a heartbeat longer!'

Elsbet's expression was defiant. She continued to glare at him whilst he merely smiled in return and held his ground. Her feistiness was just one of the many things he had always loved about her, but he could not betray her family's trust.

Finally, she said, 'you're not going to change your mind, are you?'

'No, my love, I'm not.'

In response, she attempted to look fierce and unforgiving, but the corners of her mouths soon twitched into a grin.

'By the goddess, it's impossible to be angry with you for long, Horsa son of Athelwald.' Sighing deeply, she put her head against his chest and held him close. 'I like listening to your heartbeat,' she said softly. 'It's strong and steadfast, like you.'

She did not see his grimace. Elsbet saw him as a strong, valiant warrior, but he knew himself to be a mere lackey to a cruel and dangerous man. The air was cold and the ground was damp, but they huddled up beneath Horsa's cloak, cocooned from the world. He stroked her hair and held her close, and she told him of the sea-crossing to Britannia.

Until that day she had never even seen an ocean, and she had felt in awe of its cold, grey vastness and its towering waves, of the howling wind and the eerie cries of the gulls. Until she had come to Britannia, she had never seen a hill either, but here, the ground rose and fell dizzily towards the far horizon, like the pleats of a belted gown.

'This is an alien land, Horsa - cities of stone and distaff-straight roads. I miss Saxony,' she whispered apologetically.

Horsa felt as if he had been punched in the gut. Disappointment surged through him. It had never crossed his mind that she might not be happy here. He clasped her cold hands in his.

'I'm so sorry. You shouldn't have come, sweetheart. You must go home, to your family. I will follow you, as soon as I am able.'

'That's not what I meant!' Elsbet exclaimed. 'I don't want to go home. I want to be with you. You are my family now.'

'Are you certain?'

'I've never been more certain about anything.'

Horsa's face lit up into a broad smile. Part of him knew he was being deeply selfish allowing her to stay, but the other part was relieved beyond measure. 'So, tell me about home.'

Elsbet snuggled back into his embrace.

'Where shall I begin? Your father is in good health, although he misses you greatly. When you all went away, he was lost for a time. The council urged him to take a wife. I think they hoped a young bride might distract him, but he refused to countenance the idea. It seems he will do nothing to dishonour your mother's memory.'

'He dishonoured my mother's memory by allowing Emma to be sacrificed,' Horsa said angrily.

'It was the high priest's decision,' Elsbet replied gently. 'Your father had no choice, but he has suffered terribly. I don't think he will ever forgive himself for it.'

A shadow passed over Horsa's face. 'I don't think I will ever forgive him for it. The high priest was wrong. Anya listens to the goddess. She knows Nerthus does not demand human blood.'

Sensing his deteriorating mood, Elsbet kissed him again. When they eventually drew apart she said, 'Abberlen, the little refugee boy Anya cared for, has made a good recovery. He is now an apprentice in the place of healing, and he is learning our tongue. But the Huns, the tribe that made an orphan of him, are pushing eastwards. Refugees are flooding into Saxony and your father welcomes them all, but our grain-pits are dangerously low. There is a limit to how many mouths we can feed.'

Horsa nodded grimly. How soon before the Huns, with their fast, agile warhorses and their deadly curved swords, reached the borders of Germania? Would the Germanic tribes unite against them, or would Athelwald, high king of Saxony, be forced to stand alone?

'Vortigern's men are in the city of stone. They are to accompany you to Aquae Sulis,' Elsbet said nervously.

'Yes, so I have heard.'

'They patrol the battlements, looking down on us like gods in Asgard. Tell me, why do they shave their heads? Do they have lice?'

Horsa grinned. 'I think they wish to emulate their warlord. Vortigern's scalp resembles a plucked chicken.'

Elsbet laughed but then a thought struck her. 'We came

ashore at Andereida. It is full of Saxons loyal to Hengist. Do you think Vortigern knows?'

'I am certain he knows,' Horsa replied dourly. 'Hengist is encouraging men from Germania to join him. He intends to ask Vortigern to extend the terms of the treaty.'

'Will Vortigern agree to such a demand?'

'I very much doubt it.' Cold fear was settling in Horsa's stomach.

He yearned to take Elsbet far away from this wretched island, but if he abandoned his brother now, he would break his oaths and bring dishonour to his family. He would no longer be welcome in his father's hall. He would be an outcast, an exile.

He glanced at Elsbet. Could he force such a life upon her? A life of shame and ignominy?

'Let me come with you to Aquae Sulis,' Elsbet said suddenly.

'What? No! Absolutely not! Vortigern is a dangerous man. I don't want you near him.'

Elsbet frowned. 'Do you think Anya is happy, married to such a man?'

Horsa was certain Anya was not happy. He had not found a way to save his sister from her fate, and he had to live with his shame and guilt and regret every single day.

'I have not seen her for a long time. I cannot say if she is happy,' he mumbled.

'She is my best friend. I would so like to see her again,' Elsbet persisted.

'You don't understand. Hengist's ambition has made him reckless. He has put us all in danger.'

'But you are Vortigern's kin by marriage now. Surely that means something? Surely that gives you some protection?'

'You haven't met him. You don't know what he is capable of.' Horsa's voice sounded hollow.

'If he is such an ogre, why did you let Anya marry him?' Elsbet asked, bewildered.

He lowered his eyes, too ashamed to meet her questioning gaze.

Elsbet entwined her fingers with his. 'I watched you ride away from me in Saxony and it hurt, it physically hurt. I felt as if I was being wrenched in two. And in the year we were apart, every day felt like a lifetime without you. And now, finally, we are together again, there is not the slightest chance I am going to let you ride away from me again so soon. I am coming with you to Aquae Sulis, whether you like it or not.'

Horsa looked up at her. 'I just want to keep you safe.'

'I understand that, but do you remember our betrothal oaths? You asked me to share your toils and dangers, and to be your partner in all your sufferings and adventures, be it peace or war. And I have heard the men talking. They say these borderlands are lawless. I will be safer at your side.' Elsbet paused. 'And besides, I really need to see Anya.'

Horsa let out a deep sigh. In his mind's eye, he could see Marcus's town house in Calleva. The air had been suffused with roses, too sweet a scent for what had come to pass. If he could ask the goddess for one wish, he would relive that day, and he would find a way to spare Anya. He stared searchingly into Elsbet's deep blue eyes. Perhaps, in some small way, he could make amends. And so, against all his better judgement, he said:

'So be it. Come to Aquae Sulis. I know Anya would dearly love to see you again.'

NINE

The kingdom of Siluria

Far away in the soft south, there were the first tentative signs of spring. But winter had dug its claws deep into the valley in the shadow of the mountains, and refused to let go. The snow did not thaw and nor did the icicles on the eaves of the round-houses. The clouds hung low, swathing the village in a cold, sticky mist as if Nifheim had opened its gates upon the world. The grain stores were empty now and yet no-one spoke of it. Instead, the villagers doggedly went about their daily routines, as if by refusing to acknowledge they were slowly starving, they would somehow keep death from the door.

Until Anya had come to the valley, she had never known hunger. As the daughter of a king, the table in the golden hall was always laden with food no matter how harsh the winter. But now, her belly ached and her ribs protruded from her skin like the planks of a clinker built ship. She had been drawn to this place, and she had found the sense of belonging she craved amongst Eown's kin, but she had been shocked to the core by the grim reality of their lives.

Rolling up her sleeves, she squeezed out the cloth and gently wiped Rhiannon's face. She could feel the little girl's fever burning through the linen. The child was listless, lucid one moment, the next, lapsing into long, incoherent rambles. Olwen lay at her sister's side. She had not opened her eyes for some time and her pulse was erratic, her breathing laboured. Anya could hear the fluid filling her lungs; the little girl was slowly drowning.

'Here!' Ceinwin, wheezing and out of breath, held out two wooden beakers. 'Make sure they drink all of this.'

Despite the scarcity of food, and the fact that the old woman never seemed to eat, Ceinwin's enormous body was still enveloped in rolls of soft fat. But she had long since stopped asking young men to help her up. With more than half the inhabitants of the village sick, there was no time for such frivolity. Anya took the beakers and sniffed their contents. 'Thyme?' she enquired.

'And milkwort and lungwort, hyssop, nettles, vervain, valerian.' Ceinwin rattled off the list impatiently. 'Just give it to them.'

Anya hesitated. Although Ceinwin's herbs were proven medicines, her potions were not helping the little girls. If their fevers did not break, they would soon join their parents beyond the veil.

'Is there something you want to say?' Ceinwin asked sharply. 'Spit it out, girl.'

'We need to bring their fevers down. I think we should try a yarrow-infused bath.'

'I use yarrow for wounds, not fevers,' Ceinwin said irritably.

'I use it for both,' Anya replied evenly. 'Do you have any?'

Ceinwin's expressive eyebrows darted up her forehead like startled hairy caterpillars. She let out a loud, indignant snort and heaved herself to her feet again.

'I'll fetch it,' she said, waddling away towards the herb store behind the wicker partition. She returned carrying bundles of dried yarrow, tied together with hemp string.

'You are your mother's daughter, and no mistake,' Ceinwin announced huffily as they crushed the delicate flower heads into a pot of boiling water over the fire.

Anya felt her heart skip a beat, for Ceinwin so rarely mentioned Eown. 'What do you mean?' she asked, but then Rhys arrived to take over wiping the little girls' brows, and the moment passed.

It took a long time to fill the wooden bath tub, carefully mixing boiling water with cold.

'It's too hot now,' Rhys fretted, dipping his elbow into the water yet again.

The little girls were painfully thin, their skin as pale as a kernel of unripened wheat. Olwen was barely conscious and had to be held in the yarrow infused water for fear she might drown. Rhiannon resisted, batting Anya away as if she were an unwelcome wasp. Her dark eyes were glassy, her cheeks defined by bright red splodges of fever.

'How long must they stay in the bath?' Rhys asked anxiously. He had lost both his parents and it was obvious he could not bear the thought of losing his sisters too.

'Until the water cools. The yarrow will open their pores and draw out the fever,' Anya replied, kneeling down next to him. Cupping her hands, she began to trickle the water over the girls' small bodies.

'Are you sure this will work?' Rhys persisted.

'I am certain of it.' She wasn't certain at all, but she couldn't think of anything else to try. And then, to distract him, she told him the story of yarrow's healing powers. 'Long ago, the ancient medicine men noticed that the centre of each tiny flower shimmers in the moonlight. And in this way, they learnt that yarrow was a gift from Luna, goddess of the moon. It bestows the coolness of moonlight, and it will break even the highest fever.'

She prayed she was not offering Rhys false hope. She had seen so many people die in the place of healing in Saxony. She had sung to them to ease their passing, but she did not want to sing to Olwen and Rhiannon. They were too young, too innocent, to wander in the cold mists of Nifheim for all eternity. Time passed, the bath water cooled, and Anya's thoughts drifted to Dumnonia. She had sensed Etar's spirit passing through the veil, which meant Silvanus was king of Dumnonia now, with a lifetime of duty and responsibility stretching out ahead of him. He had not relished the thought of it. In fact, he had railed against it.

'Their skin feels cooler!' Rhys exclaimed, drawing her back from her reverie.

She placed a hand on Olwen's forehead then Rhiannon's. The children were no longer burning hot. It seemed their fevers had broken.

'Will they be alright now?' Rhys asked apprehensively.

'They're not out of danger yet. There's still a long way to go,' Anya replied cautiously but, even so, she said a silent prayer of thanks. She did not know why the goddess had brought her to this claustrophobic round-house, this place of stark extremes, of sickness and hunger, of blood-ties and close kinship, of music, laughter and joy. An entire world within a world. But at least there was hope now. Hope that two little girls would live to feel the summer sun on their faces. And hope, no matter how fragile, was worth a hundred hungry nights.

TEN

Aquae Sulis, kingdom of the Dobunni

The road to Aquae Sulis was as silent as a burial chamber. Vortigern's warband took the lead; Hengist's warband brought up the rear. An atmosphere of mutual mistrust curdled the damp, still air. They passed abandoned farmsteads, the scorched and blackened timbers of burnt barns looming eerily out of the fog. The carcases of dead sheep, picked clean by wolves, dotted a nearby field, a grim parody of a grazing flock. It seemed to Horsa as if the island of Britannia was slowly dying, torn apart by bloodshed. Who had destroyed these farms? The Irish raiders who swarmed across Britannia, paying no heed to borders, leaving terror and misery in their wake. Or the Coritani, seeking vengeance for the death of their king?

He glanced at Elsbet, riding at his side. Part of him, the selfish part, was glad she was with him. The other part wished he had not exposed her to the dangers of the open road. He should have left her behind at Corinium. At least there she would have had the protection of freshly hewn gates and a sturdy palisade.

Reaching over, he touched her arm and smiled reassuringly.

'Not much further now. Look. The Romans buried their dead outside the city walls.'

Up ahead, the road was lined with stone mausoleums. Years of wind and rain had worn away the epitaphs of these long dead Romans, their names, once fondly remembered, now indecipherable and forgotten.

The gates opened, and they rode into the city. If the countryside was deserted, Aquae Sulis was a tumult of noise, the streets bustling with a thousand pinched and hungry faces. The air reeked with the stench of an overcrowded city. Blocked drains, human ordure, animal dung, midden pits, the acrid stink of stale urine in the tanners' vats, the putrid undercurrent of sickness and disease.

But no matter how crowded the streets became, the throng shrank back from Hengist's warband, pressing themselves against the walls as they rode by. Hengist ignored the crowds, but Horsa scanned the sea of faces with a mounting sense of alarm.

He could see envy in their eyes – envy for his thoroughbred stallion with its gold bridle fittings, for his finely woven woollen cloak, for his priceless sword and its jewelled encrusted scabbard, but he could also see their fear. These wretched folk were seeking refuge, not just from the Irish but also from the men of Germania – men who beached their long boats on the shores of Britannia and stole women and children, gold and silver, cattle and crops, farmsteads and land.

These people were afraid of him. He was the enemy here. How, for the love of the gods, had such a thing come to pass? All he had ever wanted was a farm, a family. He glanced at Elsbet. All he had ever wanted was her.

Elsbet's eyes were wide with amazement as she gazed at

magnificent facades of decorated stone, at majestic temples fronted by rows of graceful, soaring columns, at bath houses, their domed roofs like clusters of mushrooms. She had heard stories of these Roman cities, but this place surpassed her wildest imaginings.

'How did they build such a place?' she asked in awe.

'Surely the question should be why they built it, not how?' Horsa replied.

He hated the monstrous architecture of Rome. Every town was just like the last, a suffocating tomb of stone.

Sensing his anxiety, Elsbet smiled at him. 'Anya is here. All will be well.'

Horsa smiled bleakly in return. He wished he shared her optimism.

After the overcrowded streets, the forum was deserted, a vast expanse of flag stones and grey puddles reflecting a vast, grey sky. Horsa helped Elsbet dismount in the shadow of the basilica. It loomed over them, many storeys high.

'What is this place?' she whispered.

'I presume this is Vortigern's hall,' Horsa replied flatly.

Elsbet cast a beseeching glance at him. 'You agreed I could see Anya.'

Horsa looked into her cornflower blue eyes, his thoughts in turmoil. Vortigern was like a straw demon on a hot summer's day, creating a storm around him, bending the world to his will. He didn't want Elsbet exposed to such a storm. He wanted to keep her safe. Quite suddenly, a fresh wave of remorse crashed over him.

He hadn't kept Anya safe. She sat at Vortigern's right hand, she shared his bed.

Did his sister blame him for her fate? Did she hate him for it? He would find out, soon enough. He squeezed Elsbet's hand, his mind made up. After everything he had done, or failed to do, he could not deny Anya and Elsbet the chance to see each other again. Turning to Hengist, he announced:

'Elsbet is coming with us.'

Hengist shrugged his shoulders, disinterested.

A small, slightly built man was waiting for them at the top of the basilica steps. 'I am Rufus, second-in-command to Vortigern, high king of the Dobunni.'

'I remember you. Didn't Vortigern call you his scribe?' Hengist asked scathingly.

Rufus's expression soured. 'You will disarm here. Five men may accompany you into Vortigern's presence.'

Hengist mistook it for a negotiation. 'Ten.'

'Five, no more.'

Hengist's eyes narrowed but he turned and quickly chose Horsa, Aelfric and three others. Unbuckling his sword belt, he thrust it into the arms of the nearest guard then gestured for his chosen men to do the same.

Surreptitiously, Horsa clasped Elsbet's hand and they fell in behind the small group. To his amazement he noticed the tread of a thousand footsteps had worn down the marble steps, each shallow dip as smooth and shiny as the inside of a shell. Their footsteps echoed around the basilica hall as the scribe led them across the vast marble floor.

Horsa looked about in astonishment. The nave was more than seventy feet high, a soaring cavern of cold stone. He could not comprehend why anyone would choose to live in such an inhospitable place. The streets of Aquae Sulis had smelled foul, but the stale air in the basilica held its own kind of menace. It was hard to believe this was Anya's home now. His kind and clever sister did not deserve to live out her days in this terrible place.

Rufus opened a second set of doors and gestured for them to follow him. After the cold and damp of the basilica hall, this chamber was stiflingly hot and wreathed in wood smoke. A mosaic covered the floor, darkened by soot from the makeshift hearth at its centre.

Vortigern was sitting on a raised dais at the far end of the chamber. He was just as Horsa remembered him – as strong and solid as a watchtower, coarse-featured, his head shaved, his scalp as stubbled as freshly scythed wheat. Instinctively, he manoeuvred Elsbet behind him, out of sight.

There was a youth at Vortigern's side on the dais, a younger, slimmer version of the warlord. Horsa guessed this must be Ronan, the wastrel son he had heard so much about. The boy was biting his fingernails, tearing neat half-moons with his teeth then spitting them out.

'Where's Anya?' Elsbet whispered.

'I don't know,' Horsa replied under his breath without turning around.

Vortigern stood up. 'You have courage, Hengist, I'll give you that.'

'Lord.' Hengist gave a small deferential nod.

'Or maybe you're moon-mad. I haven't made up my mind yet.'

Despite the intense heat in the room, the air seemed to freeze.

'Our treaty laid down the exact amount of land I would give you, and the exact amount of warriors you could bring into Britannia. And yet you took it upon yourself to send for more!' Vortigern bellowed.

Hengist's reply was admirably calm and controlled.

'I swore an oath to defend the northern frontier, but the wall of Hadrian is more than seventy miles long – I did not have enough men, and so I called for reinforcements.'

'Without my permission.'

'There is peace in the north, just as you asked,' Hengist replied levelly.

Horsa tried to hide his surprise. Hengist was a good liar. Sometimes, the northern tribes fought against each other. At other times, they joined forces and over-ran the wall to pillage and plunder the people of the Brigantes. In truth, there was never a single day of peace in the north.

'Your banner flies over the fort of Andereida. How do you explain that?' Vortigern took a step forward and Horsa quickly adjusted his stance, shielding Elsbet from Vortigern's line of sight again.

'The reinforcements from Germania serve you alone, lord. They keep your borders safe. In order to fulfil my oath to you, I need a safe harbour, and Andereida serves me well. I could not risk losing my ships to winter storms.'

'You have broken the terms of the treaty,' Vortigern said loudly, menacingly. 'And now the white wolf flies over Eboracum.'

Horsa held his breath. This was the crux of it. He glanced at his brother. Astonishingly, Hengist's outward demeanour remained one of absolute composure.

'The tribes beyond the wall are cunning, lord,' Hengist replied, his tone measured. 'They raid by ship, sailing down the east coast then using the rivers to plunder far inland. As you are aware, Eboracum lies on the confluence of two such rivers. I need a presence there, to deter the Picts from striking deep into your territories. I swear on my father's life - I am, and always will be, your loyal oath-man.'

'You insult me with your lies, Saxon!' Vortigern roared. 'You have broken your oaths, and you have shown no loyalty.

You do not serve me. You serve only yourself, and you will pay a heavy price for your betrayal.' He paused, for effect. 'I hereby sentence you to death, the manner yet to be decided, but I promise you, it will not be quick.'

'No!' Elsbet cried out in horror.

Vortigern cocked his head and fixed his gaze upon Elsbet, noticing her for the first time. The smile that formed upon his face turned Horsa's stomach and the world shifted beneath his feet.

Despite the pronouncement of his own death sentence, Hengist betrayed no outward hint of alarm. Instead, he held his head high.

'You need me, lord. Without my men, you will lose control of the north.'

Vortigern climbed down the steps of the dais, each thudding footfall as ominous as a death knell. He walked across the mosaic floor and came to a halt just inches from Hengist's nose. And then he glared at him, as if willing him to buckle beneath the weight of his menace. Hengist did not flinch. It appeared to Horsa as if a silent battle was raging between the two men. Ronan continued to bite his nails. Rufus picked invisible crumbs from his tunic. Neither Vortigern nor Hengist broke eye contact, but it was Vortigern who spoke first.

'This is not a negotiation. This is an ultimatum. You are under my command. You are answerable to me. From this day forth, you will not wipe your arse without my permission. Do you understand?'

'Yes, lord.'

'No more ships, no more reinforcements, or I will personally gut you, and your men, and your women, and your children, like a barrel of bream. Do you understand?'

'Yes, lord.'

Horsa glanced at his brother. The muscles in Hengist's jaw were clenched so tightly there were veins straining beneath his skin. Horsa knew it was taking enormous self-control for Hengist to accept this public humiliation. Ronan was still studiously examining his nails, seemingly oblivious to his surroundings. Rufus, however, was glowering at Vortigern, and Horsa remembered Calleva, how the scribe had voiced his doubts about the wisdom of making treaties with Saxon warbands.

Of Anya, there was still no sign. He wondered if she was resting. Was it possible she was with child? Or perhaps she was unwell? The winter had been harsh. They had lost many strong men to fever and coughing sickness on the wall. A sudden, terrible thought struck him. Perhaps Anya was dead.

Without thinking, he blurted, 'where is our sister?'

Vortigern turned sharply. 'So, you can speak after all. I've no idea where she is,' he added carelessly.

'What do you mean, lord?' Horsa asked, confused.

'I mean, she's gone. You weren't the only ones to break the terms of the treaty.'

'Gone?' Horsa repeated faintly, struggling to understand. The warlord's casual tone belied the expression in his eyes. Horsa couldn't decide if Vortigern looked angry or ashamed. Goddess forbid, had he grown tired of Anya and found an excuse to put her to death?

'What did you do to my sister?' The words were out before Horsa could stop them, loaded with accusation.

Vortigern's eyes narrowed. 'What did you say, boy?'

Lightning fast, Hengist stepped between them. 'My brother is young and impetuous. He meant nothing by it.'

Horsa's thoughts were reeling. If Anya had passed through

the veil, surely he would have felt her departure from this world? But if she was still alive, where was she?

'So, who is this?' Vortigern's gaze had settled upon Elsbet once again.

Horsa jolted as if he had been run through. 'She is my betrothed,' he replied, in a voice that did not sound his own.

Elsbet was staring fixedly at the floor, colour rising in her cheeks.

'You're a lucky man, Saxon. She's beautiful.'

Horsa recognised the look in Vortigern's eyes because he had stared at Anya in exactly the same way. Instinctively, Horsa reached for the sword at his belt, and then he remembered he was unarmed. His hands balled into fists at his sides. He was not predisposed to violence, but at that moment, he wanted nothing more than to punch Vortigern again, and again, and again, until he had wiped the lecherous, ugly smirk from the man's face.

From the corner of his eye, Horsa saw Hengist shake his head; saw the unspoken warning in his eyes.

'I will find Anya,' Vortigern said, his gaze still fixed upon Elsbet. 'And when I do, I will have justice. In my kingdom, the punishment for runaway wives is death.'

On the dais, Ronan looked up from his nails. Rufus's hands fluttered out in front of him, as if he was trying and failing to catch an invisible butterfly. Elsbet's head shot up, her eyes wide with alarm. And something snapped inside Horsa. He launched himself at Vortigern, his fists flying in a cataclysmic storm of rage.

'You will not touch my sister! You will not hurt her! Where is she? What did you do to her?'

Hengist moved fast, forcibly restraining him.

'My brother speaks out of turn,' he shouted over Horsa's

anguished tirade. 'It is not our place to interfere in matters between you and your wife.'

Vortigern raised his eyebrows, regarding Horsa as if he were a misbehaving child.

'Evidently, your young brother has no self-control, but then why should he? He is a pagan savage. His behaviour is further proof that your barbarian kind cannot be trusted.'

Horsa's protests died in his throat, and terror coiled about his heart. He had made things worse. Much worse. Their lives were now balanced precariously on a tipping point of his own making. The tension in the air stretched and grew taut, like wool on a spindle whorl.

'What must I do to convince you of my loyalty?' Hengist asked steadily. 'Name it, lord, and it will be done.'

Vortigern was looking at Elsbet again, looking at her as if she were a ripe peach.

'You can give me hostages,' he replied and pointed at Elsbet. 'I'll take her, for a start.'

'No...' Elsbet breathed.

She glanced, horror-struck, at Horsa. The colour had drained from her face and she looked as if her legs were about to give way beneath her.

Fury exploded in Horsa's chest. 'No - you can't have her! Elsbet and I are betrothed! You can't do this, not again!'

'I don't give a fuck who she's betrothed to,' Vortigern replied. 'But if you honour the terms of our treaty, no harm will come to her.'

'I accept your terms,' Hengist replied, without hesitation.

'No!' Horsa tore himself from Hengist's hold and pulled Elsbet into his arms. Her body was trembling, hot tears pouring silently down her cheeks.

'Let go of her,' Hengist commanded.

Horsa held Elsbet tighter still. 'I will not let you do this, brother. Not again.'

Hengist's reply, spoken in the Saxon tongue, was eerily calm.

'I do what I must, because so much depends on this. You will let her go.'

Horsa's agony took physical form; it was fire searing through his veins, pulsing towards his heart. Releasing Elsbet, he turned to Vortigern.

'Elsbet is mine,' he said slowly, deliberately. 'She belongs to me. She stays with me.'

To his dismay, he realised Vortigern was laughing at him. The fire in Horsa's veins reached his heart and ignited. He clenched his right hand into a fist and swung it at Vortigern's chin. For a big man, the warlord had surprisingly quick reflexes. He ducked, and Horsa's fist flew harmlessly through the air above his head. Vortigern laughed again, goading, mocking.

Horsa raised his fists and took another swing. The searing pain in his skull was unexpected, blinding in its intensity, and his vision began to swim. Somewhere in the distance, he heard Elsbet scream.

And then Vortigern smashed his sword pommel into the back of Horsa's skull for a second time.

'Elsbet,' Horsa breathed, before his knees buckled beneath him, and his world faded to white.

ELEVEN

The kingdom of Siluria

Blood was pouring from the mountain side, choking the stream and running between the round-houses in a torrent of gore. The sword, the same sword she had seen so many times before, was held aloft, and it alone had the power to turn back the tide of blood.

Anya stirred in her sleep and the dream shifted, as if the wind had changed direction.

She was in Tintagel and she was happy because soon she would see Silvanus again. But something was wrong. There were no children playing, no bustling market in the ley of the walls. Blood ran in thick rivulets across the courtyard. Full of dread, she began to walk towards the hall…

Outside, an icicle crashed to the ground and she awakened with jolt. It took a moment to remember where she was. Turning onto her side, she buried herself deeper into her bed rugs. She wanted to go back to sleep, to continue with the dream. She needed to see inside the hall of Tintagel. She needed to know if Silvanus was safe.

But sleep evaded her, and so she lay in the semi-darkness listening to the sound of water dripping from the eaves. The thaw had begun and it seemed as if the entire world was melting. What were her dreams trying to tell her? Was she seeing things past, or things yet to come? An image of Silvanus sprang into her head, those hazelnut brown eyes, the way his short brown hair fell across his forehead. She pictured his broad shoulders and honed muscles, and an ache of longing rippled deep in her belly.

'Anya!' Olwen and Rhiannon raced around the wicker partition and jumped onto her bed. 'Get up! Get up! Ceinwin says we can help her cook today. You've got to come!'

Anya sat up, and smiled fondly. The yarrow infusion had broken the girls' fever. They were still painfully thin, but they were full of life and mischief once again.

'What are we cooking?' Anya asked.

Olwen shrugged.

'Slug soup?' Anya suggested, and the girls pulled faces and giggled.

'Or maybe spider pie?' Anya went on.

The girls giggled again.

Anya flung back her blankets. 'I like spider pie the best, because the bugs jump out of the pie and they crawl all over you - like this!' And she dived at the girls, tickling them until they laughed and shrieked so loudly, they both got the hiccoughs.

By the time Anya had dressed, Olwen and Rhiannon were already at Ceinwin's side at the hearth. They were fighting over a wooden spoon, squawking like indignant chickens. Ceinwin pulled another spoon from her wicker basket and rapped their knuckles.

'Here. One each. Now stir!'

Anya sniffed the contents of the cooking pot. The old woman was a good cook. Even now, when there was no more meat or barley, she knew how to make a watery bean broth taste appetising by adding a sprig of sorrel or a bulb of wild garlic.

One of the hounds sidled close to the pot and Ceinwin chuckled.

'No meat in there, my handsome man,' she said, kissing the tip of its snout.

Anya stroked the dog's long coat. Her sleeve fell back to her elbow and Ceinwin's gaze settled on Anya's cartwheel shaped tattoo. Leaning forward, she ran her fat fingers over its raised edges.

'You were a priestess and yet you never speak of it. Tell me, child, why did you leave Saxony?'

Anya had told no-one about Emma. She had buried the memories of that terrible day somewhere deep and dark, but she had always known they could not stay hidden forever. Emma shared kinship with these people. They deserved to know the truth.

'I -' she began, but Rhys was walking towards them.

'I need to speak to you,' he said shyly, addressing Anya.

'Yes?'

'Not here,' he said, clearly embarrassed.

Anya glanced at Ceinwin. A huge grin was spreading across the old woman's face. Olwen and Rhiannon began to giggle behind their hands. Mystified, she stood up and followed Rhys to a quiet corner.

'Thank you for saving my sisters' lives,' he stammered, his cheeks flushing scarlet.

Anya smiled. 'I am happy they are well again.'

'This is for you.' Rhys pushed a wooden spoon into her hand.

Intrigued, Anya turned it over in her palm. It was crafted from a single piece of wood. Intricate carvings of ivy wound about the handle and at its tip perched a tiny squirrel with an acorn in its paws.

'This is incredible workmanship! Did you make it yourself?'

'I made it for you, Anya.'

She looked up at him, taken aback. 'Thank you. I shall treasure it,' she replied honestly.

He was staring at her intently and she sensed he was waiting for her to say something more, but she was at a loss.

'You have an amazing talent,' she added lamely.

He nodded curtly and she saw the disappointment in his eyes as he hurried away. Puzzled, she walked back to join Ceinwin, wondering how she had caused offence. The old woman held out her hand to examine the spoon.

'He has skill and no mistake,' she declared.

'What did you say? Did you say yes?' Olwen and Rhiannon were on their feet, their eyes wide with excitement.

'Go away girls. Now!' Ceinwin commanded.

There was such mastery in the old woman's tone that the girls put down their wooden spoons and fled.

'So, tell me,' Ceinwin asked calmly. 'What was your answer?'

'What do you mean?'

Ceinwin laughed so hard, her dark, mischievous eyes were entirely swallowed up by her soft, plump cheeks.

'This is a love token, you daft goat. In Siluria, they are given by a suitor to his beloved, as a way of proving his skills.'

'Rhys was proposing marriage?'

'Yes, my sweet girl.'

Astounded, Anya glanced around, but Rhys was nowhere to be seen.

She had not meant to hurt his feelings. Was this terrible misunderstanding somehow her fault? Had she encouraged him in some way, or led him to believe she was falling in love with him?

Her mind began to race. Rhys was a kind and considerate man. She had no doubt he would make a loving husband and a good father. He was offering her a home and perhaps, if the goddess willed it, children of her own. It was a tempting thought. Hadn't she come here in the hope of finding a place to belong? Perhaps she could find contentment with Rhys, perhaps even learn to love him, in time.

But was this truly what the goddess wanted for her? This small, hard life, wreathed in eye-stinging peat-smoke. This world within a world, where laughter was commonplace but scratch beneath the surface and you would find starvation, sickness and death.

And what of Silvanus? She had not learned to love him. She had always loved him. He made her feel as if she was returning home after many years of exile, as if a bubble of happiness had burst against her heart. She did not know if she would find joy with Silvanus in this life, or the next, or the next. But one day, perhaps many years from now, if the goddess willed it, they would be together again.

'This is my home now, and I am content here, but I can't marry Rhys,' she said sadly.

'No matter,' the old woman replied, patting her knee affectionately.

'I never meant to hurt him.'

'He'll survive. Get up, I have something for you.'

With Anya's assistance, Ceinwin struggled to her feet, and scraps of herbs that had lodged on her bosom tumbled to the floor. Anya followed her as she waddled to the pile of rugs that marked her sleeping space behind the wicker partitions. It was colder here and the air smelled of dirt-ingrained rugs and old furs, of damp earth floors, of the earthy tang of the few remaining beans and beats, and the sweetness of over-ripe apples. Ceinwin's belongings were squeezed between her bed and the wall. Wheezing from the effort of walking, she sat down and pulled aside an old, foul-smelling cloak.

The sword had lain in the darkness for many years, carefully hidden from prying eyes. Ceinwin picked it up, and thrust it broadside at Anya.

'Take it!'

Anya stared at the sword, bewildered. When she did not respond, Ceinwin simply placed it in her lap. The scabbard's bronze front plate was decorated with swirling patterns, inset with red glass. The handle and the hilt were also elaborately decorated with bronze, horn, and yet more red glass. Ceinwin leant over and touched the glass with her fat fingers.

'Blood,' she said. 'The blood of your enemies.'

'Blood?' Anya repeated faintly, remembering how blood poured from the mountainside, drowning Britannia is a sea of suffering, and only the sword had the power to hold it at bay. She clasped the grip, and withdrew the weapon from its scabbard. Even in the darkness behind the partition, she could see the intertwining spiral effect that swept the length of the pattern welded blade. A sword such as this needed god-given skill to create. It felt incredibly heavy and her forearm strained with the effort of holding it aloft.

'It belongs to you now,' Ceinwin said gently.

Anya had seen this sword so many times in her dream paths. But she had never expected to find it in a round-house in Siluria, surrounded by trays of wizened apples and beans. In truth, she had never expected to find it at all. And she was a priestess, not a warrior; she was trained to heal not harm. The sword was so heavy she could barely lift it, let alone wield it in anger. What, in the name of the goddess, was she supposed to do with it?

'What makes you so sure this sword is mine?'

'It's been handed down through countless generations. We have not always been sheep farmers. We come from a line of ancient kings. Through the turning years, many things have been forgotten, but one memory has remained. The sword must be given to the outcast, the wanderer with the eternal mark.' Ceinwin glanced down at Anya's tattoo and then up into her eyes again. 'You've seen this sword before, haven't you, in your dream paths?'

Anya wanted to deny it. She wanted to pretend she had never been tormented by such dreams. She wanted to work the looms, fetch the water, and prepare the food – simple, comforting tasks. She didn't want to believe the goddess had led her to Siluria for this ancient family heirloom, its blunt blade nicked and scarred from centuries of battle. She didn't want to begin to imagine what she was supposed to do with it.

'I'm not a warrior. I can never be a warrior.'

'Of course you can't,' Ceinwin replied briskly. 'Just look at you – so skinny these days you hardly have the strength to carry the pails from the stream.'

'Then why..?'

'I don't have the answers, my sweet. All I know is that the sword belongs to you now.'

Anya was struggling to make sense of any of it. Perhaps she was wallowing too deeply in dark imaginings. This place had wrapped its arms around her and held her close. These people had not treated her as another unwelcome mouth to feed, but as one of their own. Perhaps this sword was simply an affirmation she had found the place the goddess intended for her.

And yet, Ceinwin had called her the wanderer, the outsider, doomed never to belong. Was that the life that lay ahead for her? The life of the exile, endless years of searching for a home, a hearth, a welcome? She shivered, as if someone had walked over her grave, as if a veil had blown back to reveal an uncertain future, one she had not expected, or prepared for, or hoped for.

'I want to stay here,' she said helplessly.

Ceinwin smiled. 'I know you do, my sweet.'

'I'm afraid,' she whispered.

'We are all afraid. But it's what we do with our fear that makes us who we are.'

Anya could feel her sense of belonging slipping away from her, but she did not want to let it go.

'Were you close to my mother?' she asked, desperate to reaffirm her connection to this dark and smoky world.

'I loved her as if she were my own. She had a pure soul, just like you.'

There was a lump in Anya's throat. 'I feel close to her here.'

Ceinwin patted her arm. 'Fasten the sword to your belt. It's yours now. And keep it safe. Swear to me you will keep it safe.'

'I will, I swear.' She stared into Ceinwin's eyes. 'But what am I supposed to do with it?'

'Trust me. When the time comes, you will know.'

TWELVE

The kingdom of Dumnonia

Spring came to Dumnonia, softening the air and swathing the moors in a shimmer of yellow gorse. Silvanus rode hard along the high track, watching as the clouds on the far horizon softened from grey to pink, and the first rays of the sun splashed across the wine-dark sea.

Dumnonia's coastline was stunningly beautiful but prone to rip tides, sudden squalls and treacherous storms. For all its fickleness, the sea was Dumnonia's lifeblood. It provided teeming shoals of herring and mackerel and, far beyond the breakers, the whale-roads bore the kingdom's tin and copper to the rest of the world, and brought the exotic treasures of the east in return.

Silvanus breathed in the fresh, clean air. This was his favourite time of the day. There was something deliciously illicit about these early hours, when the rest of the world was still abed, when no-one was asking for his seal on a parchment, for a judgement, a decision, a favour, a word. These were his precious hours to be alone, to mull over ideas, to plan, but first and foremost, his thoughts always turned to Anya. It was Etar who had decreed she must be sent back to

Vortigern. Would the gods ever forgive him for not defying his father? More to the point, would he ever forgive himself?

Winter had brought a dreary isolation to Dumnonia. No merchants had braved the forest of Selwood or risked the stormy sea. But the coming of spring would open the roads, and bring ships to the harbour of Tintagel once again. He prayed they would carry news from beyond the borders of his kingdom. He prayed they would bring word of Anya. He couldn't bear to think of her in Vortigern's bed. It turned his stomach, sent him spiralling into a pit of guilt and despair.

His council were pressing for him to marry, to secure the succession and the stability of the kingdom. But he was not interested in the bland daughters of his councillors. He wanted Anya. Frustrated, he kicked his stallion's flanks, quickening his pace. His mind began to calm, soothed by the sensation of the wind rushing past his cheeks and the steady thud of hooves across the sandy earth.

After several miles, Silvanus reached the brow of a hill. Reining in, he proudly surveyed the five hundred strong army assembled in the valley below him. These men were fisher folk and farmers, but they were no longer a green, undisciplined rabble. It had taken three hard months of training, but now they bore a definite resemblance to a unified fighting force.

There had been days when it had seemed an impossible task, for his people were not warriors by birth. There were potentially fatal gaps in his own knowledge too, for whilst he knew how to defeat a small Irish raiding party, he had no idea how to vanquish an army a thousand strong.

And so, shortly after Imbolc, he had sent a delegation to his neighbour, the kingdom of the Durotriges. His emissaries returned through the winter storms with tokens of friendship, and a battle hardened warrior by the name of Avernus. He

111

was from Gaul, a mercenary by trade, without any discernible morals or conscience, but he had fought in a shield wall and he had looked a Saxon army in the eye and, for a bag of gold coins, he told Silvanus everything he knew.

And now, the men of Dumnonia left their farmsteads and their fishing nets for a few hours each day to train, and each day their skills grew. They had learnt to bear arms, to ride in a cavalry charge, to stand firm in a shield wall. They threw their spears at wicker targets, and they no longer bounced harmlessly to the ground. And when foot-soldiers shouted and banged their shields amongst cavalrymen, their horses no longer reared up in terror, but held steady.

Dismounting, Silvanus tethered his stallion to the paddock fence. Stable-boys were tending the horses. Amidst a semi-circle of supply wagons, serving girls were laying out bread, cheese, meat and flagons of wine. Avernus was marshalling men in a shield wall, bellowing as he moved steadily along the line:

'Shield to shield, overlap - no gaps.'

'Each of you relies on the protection of your neighbour's shield. You carry your shield in your left hand, so you protect the man on your left.'

'Close up behind. Be ready to step forward to plug any gaps.'

'Lean into the attack. Thrust with your spear.'

Silvanus glanced to his right. Gorran, Jago and Boult were walking towards him. They were dressed for battle; mail over leather cuirasses, swords at their belts and shields slung over their shoulders. He listened to their banter with a wry smile. They were in high spirits, as usual.

'You still can't hold your drink, Gorran, after all these years,' Boult laughed.

'But it's not for lack of practice, is it?' Jago agreed.

'It's because you're too skinny,' Boult went on. 'Whereas, me, I've got hollow legs.'

'When have I ever let you down? When have I ever been so drunk you had to ride without me?' Gorran retorted indignantly.

Boult and Jago turned to one another and said in unison:

'The festival of Imbolc, two years since.'

'The roof was icy,' Gorran protested.

Boult and Jago were almost bent double with laughter now.

'By all the gods, Gorran, just listen to yourself! You were so drunk you genuinely thought it was a good idea to climb onto the kitchen roof to play your bagpipes,' Boult guffawed.

'It was a good idea,' Gorran said huffily. 'The sound of the pipes travelled better up there.'

'Yes, and you travelled too – thirty feet from the roof to the ground. You broke your leg, you mad goat!'

Boult slapped Gorran on the back with such force that he lurched forward.

'Fuck off,' Gorran replied, righting himself. Realising he was now just yards from Silvanus, he added hurriedly, 'forgive my language, lord.'

Silvanus stifled a grin. They had all been exceedingly drunk at the festival of Imbolc two years since. The evening had become something of a blur, until Gorran fell off the roof. They had all sobered up rapidly after that.

'Lord,' Jago said respectfully. 'Evric is about to demonstrate sword skills to the men. He asked if you might spar with him.'

Silvanus nodded. 'Yes, I will come.'

'Whatever happens, you must stay on your feet at all costs. Balance is the key. It's the difference between life and death.'

Silvanus turned slowly on his heel, making eye contact with the men gathered about him in a loose circle.

'Never stand head on to your enemy. Never reveal your soft underbelly. Show him your shoulder, your hip. And remember, if all your momentum is moving forward, then you are vulnerable. Imagine your body is a plumb line. Keep it centred. Let's show you what happens if you don't.'

He nodded at Evric, who lunged, his sword aimed at Silvanus's chest. Lightning fast, Silvanus struck Evric's outstretched sword arm with the flat of his own blade. It was a hard blow, catching the soft tissue of his inner elbow and Evric was not play acting when he winced and momentarily lost his balance. Seizing the initiative, Silvanus closed in, mimicking drawing his blade across Evric's throat.

'Loss of balance in close combat means death.' Silvanus released Evric and stepped away.

'Many of you are skilled at butchery. You know that you cannot cut meat by merely pressing your blade into the flesh. Like a knife, a sword is a cutting implement. It needs movement back and forth to be effective. Like so.'

Silvanus swung his blade, parrying an invisible foe with fast, incisive strikes. 'You must be quick on your feet. You must anticipate what your opponent is going to do next. You must be one step ahead of him. Let us demonstrate.'

Silvanus raised his sword, bringing it down with such force that, although Evric successfully blocked the blow, he was forced to his knees. Around the makeshift arena, the crowd gasped. Evric quickly jumped to his feet again, and attacked. Iron screeched against iron, as the two men lunged and parried. Neither held back and it made for a terrifying spectacle.

But Silvanus and Evric had grown up together, shared the

boredom of the classroom, the exhilaration of sword practice, fought side by side against the Irish. Consequently, they had learnt to read each other's thoughts. At that moment, it was the only thing keeping them alive.

'Lord!' Jago called.

Silvanus did not hear him. His veins were flooded with battle fever, his thoughts focussed solely on anticipating Evric's every move.

Jago tried again. 'Lord! Taliesin wishes to speak with you.'

This time, Silvanus heard him. He raised his left arm to halt the demonstration but Evric's sword blade was already in motion. It swept passed Silvanus's nose, missing it by barely an inch. Another collective gasp ran around the crowd.

Hastily, Evric stepped back and lowered his sword.

'Apologies, lord.'

'No harm done.' Sweat was dripping from Silvanus's forehead and he wiped it away with the back of his hand. Then he turned to face the crowd.

'That was a fine example of the dangers of losing concentration, if only for a moment. Now, I must take my leave, but Evric will stay and demonstrate how your shield can be used not only for protection, but also as a weapon.'

Under the cover of rousing applause, Silvanus turned to Evric, grinning. 'You almost took my nose off!'

'It would have been an improvement, you ugly bastard.' Evric paused for a heartbeat then added deferentially, 'lord.'

'I'll kill you next time, you insolent wretch. No mercy,' Silvanus replied cheerfully as the crowd parted to let him through.

Taliesin was leaning heavily on a walking stick. He looked weary and as frail as a dandelion clock, as if the slightest breeze would scatter him across the fields. Anya had worked at the old priest's side, bringing babies into the light, healing the sick and singing the dying to their final sleep. But Anya was gone, and Taliesin was refusing help from anyone else.

The old priest looked him up and down. 'You look tired, lord. You are working too hard.'

Silvanus raised an amused eyebrow. 'I could say the same of you. How did you get here? Did you walk?' He noticed the old man stank of piss. Without Anya, it seemed he was also forgetting to bathe.

'Yes, lord, I walked.'

'It's too far for you. You should have told me. I would have arranged a wagon.'

'What? And be bumped about like a sack of turnips? No thank you. I meant what I said - you look tired.'

Silvanus shrugged his shoulders. 'There's much to do.'

His brothers' in arms were steadfastly loyal, offering him sound advice and comradeship, but it was Anya he needed, more than he could ever admit.

'There has been no news of Anya?' Taliesin asked, reading his mind, as usual.

Silvanus caught something in his voice. 'No. Why? What have you seen in your dream paths?'

The old man clasped his hands together fretfully. His finger joints were swollen and shiny with age.

'I went to the cave of fires and I saw,' Taliesin hesitated. 'It's hard to say what I saw.'

'Try,' Silvanus said, failing to mask his impatience.

'I saw suffering. I saw a pit.'

Silvanus felt his blood run cold. 'What sort of pit? A grave?'

'Yes. No. I cannot say.' Taliesin stared at the ground.

Silvanus felt fear rise up within him. 'Tell me, do you think Anya is still alive?' he asked urgently.

The old man looked up again. 'Yes, of course she is alive. She is Epona, the girl the prophecy foretold, the girl who came from the sea to bring new life and new hope for a new golden age. She will come back to us.'

Silvanus looked askance at the old priest. Taliesin's dream paths were difficult to interpret, dismissed by many as the confused ramblings of an old and tired mind. But what if he had seen Anya's death and was simply refusing to accept it? Quite suddenly, Silvanus couldn't breathe, as if the air was being sucked from his lungs.

'She is alive,' Taliesin repeated. 'I know this to be true, so you must think no more about it.' His bony fingers clasped Silvanus's forearm, a surprisingly vice-like grip. 'Listen to me now. The council is waiting for your decision regarding your brother. There can be no more delays.'

Silvanus ran a hand through his hair, a tense, exasperated gesture.

'Lucan's fate weighs heavily upon me.'

'The council agreed unanimously. So you can take comfort that it is not your decision alone,' Taliesin replied firmly.

'Each time I lift the seal, I cannot bring myself to stamp the wax. For all he has done, he is still my blood...' Silvanus's voice trailed away despairingly.

'Your father taught you to put your kingdom above all else.' Taliesin's tone was unforgiving. 'And, besides, Lucan is too dangerous to be allowed to live.'

Silvanus let out an anguished sigh. 'I know it is my duty to see it done. And I know it must be soon, but -'

'Yes,' Taliesin nodded fervently, 'it must be done soon. Your feelings are irrelevant. Your kingdom is all that matters now. And what of Mairi? What do you intend to do with her?'

'I have not yet decided,' Silvanus replied shortly.

117

Taliesin sniffed disparagingly. 'The child is deformed, you know. A club foot.'

Silvanus glanced at the old priest in surprise. He did not share the common belief that physical deformity was a curse from the gods. But there was no denying the child would struggle in life; at best, unable to run as fast as his peers, at worst, scorned and feared as marked by a devil.

'The midwife tried to take the babe away, but Mairi wouldn't hear of it. She swore her to secrecy, but Sirona is an old friend of mine. She keeps me informed -' Taliesin broke off, overcome by a fit of coughing.

Alarmed, Silvanus offered him his water bottle but Taliesin shook his head. Fumbling in the pocket of his cloak for a handful of dried lungwort, he chewed on it until his coughing subsided.

'Despite the child's deformity, Mairi still believes her son will be king of Dumnonia one day,' the old priest went on. 'I tell you, Silvanus, she is also far too dangerous to be allowed to live.'

'Am I to murder women and children now?' Silvanus's emotions were raw to the bone. 'Enough. I will hear no more.'

'As you wish, lord,' Taliesin demurred.

A silence fell, fraught with words left unspoken. Together they watched Avernus's shield wall advancing across the valley.

'This army of yours, is it ready to fight?' Taliesin asked at last. 'If Vortigern's army marched across Dumnonia, or if a Saxon horde stood at the gates of Tintagel, would we survive?'

'You want an honest answer?' Silvanus asked bitterly.

Taliesin nodded.

'Then, honestly, I do not know.'

118

THIRTEEN

The kingdom of Siluria

The seasons turned and spring came to the valley at last. The stream was fierce and full with melting snow from the high mountains. Yellow celandines crept along its banks and a delicate white blanket of wood anemones and stitchwort lined the edges of the fields. After a winter cooped like chickens, the villagers had ventured outdoors again and the valley was filled with the sound of children playing.

Anya watched a squirt of watery milk shoot into the wooden bucket. Perched on a three legged stool, her left hand clamped around a ewe's udder, she smiled with satisfaction. A few weeks ago, she had doubted she would ever master the technique.

'We're going on a hunting trip to the black lake. Come with us?' Rhys shouted above the squeals of the children.

Anya sat back for a moment and rubbed her aching arm. A winter of hunger had left her as weak as a kitten.

Her young cousin, Abertha, yelped in indignation. 'Don't stop, Anya. I can't hold this stupid animal for much longer.'

Chastened, Anya grabbed the ewe's teat again and began to tug, strongly and rhythmically.

'What will you be hunting?' she shouted back.

Rhys shrugged. 'Hare? Duck? Anything that moves. We need meat.'

Anya smiled but she noticed he did not return her smile. She missed their easy familiarity. She had turned down his marriage proposal, and although outwardly there were no ill feelings, she knew things would never be the same between them again.

'I'll come with you,' she replied. 'Ceinwin says the lake is a beautiful place.'

Rhys shrugged again. 'I don't know about that, but there's good hunting.'

The small party set out at dawn the following day. After a claustrophobic winter in the round-house, Anya revelled in warmth of the sun against her cheeks, the exhilarating sense of space between the earth and the cold, blue sky. They climbed winding sheep tracks to the summit of windswept crests where the views were awe inspiring, and the wind so cold and harsh it took her breath away, and then wound their way down again into immense, circular valleys, scooped from the black rock.

The sun was overhead when they reached the lake. Ceinwin was right. It was beautiful, a tranquil expanse of dark water, mirroring the small white clouds that scudded across the sky. The lake was teeming with wildlife. Ducks and coots were nest building, kingfishers darted over the shallows, and herons stood as motionless as sentries amongst the reeds.

Some of the men began to lay traps, others fished. The women spread out, collecting new green shoots of mustard, ground elder, hawthorn, dill and chervil. Anya did not follow them. Instead she took the path that ran along the shoreline, looking for wild iris rhizomes. One of the old men in the village was suffering from dropsy, and she had found their harvested juice to be an effective remedy.

The lake looked as old as time, and time had not altered it, the still waters trapped forever by impervious rock and stone. The sun appeared from behind a cloud again and she enjoyed the sensation of Lugh's heat upon her skin. She felt the tension begin to leave her body, felt herself begin to relax. She was alone, and she had not been alone for a very long time. Lying down in the long grass, she closed her eyes and relished a precious moment of peace. She listened to the sounds of the lake, the gentle lapping of the water on the pebbly shore, the birdsong and further away, the chatter of the women as they gathered their herbs.

The chatter and the birdsong were beginning to fade as Anya drifted on the edge of sleep. She was dreaming of war. She could hear battle drums, louder now, startling her awake. Rolling onto her elbows, she peered through the tall grasses. It wasn't the sound of battle drums, but of a warband approaching at full gallop, their horses' hooves echoing like thunder around the peaks of the black mountains.

The horsemen reached the womenfolk first, scattering them as if they were farmyard chickens. The women ran in all directions, screaming in terror, but the horsemen rounded them up like dogs penning sheep. Two of the soldiers dismounted, pushing the women roughly to their knees. They clung to one another, sobbing with terror.

For a single heartbeat, the village's menfolk turned and stared. And then, as one, they dropped their fishing rods, picked up their hunting spears and, with a united roar of fury, began to charge towards the mounted warband.

Anya felt torn between horror and pride. Her kin were

sheep farmers, not warriors and yet they were running headlong towards heavily armed men. Their bravery was truly extraordinary, but she felt certain she was about to watch them die. They raised their spears and hurled them at the horsemen. Several missed their targets and fell to the earth, but one skewered a man's shield with such force it almost unseat him. The soldier wrenched the spear from his shield, and held it above his head.

'Come and get it!' he taunted.

Anya watched Rhys release an arrow from his bow as he ran. She did not expect it to find its mark, but to her amazement, it pierced the neck of a soldier. She saw the look of surprise on the warrior's face as he briefly clutched the shaft before he fell, lifeless, from his mount.

Galvanised into action, the warband were wheeling around. Kicking their horses' flanks, they began to gallop towards Anya's kin. Three villagers were cut down where they stood. Anya scrambled to her feet. Her legs were trembling and her head was spinning. She had no idea what do, no idea how to stop this nightmare.

Rhys was still alive, his bow hanging loosely from his right hand. His quiver was empty; he had no more arrows. He was staring into the eyes of a mounted warrior, facing death, and facing it bravely.

The soldier eyed him with a disinterested expression. 'Shall we kill them all, sir?' he shouted over his shoulder.

The commander of the warband glanced speculatively at the villagers. 'No. Tewdric was expecting us to catch fish, but a haul of slaves will be a far tastier dish.'

The breath went out of Anya's lungs as her mind struggled to comprehend the gravity of the soldier's words.

Tewdric? Slaves?

Shock and terror rooted her to the spot. She saw Rhys's eyes dart briefly in her direction, checking she was safe. The soldier turned in his saddle, following his glance. As if released from a trance, Anya dropped to her knees, shielded from sight by the tall reeds.

'What were you looking at, boy?' the soldier queried.

Rhys was staring fixedly at the ground now. The soldier dismounted, strode towards him and grabbed him roughly by his tunic. Rhys looked up and spat in the man's face. The soldier's hand flashed to his belt and in an instant, his dagger was at Rhys's throat.

'You scrawny little sheep-fucker. I'll kill you for that!'

Without thinking, Anya sprang to her feet and yelled at the top of her voice. 'He was looking at me!'

The soldier spun around, and she heard Rhys shout, 'run, Anya! Run!'

She needed no encouragement. Taking a deep breath, she began to sprint across the open ground. She stumbled in her haste, her boots catching on the hem of her cloak. She heard the commander of the warband shout dryly, 'you missed one. Go get her.'

Anya glanced over her shoulder. The soldier had mounted up again. She watched him wheel his stallion around and kick his heels. She tried to quicken her pace but the ground was dotted with raised tufts of marsh grass and when she tried to avoid them, her boots sank into wet, sinking, bog.

The hem of her cloak was sodden now, slowing her down. She grabbed the heavy fabric with both hands, lifting it out of the brackish water, and ran on. A winter of constant hunger had left her weak; she was shocked by how out of breath she felt. She changed direction, making for higher, drier ground, but the soldier was gaining on her. Above the thudding of her heart, she could hear hoof beats, feel them reverberating beneath her feet. She glanced over her shoulder again. The horseman was at full gallop, bearing down upon her. Panic gripped her. She could not out-run a mounted rider. She had been foolish to even try.

She was going to die.

Here, by the high lake, on top of the world.

Without ever seeing Silvanus again.

In the great hall, fuelled by wine and bravado, Athelwald's retinue had told stories of battle, so she knew exactly what would happen next. Tewdric's man would lean low in his saddle and he would swing his sword, and iron would connect with flesh and bone. There would be pain, agonising pain, and then she would be no more.

She didn't want to die.

And then it came to her. Why had she not thought of it before?

She had Ceinwin's sword.

The horse and rider were almost upon her, blocking out the blue sky. The animal's muzzle was foam flecked; the warrior's sword arm was flexed, ready to swing. Anya's fingers tightened around the grip of her own sword. It felt impossibly heavy and her arm muscles protested as she drew it from the scabbard.

The red glass gleamed. Ceinwin had called it the blood of her enemies.

One half of Anya's brain was telling her to kill the horse in order to unseat the rider. But the other half was wavering, for she had no quarrel with the animal, no desire to harm an innocent soul.

The soldier swung his sword. Instinctively, she blocked the stroke. The immense force of the blow jarred up her arm and she staggered backwards. The sword felt unbearably heavy now, but Anya raised it again, struggling to ignore the sharp pains that seared through her arm and shoulder. The soldier leant low in his saddle and their blades met again in a clash of iron. This time the overwhelming momentum knocked her onto her back. She fell heavily, and the sword slipped from her grasp.

She tried to get up, but her body did not respond. Dazed and winded, she watched helplessly as the man dismounted. He wrenched the torque from about her neck, running his fingers appreciatively over the creamy gold. And then he thrust the tip of his sword against her throat. She noticed his eyes lingering on the sword that lay beside her in the grass.

'Who did you steal that from?' he asked in a voice that succeeded in making the soft tones of the Silurian tongue sound harsh.

She did not reply. There was no breath in her lungs, and no feeling in the fingers of her left hand. The soldier jabbed her throat with the sword tip, and she winced as the old wound opened up again.

'Live, or die?' he asked, as carelessly as if he were toying with a fly.

The sword tip twisted, and the sharp pain intensified.

'Do you want to live or die?' he repeated.

'I will not beg this man for my life,' she thought. And so she closed her eyes, and waited for death. Strangely, she felt calm. Soon she would see Eown and Emma again. And in the space between life and death, a thousand memories flashed across her mind. But she did not see the great hall of Saxony, or the round-house in the shadow of the high mountains. Instead, she saw Silvanus. She opened her eyes.

'I want to live.'

'I thought you might.'

The pressure of the sword blade lifted, and she saw the satisfaction in the soldier's eyes.

'The bastard is taking pleasure in his power over me', Anya thought angrily. She watched him bend down to pick up her sword. Gripped with fear, she lunged for the hilt.

'No! It's mine!'

He pushed her away disdainfully, as if shaking dung from his boot. 'You are a slave now,' he spat. 'You own nothing. You are no-one.'

Tewdric's warband roped the seven survivors of the hunting party together and headed east. It was impossible to keep in step with the horses' uneven pace, and the thick rope chafed Anya's waist as they stumbled over the rocky mountain track. Mile after exhausting mile, she fixed her gaze upon the soldier who had taken her sword and wrenched its scabbard from her belt, sealing his features into her memory. She had sworn to Ceinwin she would keep the sword safe, and if it took her a lifetime, she was determined to keep that promise.

Hours passed and her thoughts drifted to Germania. She had taken her life there for granted, never imagined how easily it would be snatched away. On winter nights, around the fire in her father's hall, the bards had entertained the king with stories of a terrible monster that crept into mead halls in the dead of night. It snatched warriors one by one, and carried them back to the foul places of the earth. Tewdric was such a monster. He crept into the halls of Siluria, and carried his own people away to slavery and death. In the bard's story, a strong and brave prince called Beowulf had defeated the monster in a heroic battle.

But Anya knew she was no Beowulf. She had watched her

kin die at the high lake and she had not saved them. She had drawn Ceinwin's sword from its scabbard but she had barely been able to lift it, and Tewdric's soldier had overpowered her as easily as if she were a helpless child. She had lost the sword, lost her freedom, lost everything. It had all happened so fast. Her memory of it was blurred, like a nightmare, hardly real. But the pain from the wound at her throat felt real enough.

Exhaustion turned her bones to lead, and each weary step became a torment. Abertha, her young cousin, stumbled and fell but Tewdric's men made no allowances. The horses dragged her some twenty yards before Rhys managed to put her on her feet again. Bruised and bleeding, her cries gradually lessened to pitiful sobs.

Dusk was falling as the warband reached the hill-fort. The chain of roped humanity staggered to a ragged standstill and Anya looked about wearily. To the west, the sun was setting over the black mountains; to the east, the land fell away from the steep escarpment towards rolling farmland and forests. There were guards looking down at them from the twin watch towers, and more men patrolling the high, sturdy palisade.

The gates opened, and the warband kicked their horses forward. The rope jerked and Anya flinched as it dug into her chafed skin. The interior of the hill fort smelled of iron working and animal dung, of midden pits, latrines and cooking pots. The stronghold was both a fortress and a town, for children played in the narrow lanes, and women stood in doorways and watched the new batch of slaves stumble past.

Anya and her kin were brought to a halt before a small hut. In the fading light, rough hands searched them for any hidden valuables. They took Anya's cloak and then, by some terrible twist of fate, they tried to pull Eown's ring from her finger, but the ring held fast. Finally, their captors removed their

127

ropes and pushed them, one at a time, into the hut.

'If you try to escape, our dogs will rip you apart. We keep them hungry.' The door closed, and Anya heard the heavy locking beam drop into its slot.

There were no windows in the small hut, and she narrowed her eyes, peering into the gloom. There was no furniture either, just bare earth. The wall posts were fixed into footings of compacted chalk. Even if they dug with their bare hands, it would take far too long to try and tunnel their way out. She crawled to the door on her hands and knees. Through the tiny gap between the door and its frame, she could see two guards, talking in low voices. She glanced back at her kin. They had sunk to the ground in stunned, exhausted silence.

'We'll find a way out of here,' she said confidently, but in her heart she knew they were trapped, like hares in a snare.

Light-headed with hunger and thirst, she rested her back against the hard wattle wall and closed her eyes. She did not know how long she slept, but she was awakened by the sound of the door opening. A girl entered, carrying two wooden buckets. She placed them on the floor then went out again.

Anya sat up with difficulty. Her entire body ached, and her eyes felt heavy with sleep. One bucket contained water, the other a watery broth, with a large wooden ladle hooked over the side.

Her kin shared the meagre meal with a resolute fairness that twisted Anya's heart. And then they slept again.

Bright sunlight streamed into the darkness of the hut, and Anya blinked wildly. It seemed only moments since she had fallen into a dreamless sleep.

'On your feet!' It was the man who had taken her sword, which now hung from his belt. He didn't look much older than her, and he wasn't much taller, but he was strong and muscular, battle hardened. His red hair had been cropped short, yet curls were beginning to spring from his head again, and the smattering of freckles across his wide, flat nose muted his menace.

'On your feet! Now!' he repeated.

Anya stood up, her world spinning dizzily. The soldier was eyeing her kin one by one, assessing them like a farmer choosing cattle at market. He pointed at Rhys then turned to the men guarding the door. 'This one for the mines.'

Rhys swayed as if his legs were about to give way. Anya glanced at the soldier in horror. Ceinwin had told her the life expectancy of a slave in one of Tewdric's gold mines was just a matter of months. Rhys had been handed a death sentence. She didn't think, because there wasn't time. She simply stepped forward and positioned herself between Rhys and the soldier.

'No! Not him.'

The soldier looked momentarily astounded. And then he grabbed her by the throat. His fingers dug into her flesh and her vision began to blur. She could see the young soldier's thoughts, intertwining with hers like honeysuckle around a tree. He was angry she had dared to speak out, because slaves did not answer back. They had no voice, no opinions. They were merely commodities. In fact, he had discovered a long time ago that the only way to deal with slaves was to avoid eye contact at all costs. He did not want to see the messy emotions in their eyes because they reminded him of an uncomfortable fact he had tried very hard to forget: slaves were human beings.

His grip tightened on her throat. The wound re-opened, and her blood began to seep between his fingers. Anya clawed at his hands, desperately trying to loosen his grip, but he was too strong. Their eyes met and the familiar white mists began to roll across her mind as she trawled deeper into his memories. Once, long ago, he had been a boy just like Rhys. He had spent his childhood winters starving in a round-house, little better than an animal. But he had turned his back on that life, and learnt to fight and to kill.

He had dug a deep pit, and into it he had carefully placed his conscience and his compassion, and then he had back-filled the pit, and walked away. He was Tewdric's man now. Life in Tewdric's hall offered a table never short of meat or wine. There were no more hungry winters.

The soldier released his grip on her throat and stepped away from her abruptly. Their connection was broken and Anya blinked and swayed as her mind attempted to find its way back.

The soldier looked pale. 'You are a slave. You do not speak. Do you understand?' he said roughly.

Anya took a deep breath. 'It's been a long hard winter, and Rhys isn't strong. He won't last a week in the mines. In fact, none of us will.'

The soldier struck her forcefully with the back of his hand, and she stumbled backwards, momentarily stunned by the blow. Reaching for her arm, he caught her before she fell. His face was inches from hers. 'One more word from you, and I'll run you through.' He leant closer still. 'With your own sword.'

Pushing her to her knees, he turned to leave.

'Sir? How many for the mines?'

He hesitated for the briefest heartbeat then replied, 'none this time. They will all go to market.'

He slammed the door shut behind him, plunging the shed into darkness once again. Anya remained on her knees. Blood was dripping from the wound at her throat and her cheek bone was throbbing like a pulse.

'Thank you,' Rhys said shakily. 'That's the second time you've saved my life.'

Anya turned to face him. 'You would do the same for me.'

'Yes,' he said softly. 'Yes, I would.'

The next day was worse than the last. Much worse. They were manhandled into the spring sunshine, and bound together in a slave chain. A soldier wielding a pair of pliers forcibly closed each iron neck ring, but no-one begged or pleaded for mercy, because they all knew it would serve no purpose, and Anya felt proud of her kin's quiet courage.

The journey was long and difficult. They zigzagged up steep mountain tracks, along winding paths edged with prickly gorse and bilberry bushes that tore their bare arms. Anya's mind began to churn. When Llewelyn learnt they had been taken, how would he bear yet more grief? And what cruel trick of fate had led her to the same path her mother had walked, all those years ago? She could not begin to imagine a lifetime of slavery. Would she be sold to a compassionate owner, or to a man who treated her little better than an animal? How closely would she be watched? How easy would it be to escape? And what of the rest of her kin? If they were separated, how could she ever hope to find them again?

After a while, exhaustion numbed her mind to everything but the sheer effort required to put one foot in front of the other, mile after agonising mile. Her head throbbed with hunger and thirst, and her feet were raw with bleeding blisters. Just a foot and a half of chain separated each crushingly heavy neck ring from the next, and unless they kept in perfect step, the rings repeatedly choked them.

It was late afternoon as they began the climb towards another hill-fort, twice the size of the last, sitting high upon a natural promontory with far reaching views in all directions. Encircled by deep ditches and high ramparts topped with lime washed dry-stone walls, it dominated the surrounding countryside, an awe-inspiring statement of power and control. The ornately carved gates opened and they were herded inside.

At first glance, this settlement was much like the last, with grain pits and workshops and smithies but, mingled with the aromas of ordure and furnace and freshly hewn wood, Anya could also smell despair, and it chilled her to the bone. A large stone-walled round-house dominated the interior. As they trudged wearily by, she noticed its wooden doors were carved with intertwining patterns similar to those upon her sword.

Their neck rings were prized open, and they were made to stand in line, as if for a military inspection. The ring had chafed the wound at her throat, and it now felt itchy and hot. She touched it gingerly. It was infected, but she had no water to clean it, nor medicine to heal it.

She knew Tewdric was approaching by the way the soldiers drew themselves to their full height, the air suddenly thick with tension. She stole a quick glance at the warlord of Siluria. He was tall, lean and a full head higher than any of his warriors. A mane of thick, red hair was tied back at the nape of his neck, drawing attention to a surprisingly refined face with pronounced cheekbones, a neatly trimmed beard and moustache, and cold, intelligent eyes.

She watched him walk along the line of newly arrived slaves. She noticed the rest of her kin kept their eyes fixed firmly on the ground. Their lives lay in the palm of this man's hand and their fear was tangible.

'I can spare only one.' Tewdric's voice was deep and commanding.

An old Druid scuttled forward, his hands clasped together, his head bowed reverentially. He wore a long white gown, as was customary for the priesthood, but from his belt hung a curious collection of bleached human and animal bones, and desiccated birds.

'Just one, lord? The gods will not be -' the priest began, but Tewdric took a step towards him, and the old man physically crumpled.

'One will suffice,' Tewdric asserted.

The priest bowed his head and Anya noticed his hands were shaking. She watched him shuffle along the line and come to a halt in front of Rhys. The old man studied him for a long time, before finally moving on. And then he stopped before Anya. She lowered her gaze, staring at the old man's long, dirty, toe nails, peeking from his latticed-leather sandals, but the priest put a thin finger under her chin and forced her head up. Their eyes met and she saw something in his expression that made her stomach lurch with dread.

He edged closer and grasped her breasts in his bony hands, squeezed hard then nodded to himself. She shoved him away but, undeterred, the priest thrust a hand between her legs, and then nodded again.

'Virgin,' he announced and drew back his lips in a grim parody of a smile, to reveal a jumble of black, broken teeth. 'I have chosen.'

And in that moment Anya did not see a stinking old man, but a priest with the power of life and death over them all.

Tewdric rolled his eyes irritably.

'Why must you always choose the ones that would fetch a good price?'

133

'It is not I who chooses, lord. It is the gods.'

'Of course,' Tewdric remarked drily, and then turned on his heel and strode back to the central round-house. His warriors fell in around him, like planets around a sun.

Anya and her kin were herded into a hut much like the last. She sank to the ground, too shocked to speak. She knew what had just happened, but it was as if a shield had formed inside her head to protect her from something too terrible to contemplate. Her kin were staring at her but she did not see their shocked faces. She was floating on merciful oblivion, as if she had drunk the strongest draught of milk of the poppy.

She did not know how long she sat there, but gradually, imperceptibly, her invisible shield fell away. Reality began to seep into her consciousness as insidiously as the chill from the cold earth floor. She wondered how Tewdric's priest would send her to meet the gods. How much would they make her suffer? Would Emma be waiting for her in the world beyond? Would Eown?

Rhys touched her arm. 'We'll find a way out of here. I won't let anyone hurt you, Anya.'

'There's nothing you can do. My fate has been decided.'

Rhys's brow furrowed with concern. 'Don't say that. Please, don't say that. I swear to you, I won't let this happen!'

'We have no choice,' she replied dully.

'Do you really believe the gods want you to die?' Rhys asked incredulously.

'I know they don't want me to die.'

Then we have to do something!'

'I tell you – there's nothing to be done.'

Rhys was staring at her, his eyes wide with frustration and bewilderment. 'What is it, Anya? What is it you're not telling us?'

134

Anya could not find the words to tell him about Emma, how she had been unable to stop the events of that terrible day in the sacred grove. And nor could she find the words to explain that no-one, not even Athelwald, high king of Saxony, could deny the high priests' craving for sacrifice.

'Will you all promise me something?' she asked at last. 'Will you promise me, that no matter where fate takes you, you will try to find your way home again?'

They regarded her dolefully.

'Please,' she begged.

What makes you think we will find a way, when you have already stopped trying?' Rhys asked bitterly.

Anya put her head in her hands, racked by images of Emma, the ropes tightening about her neck, her body twitching in its final death throes. Rhys put his arms around her, drew her close, and she did not push him away. She did not want to be alone tonight. She took comfort in his warmth and the steady rise and fall of his chest. The night drew on. Dawn approached and still, neither of them slept.

'You hold your secrets close to your heart,' he said quietly.

Anya tensed. Silvanus had said much the same thing, on the beach beneath Tintagel. She could see the outline of Rhys's gentle, guileless face in the darkness. He was such a good man, a kind man.

'I'm sorry,' she said. 'I'm sorry I couldn't marry you.'

'There's no need,' he began, but she interrupted him. If this was to be her last night on earth, then he deserved to know the truth.

'There's someone else. I've loved him forever, and one day I hope we will be together again.'

Rhys did not reply but his fingers faltered for the briefest of moments before beginning their comforting caress once again.

It was still dark when the two soldiers came for her.

'Promise me you'll try and find your way home, for Olwen and Rhiannon's sake,' she whispered in Rhys's ear.

He clung to her as they tried to haul her from his arms. Irritated by his resistance, one of the soldiers punched him in the face. He cried out and fell backwards, blood pouring from his shattered nose.

Anya fought in the soldiers' strong grasp, looking over her shoulder to see if Rhys was badly hurt. He was kneeling on the floor, his hands to his bleeding face. He was surrounded by his kin, but he was not looking at them. He was looking at her, and the torment in his eyes chilled her to the bone.

The two soldiers manhandled her outside. It felt bitterly cold without her cloak and she began to shiver violently. The settlement was quiet. The sky was suffused with muted greys and lilacs, the world perfectly balanced between the stillness of night and the noisy exuberance of the dawn chorus. She fought and kicked, but the soldiers held her fast, half carrying her through the maze of lanes towards a line of storage pits in the shadow of the high palisades.

The old priest was waiting. He was standing absolutely still, and his eyes were closed. In his right hand he held a mirror and Anya's blood ran cold. The priests used such mirrors in Germania to part the veil between this life and the next, and so reflect the wishes of the gods.

The soldiers came to a halt before the largest storage pit. It was full of upright stakes, their tips sharpened to a point, and Anya felt her stomach heave in terror. Emma had walked obliviously into the sacred grove. Crushed mistletoe had dulled her senses but even without it, she would not have fought, for she did not understand.

But there was no mistletoe in Anya's veins, and she

understood very clearly what was about to happen.

'Let me go!' she pleaded, struggling in the soldiers' grasp, trying to make eye contact with them. 'This is not what the gods want! I beg you, let me go!'

But they would not look at her. One soldier shot a brief glance into the stake filled pit and she saw the distaste in his eyes. He knew as well as she did what was about to happen. She had been a little girl the last time the high priests had flung a man into a stake pit but she could still remember his terrible screams and moans. He had died hideously slowly, impaled and in agony, and his suffering had cast a shadow of unease over the golden hall for days.

The gruesome memory made her want to retch. Was this why the goddess had brought her to Siluria? Was this truly what Nerthus wanted? That she should be sacrificed by this foul smelling priest? The old man was speaking now, but his words were a meaningless jumble to her ears.

The first rays of sunlight brushed the top of the wooden palisade and the two soldiers readied themselves. Holding her tightly by the wrists they moved apart until her arms were outstretched and she resembled a giant bird, hovering over the pit.

The priest held out the mirror towards the rising sun. Raw terror consumed her. She prayed to her goddess that a stake would pierce her heart and her death might be quick, although she doubted she would be so fortunate. She struggled desperately in the soldiers' arms, her toes scrabbling at the edge of the pit, her shoulders pulsing with pain from bearing the weight of her straining body. Every nerve and muscle was on fire, trembling with a kind of terrible anticipation.

The pit smelled foul, of excrement and decaying flesh. The stakes were so close now she could see tiny pieces of dried skin still attached to some of them, and blood stains darkening the wood.

She tried to think of Emma, and Eown. They were waiting for her. She shouldn't be afraid. But she was afraid. She didn't want to die. Not here, not like this – a victim of a sacrifice she was certain the gods would not welcome.

She would have liked to have seen Silvanus again, one last time.

The sun caught the priest's mirror, and it exploded with light. He turned it fractionally and shone it directly into Anya's eyes, blinding her.

It was the sign.

The soldiers let go of her arms, and for a fraction of a heartbeat it was as if she was suspended, held aloft by an unseen force.

She heard a scream tear from her throat, a horrible, animalistic sound.

And then she fell.

FOURTEEN

Tintagel, kingdom of Dumnonia

Silvanus dismounted in the stable courtyard, and handed the reins to a yawning stable boy. Frustratingly, his ride had done little to improve his mood. He still felt on edge and ill at ease, as if the gods were angry. It had been a difficult few months. Too much conscious searching about how and when Lucan should die. Too many unresolved moot court cases that demanded his final judgement. Too many Irish raids. His fledgling army had been blooded this summer, but there was a world of difference between chasing an Irish raiding party back to their boats and slaughtering them in the shallows, and facing the massed ranks of a Saxon army.

He looked up at the watchtower, acutely aware that Lucan languished there, growing fat and frustrated from inactivity. Just as he was also acutely aware that Mairi was still confined to her chamber with their four month old son. She had named him Mordred, and although Silvanus had not seen the babe, the midwife reported he was strong but for the deformity of his foot.

Silvanus frowned. How long could Mordred be kept prisoner, how long could he be denied sunlight? And if he signed Lucan's death warrant, what future was there for his son? More to the point, how strongly would the desire for revenge burn in Mordred's heart? Silvanus turned his gaze from the watchtower. Evric was approaching.

'Lord, merchants arrived an hour since. And they have news. I just hope they're not too drunk to string a sentence together now. Their capacity for Lucius's wine is astonishing.'

'Then let's not keep them waiting a moment longer.' Silvanus strode into the great hall, his mind racing with anticipation. Had the merchants travelled through Aquae Sulis? Did they have word of Anya?

The four merchants seated at the long table put down their glasses and stood up respectfully. They were nothing like Silvanus's old friend Lucius, the flamboyant, outlandish sea-merchant who traded in exotic goods of the Byzantine world. These were merchants of the road, tinkers and chancers, their clothes blackened from the soot of countless camp fires and caked with the mud of the roads.

'Lord, I am Conumoltus.' The merchants' spokesman was older than the rest. He had thick grey hair which framed his face like a helmet and a bulbous nose which sprouted white whiskers from two large nostrils. Above pockmarked cheeks, piggy eyes peered short-sightedly at Silvanus.

'Welcome Conumoltus. You have news?' Silvanus asked, gesturing for them to sit down again.

'Yes, lord,' the man nodded sagely.

'Then I would like to hear it.' Silvanus was struggling to control his impatience.

Conumoltus cleared his throat and when he spoke, his words were a curious hybrid of Latin and the Dumnonian tongue: 'Vortigern is beset with troubles - the Coritani, the Picts, the Irish,' he broke off and shook his head apologetically. 'Forgive me, but we spend our days on the road and my tongue is often one kingdom behind.'

'I understand you well enough. Go on.'

'And as for the pagan Saxons - they are looting and killing, but what can you expect from such monstrous heathens? They are little better than animals. We travel heavily armed these days.' The merchant spoke slowly, his accent mangling the gentle language of Dumnonia. He took a draught of wine before continuing. 'Vortigern pays a Saxon warband led by Hengist, the son of the king of Saxony, to guard the wall.'

Silvanus nodded impatiently. He already knew all this. But the merchant had not finished.

'Hengist has taken the fort Andereida in the south, and the city of Eboracum in the north. He has defied the terms of the treaty, and made a mockery of his oaths. Unbelievably, Vortigern's only response to such treachery was to demand hostages! He chose a beautiful young girl who was betrothed to Hengist's brother. They say the brother fell into such a rage that he tried to kill Vortigern, right there in the hall of Aquae Sulis. But the Saxon had been disarmed at the door. With only his bare hands, he fought like a wild dog, scratching and tearing and biting. But they say Vortigern knocked him out cold with the pommel of his sword.'

'Horsa?' Silvanus asked urgently. 'Was that the Saxon's name?'

'Aye, I believe so.'

'And does Horsa live?'

'Aye, he lives. Hengist bent the knee and swore renewed oaths of allegiance to Vortigern, and he accepted their fealty. It's hard to believe Vortigern would be so naïve. They say he must be under the spell of his wife. They say the pagan witch has blinded him to her brothers' treachery.'

141

Silvanus's eyes narrowed. 'What can you tell me of Vortigern's wife?' His manner was cold, but his heart was hammering with trepidation.

'Ah, yes! The Saxon princess - she ran away!' The merchant's face lit up with pleasure at imparting such sensational news.

'What did you say?' Silvanus breathed.

'It was the day after their wedding, on the feast of Christ's Mass.'

'Where is she? Is she safe?' Silvanus demanded. He had imagined many different scenarios, but not this.

'No-one knows. Vortigern sent out riders into the winter storms. They say he sent men as far as Saxony, but he has found no trace of her. She has simply disappeared.'

Silvanus felt his heart lurch. If Anya really had run away, then where was she? Why had she not come to him? Frustration welled up inside him. He had longed for news, but Conumoltus had raised more questions than he had answered.

'They say she's possessed by the devil. They say she spirited herself out of Aquae Sulis by black magic.' The merchant was grinning broadly now, relishing his scandalous tale. 'They say the curse she has cast upon Vortigern will only be lifted when he burns her at the stake.'

Silvanus could take no more. 'Anya, daughter of Athelwald, high king of Saxony, is a healer, not a witch and I will not hear her falsely accused in my hall.' His fury was palpable and Conumoltus cowered before him.

'Please forgive me, lord, I spoke out of turn.'

Silvanus's mind was reeling. Scandalous rumours were the currency of merchants; it gave them welcome at every hearth and paid for their bed and board. Yet, whilst he wanted to dismiss Conumoltus's lurid tale as scurrilous nonsense, in his

142

heart, he sensed the man was speaking the truth.

'Someone must know where Anya is,' he said, his voice displaying a calmness he did not feel. 'What else can you tell me?'

The merchant was shaking his head. 'No-one knows where she is. There was a storm raging the day she disappeared. Some say she likely froze to death, for the snow drifts were as high as the city walls.'

Silvanus jolted, as if he had run at speed into an invisible wall. Fear was tightening like a belt about his chest and he badly needed to be alone. He stood up but the ground did not feel steady beneath him.

'I will leave you to enjoy your meal, gentlemen. I thank you for your news.'

The men at the table got to their feet in a scraping of benches across the floor.

'Sit down, sit down,' Silvanus said absently.

He walked quickly across the hall, unaware of the look of concern upon Evric's face, unaware of Breg, his favourite hound, trotting eagerly behind him. His thoughts were clashing about his head like wasps trapped inside a jar. Where was Anya? Why had she not found a way to send word to him? He prayed to the goddess she was safe, for he had no taste for this world if she had departed from it.

Lost in his thoughts, he almost bumped into Mairi. He noticed dispassionately that whilst she was pale from her long months of captivity, she was still a beautiful woman, with her dark sultry eyes, full, pouting lips and long, lustrous hair. She was surrounded by her ladies, their gazes fixed adoringly upon the swaddled child she carried in her arms.

'New hope and new life for a new golden age,' Mairi was saying, her sweet, sensuous voice ringing out across the hall.

'Why are you not in your chamber?' Silvanus demanded.

Mairi's lowered her gaze, her manner instantly demure.

'I heard merchants had arrived. I long for a new gown. I thought perhaps they carried silks and thread.' She sounded like an innocent child, and for a heartbeat Silvanus felt pity for her, but then he remembered Mairi had cold-bloodedly poisoned his father, watching him grow steadily weaker with every passing day. He raised a hand to silence her.

'Your guards should not have permitted you to leave your chamber. They will be severely punished. And you will return to your rooms immediately.'

In response, she held out her child towards him beseechingly, as if offering the babe to the gods.

'This is Mordred, your nephew.' Her voice was a husky whisper. 'He is Etar's first grand-child. Surely you would like to hold him? It is not fitting that he should be held captive, deprived of sunlight. Etar would not have wished it.'

Fury bloomed within Silvanus. 'You will be silent! You are not worthy to speak Etar's name, you who hastened his death!' He glanced over his shoulder. Evric was already hurrying towards him.

'See Mairi back to her chamber,' Silvanus commanded. 'And have her guards flogged for dereliction of duty.'

'Yes, lord.' Evric took Mairi by the arm and led her out of the hall. Her ladies drifted away to the fireside, subdued, eyes downcast.

Silvanus's fists were clenched at his sides. Mairi's feminine wiles must be considerable indeed for her guards to risk a flogging for her sake. Taliesin was right. Mairi was equally as dangerous as Lucan.

But then he thought of the child in her arms. The babe had reminded him of Lucan at that age, the shock of dark curls, the aquiline nose of the house of Etar. Mordred was his kin, an innocent child.

'She was proclaiming the prophecy of Epona, with reference to her son, no doubt.'

Silvanus spun around. Taliesin was warming his hands by the fire. He had not noticed the priest enter the hall.

'I heard her. In fact I believe everyone heard her,' Silvanus replied grimly, joining the old man.

'Mairi feeds the child herself you know, despite my offer of a wet nurse.' Taliesin sounded disdainful.

Silvanus shrugged. 'She has little else to do in her confinement.'

'She still denies the child's deformity,' Taliesin said accusingly. 'She says the foot will right itself in time.'

'And will it?'

'Perhaps – with painful manipulation, over a long period of time. But she will not let me near the babe. I believe she thinks I will kill it.'

'And would you?'

'Only if you asked me to,' Taliesin replied mildly.

Silvanus's expression darkened.

'If you do not act,' Taliesin went on, 'Mairi and her son will demand your attention today and tomorrow, and all the days that follow.'

'What do you mean by that?' Silvanus asked warily.

But Taliesin was already shuffling towards the door.

'What do you mean?' Silvanus repeated, catching up with him in a single stride.

Taliesin shook his head. 'Pay no attention to me, lord. I'm just a confused old man.'

FIFTEEN

Tewdric's stronghold, Siluria

The sunrise was pure gold, blinding in its intensity.

One moment she was staring into the pit.

And the next, they let her go.

She was falling, weightless -

Pure, raw terror -

The foul air rushing past her cheeks -

The stakes, so close now, dried flesh upon their sharp tips -

The stench of putrefaction -

And then, suddenly, she was no longer weightless, no longer falling. She felt acute pain, as if her arms were being wrenched from her sockets. The stakes had disappeared, and so too had the smell of rotting flesh. Trembling violently and as wobbly as a ragdoll, she was vaguely aware of the soldiers hauling her away from the pit.

'Forgive me, I didn't know, why didn't you tell me? I would never have chosen you. I would never offer one of our own.' The priest's voice was shaking with anxiety.

Anya tried to focus on the old man but he seemed a very long way away. She felt bitterly cold and thick fog was beginning to creep across her mind.

'My eyes are not what they once were,' he hurried on. 'But I thank the sun god for showing me what I had overlooked – a shaft of sunlight, you see, it fell on your tattoo. I don't know how I didn't see it before. Please forgive me, please forgive me…'

Anya stared blankly at him. The fog was thickening. There was a noise inside her head, a loud, brittle buzzing sound. The priest's mouth was moving but she could no longer hear his words. The buzzing was unbearable now, so loud it hurt and then, suddenly, her world turned white.

Her dreams as she drifted towards consciousness were of a land drowning in blood. Only the sword was untouched, the gory deluge shrinking back from its gleaming blade. Her dream shifted and the sword became a stake, embellished with human skin and then there were two stakes, ten, a hundred and she was falling, falling.

Voices crept into her dream, an indistinct hum at first, then louder, more persistent. And scents - the sweetness of straw, the mustiness of mould, the oily tang of sheep's wool and further away, the stench of a midden pit.

Warily, she opened her eyes. She was lying beneath rugs on a low pallet made of straw; she could feel its spiky stalks poking through the linen cover. Her gaze focussed on the wicker partition and she stared at it, perplexed. Was she in Siluria? Was she in the village of her kin? There was no sign of her cloak, but someone had placed her boots neatly beside the pallet.

A man's face appeared around the partition. 'So, you're awake at last.'

It was Tewdric.

So, she was not in the village of her kin.

147

Tewdric walked round the partition to her bedside. Grabbing her left wrist, he twisted it to reveal her cartwheel tattoo. 'Who would have believed it?' he mused. 'Vortigern's wife handed to me on a plate.'

Anya snatched her hand away and hurriedly sat up. Fear squeezed her heart. How could he have discovered her true identity?

Tewdric answered her unspoken question. 'Who else can you be? Only someone chosen by the gods would bear such a mark on their arm.'

Anya frowned, still not understanding.

'You're infamous, girl. The whole of Britannia knows Vortigern took a green eyed, red haired Saxon priestess for a wife. And the whole of Britannia knows you promptly ran away from him.' Tewdric smiled, thin lips drawing back to reveal two rows of perfectly straight, white teeth. And then he sat down on the edge of the pallet. Anya moved away from him, her back pressed against the roughly plastered wattle partition.

He was staring at her now. 'Why are you in Siluria?'

Anya's thoughts were racing. Where were Rhys and the rest of her kin? Were they still in Tewdric's stronghold?

'I've heard it said Vortigern takes no pleasure in you.' Tewdric tipped his head to one side, eyeing her thoughtfully. 'So, will he pay a ransom for you?'

Anya remained silent. Disjointed, disturbing images of the stake-pit were beginning to float across her mind.

'If I send word that I'm raping you, night after night – will that be enough to grab his attention?'

Anya's gaze focussed abruptly on Tewdric. He was a strong man, in his prime. If he tried to rape her, she doubted she would have the strength to fight him off.

'He'll kill you if you touch me,' she said fiercely.

'Ah! She speaks,' Tewdric laughed. 'I was beginning to think my priest had struck you dumb.'

Anya's mind raced on. She doubted Vortigern would pay a ransom for her, or come to her rescue. And when no ransom arrived, would Tewdric send her to the slave markets, or would he choose to put her to death?

On the other hand, Vortigern was a proud man. If a rival warlord boasted of raping his wife, surely he would seek revenge? Perhaps that was Tewdric's intention? Perhaps he hoped to draw Vortigern out?

'I can't believe he took no pleasure in you.' Tewdric's eyes were roaming appreciatively over her body.

Anya shifted uncomfortably. 'Where are my kin?' she asked, attempting to distract him.

'Your kin? I thought you were of Saxon blood?'

When she did not reply, he said carelessly, 'they've gone to market at Caerwent.'

Anya's expression faltered. He spoke of them as if they were animals. Where was Caerwent? How could she ever hope to find them again?

'There's something very appealing about another man's wife.' Tewdric's handsome face was breaking into a broad grin. Seizing her by the shoulders, he flung her backwards onto the pallet, his hand sliding beneath her gown. Horrified, Anya dived to her right, rolled off the pallet and scrambled to her feet. She did not get very far. Tewdric grabbed her by the hair and threw her roughly against the wall. Her head met the stonework with a sickening crack and she cried out in pain.

Tewdric manhandled her back to the pallet. With one hand at her throat, he fumbled to unfasten the brooches at her shoulders with the other. Anya tried to wrench his fingers from her throat but he was too strong. In desperation, she went for his eyes.

He jerked his head away from her raking fingernails, and his hand momentarily lessened its suffocating grip about her throat. Anya took a deep breath and screamed so loudly that the distant hum of conversation instantly ceased.

Moments later, a girl appeared around the wicker partition. She looked down at the bed and then cried out in distress.

Tewdric cursed under his breath, raised himself up on one elbow and rolled his eyes. The girl was very young, perhaps no more than fourteen summers old. She was slim and beautiful with long brown hair that fell un-braided to her waist. Her feet were bare, and her flimsy gown was transparent. She was naked beneath it. Anya watched Tewdric's gaze linger over the young girl's body, clearly outlined beneath the fine linen.

'Come back to bed,' the girl said in a voice as soft as silk, sliding her gown provocatively over her upper thighs.

Tewdric laughed. 'My barren wife is so desperate for a child in her belly, she ruts like a bitch on heat.'

Over his shoulder, Anya watched the young girl's face crumple in hurt and shame.

'Maybe I'll cast her aside,' Tewdric said thoughtfully. 'You'd give me strong sons, wouldn't you, Saxon?' His hand was sliding up her thighs again.

Anya tried to push him away, but he was as strong and immovable as a standing stone.

'Husband, please…' His young wife was crying now.

'Go away!' Tewdric bellowed. 'You'll have your turn tonight, but only if you stop whining.'

But the girl did not go away. Instead, she tried to haul her husband off Anya, tugging ineffectually at his shirt.

'Please don't do this, please,' Tewdric's wife sobbed

pitifully. 'She's a priestess, she belongs to the gods. If you lie with her, you'll curse us all!'

Anya could see conflicting emotions in Tewdric's eyes now: fury, doubt, indecision, frustration. After what felt like an eternity, he swore loudly, rolled off her and stood up. Tying his breeches, he pushed past his wife without a word.

Anya sat up and pulled her gown over her knees with trembling hands. Tewdric's wife was staring at her with an intensely hostile expression.

'Thank you,' Anya said shakily.

'I didn't do it for you,' the girl replied coldly. 'My husband's seed belongs in my belly, not yours. And I warn you, priestess, if you touch my husband again, I swear I'll slit you from groin to gullet.' And then she turned on her heel and walked away.

Anya lay down on the pallet again, curled into a ball, and pulled the rugs about her. She felt bitterly cold, her body trembling violently. Tentatively, her fingers explored the wound at her neck. The infection was spreading; she could feel its heat beneath her skin. She closed her eyes and felt a tear trickle down her cheek.

In Germania, she had led a charmed life, a protected life. As a priestess and an unwed princess, no man had dared to touch her. In Britannia, she had no such protection and she had never felt more vulnerable or more alone. She wondered what future awaited Rhys and the rest of her kin, human souls bartered like livestock. She felt deeply ashamed she had not found a way to save them.

At last, she fell into a disturbed sleep. When she awoke, all was quiet. She sat up and looked over the wicker partition. The fire was low. As her eyes grew accustomed to the gloom she began to make out the sleeping figures of Tewdric's men lying beneath their cloaks at the hearth side.

Rubbing her tired eyes, she forced herself to think. She had to get away from here, but she had made a promise to Ceinwin – she couldn't leave without the sword. She stood up, searching for her cloak and then she remembered it had been taken by Tewdric's men. Draping a blanket over her shoulders, she pulled on her boots and crept around the wicker partition. The snores of Tewdric's sleeping men sounded like frogs on a pond. She crouched down beside each man in turn but the soldier who had taken her sword was not amongst them. Perhaps he was on guard duty? But even if she found him, how, for the love of the goddess, was she supposed to take the sword from him?

She stood up again, and her world began to spin. Gingerly, she touched the wound at her throat; pus was oozing from the scab and the skin surrounding it was tender to the touch. The infection was much worse now. She tiptoed to the door. A wolfhound stirred, raised its snout and sniffed the air. Anya froze, her heart pounding in alarm, but the dog merely scratched itself then settled again.

She lifted the latch and opened the door a fraction, wincing as its hinges creaked loudly. A soldier mumbled in his sleep. One of the wolfhounds farted. A tiny mouse scurried across the floor, and finally the round-house quieted once again. Anya opened the door still further and peered into the darkness. She couldn't see any guards but she knew they must be close by.

As she stepped out into the alley a strong gust of wind swept the door from her hand and banged it loudly against the frame. Cursing under her breath, she grabbed it and held it fast, anxiously looking about. But all was silent.

After the warmth of the round-house, the air felt bitterly cold. Tugging the blanket about her shoulders, she hurried along the track, trying to remember the route back to the gate. She stopped beneath the overhanging eaves of a small store shed and attempted to get her bearings, but the hill top was a maze of narrow alleyways and in the darkness, nothing looked familiar.

Footsteps sounded to her left, splashing through the mud. She stared into the gloom. A man was approaching but she couldn't see his face. She glanced around. Loom weights were stacked against the wall of the shed. Bending down, she picked one up. It was heavy. Wielded forcefully, it could crush a man's skull.

Should she run, or should she put her makeshift weapon to the test? The man was close now. She stepped back a pace, until she felt the dry-stone wall of the shed pressing into her back. Her heart was hammering against her ribs, so loud she felt certain he must hear it.

'Who's there?'

He was looking straight at her, peering into the darkness. Fear gripped her lungs. What possible explanation could she find for cowering beneath the eaves in the dead of night? Anya watched as the soldier drew his sword.

She dropped the loom weight, and then she ran. Ducking her head to avoid the overhanging thatch, she hurtled along the track, her boots sliding through the mud. She glanced over her shoulder. The soldier was just yards away from her and closing fast. Anya's heart was pounding, her eyes darting frantically from left to right.

There was no point crying for help, for who would risk their necks to help a slave? Perhaps if she could find a way to slow the man down, to put some distance between them, it might give her chance to find somewhere to hide. From the corner of her eye, she spotted a narrow alleyway to her right.

Turning on her heel, she plunged into the darkness. Her nostrils were instantly assaulted by the smell of rotting meat. She guessed there must be a butcher's midden close by. Gagging, she put a hand over her nose and mouth. She came upon two dogs fighting over a rope of tangled intestines. They snarled at her, hackles raised. She dodged around them, rats scurrying between her feet as she ran.

The man was close now, very close. Panic welled within her. She had made a mistake. She should have kept to the wider track. The walls of the alleyway seemed to be closing in, pressing upon her lungs until she could barely breathe.

The voice inside her head was harsh. *'Keep going. You have to keep going!'*

Up ahead, in the shadows, she could just make out the outline of a door. Were her eyes deceiving her, or was it slightly ajar? Perhaps it was the entrance to a store shed. Perhaps she could find somewhere to hide.

Strong hands grabbed her shoulders and she cried out with alarm. Twisting her torso, she wrenched herself from the soldier's grasp and ran on. She heard the man snarl with frustration. She felt dizzy and nauseous now, the wound at her throat throbbing, her breath coming in short, sharp gasps, every step an effort. A figure emerged from a side alley, an old man, bent almost double, pushing a hand-cart. She darted around him, glimpsed the startled look on the old man's face and then she was running once more, splashing through stinking puddles.

She glanced over her shoulder again. The man with the cart had briefly slowed her pursuer down, but he was rapidly catching up. In her haste, she did not notice the pile of refuse until the last moment. Changing direction, her boots began to slide through offal and gore. Her left shoulder rammed hard into the side wall and shooting pains tore down her arm. She swayed for a moment, stunned. The soldier grabbed her shoulder, wrenching her around to face him. She saw a brief glimpse of a high forehead and pale, unhealthy skin before she jabbed her knee sharply into his groin. He let out a grunt, his face contorted in agony as he staggered backwards through the stream of filthy water running down the middle of the alley.

Anya fled. Light headed now, her world was narrowing to the deafening thud of her heartbeat pounding in her ears, and the sound of her ragged breathing. There were two more men in pursuit now. Where had they come from? She felt the wicker crate before she saw it, felt its sharp edge slam into her shin bone. Off balance, she stumbled and fell, landing face down in stinking mud.

It was in her nostrils and in her mouth. It tasted of piss and shit and rotting meat and her throat heaved as she tried to spit it out. The two soldiers hauled her upright. She fought and kicked but they held her fast, manhandling her back the way she had come.

Tewdric was striding towards them. 'How did she get out?' he bellowed furiously. 'Where are the guards? I want their names. And then I want them dead.'

Tewdric's priest was not as skilled in the healing arts as Taliesin and his infusions and poultices did not stop Anya's infection from spreading. Tewdric's soldiers guarded her day and night but in reality she was too sick to move. Her fever worsened. She tossed and turned on the pallet, one moment uncomfortably hot, the next, bitterly cold.

Her thoughts ran wild. What miseries were Rhys and the rest of her kin enduring, if they were even still alive? Would

155

Vortigern see her as damaged goods now? Would he leave her here to die? And what of Silvanus? Had he taken a wife, as all kings must to ensure their succession? She did not want to imagine him sharing a marriage bed with another woman; the thought felt like a dagger through her heart.

Meanwhile, life in the round-house went on beyond the partition. She could smell spit-roast, and hear the rowdy sounds of feasting, women laughing, children playing. Occasionally, Tewdric peered over the partition. She saw his brow furrow and she supposed she must look very sick indeed, for he did not come any closer.

The days began to blur, marked only by the grey light waxing then waning between the tiny gaps in the dry-stone walls. The priest came and gave her foul tasting potions and applied poultices to the wound at her neck, but she knew they were having little effect.

'Yarrow,' she told him insistently. 'Yarrow will heal me.'

But the old priest did not seem to hear.

Her fever peaked and her world spun. One minute there were a thousand spiders crawling across her skin, the next there were a thousand swords protruding from the walls. Their blades glinted in the moonlight and they jabbed at her flesh until she cried out in her delirium.

And as she sank into oblivion, her last rational thought was the irony of surviving the stake-pit, only to die from a festering wound that a bucket of lye and a poultice of yarrow would have healed.

SIXTEEN

Aquae Sulis, kingdom of the Dobunni

Rufus hurried along the corridor that led to the council chamber, his mood as black as the mould on the flaking wall plaster. It seemed as if Aquae Sulis was an island surrounded by a sea of enemies, and to make matters worse, the disparate Saxon warbands terrorising the south coast were uniting under the banner of a warlord by the name of Cerdic. Vortigern's spies reported he was a warrior of great renown amongst his people. He had laid claim to Heytesbury Head, an easily defended promontory, and the men of Germania were flocking to him to bend the knee.

But there were more immediate concerns, for pestilence had come to Aquae Sulis. Some said it was carried on the warm spring air, whilst others blamed the merchants who travelled the great Silk Road and crossed the broad eastern deserts.

Vortigern had ordered the gates of the city to be closed to all merchants, journeymen and refugees, but everyone knew it was too late. The plague was already walking the streets and creeping along the narrow, fetid alleyways. The citizens of Aquae Sulis barricaded their doors, but pestilence had no need to knock. In the overcrowded city, it was spreading like wildfire. A splash of cold water landed on Rufus's shoulder and he looked up. The roof was leaking now.

The long, harsh winter had taken its toll on the ancient building. The damp plaster was crumbling from the walls and even the coming of spring could not disguise the smell of festering rot.

Entering the council chamber, he saw Vortigern sitting on the raised dais with Ronan at his side. The boy was the spitting image of his father, the same coarse features, the same surly demeanour, and Rufus felt a familiar stab of bitter resentment. Why did the wastrel boy sit at Vortigern's side, not he?

Rufus noticed Vortigern was holding a parchment at arm's length, squinting as he tried to read it. He felt somewhat cheered by this, for it proved Vortigern was not immortal or invincible. The high king of the Dobunni's eyesight was failing; he was finally beginning to show his age. From the expression upon Vortigern's face, Rufus knew in an instant that something was terribly wrong.

'What is it?' he asked, approaching the dais.

'My wife is in Siluria.' Vortigern stood up and threw the parchment at Rufus. It hit him in the chest and he clutched it with both hands to stop it from falling to the floor.

'Why is she in -' he began tentatively but Vortigern was shouting now.

'Tewdric has her. That sheep-shagging, inbred half-wit has my wife!'

Rufus felt sick to his stomach. How had Anya come to be in Siluria? Ronan was biting his finger nails, seemingly oblivious of his father's outburst, but Rufus had known the boy all his life. He recognised the hint of concern in his eyes.

'He says he's fucking her and he'll keep on fucking her until I pay a ransom! Read it yourself!' Vortigern roared.

Rufus turned cold with shock and revulsion. Anya was brave and feisty, and gave the world the impression of fire and steel, but he knew that, underneath, she was as delicate as glass. It was said Tewdric was a brute who sold his own people into slavery. He did not want to imagine Anya in Tewdric's bed, just as he had not enjoyed thinking of her in Vortigern's bed. Neither of them knew how to care for such a rare creature, but if she were to belong to him, he would treat her gently and with respect.

'What the fuck is she doing in Siluria?' Vortigern yelled.

'I don't know, lord,' Rufus replied hesitantly.

'If he thinks I'll pay him an ounce of silver then he's sadly mistaken.'

'You don't want her back?' Rufus asked, appalled.

Vortigern thudded heavily down the steps of the dais.

'Why would I want her back?'

'Because she's your wife?'

'She ran away from me. She humiliated me. And now she's despoiled by that Silurian sheep-fucker, she's no use to me.'

Rufus could not bear the thought of never seeing Anya again. Most women treated him with scorn, but despite everything he had done, or failed to do, Anya had never judged him. Her green eyes had looked into his soul and she had understood him, and accepted him for what he was.

He thought fast. It was unlikely he could persuade Vortigern to pay ransom; he would believe it made him appear weak. But perhaps there was another way. Tewdric and Vortigern had been eyeing each other for some time now, each threatened by the other's power, like two fighting cocks circling in a pit no longer big enough for both of them.

159

'This is a perfect opportunity to mount a legitimate attack on Tewdric's kingdom,' Rufus said, choosing his words carefully. 'No-one can accuse you of aggression when you are taking back what is rightfully yours.'

From the corner of his eye, he saw Ronan look up from his finger nails.

'I've never heard such a fucking stupid suggestion. I thought we'd agreed you'd keep out of politics?' Vortigern barked.

'If you don't respond to Tewdric, he will see it as a sign of weakness.' The thought of never seeing Anya again was making Rufus bold.

Vortigern took a step forward until he towered over him, a solid mass of belligerence and brute force. 'Tewdric has been trying to goad me into attacking him for years because he knows ambush and massacre await any army foolish enough to venture into those valleys.' He grabbed Rufus by the tunic, shaking him as if he were a dusty rag. 'I won't do it, do you hear? I won't do it!'

Rufus's teeth were rattling and he wondered if he was about to be sick. Vortigern released him abruptly, shoving him backwards so he skidded across the mosaic floor. He came to a halt, his pale cheeks spotted with fury and humiliation. Righting himself, he primly adjusted his tunic.

'She is your wife,' he repeated, struggling to catch his breath. 'You can't abandon her!'

'Tewdric is welcome to her. I don't need her any more. I have another Saxon whore in my bed, and believe me, Horsa's girl tastes sweet.'

Rufus pursed his lips. The hostage was rarely permitted to leave her chambers. On the few occasions he had caught sight of her, she had that 'dead behind the eyes' expression only

160

seen in slaves. 'You married Anya in the sight of God. You swore an oath to protect her, for better for worse,' he said anxiously.

'I am king of the Dobunni, whilst you are a jumped up cowardly quill-pusher. No-one tells me what I can or cannot do! Not you, not Tewdric, not even God!' Vortigern roared.

Rufus shivered. The ancient Greeks had a word for such conceit. They had called it '*hubris*,' and no good ever came of it.

'We have to get her back.' Ronan's voice rang out from the top of the dais.

As one, Rufus and Vortigern turned to look at him.

'You've told me time and time again that a king must never show any sign of weakness, father,' Ronan went on. 'If you leave your wife in Tewdric's hands, you will seem weak.'

Vortigern glared at his son. 'The Picts are on the move again. The Irish swarm across my land. The Catuvellauni are burning my granaries on the borderlands. My spies say the Coritani are amassing an army. Aquila, their boy-king who, incidentally, you failed to kill, is desperate to avenge his father. That Saxon whore-son at Heytesbury Head is raiding further and further inland. And with all this, you honestly expect me to go into Siluria for a frigid Saxon bitch?'

'No, father. I'll go into Siluria, with a warband, not an army. We'll travel at night. No-one will see us coming. We'll be in and out before Tewdric has time to pull up his breeches.'

Vortigern's frown deepened. 'You would do that for Anya?'

'No father,' Ronan replied levelly. 'I will do it for you.'

Vortigern's eyes were darting to and fro. Rufus knew that expression well. Vortigern was weighing the pros and cons, assessing the risks.

'Then just make sure you bring her back alive,' Vortigern

161

said at last. 'She's humiliated me in the eyes of the world. And I intend to make her pay for it.'

From the tiny window of her chamber, Elsbet watched Ronan's warband assemble in the forum far below. She wondered where he was going and why. She closed her eyes for a moment, overcome with weariness and despair. She had pleaded with Vortigern to respect her betrothal oath to Horsa. But he had locked the door, and turned to face her with that look on his face she had come to know so well. He took her to bed each and every night, even during her monthly cycle, until the bed rugs were stained dark red with her blood.

She had tried to fight him. She had bitten and scratched and screamed, but her resistance had merely increased his desire. He had hurt her, and humiliated her, and shamed her. It was her fault she had not found a way to stop him. She was weak and worthless, and she hated herself.

There was no doubt in her mind that she had to die. To go on living for even a day longer would be intolerable. In her mind's eye, she could see the moment the pommel of Vortigern's sword had smashed down on Horsa's head. The moment he had crumpled to the floor. She had cried out as Hengist's men carried him from the chamber, leaving a trail of his blood across the floor. She had made to follow them, but Vortigern had held her back, and when she fought against him, he had grabbed her by the throat and squeezed until there was no more breath in her lungs.

Elsbet did not blame Anya for turning her back on her wedding vows. She understood why she had run away, for who could bear to be married to such a brutish man as Vortigern? Many said Anya had died in the winter storms, but she did not want to believe that. She prayed her closest friend

162

was safe, prayed she had found sanctuary. They would not meet again in this life but she prayed they might be reunited one day in the world beyond the veil.

She watched Ronan's warband ride away through the imposing arched entrance of the forum then out into the streets beyond. Although the sun was shining, the city appeared deserted. The people of Aquae Sulis were locked away behind closed doors, dying in the stifling, stinking darkness of shuttered rooms, away from the warmth of a bright summer day.

Elsbet had given considerable thought to how she might die. At first she had hoped the pestilence might make the decision for her but, frustratingly, she had not sickened. She watched a cart trundle past, a pile of bodies heaped upon it. Death would not be so terrible after all. Outside the thick walls of the basilica, people were dying all the time.

Steam was rising from the rose-perfumed bath the slaves had prepared for her. She began to undress, taking her time, her mind calm and deliberate. When her monthly bleeding had stopped, her first thought was to take a knife and cut Vortigern's child from her belly. She didn't want it, this cuckoo in the nest, this monstrous, loathsome creature growing inside her, sapping both her strength and her sanity. But she couldn't bring herself to do it, and she despised herself for her weakness.

Now, she was simply too tired to bear the shame any longer. Too tired to live with the knowledge that Horsa was lost to her forever, for there was no doubt in her mind that he would never bring himself to look upon her again. She was violated, defiled, and carrying another man's child. She was no longer worthy of Horsa, a man of unfailing integrity and honour.

Vortigern had refused to speak to her of Horsa's fate, but

163

the slave girls knew everything: Horsa had survived Vortigern's assault, and returned to the wall with Hengist. She worried about him, so far away in barbarian lands, but it was a huge comfort to know he was still alive.

Elsbet lowered herself into the warm water. She had never known childbirth, never held the children she and Horsa had so desperately craved, never watched them grow and learn. But she had known love. Her love for Horsa had been pure and untainted. At least she had something good to take with her into the world beyond.

She reached for the knife beside the bath. Carefully she ran the blade across her finger-tip. It was sharp. A droplet of blood fell to the water, and spread across the surface. It reminded her of a sunset across the fields of Saxony. She took the knife and drew it quickly across her wrist. The pain made her cry out, and her face contorted, every muscle tensing against it. There was a heartbeat's delay and then the wound opened, blood beginning to run down her arm towards her elbow.

Hurriedly, she switched hands, and drew the dagger across her right wrist. She gritted her teeth as pain engulfed her, and tears squeezed from her tightly closed eyelids. The dagger fell from her fingers and clattered against the wooden floorboards. She pushed her hands deep into the scented water. Its warmth soothed the pain and she slid deeper into the bath.

The perfume of the rose water was sweet and comforting. Her mind returned to Horsa, his smile, and the kindness in his eyes. She remembered their kisses, their secret embraces. The feel of his body pressed against hers had made her melt and yet burn at the same time.

Her thoughts turned to home, to Germania. The flat fields

164

against a brilliant blue sky, the companionship in the great hall, the comforting scent of wood smoke. The laughter at the fire side with Anya, her dearest friend in all the world. They had shared so many secrets together, so much joy.

And then she thought of her parents, and her brother and sister. It seemed her mother was always large with child. She had brought so many babies into the world who had struggled for life and then simply fallen asleep, worn out by the battle. They had been sad times, following those tiny, shrouded bodies to the burial field.

She drifted, her eyes closed. The summers in Germania were long, always sunny, the endless hours to play. It had been a long tiring day. Her mother was tucking her up in bed. She felt her kiss across her cheek.

And Elsbet fell asleep.

SEVENTEEN

The kingdom of Siluria

Ronan and his warband of thirty men travelled incognito, no banner unfurled, no white boar etched upon his men's cuirasses. They travelled at night, although at this time of year, it was never truly dark. No sooner had the sun set than the birds were singing again. They followed ancient drovers' tracks into the west and the way was quiet.

It was easy to disappear in a kingdom of dense forests, easy to find food and water in a land of streams filled with salmon. The weather was kind; hot cloudless days warmed the earth, giving the nights a soft, balmy stillness. They reached the pasturelands of Tewdric's kingdom on the third night. Moonlight illuminated a lone shepherd, watching over his flocks. At the sight of the approaching warband, the man turned tail and ran away, disappearing into a swathe of dark woodland.

'Should we hunt him down, lord?' A strand of spittle flew from Julianus's lips, a symptom of his misshapen jaw.

With practiced ease, Ronan turned his head to avoid the glistening thread. He found it curious that a man of such profound ugliness should have found favour with Vortigern, but there was no denying Julianus was the most steadfastly reliable of his father's warriors.

'No, let him go,' he replied. 'He saw a warband, that's all. I'd wager he thinks we're Tewdric's men. He's likely pissing his breeches.'

They rode on through the night. Dawn was breaking when Tewdric's stronghold finally came into the view. It dominated the distant hilltop, its chalk ramparts gleaming in the half light.

'We'll make camp there,' Ronan gestured to the nearby woodland. 'Eat, get some rest. We attack tonight.'

Ronan crouched in the shadow of Tewdric's stronghold. He had an uneasy relationship with God, but someone deserved thanks for the cloud cover that hid the bright full moon. He had left five men to guard the horses in the woodland camp; the rest were beside him. He raised his hand and his men rose up from the darkness. An arrow felled an approaching sentry guard and moments later, bill-hooks attached to ropes flew through the blackness and embedded in the wooden palisades. Ronan and his men climbed over Tewdric's defences, slid down the steep rampart and dropped unobserved into the sleeping hill-fort. They moved along the narrow pathways, keeping to the shadows, as fast and silent as owls on the wing.

Ronan came to a halt at a crossroads, peering cautiously around the corner of a shed. Three men were approaching from the left, talking in low voices. Pressing his back against the wall, he gestured for his men to shrink back into the shadows. He held his breath, praying the Silurians would not turn into their path.

Perhaps God was listening, for the men passed by, their hands on the pommels of their swords. Ronan eyed them curiously. He thought they looked like savages, half man, half

167

bear, with their unkempt hair, thick beards, and furs about their shoulders despite the warmth of the summer night.

He waited until their voices had faded into the distance then nodded to his men to proceed. Tewdric's stronghold reeked of the sickly-sweet stench of rotting midden pits, of fresh animal dung, of the dirty tang of metalworking. It smelled different to Aquae Sulis, Ronan mused grimly. Vortigern's stronghold smelled of pestilence, of misery and of death.

The central round-house was not hard to find. It dominated the hill-top, its huge doorframe carved with pagan decorations, circles within circles, like some nightmarish maze. There was a guard by the door, his eyes glazed with boredom and fatigue.

Ronan nodded to one of his bowmen. The soldier nocked an arrow and drew back his arm. The arrow flew like a whisper, sinking into the guard's neck. The man's face registered his shock. He made a fumbling attempt to pull the arrow from his throat before blood began to ooze between his teeth and he collapsed to the ground. Ronan lifted the guard by his ankles and dragged him aside.

Cautiously, he tried to open the round-house door. It was locked from the inside, as he had expected.

'I need an axe,' he hissed, holding out his hand.

A soldier stepped forward and handed him the weapon. Gripping the axe by the neck, Ronan slid its blade into the gap between the door and the jamb. He felt it meet the latch. Leaning against the door frame for leverage, he forced the axe head up and lifted the beam. The door creaked on its hinges and he pushed it ajar with his foot.

Turning, he mouthed at his men. 'Now.'

They spilled into the round-house, black shadows against

the fading embers of the fire. Ronan's first instinct was to wait for his eyes to become accustomed the gloom, but they had surprise on their side and it was too valuable to squander. They moved fast, driving their swords into the haphazard mass of sleeping bodies.

A hound stirred. Ronan watched Julianus grab it by the scruff of the neck and draw his blade across its throat. The animal was still twitching as he lowered it back to the floor with surprising tenderness.

By the fourth kill, Ronan could feel battle fever coursing through his veins. His sword felt as light as air in his hand and despite the darkness, he could see as clear as day. He moved with ease, his limbs fluid and agile, each motion as polished and perfected as a dance. He raised his sword, ready to plunge its blade into the next prostrate body, but the man was sitting up, looking about in confusion, reaching for his dagger at his belt.

Ronan kicked the man in the face. He toppled onto his back, his arms flailing. Stepping closer, Ronan drove his sword through the man's throat then moved on. He needed to find Tewdric. And then he needed to find Anya. Moving quickly, he began to search behind the wicker partitions. Tewdric's sleeping quarters were unmistakeable, dominated by a huge bed. Raised above the beaten earth, it was embellished with an intricately carved wooden head-board, patterned woollen rugs and linen sheets. Finely embroidered fabrics masked the dry-stone walls whilst silver cups and platters were strewn across a low table at the end of the bed.

There was a young girl beneath the rugs, her long dark hair falling across the pillows. There was no sign of Tewdric and Ronan felt a surge of frustration. He stepped closer and pulled the rugs away from the girl. Her slender, flawless body was naked. The cool night air fell upon her skin and she stirred and opened her eyes sleepily. Catching sight of him, her expression crumpled into terror.

Ronan clamped a hand over her mouth to silence the scream that was forming on her lips. It had been several days since he had taken a girl to his bed. Tewdric's wife was young, pert, and she smelled good. It was a pity there was no time to have her, for it would have been sweet revenge. She struggled in his arms but he grabbed her hair and held her fast.

'If you make a sound I will kill you,' he said roughly.

It appeared she understood him, for she stopped struggling, her eyes wide. He released her and she reached for the sheet, but he tugged it away from her grasp. She would be more likely to talk if she was naked and vulnerable.

'Where is he? Where's Tewdric?'

She looked blankly at him and he felt his patience snap. He took the dagger from his belt and pressed it to her throat.

'I know you understand me. Tell me where he is, or I'll slit your throat.'

He felt her soft body beginning to tremble.

'Hunting. Three days since.' Her tongue stumbled awkwardly over the Latin words.

'Are you lying, woman?'

He pressed the dagger harder against her pale skin and she whimpered with terror.

'No lie,' she breathed.

He let her go, thinking fast. What to do with her?

He could take her as a hostage, but he had come to Siluria to end a feud, not perpetuate one. He knew what his father would do. He would kill her without hesitation, for fear she carried Tewdric's child. Ronan eyed her slender limbs and tiny breasts. She was beautiful, but she was little more than a child herself. And he didn't kill children. He stood up. Balling his right hand into a fist he aimed for her temple. It was a clean blow. She gave a tiny gasp and fell back onto the rugs, out cold.

In the round-house, the slaughter was complete. The air no longer smelled of spit-roast but of an abattoir, of spilled guts, and fresh blood. Ronan moved quickly, peering into corners and over wicker partitions, searching for Anya.

She was still fast asleep. He crouched beside her pallet and shook her hard.

'Anya! Get up!'

She moaned incoherently.

'What's the matter with you?' he asked impatiently. 'Are you drunk?'

'No…'

'We have to go. Come on!' he urged.

She tried to sit up but sank back onto the pallet. 'I don't think I can.'

What was the matter with her? Ronan lifted the soaked bandage about her neck. It looked as if someone had tried to cut her throat. The wound was oozing yellow pus, the surrounding skin puckered and inflamed. He put a hand to her forehead and felt her fever.

Cursing under his breath, he put an arm around her waist and lifted her from the pallet. He was shocked by how little she weighed. Stepping over the bodies of Tewdric's slaughtered men, he carried her to the door.

'I can't go. Not yet. I have to find my sword,' she protested.

'You don't have a sword,' he snapped. Was she delirious?

'Put me down!' Anya disentangled herself from his arms, but the world swayed and she gripped the door frame for support.

He grabbed her shoulders. 'Come on, Anya, we have to go.'

But she held her ground. 'No! I can't leave until I find it.'

She pushed past him, back into the darkness of the round-house. Ronan stood in the doorway and watched her in amazement. By the light of the dying embers of the fire, she was stumbling over the corpses of Tewdric's men. It was as if she knew exactly who she was looking for, as if she had imprinted a face into her memory.

Ronan could feel battle fever pumping through his veins from the short, sharp massacre; his muscles twitched and his eyes darted back and forth across the sleeping hill top. The light was softening towards dawn. This was all taking too long. It was only a matter of time before someone passed by, noticed the doors were open, smelled the blood, sounded the alarm.

He turned towards Anya again, watching as she heaved a bloodied corpse onto its back, looked at the man's face then moved on. Why was he standing in the doorway like a humble sentry while this insane Saxon girl kicked over corpses like a battlefield scavenger? He did not think she even possessed a sword. But he had seen something in her eyes. Not the delirium of a fevered mind, but not exactly rational thought either. It had been something else entirely, something he couldn't name, but something so absolute it had frozen him to the spot like an obedient hound.

He watched her approach another of Tewdric's slaughtered warriors. The man lay on his back on a wall bench, one arm dangling to the floor. His eyes were closed as if he was still sleeping, but his throat gaped open. Blood ran from the deep wound and dripped onto the floor rushes. Ronan noticed the girl's fingers were trembling as she unclasped the sword from the dead man's belt, and fastened it to her own.

She stood up and walked unsteadily towards the door.

'We can go now.'

Ronan eyed the extraordinary sword and scabbard that now hung from her belt. He had a lot of questions for his father's wife, but they would have to wait. Anya was shivering uncontrollably and he suspected her legs might give way at any moment. She did not protest as he scooped her up into his arms. She felt hot, her skin burning up.

Ronan led his men through the sleeping hill fort. They moved fast and silently, scanning the narrow alleyways for signs of trouble, but was all quiet save for the distant crowing of a cockerel, and a blackbird's song in the branches of an ash tree. Ronan narrowed his eyes as the first rays of the sun flooded over the high palisade. The day had begun; they no longer had darkness on their side. And although Anya wasn't heavy, she was slowing him down.

'Put me down. I can run,' she said, as if she had read his thoughts.

'You can hardly walk! Put your arms about my neck and hold on tight!'

He knew they would not be able to leave the way they had come. He couldn't manhandle a barely conscious woman up a thirty foot high chalk rampart and over a sharp tipped palisade. They would have to take their chances at the gate. Ronan looked cautiously around the corner of a leathersmith's workshop. His boots were sinking into a deep layer of off-cuts, the air pungent with the aroma of freshly tanned hide.

There were two guards at the gate. They looked half asleep, slumped wearily against the rampart. At that moment, the urgent blasts of a war-horn reverberated loudly through the stronghold. Ronan shot a glance over his shoulder. He could hear raised voices, cries of alarm coming from the direction of

Tewdric's round-house. And then he looked back at the gate. The guards had sprung to life, instantly alert.

'Get those gates open!' Ronan yelled.

With Julianus leading from the front, Ronan's warband charged towards the gates. Tewdric's guards had barely drawn their swords before they were cut down where they stood. Julianus stepped over the bodies, heaved the heavy locking beam from its socket and pulled the gates open.

And then they were running again, hurtling down the hillside, leaving the ramparts and ditches of Tewdric's fortress behind. Ronan's heart was racing with the effort of carrying Anya in his arms. He worried he might lose his footing in the slippery grass, but he dared not slow his pace. He had noticed stables in the fortress. It was highly likely they were about to be pursued by mounted warriors.

Curious sheep lifted their heads from the pastureland as Ronan's warband ran past. He looked over his shoulder. As he had suspected, a tight knot of horsemen had left the fort and were galloping after them. The sheep were scattering in alarm.

'Fuck!' he said under his breath and then louder, to his men, 'keep going! Almost there!'

Up ahead, he could see the woodland where they had made camp, where their own horses were waiting for them. It was tantalisingly close, no more than three hundred yards away, but the horsemen were rapidly gaining on them.

Ronan's men instinctively closed up, forming a protective shield around him as he ran. His thoughts were whirring. He didn't want to die surrounded by sheep shit in a skirmish that no-one would remember. And he certainly didn't want to die for this Saxon girl his father had married in haste and now despised. She wasn't particularly heavy but nevertheless, she was slowing him down.

Perhaps he should just let go of her, and leave her to her fate. And yet, he had come this far. He had made a promise to his father, and it would mean so much if once, just once, he could see pride in Vortigern's eyes, not disappointment. And besides, if he abandoned the girl now, Tewdric had won. He glanced over his shoulder again. The horsemen were closing fast. His arms were aching and his legs felt heavy as lead, but he gritted his teeth and quickened his pace.

Julianus reached the woodland first. Ducking his head to avoid the low branches, he began to charge through the undergrowth like an angry bear.

'Make haste!' he shouted, but Vortigern's soldiers had been keeping watch. They had saddled the horses in readiness, holding out the reins to the rapidly approaching warriors like competitors in a relay race.

Ronan lifted Anya into the saddle and then mounted up. With one hand firmly around her waist, he reined around.

'We ride hard. We put distance between us. And then we stop, we ambush, and finish these sheep-fuckers!'

Digging in his heels, he led his men along the forest track at full gallop. Anya's head fell heavily against his chest. From the looseness of her limbs, he knew she was slipping in and out of consciousness. A warm wind blew in from the south, thrashing the branches above their heads. The gap between his men and Tewdric's riders steadily widened. Their stocky ponies were no match for the thoroughbred stallions of the Dobunni.

After several miles, the track began to climb steeply towards the crest of a hill. Reaching the top of the rise, Ronan slowed his mount to a walk and quickly assessed his surroundings. The track fell away, a steep drop of baked earth overlain by loose stones. The forest pressed in on both sides, dark and dense, blocking out the early morning sunlight. The Silurians were perhaps half a mile behind. There wasn't much time.

'We ambush half way down the hill – there, by the fallen tree. Get out of sight, behind the tree line, both sides of the track. Archers – wait until all the horsemen are over the hill and on the downward slope. Spears - follow on my command. Go! Now!'

His men steadied their horses as they began to slip and slide down the steep track. At the fallen tree, they quickly divided into two groups, turning into the forest and disappearing into the darkness. Ronan followed the archers into the undergrowth. He could hear the ponies' hoof beats; Tewdric's men were almost upon them. He slid from his saddle, drawing Anya down with him.

'What's happening?' Her words were slurred, almost indecipherable. She clung to his shoulder, looking about in alarm.

He silenced her with a shake of his head and half carried, half dragged her into the woodland, depositing her against the trunk of an oak tree. She looked up at him with glazed eyes.

'Stay here. Keep quiet. I'll come back for you,' he whispered then strode back to his men.

His archers had taken up position in a staggered formation, as still as statues. Ronan mounted up in time to see the first Silurian appear over the brow of the hill. Another crested the hill, then another. All the horsemen slowed to a walk as they began to descend the steep track.

At Ronan's signal, a storm of arrows flew from the tree line. The first found its mark in the chest of a Silurian and the man let out a strangled cry. As he fell towards the ground, his foot caught in his stirrup. The pony began to rear in fright, dragging the man down the stony track. Another pony took an arrow to its flank and let out a high pitched squeal of pain. Its rider fought to control it, but the animal was sliding helplessly through a cascade of scree. The next arrow found the rider's throat, sinking into his flesh with a wet thud. He let go of the reins and hit the ground hard, his body trampled beneath the hooves of his terrified pony.

The remaining Silurians were attempting to break free of the killing ground. With their shields above their heads against the cloud of arrows, they dug in their heels and began to gallop back up the hill.

'Don't let the bastards get away!' Ronan yelled.

Tewdric's men died a coward's death, their backs a pincushion of arrows shafts. They fell from their saddles, sliding back down the hillside amidst tumbling rocks and stones. Ronan dismounted and stepped out from the tree line. The wounded horse had collapsed but it was still thrashing wildly, sending storms of dust into the air.

'Someone put that beast out of its misery.'

One of his men stepped forward and Ronan turned away. He always found it more disturbing to watch a horse die than a man. For a brief moment, he wondered what that said about him, but then he noticed Anya approaching through the trees.

'I told you not to move!'

But the girl walked straight past him. He noticed she was shivering uncontrollably, her hands clasped about her thin frame as if hoping they might offer some warmth.

'Here.' Ronan unfastened his cloak and slung it around her shoulders.

She did not acknowledge his gesture. Her gaze was fixed on the dead Silurian at her feet. 'That's Tewdric,' she said.

'What did you say?' She had spoken in a language he did

177

not understand. It didn't sound like Saxon and he wondered if she was speaking the Silurian tongue.

She turned to look at him and he saw a flash of confusion in her eyes.

'That's Tewdric,' she repeated, this time in Latin.

'Are you sure?' he asked sceptically. Where had the bastard been hiding whilst his men died?

Anya's fingers tightened around the edges of Ronan's cloak and she pulled it about her, as if she had just realised it was there.

'I am certain,' she said, her expression hardening.

Ronan knelt down beside Tewdric's corpse. In death the once-powerful warlord of the Silures was nothing more than torn flesh and shattered bones. He smiled grimly.

'Then this day just keeps on getting better and better.'

Ronan did not linger. He left the dead for the wolves, but he took Tewdric's head as a trophy for Vortigern, and the four remaining ponies. *Waste not, want not,'* as his mother always used to tell him. Strange how he remembered her words, even now, after all these years.

They rode all day, resting the horses briefly at midday, and did not make camp until sunset. They were still deep inside the forest. Ronan sat down next to Anya at the fireside. She looked weak and sick and he realised she had lost a great deal of weight since her wedding day. Her eyes were sunken, her cheeks flushed with fever. He put a wooden beaker into her hand and closed her fingers around it. It was filled with ice cold water from the stream.

'Drink.'

She took a sip and nodded her thanks.

'How did you get that wound on your throat?' he asked.

'It's a long story.'

'I have time.'

Her hand strayed to her throat. 'If you don't get me back to Aquae Sulis, to my medicine box, you may as well have left me for dead in Tewdric's stronghold.'

'I'm aware of that,' he replied drily.

He waited for her to speak again, but she was staring blankly into the fire. She looked very young, very vulnerable. Ironic then, to think this girl was his step-mother.

'I should warn you there is pestilence in Aquae Sulis,' he said. 'Many people are sick, many are dying.'

'The plague?' Anya asked nervously. 'Where are my brothers? Are they safe?'

'Your brothers are in the north. As far as I know, they're alive.'

He saw the relief in her eyes.

'I have medicine in my chamber. Perhaps I can help the people of Aquae Sulis,' she began.

'If you live long enough,' Ronan replied bluntly.

Anya stared at him for a long moment. He had a curious feeling she had made an assessment and found him wanting. His shifted uncomfortably. Anya's brothers were dangerous men. Vortigern was a fool to trust them, and a fool to allow their reinforcements to flood into Britannia. A fool to stand by and do nothing as Hengist steadily claimed the territory of the Brigantes. And Vortigern had been a fool to marry this girl. She was weak and sick, but there was something about her, something unnerving. It was not difficult to see why many believed her to be a witch.

Taking the beaker from her hand, he took a long drink of water. Although his father had never spoken of it, he suspected something had happened on his wedding night, something which had tormented Vortigern from that day to this. Anya was trouble. Perhaps he should have left her to die after all.

'So, tell me, did you enjoy being a guest of the late king of Siluria?' he asked sarcastically.

'He didn't rape me, if that's what you are asking. But he would have, if his wife had not been so…possessive. And if I had not been…'

'Half dead?' The corners of Ronan's mouth twitched into a wry smile.

The girl did not return his smile. 'There is something I would ask of you,' she began tentatively. 'My kin were taken as slaves by Tewdric. He spoke of a slave market in a town called Caerwent. If you were to send out riders, if you could find my kin -'

But Ronan interrupted her. 'Even if we had the men to spare for such a task, it would be a fool's errand. Your kin will be long gone by now, most likely shipped overseas, to Ireland or Gaul or beyond.

'But they are my blood -' she said wretchedly, but Ronan cut her off again.

'You must accept it. There is nothing anyone can do for them. They are lost.'

Anya's expression faltered. She felt tears of frustration and grief welling in her eyes but she brushed them aside, determined not to show her feelings to this man. Swallowing hard, she asked, 'how fares Dumnonia under its new king?'

Ronan wondered why she would ask such a thing, and then he remembered the long months she had spent hiding in the kingdom at the edge of the world. 'How did you know Etar was dead?' he asked sharply.

'I heard Tewdric speak of it.'

Her eyes did not meet his and he suspected she was lying. Not for the first time, he wondered if this strange girl was a spy.

'I know little of Dumnonia. They trade with us, and their horses are without equal, but Dumnonia has always kept itself to itself,' he replied carefully.

'Has Silvanus taken a wife?'

Bemused by her question, Ronan laughed out loud.

'I'm sorry.' The girl looked disconcerted. 'I don't know why I asked that…' her voice trailed off again.

To his immense surprise, Ronan realised he pitied her. Her throat was threaded with ominous black veins. He had seen enough men wounded upon the battlefield to know that poison was beginning to spread through her body. He estimated they would reach Aquae Sulis by nightfall tomorrow. He doubted she would be alive to see it.

'You should rest. Save your strength. We have a long ride ahead tomorrow.'

'You know as well as I that if I sleep, I might never wake up again,' she said quietly. 'Talk to me a while, please?'

Ronan had no skill for small talk; he took after his father in that respect. He knew even less about talking to women. His mother had died when he was twelve years old, and since then he had not had a single meaningful relationship with a member of the opposite sex. He either bedded women or he ignored them. There was nothing in between. He racked his brain, struggling to think of something to say.

'Is that truly your sword?' he asked at last, glancing at the scabbard at her belt.

'Yes.' Her fingers tightened possessively about the hilt.

'Who gave it to you?'

'A friend.'

181

Ronan waited, but the girl did not elaborate. His eyes fell enviously upon the scabbard again. The sword was obviously ancient, a thing of beauty, a work of supreme craftsmanship. He would like to own such a weapon, feel the weight of it in his hand.

'What news from Aquae Sulis?' the girl asked.

Ronan took another drink of water, weighing up how much he should tell her. At length he said, 'your brothers came to Aquae Sulis, and my father demanded hostages.'

'Hostages? Why?'

'Because they are traitorous bastards who can't be trusted.'

'They're not traitors -' Anya began, but he cut her off.

'Save me the speech in their defence. I've heard it all before and I don't believe a word of it.'

Fear flickered in Anya's eyes, but Ronan didn't notice. His thoughts had turned to the young Saxon girl Vortigern had taken to his bed.

'One of the hostages is such a pretty little thing - hair the colour of ripe wheat,' he mused out loud.

'A girl?' Anya asked, surprised. 'What is her name?'

'I can't remember, but your brother wasn't pleased.'

'My brother?'

For a fleeting moment, Ronan wondered why Anya's entire body had tensed, as if her every muscle had turned to stone. And then, just as quickly, he gave up. Women were impossible to understand, too many baffling emotions seething beneath all that soft, enticing flesh.

'Your brother, Horsa, wasn't pleased,' he repeated carelessly.

'Elsbet? Is her name Elsbet?' Anya asked.

She was leaning forward now, starring intensely at him, suddenly, startlingly alert.

182

'Yes, I think that was her name.'

'And does Vortigern treat her honourably?'

In reply, Ronan merely snorted. The girl had not left his father's bed in weeks.

'Answer me.' Anya's voice was trembling.

'You know my father. What do you think?'

He did not expect what happened next. Anya launched herself at him, shouting incoherently. He grabbed her arms, pinning them to her sides, but still she thrashed wildly in his grasp, tears streaming down her cheeks. He had no idea what had caused this outburst. Was she delirious?

'Stop it! Calm down! Take a breath!'

But she did not stop. If anything, she grew more hysterical, screaming at him in the Saxon tongue. Out of his depth, he looked helplessly at Julianus, but he merely raised his eyebrows and shrugged his shoulders. And so Ronan resorted to the tactics he knew best. He clenched his fist and punched her in the temple. It was not a hard blow, just enough to silence her. Her head jerked back, her eyes rolled up and he caught her as she fell.

Ronan awoke just before dawn. His men were already breaking camp, dowsing the fire, tending the horses, packing saddle bags. He stood up, stretched and walked over to Julianus.

'We cannot linger. We're still in the territory of the Silures, and we've just killed their king.'

'I'll give the order to move out, lord.'

Ronan turned next to the girl. She lay beside the smoking fire, motionless beneath his cloak. Crouching down, he pushed her hair from her face and eyed her dispassionately. He had not expected her to last the night, but she was still alive; her eyelids fluttering in her sleep. There was a vivid purple bruise and a swelling the size of a small egg on her temple where he had struck her.

'Anya!' He shook her shoulder.

Her gaze focussed on him and he saw confusion in her eyes, then anger.

'You punched me,' she began, her fingers tracing the bruise at her temple.

There was no time for apologies or recrimination. 'Time to go,' he said, and hauled her upright.

She swayed on her feet, so he lifted her in his arms and carried her to his horse. Dawn broke as they rode on, shafts of sharp sunlight breaking through the tree canopy and piercing the narrow track. Ronan was half expecting to see a warband close on their heels, but all was quiet. Anya's head fell against his chest and he could feel the heat of her fever radiating from her skin.

As they neared the edge of the forest, they came upon isolated settlements of charcoal burners, swine herders and potters. And soon after, they entered the kingdom of the Dobunni, and found themselves in open countryside, riding beside fields of ripening wheat, barley and beans. Ronan ordered the unfurling of the banner and felt his body begin to relax for the first time in days. They were almost home.

It took five crossings to ferry his warband across the river in the shadow of the old Roman temple. Ronan dismounted and carried Anya to the boat. She did not stir, a dead weight in his arms. Tired, hungry and caked in other men's blood, his warriors were unusually taciturn. They led their horses onto the flat bottomed boat and stood in silence, staring blankly ahead.

It was peaceful upon the river, the only sound the rhythmic

plash of oars, and Ronan's mind began to drift. The ambush in the forest was a job well done. Tewdric was dead; the kingdom of Siluria belonged to Vortigern now. Surely his father would praise him for this?

The girl stirred in his arms and his brief sense of well-being vanished. Her lips were moving in her delirium, and he realised he didn't want her to die. He had promised his father he would bring her back alive and he didn't want to fail him, didn't want to see the disappointment in his eyes.

The ferry beached with a gentle bump. In sharp contrast to the tranquil river, the fishing village was bustling with life. At the sight of a warband regrouping in their midst, the villagers stopped what they were doing, watching them warily.

'We're not your enemy!' Ronan snapped. 'Don't you know the banner of your king?'

His words did not appear to reassure them. He realised many of them were staring at the girl in his arms. Did they recognise her? Had she passed this way before? He could not begin to imagine why she had chosen to make the long, dangerous journey to Siluria. Heaving her back into the saddle, he threw a coin at the nearest ferryman and rode on.

They reached Aquae Sulis at dusk, their horses foam flecked with fatigue. Ronan dismounted in the forum, and Anya's unresponsive body slipped from the saddle and into his arms. His men hurried up the basilica steps ahead of him to open the doors. He strode inside, shivering as the cold, musty air enveloped him. Rufus was scurrying towards him.

'What's the matter with her?' the scribe asked anxiously.

Ronan was already half way up the stairs. 'Isn't it obvious?' He nodded at the festering wound at Anya's throat.

Rufus bridled at his tone. 'Your father wants to see you,' he said coldly. 'The Saxon girl, the hostage, slit her wrists.'

Ronan swung around to face him. 'And is she dead?'

Rufus nodded.

'Then there's nothing more to be done, is there? Tell my father I will join him shortly.'

'But he said he wanted to see you immediately.'

'He'll have to wait! There's something I need to do.'

Ronan carried Anya up the stairs, along the dark corridor and pushed the door of her chamber open with his foot. He laid her on the bed and pressed two fingers against her wrist. There was a faint, erratic pulse. He glanced quickly about the room. She had spoken of a medicine box, but there was no sign of it. The room was startlingly empty, no trinkets, no jewellery, no clothes. He prowled about the room until he came to the bed again. 'Were you delirious? Do you even have a medicine box?' he shouted irritably but Anya did not stir.

'It's under the bed, lord.' A slave girl was standing in the doorway, her eyes downcast.

Ronan recognised her. She was tolerably pretty and he had fucked her more times than he could remember, usually up against the nearest wall. She cried every time which always annoyed him. He thought she'd have grown used to it by now.

Crouching down, Ronan peered under the bed. Amidst the dust and spider webs, there was a wooden box. He pulled it towards him and opened the lid. It was full of medicine vials, bottles, linen pouches of dried herbs. He picked them up one at a time. Not one of them was labelled.

'Jesus Christ!' he hissed in frustration. Sitting down on the edge of the bed, he put a hand to Anya's cheek. 'Can you hear me? Which medicine will help you?'

But she was as still as death. He put an arm around her shoulders and hauled her upright. 'Unless you want to die in the next few hours,' he said loudly, 'you have to open your

186

eyes and tell me which one of these bottles I am supposed to tip down your throat.'

Anya stirred slightly and mumbled something.

'I can't hear you. Say it again.' He leant closer.

'Green one...'

Ronan ripped open the wax seal of the green glass bottle, sniffed its contents cautiously, and recoiled in disgust. It stank of fermenting grain. Tipping her head back, he poured the thick syrup down her throat. She choked repeatedly, but he kept going until the bottle was empty. He laid her down again and turned to the slave girl.

'Come and find me if she wakes up.' And then, as an afterthought, 'or if she dies.'

Ronan strode back down the corridor, his mind churning. He had been gone from Aquae Sulis for six days and in all that time he had managed to snatch no more than a couple of hours sleep at a time. His battle fever had long since waned and his body felt heavy with fatigue. He longed for a hot bath and a clean bed but first, he had to face his father.

Vortigern was sitting on the raised dais of the council chamber, staring broodily into space. Rufus was at the table, quill in hand, writing on a parchment scroll. His brow was furrowed in concentration but he looked up as Ronan approached.

'How is she?' he asked plaintively.

Ronan ignored him, climbing the steps of the dais two at a time and sinking wearily into the chair beside his father.

'What is God's name did the bitch think she was doing?' Vortigern growled at his son.

'I believe she was running away from you, father.'

'Not Anya! Elsbet. Suicide is a sin in the eyes of God. What was she thinking?'

'She's a pagan,' Ronan replied. 'She doesn't care, I mean, she didn't care, about Christian laws.' He glanced at his father. 'Was it truly suicide?'

'What are you suggesting? That I killed her? No, the stupid girl slit her wrists and bled into her bath tub like a stuck pig.' Vortigern shook his head in disbelief then waved his hand disparagingly, as if the matter was closed. Turning to face his son, he said accusingly, 'you promised me you'd bring my wife back alive.'

'She's not dead, father.'

'She is not dead yet,' Vortigern corrected him. 'Julianus tells me it's not likely she'll survive.'

Ronan saw the displeasure in his father's eyes. The same look that never failed to get under his skin. The same look that never failed to make him feel small.

'I killed Tewdric -' he began, determined to make amends.

But Vortigern talked over him. 'I told you I wanted her back alive. I told you I wanted her to pay.'

Ronan felt a flare of anger. His father wasn't listening. His father never listened. 'Tewdric is dead,' he reiterated forcefully. 'His kingdom is yours now.'

There was a flash of excitement in Vortigern's eyes before he quickly masked it with a show of indifference. But Ronan knew he had his father's attention at last.

'Did he rape her, like he claimed?' Vortigern asked casually.

'Anya says he didn't touch her.'

'Well, she would say that, wouldn't she? Do you believe her?'

'Yes, I do.'

Vortigern did not look convinced. 'God's blood, I should never have married that girl. It's time I was rid of her. I assume you remember how the church deals with witches?'

Ronan examined his fingernails. A few years ago, Vortigern had taken him to witness a burning. The young girl had survived the smoke and flames long enough to watch her own skin melt from her bones. Her terrible shrieks and moans, and the smell of her burning flesh were etched on his memory forever.

Ronan was about to bite a fingernail when he noticed they were stained to the quick with other men's blood. Men who had died in their sleep, and all so Vortigern could enjoy inflicting a truly horrific death upon his Saxon wife. Better for Anya to have died from fever in Tewdric's round-house than endure such a fate.

Rufus was on his feet, scuttling towards the dais, the quill trembling between ink stained fingers.

'You can't burn her,' he stammered.

'I'll do what the fuck I like to my wife. Now sit down before I rip out your interfering tongue.'

Rufus's entire body began to shake with barely suppressed rage. He glared at Vortigern for a long moment, his expression one of unadulterated hatred, before he finally retreated to the table. Vortigern turned back to his son.

'So, did you bring me his head?'

Ronan found it difficult to share his father's relish for such barbaric displays of victory. After the battle against the Coritani, he had handed Pascent's severed head to his father like an offering to a pagan god, but the act had left him cold and he had found no glory in it.

'Yes, father,' he replied. 'And I left the rest of his warband for the wolves.'

'How do I know it is Tewdric's head? How do I know he truly is dead?'

'Trust me, he is dead.'

'Why should I trust you?' Vortigern asked coldly. 'Trust has to be earned.'

The hurt was almost physical, his father's words as painful as a dagger thrust. There would be no thanks from Vortigern, no praise. His father had not changed. His father would never change. Gritting his teeth, Ronan pushed aside his self-pity. His mother had been dead for more than ten years. His siblings had not survived into adulthood. Vortigern was his only family. His father was thoughtless, callous and cruel, but he had no-one else. And so he squared his shoulders and said evenly, 'your Saxon hostage has killed herself, and it's possible Anya will not survive either. How are we to explain this unfortunate turn of events to Hengist?'

'He's a hired mercenary. I don't need to explain myself to him. It's not my fault Elsbet slit her wrists. And it's not my fault Anya chose to run into Tewdric's hands.' Vortigern leant back in his chair and scratched the stubble on his chin. 'When women try and think for themselves, they become incredibly troublesome.'

Ronan nodded grimly. His father had a point.

'That's why I stick to whores,' he replied.

EIGHTEEN

The darkness closed over Anya for a long time, but gradually she became aware of noises around her, footfall on the wooden floorboards, the door opening and closing, voices, and birdsong. She could smell the sweetness of the honey compress against her throat, and feel the fur rugs itching her bare arms. And later, she opened her eyes, and noticed cobwebs hanging like forgotten garlands between the wooden rafters, and the simple fresco running around the walls at waist height, a thin band of intertwining geometric design.

Days and nights came and went in a blur of troubled dreams and a slave girl who persistently encouraged her to eat. She dreamed of Dumnonia, the same dream, again and again.

It was as if a forest of rotting vines had trapped Tintagel's great hall in its creeping tendrils. They dripped from the high rafters, clung to the walls, and matted the floor like a thousand slithering serpents.

The hall was littered with corpses, decayed, rotting, left where they had fallen, the tattered remnants of their cloaks billowing in the wind like ancient battle banners...

Anya opened her eyes and looked about, confused. Ronan was standing at the end of the bed. She stared at him, her mind suddenly filled with muddled images of the dark round-house, the corpses of Tewdric's men. The air had reeked like

191

an abattoir. And later, she had sat with Ronan beside a camp fire, and he had told her about Vortigern taking Elsbet to his bed.

The memory hurt. It felt like fire beneath her skin, rekindling her anger and rage and fury. She sat up and tugged a blanket about her shoulders, eyeing Ronan suspiciously. She had spent days in his company on the journey from Siluria. They had shared a saddle, a drinking cup, a fireside, and yet her recollection of their time together was contradictory and confusing. She had a vague, disturbing memory of him punching her. Gingerly, her fingers probed her right temple. It still felt sore.

And yet she also remembered being carried in his arms as he raced across an open field, the thud as her head banged against his chest, the smell of his leather cuirass against her cheek. And she had the faintest recollection that he had tipped Taliesin's foul tasting fever-balm down her throat.

It was almost impossible to comprehend, but it appeared Vortigern's son had saved her life.

Perplexed, she asked, 'where's Elsbet?'

She longed to see her friend again. And yet at the same time, she dreaded their reunion, for what could she possibly say to make amends? Elsbet had been forced into Vortigern's bed against her will and she could not begin to imagine her humiliation and misery.

'You look better. It seems you are going to live,' Ronan replied dispassionately.

'You didn't answer my question.'

Ronan looked away, seemingly unwilling to meet her gaze. Why wouldn't he look at her? Why wouldn't he answer her?

'Where is Elsbet?' she repeated.

And still Ronan did not reply. She could see the tension in

his body, and the muscle flickering at his jaw. Fear gripped her heart. 'What is it? Is she unwell?'

Ronan remained motionless.

'Tell me!'

He turned to face her then. 'Elsbet is dead. She took her own life.'

Time stopped, suspended in that single, terrible moment. At first Anya thought she had misunderstood him, for she had spoken many different languages of late - Saxon, Latin, Silurian. But, no, she had understood him well enough.

And then she thought perhaps he was lying, a cruel trick to torment her? But no, he wasn't lying. He was telling the truth. She could see it in his eyes.

And then suddenly, time speeded up again. Anya had always tried to avoid hatred, for it was such an ugly, destructive emotion. But she was drowning in it now, and it felt cold and vile. She hated Vortigern for taking Elsbet, and she hated Hengist for allowing it, and she hated Ronan for doing nothing to stop it. First Emma, and now Elsbet. Another wasted life, over before it had truly begun.

'You did this,' she breathed. 'You killed her.'

'No. She took her own life, when I was in Siluria, looking for you.'

Throwing back the rugs, Anya crawled to the edge of the bed and stood up. Her head throbbed violently and she could feel sweat breaking out across her skin. Her legs trembled beneath her, but she had to do something, anything to be rid of this black hatred, this poison filling her lungs.

'I think you should rest,' Ronan began, reaching out to steady her.

'Don't touch me! Don't you dare touch me!' she screamed. 'You raped her too, didn't you, you bastard?'

He backed away from her, his hands raised in a gesture of surrender. 'I never laid a finger on the girl. My father has never been good at sharing.'

Anya shuddered with revulsion. How could he make a joke about something so terrible? But the longer she stared at him, the more she realised that beneath his cocky demeanour, there was genuine indignation. Much as she didn't want to believe him, he was telling the truth; he hadn't touched Elsbet.

And it came to her then, in a flash of clarity. Vortigern was responsible for Elsbet's death. He had defied the goddess, unbalanced the natural order, and Nerthus would not rest until the debt was repaid and equilibrium was restored.

'Vortigern will die for this,' she said with resolute certainty.

Ronan felt a sudden flicker of unease which he promptly disguised as sarcasm. 'Don't tell me you're throwing a curse?'

'I am not a witch.'

Ronan frowned. His father thought otherwise. His father intended to burn her at the stake and the thought discomforted him. Should he warn her? For a fleeting heartbeat, he wrestled with his conscience but in reality, there was no decision to be made. He could never betray his father. And besides, Anya was a Saxon, and deserved no mercy.

'Lord?'

Ronan turned. A soldier was standing in the doorway.

'Cerdic has taken the city of Venta, lord.'

Ronan let out a roar of frustration. 'I prayed the plague might take him! God's blood, will that Saxon never die?'

Anya remembered her father talking about Cerdic, the son of the high king of Frisia. Her father had called him a potential threat to Saxony, a renowned and ferocious warrior with a thirst for land and wealth and glory. But it seemed Cerdic had turned his sights on Britannia instead.

'He's not a Saxon, he's a Frisian,' she began, but Ronan rounded on her furiously.

'You're all the same. You're all from Germania - you carry the plague, you steal our land, you slaughter our people. If it takes my last breath, I'm going to drive every single one of you back into the sea!' He turned to the soldier again. 'Tell my father I'm coming.'

With one last venomous glance at Anya, Ronan left the room, slamming the door behind him.

Anya lay down on the bed, curled into a ball and closed her eyes. Her body was trembling violently. Memories of Elsbet crowded her thoughts - her kindness, her laughter, her smile. What torments had she endured at Vortigern's hands to believe death was the only solution? And what of Horsa? Did he know Elsbet was dead? How would he ever bear such terrible, heart-breaking news?

'My lady?'

Anya opened her eyes again. A young slave girl stood beside the bed, her demeanour timid and afraid. She was painfully thin, her red hair scraped back to reveal a tired, pinched face.

Anya sat up. 'I remember you. You put pearls in my hair on my wedding day. Have you been caring for me?'

'Yes, my lady.'

'Then I owe you my thanks.'

The slave looked astonished and Anya guessed she was not accustomed to gratitude.

'Tell me, the Saxon hostage who took her own life – do you know where she is buried?'

The slave girl nodded. 'They took her body to the plague pit with all the rest, my lady.'

Anya stared at the girl, horror-struck. So Elsbet would not

have a funeral pyre, adorned with her most treasured possessions. There would be no loved ones to witness her soul's journey to the gods upon a veil of sacred smoke. Instead, her spirit would be trapped on earth, restless, endlessly searching for peace.

As a child, Anya had viewed vengeance as something for the heroes of epic poems. As a healer, she had scorned its endless cycle of bloody vendetta. But today, she thought she understood what drove men to seek justice and retribution no matter what the cost. Grief and rage consumed her, until it was impossible to know where she ended and they began.

Time passed, perhaps a matter of moments or perhaps much, much longer. Gradually, the physical pain crushing her heart began to subside, to be replaced by a feeling of intense fatigue. And slowly, she became aware of her surroundings again - the cold, damp chamber, and the pale, sickly slave, eying her warily at her bedside. The girl had red hair, the same colour as her own.

'Are you of the Silures?' Anya asked dully.

'No, my lady. My people are the Votadini, from beyond the wall.'

'If you could, would you return to them?'

'My family are all dead. The Picts stole our cattle and burned our village.'

'I'm sorry.'

Instinctively, Anya reached out and lightly touched the girl's arm. The slave recoiled as if she had been struck, as frightened and cowed as a beaten dog.

Anya hurriedly withdrew her hand. 'I didn't mean to scare you. I won't hurt you.'

In Germania she had never given much thought to the slaves in her father's hall but as she looked into the young girl's frightened eyes, she felt once again the heavy weight of the slave chain about her own neck, felt the terror and shame as her dignity was brutally stripped away. She took a deep, shuddering breath. She had to find Rhys. And she must send word to Llewellyn. She must let him know she was safe. And what of the promise she had made to Ceinwin?

'Where's my sword?' she asked anxiously.

'It's under the bed, my lady. It looked so precious I thought it best to hide it from prying eyes.'

Anya felt a rush of relief. 'What's your name?' she asked.

'Maud,' the girl replied nervously.

'Well, thank you, Maud.'

The slave's thin face broke into a hesitant smile. 'Shall I bring you some food, my lady?'

Anya had no appetite but she nodded, if only for the pleasure of seeing Maud's tentative smile widen still further.

Vortigern stormed down the corridor towards the kitchens. If he was to march to Venta then he intended to do so with a full stomach. The kitchen slaves would no doubt piss themselves with terror at the sight of him in their midst, but there was no time to be waited upon in the council chamber because Julianus was already mustering the men.

He saw the slave girl from the corner of his eye. She was trying to avoid him, turning back the way she had come. He had made good use of her in the last few months. Red haired and pale skinned, she reminded him of Anya but without the feistiness, without the fire.

'How fares my wife?' he shouted down the corridor, but Maud kept on walking.

'Come here!' There was an edge to his voice now.

Maud turned. 'She is still weak, lord.'

197

'But will she live?'

'I believe so, lord.'

Vortigern's belly rumbled loudly, his hunger pangs exacerbated by a disagreeable sense of unease. Anya had unmanned him with her pagan devilry, and a part of him badly wanted her to die. But another part, the part that lusted for her firm, young body, wanted her to live. Should he visit her chamber? Should he finally consummate the marriage? But what if she found a way to unman him again?

He had ruled the kingdom of the Dobunni for more than twenty years and in that time he had learnt to make important decisions quickly and rationally by assessing any situation then weighing the odds. So why did Anya, a mere girl, make him feel like a floundering fish out of water?

Unsettled, he seized Maud by the shoulders and slammed her against the wall. She whimpered but did not attempt to push him away. And as he thrust into her again and again, it was not Maud's face he saw, but Anya's. His release came quickly. He experienced a brief moment of soaring elation, of triumph, but then he remembered this snivelling girl was not Anya, and his sense of euphoria quickly passed.

Why could he not rid himself of his need for Anya? He desired her, and he hated her, and there were days when he felt driven mad with the torment of it. In truth, he had begun to suspect that only her death would set him free. But that would have to wait. Today, he had to fight Cerdic, another Saxon who tormented his every waking moment. Today, if God was just, Cerdic would die.

Vortigern's army was assembled in the forum, awaiting his command. Two hundred battle-hardened mounted warriors, and three hundred grim faced foot-soldiers. He took the reins of his stallion from the stable boy and mounted up, his back protesting as he settled himself in the saddle. Raising his right hand, he kicked his horse's flanks, and led his army across the forum, beneath the monumental arch and out into the streets of Aquae Sulis.

Despite the hordes of refugees within its walls, the city was ominously quiet. It was distressing to see his once proud and prosperous city sinking into a stinking cess pit of contaminated wells, blocked drains, and disease.

Despite his best endeavours, the plague had reached the basilica several weeks ago and quickly decimated his under-fed slaves. It had then moved on to the barracks and he had lost some of his best fighting men. He would have lost many more but for the fact he kept their bellies full, which in turn kept them strong.

Vortigern glanced over his shoulder. Without his warriors, he was nothing. It was for them he protected his well-stocked granaries, filled with the tribute from his grain-rich client kingdoms. If the refugees and the plague-sick citizens of Aquae Sulis went hungry and died, then it was unfortunate, but it was for the greater good.

His father had taught him true kingship was the ability to make difficult decisions. No one said it was easy. Few had the strength of character to see it through. Vortigern's gaze settled on his son, riding at his side. There was no denying the boy had shown skill and bravery in battle, but he wondered if Ronan would ever show the cold-hearted resilience necessary to hold the kingdom together.

NINETEEN

Anya's body began to mend. Day by day, she could feel her strength returning, but her mind took longer to heal, her grief for Elsbet still raw. At night, her dreams returned. She no longer saw the village in the shadow of the mountain. Instead she saw the sword. The intertwining patterns in the iron blade heaved like writhing serpents straining to be free from molten metal. And the red glass on the hilt shimmered as brightly as droplets of freshly spilled blood.

She pulled the sword from its hiding place. The decorations upon its scabbard reminded her of the undulating outline of a dark forest silhouetted against a pale horizon, or the soft curves of a bank of fair weather clouds. Irrevocably intertwined, with no beginning and no end, their sweeping arcs surged with all the unstoppable force of a wave about to break upon a shore.

She unsheathed the sword and swung it to and fro. The weapon sliced through the air, each cut a deadly whisper. Despite its weight, it was beautifully balanced, a work of pure craftsmanship. Ceinwin said her kin were descended from great kings of old. How many generations of high kings had wielded this blade? How much blood had it spilled? What stories would it tell, if it had a voice?

And now it had found its way into her hands. Why? For what possible purpose? She could not believe the goddess wanted her to ride into battle wielding such a weapon. She could barely lift it and besides, she did not know how to fight. She closed her eyes but the sacred grove felt far away, unreachable. Instead she saw an image of the baths of Sul.

She wondered why her mind had skipped to that forlorn, forgotten place. She blinked as the mists of vision crept across her eyes. She could see the steam rising from the hot, swirling water, and she could smell the sulphur and the reek of decay. But the baths were no longer empty; their damp, echoing chambers were crowded with sick people. Men, women and children were gathered by the waters, crying out in pain, in suffering, in sorrow.

She clamped her hands to her temples, willing away the searing pains, thinking about what she had seen. As a last desperate hope, plague victims were reaching out to the old god's healing powers, but Anya knew it was a vain hope. She had drunk the water and recognised its foul taste. The sulphur might heal an inflamed wound or an open sore, but it would not cure a plague sufferer, if anything it would only speed their end.

Her thoughts turned to home. In Saxony, her kin lived in terror of the plague. It came without warning, carried across the plains on the biting east winds, sweeping whole families away with its terrible destructive force. She had treated many plague sufferers in the place of healing. More often than not, there was little to be done for the afflicted, save make their final hours as comfortable as possible. But sometimes, just sometimes, if the disease was caught quickly enough, she had successfully saved a life.

She returned the sword to its hiding place, and pulled out

Taliesin's medicine box. Opening the lid, she chose a handful of neatly labelled linen bags: elderberries, yarrow, coltsfoot, heartsease. Carefully placing them inside the pocket of her new cloak, she stood up and walked to the door. To her surprise, it was unlocked. She looked up and down the dark, empty corridor. Six months since, she had been forced to resort to trickery to escape the basilica but now her chamber was unguarded, and she wondered why. Did Vortigern believe she was still too sick to try to escape?

She stared into the darkness, torn with indecision. One part of her brain was urging her to run and keep on running until she was far away from Vortigern's pestilence-ridden city of stone. But the other part was telling her to go to the baths of Sul. She was a healer. She could not leave the people of Aquae Sulis to die, not if there was just the smallest chance she could ease their suffering.

Anya hurried down the sweeping flight of stairs and into the basilica hall. The chamber was cold and empty and her footsteps echoed eerily. Torches cast long shadows across the marble floor. In their niches, the statues of long forgotten emperors stared back at her with blank, impervious eyes.

She glanced about, unnerved. To her right, the huge bronze doors led to the forum, but she knew Vortigern posted guards on the colonnade. Would they allow her to pass freely? Somehow, she doubted it. Turning on her heel, she went to the kitchens. As she pushed open the double doors, she was greeted with a rush of warm air infused with the yeasty tang of baking bread. A young boy slept by the hearth. A slave girl was standing at the long table kneading dough, her thin arms dusted in flour.

'My lady,' she began nervously but Anya paid her no heed. She had passed this way before, on her wedding night and her mind was churning with unwanted memories. Willing them away, she opened the door at the far end of the kitchen and stepped out into the courtyard. Dawn was trailing wisps of pink cloud across a pale lilac sky. Somewhere in the distance, a cock crowed. Dilapidated lean-to buildings clung to the walls of the basilica: stables, workshops, storerooms, a laundry. Six months ago, this courtyard had been bustling with life but today it was deserted. No slaves, no merchants and no guards. Had the plague taken them all?

The gate that led to the street was locked. Despairingly, Anya stepped back a pace then noticed a key hanging from a nail in the wall. Unhooking it, she turned it in the lock. The mechanism sounded deafeningly loud in the silence. She glanced over her shoulder anxiously but saw only a prowling cat, which ignored her disdainfully.

Anya opened the gate and walked out into the street. The stench of the city assaulted her senses, piss and shit and midden pits, swarming with flies. And there were other more alarming odours - stagnant water, blood and putrefaction, the unmistakeable scents of the plague.

Dizzy and out of breath, she put a hand against the wall to steady herself. What was she thinking?

She was still weak from the fever which had almost killed her. It was madness to go amongst the plague victims, to breathe in their corrupted breath. Why not take a horse from the stables and ride to Siluria, to her grandfather? Or to Caerwent, wherever that might be, in search of Rhys and the rest of her kin.

Or to Dumnonia. For wasn't that where she yearned to be? Where her thoughts returned in the long, dark hours before dawn? Even now, if she closed her eyes, she could see Silvanus's face, those hazelnut brown eyes, sometimes troubled, often tortured, always kind. She felt empty without him. But she was still Vortigern's wife and she had seen the fate of those who dared take what belonged to him.

She put a hand to her head, trying to clear the image of Silvanus from her mind but he lingered, as if he walked the quiet streets beside her, guiding her towards the monumental archway of the temple precinct. Even at this early hour, she could already feel the sun's heat beginning to warm the ancient stones. She passed Sul's temple, the four giant pillars of the portico soaring towards the cloudless sky. The sculpture of the god's fearsome face glared down at her from the pediment, wide eyed in his battle-fury.

A flight of steps led to the grand atrium of the bath complex. Anya passed a series of small chambers and came at last to the high-vaulted hall of the great bath. It was stiflingly hot; steam rose from the swirling water and the air smelled as foul as rotten eggs. Fine frescos were crumbling in the steamy air, green algae floated upon the water and the bath was overflowing, puddles lapping against a row of water-marked pillars.

Through an archway on the other side of the hall she could hear the sound of Sul's spring waters, cascading into their deep, stone tank. It was just as she remembered it, all those months ago, save for one marked difference. Today, the hall was full of men, women and children. Some were alone, sitting propped up against the walls, staring blankly into space, their faces sheened with sweat. Others lay on the wet floor, ugly black swellings at their throats, perhaps already dead. Still more lay upon makeshift pallets, surrounded by family members whose stricken faces revealed their despair.

Anya came to a halt. She felt suddenly overwhelmed. So many sick, so many dying. Hot sulphurous air and the stench of putrefaction hit the back of her throat. She bent double and gagged. As she straightened up, she realised many pairs of eyes had turned in her direction. They looked so distraught, so terrified and so helpless that she felt her own apprehension dissolve.

'I am a healer,' she said loudly, in Latin. 'I have come to help you.'

Crouching down, Anya put a hand on the young boy's forehead. No more than six years old, he lay on a bed of folded rugs, his eyes closed, his face contorted with pain. The swelling at his jaw line had blackened and burst. It was now oozing foul green pus onto his heaving chest. The boy's mother was kneeling at his side, his small hand clasped tightly in hers.

'There must be something else you can do!' she pleaded, her face grey with distress and exhaustion. 'Perhaps he should drink more of Sul's water?'

Anya laid her hand on the woman's arm. 'Sul's water won't help him. It will only make him vomit, and he's too weak for that. I'm not going to lie to you. My remedies have not stopped the spread of the disease, they have merely slowed it. All we can do now is pray.'

The woman let out a howl of despair. Lifting the little boy's frail body, she rocked him against her chest, tears streaming down her cheeks. Anya swallowed hard. Her infusions of elderberries, restharrow root and violets were easing the merciless bouts of coughing, and her coltsfoot and heartsease compresses were reducing the terrible bulbous swellings. But she knew in her heart that, for the majority of these desperate men, women and children, she was only delaying their fate for a few days at most.

She stood up wearily and wiped her hands on the cloth tucked into her belt. It was soaked with the oils of dried juniper and fennel fruits, both powerful antiseptics, but both were proving useless against this terrible disease. Why was the goddess allowing innocent children to be punished so cruelly?

Tucking the cloth back into her belt, she nodded to the next family in the long queue. The husband was healthy, but the girl-child in his arms was barely conscious. His wife already had the first signs of fever, her face flushed, her eyes unnaturally bright. Grief was just days away for this family. Forcing a smile, Anya turned to the husband.

'So, tell me, what's your daughter's name?'

Hours turned to days and Anya lost track of time. As was her way, she worked steadily and methodically, too preoccupied to remember to eat or drink, or to sleep for more than a few hours at a time.

'Anya? What on earth are you doing here?'

She started at the sound of her name and glanced over her shoulder. Rufus was standing in the doorway, a cloth over his nose and mouth.

'I want to talk to you!' his voice was muffled by the cloth. 'Come here!'

'I can't. I'm busy. You will have to come here.'

'No! This is close enough for me.'

Anya put down her pestle and mortar and stood up. Her world revolved dizzily, a sudden reminder of her hunger and exhaustion. The waters were over-flowing again and her gown trailed through warm puddles as she approached Rufus. She had not seen him since her marriage to Vortigern, on Christ's Mass Day. He was unchanged, his hair lank and greasy, his shoulders hunched as if he carried the weight of the world.

She remembered how he had chosen to jump from his horse and hide in the bracken as the Irish warband had slaughtered Vortigern's men on the road to Aquae Sulis. He was such an unassuming figure, so easy to dismiss as a coward, but behind his mousy demeanour, she had always sensed a shrewd, calculating brain. Not for the first time, she wondered if Vortigern was wrong to ignore and humiliate him.

'I thought you had gone to Venta with Vortigern,' she said wearily.

'No. He does the killing. I tax the unfortunate bastards who survive his sword.'

Anya was too exhausted to decide how to respond to that so she said nothing.

'You shouldn't be here. It's too dangerous.' Rufus glanced about. 'Where are your guards? Vortigern ordered your chamber to be guarded night and day.'

Anya shrugged. 'Perhaps they prefer to face a flogging than stand outside my door. Isn't it common knowledge all Saxons carry the plague?'

'Vortigern wouldn't approve of this,' Rufus said fretfully.

'Then it is fortunate he is in Venta, isn't it. Although, to be honest, I don't think he much cares whether I live or die.'

'Come away from here, Anya. Please. You can't help these people. You're wasting your time, and risking your own life needlessly.'

Anya was surprised by the strength of feeling in his voice.

'I am a healer. I have to stay.'

Rufus kept the cloth firmly clamped to his nose and mouth but his beady eyes were gazing intensely at her. 'Am I right in thinking you went to Siluria because you have kin there?'

Anya was instantly on her guard, for the village in the shadow of the mountains was her secret, and its isolation was

207

its only protection. 'No, you are mistaken. I am a Saxon…' her voice trailed away, her brain sluggish with fatigue.

'You do realise that, thanks to you, Tewdric is dead and Vortigern now holds dominion over Siluria,' Rufus said slyly. 'Perhaps you should have thought about the consequences of running away to find your kin?'

Anya frowned. So, she had not fooled him with her half-truths.

'And, as usual, Vortigern rides away and leaves me to pick up the pieces.' Rufus lowered the cloth, his thin face twisting into a snarl of frustration. 'Slaves, tribute and taxes, the gold and silver hewn from Tewdric's mines. I suppose Vortigern should thank you, because you've brought him riches beyond imagining.'

Anya had been too overwhelmed with mourning for Elsbet to think about the ramifications of Tewdric's death. And these last few days she had been too preoccupied caring for the plague victims to think about Vortigern. Her heart began to hammer fiercely. Much as she wanted to help the people of Aquae Sulis, she knew she had to escape the city before he returned.

'How much longer will Vortigern remain at Venta?' she asked. It felt painful to say his name out loud.

'I expect word from him any day now. I am quite sure he will have wasted no time in storming the city. Vortigern is not a man possessed of patience.'

Rufus was staring at her, mesmerised. Despite her hollow cheeks and the dark shadows beneath those astonishing, sea-green eyes, she was still startlingly beautiful. Why did Vortigern have so much and yet appreciate none of it. How could he even consider killing something so exquisite?

Rufus stifled a shudder. He yearned to protect this girl, to keep her safe, but she would never be safe, not whilst she belonged to Vortigern. In his heart, he knew he should urge her to leave Aquae Sulis. But another part of him knew he would say nothing, the selfish part that could not bear the thought of watching her walk away.

He stepped closer and Anya caught a hint of his perfume, a heady exotic scent. He raised a neatly manicured hand and for a moment she wondered if he was about to touch her cheek, but then a shadow passed over his thin features and his arm fell back to his side, a strangely defeated gesture.

'We share a bond, you and I.' Rufus's expression had soured, his tone bitter.

'A bond?' she repeated, mystified.

'Yes. Vortigern – he defines us, does he not? We are the flies in his web, at the mercy of his whims. And there is no escaping from him. He found you, didn't he, even in the wilds of Siluria – and he brought you back.'

TWENTY

Tintagel, kingdom of Dumnonia

Lucan prowled back and forth across the small watchtower room. He counted one thousand paces then he dropped to the floor. Keeping his legs and back straight, he raised his body fifty times using the strength in his arms alone. Springing up again, he wiped the sweat from his face, took a long drink of water then walked to the open window.

From his high vantage point he could see Tintagel in its entirety: the great hall and the small market in the courtyard; Taliesin's round-house, its herb garden overgrown now without the Saxon witch to tend it; the cliff path edged with sea pinks and beyond, the sea, shimmering under a hot summer sun.

Tintagel was full of noise, the shouts of the market traders mingling with the cries of the gulls and the crashing of the waves on the cliffs beneath the fortress. They were the sounds of his home, as familiar to him as breathing. But his home had become a prison of Silvanus's making.

He had never liked his older half-brother. Even as a child, Silvanus had been a smug bastard, secure in the knowledge he was Etar's chosen heir. Lucan threw the leather water bottle across the chamber. Un-stopped, it hit the opposite wall and water cascaded down the stonework.

The injustice of his situation was intolerable. Etar had never loved Silvanus's mother. He had not mourned her passing. But Etar had adored his second wife, Branwen. Lucan's mother had been young and beautiful, and Etar had showered her with gifts and gold, and loved her until her dying day.

'I am Branwen's only child. I should be king of Dumnonia,' Lucan shouted out of the window, but his words were carried away on the strong westerly wind. No-one looked up. No-one heard him. It was as if he had become invisible. As if he no longer existed.

He sat down on the edge of the bed and ran his hands through his unruly black curls. Neither as tall nor as handsome as his older half-brother, he was as short and stocky as a mountain pony. He was twenty years old, but his cheeks were still marred by unsightly pimples. A thin, wispy moustache hugged his upper lip.

Lucan's fury was a storm of rage now. Slowly but steadily, Silvanus had connived to turn their father against him. He had refused Lucan a place in his warband, claiming he wanted to keep his younger brother safe from harm. But what chance had there been for him to make his mark, or to make his father proud, if he was denied a sword and shield?

It was a travesty he was held accountable for Etar's death. The old wise woman on the moors had told him his son would be king. Mairi had dropped crushed laburnum seeds and essence of belladonna into Etar's drinking cup because no-one should deny the wishes of the gods. And besides, the old man was dying anyway.

Lucan's hands balled into fists. There were days when he wondered if he might be losing his mind, locked away in this small chamber, denied the right to see his new-born son, the boy who would be king. Fighting to control his mounting claustrophobia, he took a succession of deep breaths and tried to calm his pounding heart. He knew the council had voted unanimously in favour of putting him to death. But he also knew Silvanus was a coward, lacking the courage to sign his own brother's death warrant.

And so he felt confident his life was not in immediate danger, and he still had a few friends in Tintagel - men who remembered Branwen's hold over Etar, men who had themselves been enslaved by her seductive powers. They counselled him on the world beyond Dumnonia's borders. Vortigern was under threat from all sides, and never more in need of an alliance. If he could get word to Aquae Sulis, this time he felt certain the warlord of the Dobunni would ride to his aid.

Lucan stood up again, swinging his arms to loosen the tension in his shoulders. He had already decided how Silvanus would die. He envisaged tying him to a rack on the cliff edge. The sea birds would take his eyes first. It would be a very slow, very painful death. And he intended to savour every moment of it.

TWENTY ONE

Scardunum, territory of the Brigantes

The air was wet and clammy and Horsa tugged the edges of his cloak together. The forts and signalling stations along the east coast had been built by the Romans to keep watch against the Picts who often avoided the wall and arrived from the sea instead. But it had not taken Horsa long to realise these forts had always been a waste of time, for the weather was rarely clear enough to send a signal from one to the other along the coast, let alone send a signal inland to Derventio or Eboracum. Today, as was so often the case, a sea fret had settled, and visibility had been reduced to a matter of yards.

The arrival of summer had meant little in the north; the air remained unseasonably cold, the wind harsh. But it had brought merchants, carrying news of war and pestilence. It had also brought messengers from their lands at Corinium, bringing word of Anya's enforced return to Aquae Sulis - and of Elsbet's suicide.

Grief had not been kind to Horsa. It was a strangely clinging thing, and it had shrunk his soul and hollowed his heart. He had lost weight, his face was gaunt, his eyes blank. For many weeks, he was an empty shell, existing rather than living. He felt as if nothing could touch him, neither joy nor pain, and he no longer cared whether he lived or died.

But time passed and emotions gradually awakened within him again. First, he felt anger that Elsbet could have misunderstood him so completely. Anger that she could have underestimated his feelings for her, with such devastating consequences. He loved her unconditionally. There was nothing under the sun, no evil powerful enough, that could ever change how he felt about her.

After the anger, came hate. He had learnt many things since he had come to Britannia but, more than anything, he had learnt to hate. He hated Hengist because he had thrown away not only his sister but also his betrothed, the two women he loved most in the world. And he hated Vortigern because he had taken them both, carelessly, casually, without any thought of the cost.

And finally, his thoughts had turned to revenge. He wanted Vortigern to pay for the suffering he had caused, before the sun set on another achingly empty day.

Hengist was gesturing from the courtyard for Horsa to join him. A messenger was waiting to speak. Horsa was inclined to ignore his brother because he truly didn't care what the messenger had to say.

'Get down here, brother!' Hengist shouted.

Horsa turned away from the sea and walked slowly down the narrow steps that hugged the wall.

'Cerdic of Frisia has fought against Vortigern at Venta, lord,' the messenger began breathlessly. 'Vortigern regained control of the city but both armies suffered heavy losses. Vortigern has returned to Aquae Sulis. Cerdic has retreated to his stronghold on the coast and is rebuilding his army.'

Horsa stared at the messenger, his thoughts reeling. He

yearned for Vortigern's death. He needed it as much as he needed air. So why was the bastard still alive? How could the gods be so capricious, so cruel?

He turned to his brother. 'We must move against Vortigern now,' he said urgently. 'Even here in the north, the harvest is in. We can feed an army on the march. Britannia's granaries will be full.'

Hengist shot him a quick glance, his pale blue eyes glacial, but remained silent.

'If we delay any longer it will be Cerdic who rules Britannia, not you!' Horsa went on. He could feel the muscles tightening across his chest, the tension building in every nerve, every sinew. He knew vengeance would not bring Elsbet back, but it was all he had to offer her now, one last precious gift.

Hengist was staring into the middle distance, his brow furrowed, deep in thought. The silence stretched on. Horsa could not understand why his brother was hesitating. Torment welled within him, as hot and deadly as a vat of boiling pitch.

'What has become of you brother? I never took you for a coward!' he hissed. 'Thanks to Cerdic, Vortigern is weak. If we march on Londinium now, we give him no time to regroup. Just think on it! Your banner will fly over the greatest city in Britannia. You will control its quays, its trade. You will have wealth. You will have your gift throne and your -' Horsa froze, for Hengist's knife was at his throat.

'How dare you call me a coward, you ugly runt! May the gods take you in the battles to come, for I swear I have no use for a worthless half-breed.' Hengist's cold eyes glinted with a lifetime of accumulated hate.

The two brothers glared malevolently at one another for a long moment before Hengist finally lowered the knife, and turned to Aelfric.

'Send word to our kin at Corinium and to the garrison at Andereida. Tell them to meet us on the old road north of Londinium. Tell them to prepare for battle.' Hengist's gaze slid back to his brother. 'I'll give you the vengeance you seek. Perhaps then you'll stop mourning for that stupid, simpering girl and find a proper woman who will give you strong sons.'

Horsa's mouth fell open, dumbfounded. Hengist had never hidden his dislike for Elsbet, but how dare he speak ill of the dead? Rage coursed through him, burning like poison. At that moment, he wanted nothing more than to drive his sword through his own brother's heart.

He knew that for such a heinous crime he would never enter the halls of Valhalla, never feast with his ancestors. Instead he would wander in the cold mists of Nifheim for all eternity. But he would bear such punishment gladly, for Hengist deserved to die; he was as much to blame for Elsbet's death as Vortigern. He began to withdraw his sword from its scabbard; one inch, two…

And it was then that he heard the voice inside his head, as clearly as if the words were spoken aloud:

'Fratricide defies not only the laws of Saxony, but also the will of the gods. If you kill Hengist, you will bring down chaos and destruction upon your people. Is that truly what you seek?'

'What's the matter with you?' Hengist growled. 'You look as if you've seen a ghost.'

Horsa's gaze focussed on his brother. He would never forget what Hengist had done, and nor would he ever forgive but, nevertheless, he loosened his grip on his sword.

And so Horsa marched south with Hengist's army along the old Roman road that ran as straight as a corn stalk from Eboracum to Londinium. His army was seven hundred strong, bolstered by both Pictish and Irish warbands, bribed with promises of the spoils of war. Hengist took his time on the march, ransacking towns and villages along the road. He took treasures from the Christian churches, livestock from the fields, freshly-harvested grain from the granaries, and men, women and children to sell in the slave markets of Gaul and Germania. He left behind him a smouldering path of burning, as if a dragon had scorched the earth. But he halted some thirty miles north of Londinium in the territory of the Catuvellauni, for he had a proposition for their young king, Cunedda.

Horsa had heard stories of the fate of the Catuvellauni. Their city of stone had prospered even after the Roman withdrawal, until the Catuvellauni had refused to accept Vortigern as their overlord. In retaliation, Vortigern had reduced their city to a charred ghost town, and razed the surrounding villa estates to ashes, leaving smoke rising to the heavens like a hundred funeral pyres. And then, some five years since, Vortigern had met the army of the Catuvellauni in battle, and sent Vegetius, their king, to meet his gods.

But the Catuvellauni were a proud people, not easily broken. Vortigern may have destroyed their city of stone, but their ancient hill-top stronghold had survived. And so Cunedda, son of Vegetius, rebuilt its palisades, re-cut its deep ditches, and built his long-house on the highest point of the hill top. He used wood and thatch, and wattle and daub, and his home so strongly resembled a Saxon hall that Horsa smiled to himself as they rode up the winding track to the summit. Dismounting, they handed their weapons to the guards at the door of the long-house. Without his sword at his belt, Horsa felt acutely vulnerable as he walked towards the raised dais at the end of the hall.

Cunedda remained seated as the Saxon warriors drew near. To his surprise, Horsa realised he was no more than sixteen summers old, not yet a man. His body was slight, his beardless cheeks covered in the unsightly blemishes of youth. Watchful, brown eyes peered out from behind a curtain of lifeless, brown hair.

'You come bearing white linen upon your spears, but your army is not a mile from my hall. I know the destruction you wreak. Why should I trust your truce? Why should I welcome you?' Cunedda spoke in Latin. Despite his youth, his voice was strong, his manner confident.

'We come to offer you an alliance against Vortigern, king of the Dobunni,' Hengist replied calmly.

Cunedda laughed humourlessly, brushing strands of hair from his face. 'I am a Christian, like my father before me. In his day, Verulamium was a civilised city, a place of culture, ideas, philosophy. Those days are long gone. Verulamium is in ruins, thanks to Vortigern of the Dobunni. But you - your people are worse, much worse. You loot Christian churches, you murder our priests, you desecrate our holy altars.'

Hengist held his hands out, palms up, as if weighing two invisible objects. 'Vortigern of the Dobunni on the one hand. Hengist, son of Athelwald, high king of Saxony on the other. You might say, six of one, half a dozen of the other. You have a difficult choice to make, Cunedda, son of Vegetius.'

Horsa shot a glance at his brother, staggered by his lack of respect.

Cunedda's expression hardened. 'Until recently you were in Vortigern's pay. Does treachery come easily to all Saxons, or just you in particular?'

'You insult me, Briton,' Hengist replied, and there was an edge to his voice now.

'If asking a valid question can be perceived as an insult, then yes, I am guilty of it,' Cunedda replied evenly.

'It seems you are also guilty of a marked lack of hospitality. I am a guest in your hall and yet you treat me with contempt.' Hengist's demeanour remained controlled, but Horsa knew his brother well. The clenched muscles flickering at his jaw spoke of his mounting anger.

'I did not ask you to come here, Saxon. I did not choose to invite pagan barbarians into my hall.'

Horsa looked from one man to the other. The situation was deteriorating. He needed to do something, and fast.

He stepped forward. 'Vortigern took my betrothed as hostage. He abused and defiled her until she believed she had no choice but to take her own life.'

Giving words to Elsbet's suffering felt like a knife through Horsa's heart. He swallowed hard. 'And so I must seek vengeance, or be found wanting before my gods. If that makes me a pagan barbarian, then so be it.'

Cunedda stared at Horsa for a long time and when he finally spoke, his tone had softened slightly.

'Vortigern severed my father's head from his body and carried it from the battlefield on the tip of his spear. I was just a child of ten years old, too young to defend him, or to avenge him. So, perhaps we do have some common ground after all.'

'Yes,' Hengist agreed. 'Common ground. That's a good place to begin, is it not?'

Cunedda brushed his hair from his face again. Horsa could see the doubt and uncertainty in the young man's eyes, his unwillingness to forge an alliance with a pagan army that had already proved itself treacherous.

'We will eat and we will talk,' Cunedda said at last. Standing up, he gestured to the long oak table. 'Come, join me.'

Horsa had little appetite and ate sparingly. Unarmed and surrounded by Cunedda's warriors, who watched them with ill-disguised suspicion, he felt defenceless and ill at ease. He was also aware that Cunedda had not agreed to march beneath the banner of the white wolf. He had agreed to talk, nothing more.

Hengist however, was eating hungrily, shoving large slabs of beef into his mouth and washing them down with glasses of Cunedda's wine, which Horsa thought tasted like vinegar.

'I apologise for the inferior wine,' Cunedda said smoothly, as if guessing Horsa's thoughts. 'But we have not had the best of years, and I am not just referring to the grape harvest.'

Hengist ignored him, intent on his meal, but Horsa caught the young boy's eye, and a slight smile passed between them. When they had eaten their fill, Cunedda gestured for their plates to be removed and their glasses refilled.

'So, tell me about this alliance you propose.' His tone was light, amenable.

Hengist took another long draught of wine, stifling a shudder at its bitter taste. 'Vortigern has fought against Cerdic the Frisian. Both armies suffered heavy losses.'

Cunedda nodded. 'So I have heard.'

'We intend to take Londinium while Vortigern is still weak, before he has time to rebuild his army,' Hengist continued. 'I ask that you march with us.'

Horsa noted Hengist did not give details about the precise location he had chosen to make his stand, nor did he mention the reinforcements he had requested from Corinium and Andereida. If Cunedda ultimately refused to join forces with them, the less he knew of their plans, the better.

'Vortigern was a fool to trust you. If I decide to ally with you, then am I not also a fool?'

'I can see plainly that you are no fool, Cunedda,' Hengist replied flatly. 'We both want the same thing. We both want Vortigern dead.'

'And if I decide to march with you, what would my people gain?'

'Aside from the pleasure of seeing Vortigern's head upon a spear?' Hengist asked dryly.

'Yes, aside from that.'

'We will divide Vortigern's kingdom between us and enjoy the spoils,' Hengist replied.

Horsa shot a glance at his brother. Hengist was lying again. As soon as Cunedda was of no further use, the only thing the boy would enjoy would be a Saxon blade through his gullet.

'I should warn you, Vortigern has a son,' Cunedda said. 'If we succeed in killing Vortigern, Ronan will seek vengeance.'

Hengist shrugged. 'We've met him. He's a sulking youth. We'll find another spear tip for his head.'

'If I agreed to march with you, I would need your assurances that the people of Londinium would remain unharmed, and that the Christians would be protected and allowed to practice their religion without fear of persecution.'

'I give you my word,' Hengist replied solemnly, but Horsa knew full well his brother was lying yet again. Hengist had no intention of protecting Christians. Their gentle natures made them excellent slave market fodder.

Horsa glanced at Cunedda. The young man's expression betrayed his inner turmoil. He was being forced to make an impossible decision and Horsa felt a pang of sympathy for the youth.

'The bible tells us to turn the other cheek,' Cunedda said at last. 'But in times such as these, it's hard to believe the meek will inherit the earth. If I refuse to accept your offer of an alliance, you will march over my lands regardless. You will meet Vortigern in battle - the man who murdered my father - and you will claim his kingdom for your own. In all conscience, what kind of king would I be if I do not march with you?'

Horsa saw a flicker of confusion cross his brother's face and suspected he was struggling to grasp Cunedda's rapidly spoken Latin.

'Is that a yes?' Hengist asked.

Cunedda nodded. 'For my father's sake, I will march with you.'

'I want Londinium,' Hengist said hastily.

'You're welcome to it,' Cunedda replied. 'The city's dying. There's no trade. The quays on the river Thamesis are deserted. Starvation is killing half the people, the plague is taking the rest. Believe me, Londinium is yours, as long as you protect the Christians.'

'Of course, of course,' Hengist replied, although it was painfully obvious to Horsa that his brother was no longer listening to the young king of the Catuvellauni.

TWENTY TWO

Aquae Sulis, kingdom of the Dobunni

Dismounting before the steps to the basilica, Vortigern handed his reins to the waiting stable boy. His body was stiff and sore after the long ride. A foul, putrid stench was drifting from the plague pits beyond the city walls and Vortigern felt his weary stomach heave. He glanced heavenwards then quickly lowered his gaze again. The canopy of stars over the earth always unsettled him, made him feel small, insignificant.

His mother had believed in the Christian God of love who watched over men from the heavens. He paid lip service to her God, but he had never truly shared his mother's faith. His soldiers had dug a deep burial pit at Venta and filled it with the corpses of fathers, brothers and sons who would never return home. Would a God of love condone such waste, such suffering?

Ronan bounded up the steps two at a time, but Vortigern took them slowly. For the first time in his life, he felt old. Cerdic on the other hand, had proven youthful, courageous – and reckless. The Frisian had given up the protection of Venta's high walls and marched out of the city to meet the army of the Dobunni face to face. Cerdic had been easy to

223

spot on the battlefield, head and shoulders above the rest, his long yellow hair bound in two thick braids. He had worn no armour, choosing to fight naked from the waist up, his muscular torso glistening with sweat, and the blood of Vortigern's men.

Cerdic's warriors had fought ferociously but with no discernible battle strategy, as if each man was engaged in his own personal blood vendetta. Vortigern, schooled in Roman tactics, had assumed his own disciplined troops would easily quash the enemy's chaotic charges but when need arose, the Frisians had proved capable of collaboration. No matter how hard he had fought to get near Cerdic, each time he had been driven back by a hastily formed, impenetrable Frisian shield wall.

And now, rumours were beginning to circulate amongst Vortigern's men that pagan devilry had enchanted Cerdic to safety. Such stories were dangerous, and bad for morale. Vortigern walked across the basilica hall, exhaustion fanning the flames of his anger and frustration.

A slave was waiting in the council chamber, a bowl of warm water in his hands and linen cloths draped over his arms. Ronan quickly stripped to the waist, dropping his blood stained cuirass and tunic on the floor. Grabbing a cloth, he began to wash. Sprays of water drenched the slave and ran down Ronan's muscular chest and taut stomach.

Vortigern, envious of his son's honed figure and acutely aware of his own sagging belly, kept his filthy shirt on. He washed his hands, pushing aside the rose petals floating upon the water. They looked incongruous and out of place, when his mind was still raw from the carnage of battle.

'Lord, I have news.' The messenger was grey with fatigue, his cloak covered in the dirt of the road.

Vortigern turned. 'Yes?'

'Hengist has left Eboracum. He is marching towards Londinium. He leads a great army.'

Vortigern froze, his mind grappling to make sense of the messenger's words. There must have been a mistake, a miscommunication. This could not be happening. From the corner of his eye, he saw his son shake his head and raise his eyes heavenward, a gesture he took to mean, 'I told you so'.

The mosaic floor no longer felt solid beneath Vortigern's feet. He had been advised on countless occasions not to trust the Saxons, but he had not heeded the warnings. He had not believed an illiterate band of pagan barbarians capable of such treachery, or such audacity.

This was not his fault. He was the most powerful king in all Britannia. He did not make mistakes.

But something had gone wrong. Someone must be held responsible, someone must be to blame.

It had all begun with Anya.

She had cursed him. How else could he have lost his virility in the marriage bed?

Fury exploded in his chest.

'Where's Anya? Where's that conniving bitch? She ran away for the sole purpose of distracting me. And while my back was turned, her barbarian brothers rise up against me! She is a traitor and I want her dead!'

Ronan threw his wash cloth at the slave, who caught it in both hands, the sodden cloth dripping dirty, bloodied water down his tunic.

'Forget Anya, father! We have more pressing matters to consider. Half your army lie in burial pits before the walls of Venta, the rest are desperate to go home and harvest their fields. Even if we reach Londinium before Hengist, which would be a miracle in itself, how are we to defeat him?'

Vortigern was breathing so heavily, he sounded like an enraged bull. As hard as he tried to focus his mind on matters of war, his thoughts spun back to Anya. Her kin carried plague and chaos in their wake. He wanted rid of her. He wanted rid of them all.

'Father?' Ronan queried.

'Whatever happens, Londinium must not fall into Hengist's hands. We leave at dawn, and raise troops as we march. We'll stop at every village, every farm, and we'll take every man and boy able to lift a spear.'

Still naked from the waist up, Ronan sat down at the table and reached for the wine jug.

'Farm boys will be more hindrance than help,' he said languidly.

'Don't question me, boy!' Vortigern snapped.

But he knew Ronan was right. A rabble of terrified farmhands would not stand firm in the shield wall, but what choice did he have? As usual, he took out his frustration on his son.

'What do you think you're doing? Now is not the time to drink yourself senseless. Go and find Julianus at the barracks. Tell him the men cannot go home. They'll have to wait a few more weeks to tend their fields. And find out how many horsemen Julianus can muster. From what I saw at Venta, the Germanic tribes fight like a drunken tavern rabble. A few strong cavalry charges and we'll trample Hengist's foot-soldiers into the mud.'

'Yes, father,' Ronan replied. There was no discernible trace of animosity in his voice, but he made a point of taking the wine jug with him. With his free hand, he picked up his cuirass and tunic and headed for the door.

'I'm going to burn Anya for this betrayal,' Vortigern shouted after him. 'But first, she's coming with us to Londinium. I want her to watch her brothers die.'

Anya was sitting on the floor of her bed chamber with Maud at her side. Taliesin's medicine box lay open between them.

'We have run out of coltsfoot leaves, and we have barely enough heartsease to brew another infusion,' Anya said grimly.

Maud held up a linen bag. 'Isn't this coltsfoot's root? Perhaps we could use this instead?'

'For a poultice, yes, but not for an infusion. Too strong a dose and it's poisonous -' Anya broke off. Someone was approaching; she could hear the sound of footsteps in the corridor. A moment later, the door opened and Ronan stepped inside.

Maud tensed like a frightened hare. Anya's heart began to pound with alarm. She had been so preoccupied with caring for the sick, she had given little thought to Vortigern's return.

'What are you doing here?' she asked, shocked. 'Is Vortigern... is he...?

'Your husband lives,' Ronan replied curtly.

Anya stood up, smoothing down her gown, a nervous gesture. 'We did not expect you so soon. What happened?'

Ronan's laugh was devoid of humour. 'I will tell you what happened. Bloodshed, slaughter, men crying for their mothers. Such is the way with battles.'

He sounded bitter and Anya felt an unexpected stab of pity for Vortigern's son. 'I'm sorry,' she said softly.

'Are you?' he replied sceptically, his eyes narrowing. 'I hear you have been a regular visitor to the baths. Why is that?'

'Your city is riven with disease. I am a healer,' Anya replied,

227

struggling to control her mounting panic. She had promised herself to be far away from the city by the time Vortigern returned. And now it was too late.

'You risked your life for the people of Aquae Sulis?' Ronan sounded incredulous. 'They are not your kin.'

'I have no kin. I am an exile.'

Ronan looked astounded. In a rush of confusion, Anya remembered he did not know why she had come to Britannia.

'An exile,' Ronan repeated curiously. 'Why? What did you do?'

Cursing her indiscretion, Anya shook her head wordlessly.

'Well, it doesn't matter now,' Ronan replied carelessly. 'You won't be able to escape from my father's clutches again. He intends to burn you as a witch.'

'What?' For one terrible moment, Anya heard the crackle as the green kindling took light, and smelled the wood smoke as the logs began to burn. She could see her own legs blacken as the flames licked her flesh and she could feel the indescribable agony.

'You two look alike - pale skin, red hair.' Ronan had turned his attention to Maud, his eyes wandering over the slave girl's slender body. 'Can't say why, but you look prettier than I remember.' Hauling Maud to her feet, he began to drag her from the room. 'I haven't much time. This will have to be quick.'

Appalled, Anya pulled the sword from its hiding place beneath the bed. Wrenching it from its scabbard, she scrambled to her feet.

'Let go of her!'

Ronan turned around, grinning broadly. 'Don't hurt yourself with that!'

Anya took a step towards him, brandishing the sword. It felt impossibly heavy and she struggled to keep it aloft. 'I mean it, Ronan. Let her go.'

Ronan moved fast. Shoving Maud roughly aside, he grabbed Anya's wrist, tightening his grip like a vice. She cried out with pain, and the sword slipped from her nerveless fingers. Catching it with his free hand before it fell to the floor, Ronan swept it out of her reach.

In a heartbeat, Maud was on her feet again. She darted between Anya and Ronan, squaring up to him defiantly, a shield in human form. Anya was incredulous. Her father had taught her of the virtue of high kings, and the worthlessness of slaves. But her father was a king who had murdered his own daughter, and Tewdric was a king who sold his own people into servitude, whilst Maud, a mere slave, was selfless and brave.

'There's no need for that, Maud,' Anya said firmly. 'Come, stand beside me.'

And then she turned her gaze on Ronan. 'I am a priestess of the sacred grove. If Vortigern tries to burn me, he will invoke the wrath of the goddess.'

'My father doesn't believe in your pagan gods. And anyway, he's too busy to burn a witch today.' Ronan adjusted his grip on her sword, then began to sidestep and parry, slicing the air, as if fighting an invisible foe. Anya felt her chest begin to tighten.

She wanted the sword back. She needed it back.

'You are to come with me,' Ronan said, his eyes fixed on the pattern welded blade. 'My father wants you to watch your brothers die.'

'What did you say?' Anya breathed.

'Your brothers have left Eboracum and are marching on Londinium. Our spies tell us they mean to take the city.'

Ronan's eyes had not left the sword, as if he were a moth and the blade a flame.

Anya's skin turned to ice. She could have wept for Horsa, swept up in a maelstrom not of his making. Horsa, who had wanted only to live peacefully with Elsbet, but instead was marching to war. Her thoughts hurtled on. How big was Hengist's army? Did he stand any chance of defeating Vortigern, or was he leading the army of the white wolf to certain death?

'I'd forgotten you had this. It's beautifully balanced,' Ronan said appreciatively. 'A good sword. I think I'll keep it.'

Anya had lost the sword once before, and she did not intend to lose it ever again, and so she enunciated her next words as if they were a curse.

'It belongs to me. You cannot keep it.'

Her fury was a physical thing, merging with the blood in her veins and the marrow in her bones. Her skin was no longer cold but red-hot, as if she was standing too close to a fire.

Suddenly, Ronan swayed as if struggling to remain upright in a vicious storm, and a look of confusion crossed his face.

'You!' he said gruffly, holding out the sword to Maud. 'Take it.'

Maud took it from him, holding it awkwardly, like a man might hold a baby. And then Ronan visibly relaxed, as if a heavy burden had been taken from him. Anya noticed he was rubbing his sword hand gingerly, as if he had injured it in some way.

When he finally turned to face her, his manner was unusually subdued.

'The sword stays here, but you - you're coming with us.'

'Vortigern is taking me into battle?'

Ronan nodded. 'We leave within the hour.'

Anya stared at him, aghast. She had heard the bards tell stories of the shield wall, of the Valkyries riding through the tumult of battle, choosing Odin's followers from the slain. At the fireside, it had sounded heroic, glorious. But since coming to Britannia, she had seen enough bloodshed to understand it would be neither heroic nor glorious. A small part of her couldn't bear the thought of watching her brothers fighting for their lives. But the larger part felt ashamed of her cowardice.

'I'll go with you, my lady,' Maud said.

Anya was struggling to control strong emotions which threatened to overwhelm her. 'No, you must stay here. You must go to the baths every day, use what's left of the medicines and do what you can to help.'

She turned to Ronan again. 'I'll go to Londinium with you. But it will not be to watch my brothers die. The goddess will protect them.'

Ronan shook his head scornfully. 'Your heathen gods are finished, crushed beneath the might of God, the one true god. He has swept aside your pagan groves and your blood-stained altars. When we ride into battle against your brothers, God will be riding beside us, for God fights on the side of the righteous.'

Anya eyed him thoughtfully. 'That's a fine speech, Ronan, but you don't actually believe a word of it, do you?'

An hour later, Anya descended the steps of the basilica at Ronan's side. Despite the warm sunshine and the soft southerly breeze, she felt bitterly cold. The forum was packed with Vortigern's horsemen and foot-soldiers. They looked exhausted, and Anya could see the resentment in their eyes. These men had fought a bloody battle before the walls of

Venta. They had dug burial pits for lost friends and comrades. They had marched back to Aquae Sulis, but there had been no time to wash the blood from their hands, before they had been ordered to march into battle again.

Her presence at Ronan's side had not gone unnoticed and she felt the men's animosity as if it were a chill wind. One soldier muttered 'Saxon traitor' as she passed. Another spat at her feet. Ronan turned on his heel and in a heartbeat, his hands were at the man's throat.

'Show some respect to the wife of your king,' he snarled, squeezing until the man's face turned purple and his eyes began to bulge. When Ronan finally released him, the man clutched his bruised windpipe and gasped for air. Ronan walked on and Anya instinctively edged a little closer to him, matching his step.

She spotted Vortigern easily. Surrounded by his household guards, he stood head and shoulders above them all. Memories of their wedding night, that terrible night of pain and humiliation, crept unbidden into her mind. It was not easy to will the images away.

Perhaps sensing her gaze, Vortigern turned to Anya, and found he was unable to look away, his mind in spate like a river after rain. He noticed the signs of her grave illness still clung to her. She appeared physically fragile, but her eyes held the same feisty defiance that had entranced him all those months ago. Despite everything she had endured, she was not a broken, cowering creature, but a girl whose spirit was undimmed. And he hated her for it, this Saxon witch whose kin were treacherous, pagan, oath breakers.

And yet, from the first moment he had seen her in Calleva all those months ago, he had yearned to take her to his bed, to tame her, to control her, as he yearned to control everyone,

232

and everything. Lust flared, unexpectedly and confusingly. He quelled it, because Anya was worthless now. Tewdric had raped her night after night, taken pleasure in her, and gloated of it.

Leaving his men, he walked towards her and whispered in her ear, 'did you cry out like a whore when Tewdric fucked you? I've heard the Welsh like to arse-fuck. Did you like that too, you dirty, traitorous, Saxon slut?'

He drew back a little, and took pleasure in watching Anya's discomfort.

'Tewdric did not touch me. I am a virgin still,' she said, her cheeks flushing.

'You lie as easily as your brothers,' he replied coldly and then his gaze settled on the vivid scar at her throat and his eyes narrowed. No-one had expected her to survive that wound. It would have been so much simpler if she had died in Siluria.

Anya's heart was thudding fiercely against her ribs. It was almost impossible to comprehend this brutish man was her husband, this man she hated and feared in equal measure. This man who held her own life, and that of her brothers, in the palm of his hand.

What could she possibly do or say to prevent more bloodshed and suffering?

She took a deep breath for courage. 'Your army remains undefeated. Hengist must know he cannot win this battle. He may be willing to negotiate -'

But Vortigern shouted over her. 'There is nothing to negotiate! Your brothers have repeatedly betrayed me, and this time they're going to die for their treachery. By God, I won't rest until every last Saxon in Britannia is dead. And that includes you!'

'But the price will be too high!' Anya persisted. 'The men of Germania are renowned for fighting in the grip of frenzy. If you meet Hengist in battle, the field will be strewn with the corpses of your finest warriors. My brother seeks renown, but more than that, he seeks wealth. If you give him enough silver, he will leave Britannia. Isn't that a worthy trade for the lives of your men?'

'Trade?' Vortigern roared. 'I would sooner cut off my right arm than trade with Hengist! Be silent, woman! I wager you'll be less talkative when you've watched your brothers gutted like lambs on a butcher's block.'

Anya felt as if she was standing on a precipice, the cliffs crumbling away beneath her feet. She had failed. There was nothing she could do against such a man as Vortigern. She could not change his mind. But she could speak her own mind. The words tumbled from her lips before she could stop them.

'Elsbet was not yours to take. You are responsible for her death, and the goddess will not rest until you answer for it.'

'I told you to shut your mouth!' Vortigern raised his right hand and struck her viciously across the cheek. The force of the blow sent her reeling. She had bitten her tongue; she could taste the metallic tang of blood. Vortigern turned away to re-join his men. Several heartbeats passed before Anya became aware she had stumbled backwards into Ronan's path, and that his hands were upon her shoulders, steadying her.

'My father is like pumice stone,' he said quietly. 'No matter how hard you fight against him, in the end, he just grinds you down.'

Vortigern's army marched out of the city and headed east along the old Roman road, the banner of the black boar fluttering above the massed ranks of cavalry, foot-soldiers and supply wagons. They gave Anya a piebald mare, a meek and docile beast. She rode near the back of the column, surrounded by four surly bodyguards. Her emotions were veering wildly. On the one hand, she did not want to watch her brothers die. On the other, if Hengist was the victor in the battle for Londinium, she knew he would turn next to Aquae Sulis, and she had no doubt his soldiers would burn and rape and slaughter.

In the countryside, the Dobunni were at harvest. With most of the men conscripted, the womenfolk were scything oats, rye, wheat and barley, whilst their children followed on behind, gathering and binding the sheaves. Above their heads, noisy clouds of seagulls swirled greedily.

Vortigern collected new recruits like sticky burrs to a sheep's tail, often dragging them forcibly from the fields. Boys barely out of childhood, armed only with pitchforks for harvest, and spears for hunting boar in the forest. Mothers wept for their sons, but no-one challenged Vortigern's authority. The people of the Dobunni seemed too wearied by war and by disease to risk open dissent. Anya pitied them. This year's crop promised to be bountiful, but how much of it would find its way into their granaries once Vortigern had commandeered his share?

The further they rode from Aquae Sulis, the emptier the countryside became. They passed many deserted villages and fallow fields. Some of the settlements were burnt to the ground. Others seemed simply to have been abandoned and Anya wondered if either pestilence or her own Saxon kin had played their part.

They spent a night in Calleva. Anya rode through the decaying city, unsettling memories crowding her thoughts.

Here, she had met Vortigern for the first time. Here, Hengist had bartered her away to bolster a treaty few thought was wise. And here, she had said goodbye to Horsa and watched him ride north, to the land of the painted Picts.

Vortigern's garrison commander had taken up residence in Marcus's once fine townhouse. The garden had been requisitioned by the blacksmith and the marble atrium was now a weapons store. When Anya had first come to Calleva, this house had been sweet with the fragrance of freshly cut roses and lilac, but now the air was thick with the stench of metal working and unwashed men.

The evening meal was taken in the dining room. It was a hurried affair, the pork was dry and the lentils and beans were overcooked. Anya had no appetite and picked at her food. She remembered how light and airy the room had appeared under Marcus's wife's genteel touch. Tonight, it was lit only by a handful of guttering torches. She knew Vortigern had killed Marcus, but she wondered what had become of Marcus's refined wife. Was she now for rent in some back street brothel?

Vortigern and his men were discussing the news from his scouts. Hengist was pillaging and burning a trail of destruction as he marched towards Londinium. And then they talked of war, of battle strategy. A shiver ran down Anya's spine. These men were discussing how best to kill her kin and suddenly, she could remain silent no longer. 'Let me ride out and meet with Hengist. Let me at least attempt to broker for peace.'

Vortigern rounded on her, his face like thunder. 'How dare you speak in council? Leave us. Now!'

Anya remained seated. 'This room - don't you remember? This is where you sealed the treaty with my brother. If I could just speak with him -'

236

'You will be silent! Get out of my sight, before I have you flogged!' He gestured to one of his guards who took her arm, manhandling her out of the dining chamber and into the atrium. A huge harvest moon was rising above the rooftops of the city, flooding half the courtyard with brittle light, and casting the rest in cold shadow. The soldier kept a firm grip on her arm as he led her along the colonnaded corridor and into the west wing of the house.

To Anya's surprise, roughly hewn partitions now divided the once spacious reception chambers, creating separate bed chambers for the garrison commander's officers. The partitions cut across intricate mosaics; proud Poseidon dismembered, his head and trident in one room, his naked torso in the next. The guard came to a halt outside one of the small makeshift rooms, and pushed her inside.

'I will be outside all night, so don't bother trying to escape,' he said gruffly and closed the door behind her.

Anya looked about. The chamber was dark and cold, the only furniture a narrow bed and a small table bearing a solitary oil lamp, which was not lit. She sat down on the edge of the bed and unfolded the blanket. It smelled of horses and sweat and she wondered about the man who had slept here and why he no longer needed his bed.

The thin, straw filled mattress was stained and lumpy and smelled rancid, but the alternative was sharing the floor with the rats. Despite her exhaustion, she could not sleep. She had seen the look in Vortigern's eyes. He hated her but at the same time, he wanted her. Would he come to her bed tonight?

She stared into the darkness, her entire body on edge, her ears straining at every sound, every creaking door, every footstep. The night wore on but Vortigern did not come. She tossed and turned, her exhausted mind roiling with

237

helplessness and despair. Tomorrow she would see Horsa again. Upon a battlefield.

They left Calleva at sunrise, the peaceful rolling fields of the Atrebates swathed in the soft mists of a late summer dawn. Above the pulsing footfall of marching men and the rumbling wheels of the supply wagons, Anya could hear the familiar sounds of the countryside: skylarks trilling high above her head; crows cawing irritably at one another as they scavenged the newly harvested fields and, closer to hand, the warning cries of blackbirds in the hedgerows.

Vortigern's army caught up with Hengist less than ten miles from Londinium, bringing the Saxons' progress to a decisive halt. And Anya could no longer hear the sound of skylarks or blackbirds. There was only the tumult of men preparing for war, as the army of the white wolf and the army of the black boar took up their battle formations, and eyed each other across a field of yellow stubble.

Vortigern placed Anya on the brow of the hill, surrounded by her bodyguards. 'This is an excellent vantage point for you to watch your brothers die,' he told her, then he reined around and rode back down the hill.

Anya looked about in shocked disbelief. It was almost impossible to comprehend that the men in the field below were assembling for the sole purpose of killing each other. Some, like Hengist, were here for personal gain and glory, but many others were here because they had no choice, young men torn unwillingly from their families and their homes.

Vortigern's scouts had not exaggerated. Hengist had succeeded in amassing a vast army. The Picts were on the front line, Anya presumed in the hope of instilling terror into the men of the Dobunni. Their half-naked bodies were adorned with vivid blue tattoos, their long hair coated with clay and formed into wild peaks. On the left flank, the Catuvellauni were clad in ancient Roman mail. She had heard stories of how Vortigern had severed their old king's head in battle, and here was the old king's son, still a boy, but come for revenge, come to perpetuate the endless cycle of the blood vendetta.

And then there were her own kin, so proud, so aloof, like gods amongst men. Unlike the Britons, the Saxons fought suitably attired for a place at the tables of Valhalla should the battle go ill, in sand-scoured mail, and bedecked with gold, garnets and lapis lazuli. Hengist was easy to find, his distinctive, crested battle helmet gleaming in the sunlight. Anya stared at him, her emotions spiralling. She had so many reasons to hate him but he was still her kin. And in that moment, she realised she didn't want him to die.

She could not find Horsa in the Saxon ranks, but she knew he must be there, for Hengist would expect his brother to be at his side. She wanted to see him again so badly. She wanted to gallop to him, fling her arms around him and hold him close and tell him she was sorry, sorry for everything. And yet the stubble field separating the two armies might as well have been the widest ocean.

At first glance, Vortigern's army appeared heavily outnumbered, even with his ranks supplemented by farm boys. They looked pale faced and terrified and she wondered if they would stand firm in the shield wall, or simply turn and flee. Did they even know what they were fighting for? And then she noticed Vortigern's horsemen massing on the brow of the hill. He may be outnumbered, but he had something Hengist did not: a fast, flexible cavalry unit that could cut down men like a scythe through a field of wheat.

The Saxon drums were filling the air now, their pulse fast and full of fury. Unused to the sounds of battle, Anya's mare began to stamp its feet and toss its head. She leant forward and stroked the animal's neck, whispered soothing words in its ear. And then, above the drums, she heard four short blasts from a battle horn. Moments later, a storm of Saxon spears flew across the field. The air was filled with the sound of their flight, like a strong wind surging through a narrow valley. Time seemed to slow then rapidly speed up again as spears found flesh, and the first men fell. There was a strange singing sound as spear tips pierced chain-mail and a look of terrible surprise on the faces of men as they died.

Vortigern's army responded with its own deadly volley of spears and the front lines of Hengist's army began to fall; Picts, Catuvellauni and Saxons united in death. Anya closed her eyes. She was a healer. She did not want to witness this slaughter. She wanted to rein around and ride away, far, far away. But Horsa was somewhere amidst the Saxon battle lines. How could she turn her back on him now?

When there were no more spears, the shield walls began to advance across the field. Swords beat against iron bosses, faster and faster, keeping time with the rapid pulse of the Saxon battle drums. And then the two armies were running, charging towards each other across the stubble, screaming to their gods for victory, for deliverance.

The shield walls met and it was as if the very earth shuddered and convulsed. Amidst the thrusting, hacking savagery, men began to fall, trampled underfoot by others who quickly took their place. Vortigern and Ronan were riding back and forth behind the shield wall, shouting commands, holding the line, the banner of the black boar fluttering close by. Clad in a cloak of imperial purple over a cuirass of Roman mail, with his sword held aloft, Vortigern looked every inch the warlord-king.

The sounds of battle swept up the hillside towards Anya, the grunting, animal effort of killing, the terrible screams as men went down, the stench of blood and shit and terror. She turned in her saddle and retched. There was no question of taking sides; her father was a Saxon, her mother a Briton. She wanted only for the slaughter to stop. Forlornly, she sought the goddess, but no matter how hard she searched, she could not find the soothing calm of the sacred grove. Why was Nerthus silent? Didn't she care who lived or died today?

Anya narrowed her eyes. There was a cloud of dust on the horizon. At first it was no more than a smudge upon the road, but then she saw the glint of sunlight upon spears. Hengist's reinforcements from Corinium were late, but their impact was devastating. His foot-soldiers charged full pelt across the stubble field, attacking Vortigern's shield wall from the rear. Taken by surprise, his unshakeable battle-lines began to falter. Anya heard Vortigern's voice bellow above the tumult.

'Engage the cavalry!'

More battle horns sounded, and she watched Vortigern's horsemen gallop down the hillside, gathering speed as they approached Hengist's reinforcements. Many of the Saxon foot-soldiers wore no helmets, and the slashing blades of Vortigern's cavalrymen sliced skulls and severed heads, until the churned field ran red with blood. With the Saxon reinforcements in disarray, the cavalry swept wide then regrouped and charged headlong into the rear of Hengist's own shield wall. The Saxons broke into fragmented confusion. Many of Hengist's men, Picts, Saxons and Catuvellauni alike, began to flee the field. Even as they ran for their lives, Vortigern's cavalry pursued them and cut them down.

A tight knot of mounted Saxon warriors were galloping hard towards the nearby woodland. Anya shielded her eyes, trying to focus over the long distance. One of the retreating horsemen was Hengist; she recognised his battle helmet. Did that mean Horsa was also part of the fleeing group? She knew the doors of Valhalla would not open for warriors who fled the field of battle. There was no glory in surviving a defeat such as this. But at that moment, she did not care about glory. She felt only relief that her brothers were still alive.

And yet, even as the thought crossed her mind, she realised the battle was not over. A Saxon warrior had broken away from the retreating group. Jumping down from his horse, he tore his leathers from his chest as he charged back the way he had come, roaring like a man possessed. His boots were sinking into the churned and bloodied stubble but he kept running, charging towards Vortigern, stripping his clothes from his body as he darted around dead and dying men. He was almost naked now but for his breeches and the helmet that covered his face. And still, he kept coming.

Vortigern's guards closed ranks around him, their horses towering over the Saxon, but the half-naked man showed no fear. Holding his shield above his head in defence against their swinging swords, he plunged into their midst, his rune-protected blade stabbing, thrusting and slicing. Trails of blood swept through the air as his sword cut the flesh of horses and men alike. Horses buckled and crashed to the earth, screaming in pain and confusion. Their riders tumbled into the mud, where the Saxon despatched them with ruthless efficiency. And as the last bodyguard fell, the Saxon grabbed the reins of Vortigern's stallion.

Anya watched as Vortigern attempted to bring the animal under control, but the beast was wild with fear. The Saxon leapt sideways to avoid its flailing hooves and wrenched on the reins again. The horse reared up in panic then crashed to its knees. Vortigern was flung from the saddle and fell heavily to the ground, winded and dazed. His helmet flew off and landed in the mud several yards away.

The Saxon raised his sword, bringing it down like an axe. Vortigern parried the blow, scrambled to his feet then immediately retaliated. From the angle of his blade, Anya guessed he was aiming for the Saxon's neck but the man twisted his naked torso at the last moment and Vortigern's sword sliced through the Saxon's left shoulder. She saw a flash of bone and then blood began to ooze from the deep wound.

The Saxon was moving forward, showing no indication that he was even aware of the deep gash in his shoulder. Vortigern swung his sword again, but the Saxon jabbed viciously with his shield, deflecting the blow. Anya heard a sharp cracking sound as the bones in Vortigern's hand shattered on impact with the shield boss, heard him grunt with pain as his sword slipped from his grasp.

The Saxon kicked the sword out of Vortigern's reach and rammed his shield hard into Vortigern's face. More bone splintered and Vortigern fell onto his back, blood pouring from his split nose. His right hand was grasping the mud wildly, searching in vain for his sword.

The Saxon was straddling Vortigern now, leaning over him like an avenging fury. Anya thought she caught a glimpse of the Saxon's lips moving before he plunged his sword directly into Vortigern's heart. He wrenched the blade out, and then he repeated the action again, and again, and again.

Ronan dug his heels viciously into his stallion's flanks, charging across the field towards his father. Deep inside, he knew he was too far away, but hope still clung to him, hope he would reach his father in time, hope he would save him.

He was close now, so close. Twenty yards, ten.

Even when he saw the Saxon drive his sword into his father's chest, he thought he must be dreaming and at any moment he would wake from this unthinkable nightmare. But then he saw Vortigern's head fall to one side, a gush of arterial blood surging from his mouth. And then he knew it was not a dream but real, and his father was truly gone.

He had not reached Vortigern in time. He had not saved him. In this last battle, he had proved himself to be the disappointment his father had always expected him to be. Fuelled with grief and fury, he swung down from his horse and charged towards the Saxon who straddled his father's body like a carrion crow.

'Get away from him!' he bellowed as he ran. 'Get away from him!'

The warrior appeared disorientated for a moment, as if uncertain where he was, and then he stood up and stepped away from Vortigern's corpse. The Saxon's arms and torso were splattered with blood.

Vortigern's blood.

Almost blinded by rage, Ronan raised his sword high above his head and kept running. The Saxon held fast. He waited until Ronan was almost upon him and then lunged to his right. Ronan's blade tore harmlessly through the air, missing the Saxon's left arm by a hair's breadth.

Ronan caught his breath. Somewhere in his tortured mind, a voice was urging caution. The Saxon was no longer in the grip of battle frenzy. He was now thinking rationally, and that made him a dangerous adversary. They began to circle one another, slowly at first then faster. The Saxon struck first, bringing his sword down with savage strength. Ronan held his ground, ducking and weaving, parrying the stream of blows, his eyes swiftly returning to the Saxon after each feint. Although his father had never acknowledged his skill, Ronan knew he was good at this. In the heat of battle he gained a sort of clarity, his sword light, his body agile, as if dancing to a tune only he could hear.

The Saxon brought his sword down again, but Ronan was quicker. He anticipated the move then darted back with another vicious slice of his blade. The force of the blow knocked the Saxon back a pace. He swayed slightly, momentarily off balance. It was all Ronan needed. Springing forward, he plunged his sword deep into the man's naked chest, felt the blade crunch between ribs. Clasping the hilt with both hands, he drove it deeper. Then, placing his left hand on the man's shoulder as leverage, he twisted the blade and wrenched it from the Saxon's chest. The wounded man gave a low moan and staggered backwards, his hands outstretched, as if searching the air for support.

And then a strand of red hair slipped from beneath the Saxon's helmet.

And in that finite speck of time, Ronan looked into the warrior's deep green eyes and to his immense surprise, he saw Anya's eyes. And in that briefest of moments, he faltered. It was the tiniest pause between a heart-beat but he knew instantly he had made a fatal mistake. How many times had his father told him never to hesitate in battle? He watched the Saxon lurch forward. Despite the terrible wound in the man's chest, it seemed as if pure instinct was driving him on.

And in that same blink of an eye, the Saxon drove his sword into Ronan's belly. It was the last effort of a dying man for his legs gave way beneath him and he sank to the ground, tugging the blade from Ronan's belly as he fell. Ronan felt a fleeting sense of elation as he watched the Saxon collapse into the mud. He had avenged his father. It was what Vortigern would have wanted.

And then the pain caught up with him, searing, white hot, knocking him to his knees. It was so unexpected, so intense, he could not catch his breath. He clasped his hands to his belly and felt his own blood, thick and warm, oozing between his fingers.

The pain was overwhelming; he had never experienced anything like it before. His mind was filled with it and there was no space for anything else. He gritted his teeth against it, tried not to cry out as he collapsed into the stubble. Blood was pulsing from the jagged wound now. His hands, cold and slippery, could not even begin to staunch it. He wondered how long it would take for him to die. To his vague surprise, he felt no fear, no regret. He realised he would welcome death, for it would bring an end to this unbearable pain.

Anya saw the strand of red hair slip from its leather tie, saw it flutter like a flimsy banner in the wind. She had seen this image in her dreams.

Horsa upon a nameless battlefield.

'No!' The scream tore from her throat.

Her bodyguards were no longer at her side. They were already galloping across the field, racing to Ronan's aid. Anya dug in her heels and charged after them. The field was littered with the dead and dying but her eyes were fixed solely on Horsa and Ronan, wielding their swords like axes as they spun around each other in some terrible parody of a dance.

And so when the fatal blow was struck, she was not immediately aware of its terrible significance. It was only when

Horsa fell to his knees and she saw the black shadow of death lingering above him, like smoke rising from a pyre, that she realised the truth of it.

Slipping from the mare's saddle, she ran towards her brother. Horsa lay on his back, blood surging from the wound in his chest. A few yards away, Ronan lay clutching his belly, curled up in agony, but she barely noticed him. Kneeling at Horsa's side, she gingerly probed his wound. There was nothing she could do. He did not have long. Carefully, she removed his helmet and cradled his head in her lap.

'I'm here,' she said gently. 'Horsa, I'm here, I'm with you.'

His red hair was dark and matted with sweat. There was blood everywhere, pulsing from his wounds, dripping onto her cloak and into the stubble. He was struggling to breathe, his face a rictus of agony.

'Anya, I hoped I might see you again one day...'

'Yes, I'm here. I'm with you.'

'Vortigern is dead. I have set you free...'

'Yes. Yes, you have. Thank you, Horsa.'

She could hear blood filling his lungs with each wet, gurgling breath he took. Anguish constricted her throat, pushing stinging tears to her eyes. She had never felt more helpless. She had no milk of the poppy, nothing to offer him to ease his pain.

She had seen so much suffering and death in the place of healing. There, it had been her duty to be kind and yet detached. But she could not distance herself from her brother's suffering. She did not want him to die drowning in his own blood, in this terrible place of carnage.

But she could not save him, just as she had not saved Emma or Elsbet.

'I avenged Elsbet...' he breathed.

247

She heard the terrible gurgling in his lungs again and she nodded, wiping away a treacherous tear from her cheek.

'Yes. Yes, you have,' she repeated.

Horsa's chest began to heave, his eyes suddenly filled with fear. Blood bubbled between his teeth, trickled from the corner of his mouth.

'I love you Horsa,' Anya said gently. 'I will always love you. You are the kindest of brothers and the best of men.'

His eyes were losing focus.

'Go to her. She is waiting for you,' she whispered.

And then she shut out the sounds of the battlefield, the moans of dying men and the screams of wounded horses. Focussing her gaze solely on her brother's face, the song she sang to him was sweet and soft. And there she remained, cradling him in her arms, long after the terrible tension had left his body, long after his soul had fled the field.

Strong hands were pulling her upright. 'My lady, we have to go.' It was Julianus.

Disorientated, she tried to shrug him off. 'Let go of me!'

'The Saxons are re-forming their battle lines. You can't stay here!'

'What did you say?' she asked, her bruised mind slow to understand. Her gaze focussed on Horsa's lifeless body, lying heavily across her lap.

'I'm not leaving him. He must have a funeral pyre. It must be hung about with shields and -'

'Not now. No time.' Julianus lifted her to her feet and began to drag her forcibly across the field.

'I won't leave him!' She was struggling to break free of Julianus's grasp, but he grabbed her shoulders and turned her to face the tree line. 'Look!'

248

Emboldened by Vortigern's death, Hengist had re-formed his shield wall. But the remnants of Vortigern's army were in retreat. Their warlord was dead and they had no stomach for battle now. Ronan's body was being lifted onto a covered wagon. She wondered vaguely if he was still alive.

Numb with misery, Anya watched the Saxon shield wall begin to advance, the sound of their drums drowning out the cries of mortally wounded men. Hengist was leading from the front. She could sense his thirst for vengeance; it seemed to ignite the air around him.

'We have to go. Ronan is alive and it is our duty to protect him,' Julianus insisted.

Without waiting for her response, he lifted her onto the mare and thrust the reins into her hands. Defeated by grief, she did not resist him. And so she dug in her heels, keeping pace with Vortigern's warriors as they galloped away from Hengist's advancing shield wall, away from Vortigern's corpse, abandoned in haste, and away from Horsa, the brother she had loved so dearly, her last link to home.

On the long, grim march to Aquae Sulis the image of Ronan's sword blade sinking into Horsa's chest played repeatedly in her mind, an endless cycle of horror. She had been shocked by Julianus's decision to leave the dead and mortally wounded behind, their worldly goods booty for the Saxons, their flesh a feast for the carrion crows, but she understood he had no choice. The king was dead. Long live the king. She turned in her saddle, glancing over her shoulder at the covered wagon. She could hear Ronan's moans as the wheels lurched over the uneven road. Why was he still alive?

Was there no justice in this god-forsaken land?

TWENTY THREE

The army of the Dobunni straggled into the forum of Aquae Sulis four days later. Exhausted and leaden with grief, Anya dismounted and watched as Ronan's makeshift stretcher was lowered from the wagon and carried into the basilica. She could see from the rise and fall of his chest that he still breathed, and she hated him for clinging to life, when her brother had fallen beyond the veil. Why had Nerthus allowed Emma, then Elsbet, then Horsa to die? For the first time in her life, she felt her faith in the goddess waver.

Vortigern's soldiers were milling around aimlessly, their expressions unsettlingly blank, as if they had left part of themselves behind on the battlefield. She eyed them warily. Ten days previously, these men had spat at her feet and called her a witch. Did they now blame her for Vortigern's death, blame her for bringing shame and ignominy upon the previously undefeated army of the Dobunni?

She sensed it would be unwise to linger in Aquae Sulis now. What had Horsa said? *'I have set you free.'* With Vortigern dead, she was free to leave the city. Free to ride to Dumnonia, to Silvanus.

The vision came upon her without warning.

The great hall of Tintagel was mired in stinking slime and littered with corpses. And then she saw Mairi. She held a child in her arms, holding him high as if in offering to the gods. She was speaking now and her voice was magnified, echo upon echo resounding about the hall. 'And he will bring new life and new hope to a new golden age.'

The image faded as quickly as it had come. Cold fear settled in Anya's stomach, and then she let out an anguished sigh. Her visions were not blessings but torments, taunting her with their mystifying, maddening vagueness. Time and time again, she had seen Horsa upon a nameless battlefield with death lingering close by. And yet she had not found a way to save him.

The hairs on the back of her neck began to prickle and she turned around. Rufus was staring intently at her, his expression unfathomable. She could not decide if he wanted to kiss her passionately, or kill her extremely slowly. Unnerved, she looked away again. Maud was hurrying towards her, weaving between the groups of exhausted soldiers. Her eyes were downcast, as if attempting to appear invisible.

'The plague?' Anya asked her urgently.

'No new outbreaks since you left, my lady. I believe the worst is over.'

Anya nodded, profoundly relieved. She felt weary to her bones, weary of misery and suffering and death. And then she thought of Horsa, lying in her arms, his life blood leeching into the dark earth. There was not enough space in her heart to hold her grief for her brother's death. Like a river bursting its banks, quite suddenly, she was engulfed by it. She felt her eyes begin to fill with tears and she no longer had the strength to hold them back. A sob rose in her throat.

'My lady, let's go inside,' Maud said kindly.

Putting an arm around Anya's shoulders, the slave girl guided her up the steps and into the basilica.

251

Rufus watched Anya's tears begin to fall, his mind a tumult of conflicting emotions. Anya's brother had killed Vortigern, and part of him hated her for it. But the larger part pitied her, for how was any of this her doing? When the advance scouts had brought the word of Vortigern's death he had felt as if he was physically shrinking, dwarfed by the magnitude of the news. In the privacy of his own bedchamber he had put his head in his hands and wept. How was it possible to hate a man and yet to love him at the same time, to be glad he was dead, and yet mourn him deeply?

Even now, several days later, he was finding it difficult to accept that a lifetime of abuse and humiliation was suddenly over. Like a slave unexpectedly released from servitude, he had no clear idea of what to do next. He had danced to Vortigern's tune for so long, that now the strings were finally cut, he felt as if he had simply fallen to the ground, as spineless and useless as a discarded marionette.

Julianus was issuing orders, and his commanding voice interrupted Rufus's reverie. 'Take Ronan to his chamber. Find him a physician, quickly. Help the lady Anya. The men are to go to the barracks in the old fort. Check supplies. See the horses are watered.'

Rufus felt a flash of familiar resentment. Yet again, he was being passed over and ignored. Without Vortigern's patronage, would he simply become invisible now? No, that could not happen. That must not happen. Squaring his shoulders, he followed Julianus and his men into the council chamber, watching as they heaped their sword belts and mail upon the long table in a clatter of iron and steel.

Rufus frowned. He took pleasure in beauty, wherever it was to be found – in the high, sweet notes of a flute, or the exquisite chase-work on a silver feasting bowl, or the idyllic perfection of Virgil's pastoral poetry, or the colour of Anya's eyes. But Julianus's very existence offended him, for he was an ugly brute of a man, with flat cheeks, a misshapen nose, and a mouth full of broken teeth. If he was honest, he felt intimidated by all Vortigern's men, these coarse but fearless warriors who did not run from danger as he had done on the road from Calleva all those months ago. How would he ever find the courage to say what he must?

'Julianus, I would speak with you.' To his chagrin, he realised his voice was high pitched with fear.

Julianus turned around. He had not realised Rufus was in the room. 'What is it?'

'Our kingdom is vulnerable,' Rufus began, but Julianus cut in. 'I am well aware of that.'

'It needs a strong ruler, or everything Vortigern fought for will be lost,' Rufus stammered.

'Are you just going to stand there spouting the obvious or do you have something useful to say?' A strand of shiny spittle flew from Julianus's misshapen mouth It reminded Rufus of a slug-trail and he stifled a shudder of revulsion.

'I know this kingdom like the back of my hand – its towns, villages, farms, forests, mines,' he said hurriedly. 'I understand the threads that hold it together.'

'You gather taxes,' Julianus replied disparagingly. 'What's your point?'

Rufus was finding it hard to catch his breath. 'I should rule the Dobunni. The kingdom will be safe in my hands. It will be prosperous, stable -'

'You?' Julianus scoffed. 'What gives you the right to rule? Ronan is Vortigern's rightful heir.'

'Ronan is bleeding to death. He'll be dead by nightfall,' Rufus replied bluntly.

Julianus's eyes narrowed. 'Ronan's fate is in God's hands, but even if you are right and he dies, the Dobunni need a strong warrior to lead them, not a weakling scribe.'

Rufus pulled himself to his full height, but he was still at least a foot shorter than Julianus. 'I am not weak. I served Vortigern faithfully and wisely, all these years.'

'And Vortigern despised you, all these years. He suffered your company out of some misplaced loyalty because you grew up together, but Ronan will not be so forgiving, and neither will I.' Julianus took a step towards him, his eyes hard and scornful. He towered over Rufus, a giant oak above a spindly sapling, stealing his light, just as Vortigern had done.

And it was at that precise moment Rufus realised how foolish he had been to believe the old adage, 'the quill is mightier than the sword'. Unlike Ronan, he had no God-given right to sit upon the dais in the basilica of Aquae Sulis. He needed a show of strength. He needed warriors. And he needed them now.

Anya stood outside the door of Ronan's bedchamber. She reached for the latch but quickly withdrew her hand, her thoughts in disarray. Conflicted and confused beyond measure, she walked away. She had taken barely five paces before she turned around and walked back the way she had come. Opening the door, she stepped inside. She had half expected to see a Christian priest or a man of medicine at Ronan's bedside, but he was alone. The shutters had been pulled across the window and in the half-light the fading frescoes looked nothing more than mottled mould. The room smelled foul, an acrid mix of blood and sweat, of stale air and stale wine and unwashed clothes.

Ronan was lying flat on his back on a low, slatted bed

strewn with furs. His leather cuirass had been removed but he still wore his tunic and breeches. His sword and scabbard had been placed at his side. His heavy leather boots were stained with blood, and a blade of grass protruded from a thick lump of dried mud on his sole. Someone had bound his wound, but fresh blood was already beginning to ooze through the linen.

'They expect him to die,' Anya thought, *'and he is to die a warrior, with his sword close at hand.'*

She took a step into the room then came to an abrupt halt. Vortigern was dead. She was no longer bound to him. She was free to ride to Silvanus. She yearned to be at his side, dreamed of it. So what was she doing here?

She realised she had no answer. She walked towards the window and flung back the heavy shutters. Daylight streamed across the room, and she breathed in the warm, late summer air. A blackbird flew off across the red-tiled roof tops, crying a tuneless alarm.

She suspected the room was just as Ronan had left it on the day they had marched to meet the army of the white wolf. He was a staggeringly untidy youth. The floor was strewn with his undergarments, tunics, breeches, belts, cloak clasps and hunting knives. She stepped closer and examined his grey, sweat sheened face. From the look of him, she doubted he would ever have need of such items again.

This man had killed her dear, kind-hearted brother, and she hated him for it. She hated him so much she wanted to pick up the sword at his side and drive it through his heart. Surely it was revenge that had drawn her to this room that stank of the battlefield? She watched Ronan's chest rise and fall. His breath was coming in short, sharp rasps and they sounded like dagger thrusts in the silence. She noticed his hands were encrusted with dried blood. Was it his blood, or Horsa's?

Perhaps sensing he was no longer alone, Ronan opened his eyes. 'Ah, Anya. So you have found me. Show some mercy, and make it quick.'

'I...' Anya's words faded in her throat.

Ronan did deserve to die, and she suspected Vortigern's son would go to meet his god without regrets. He had avenged his father, his conscience was clear. She sensed there would be no emotional confessions, no pleas for forgiveness. Even at the moment of his death, Ronan would see the world through a warrior's eyes, in clear cut, absolute certainties.

Silvanus, of course, viewed life very differently. For him the world was never black and white, but a patchwork of grey, of endless possibilities and outcomes. It was just one of the many reasons why she loved him. So what was she doing here?

She closed her fingers about the grip of Ronan's sword. She had watched men killing each other. It would not be difficult to find Ronan's heart, just as he had found Horsa's. And she wanted to do it. She wanted to do it so much.

She watched the pain overwhelm Ronan again, watched him close his eyes against it. With Vortigern dead, and his heir mortally wounded, she wondered who would rule the Dobunni. Rufus knew how to collect taxes, but he could not lead men into battle. Julianus was a proven warrior, but she doubted he had the strength of personality to maintain power. So would an outsider seize control of Vortigern's weakened kingdom? Would another tyrant warlord bring yet more suffering and misery to the people of the Dobunni?

Anya felt a sudden sense of despair. Britannia needed a very different kind of king if it was to survive, someone who would bring unity, not division.

Ronan's breathing was shallower now. She doubted he had long for this world. She wondered if he would have ruled the

Dobunni as his father had ruled - with brutality and cruelty. Or would he, by some miracle of fate, have chosen a different path? She leant forward and touched the sword at his side, running her fingers over the grip.

Ronan deserved to die. A life for a life.

'Now! Do it now!' the voice inside her head urged.

And yet...

'It won't bring Horsa back, will it?' she said out loud, letting go of the sword. 'Or Elsbet.'

'What did you say?' Ronan opened his eyes.

She wanted to avenge Horsa. It shocked her how much she wanted to kill Ronan but it wouldn't solve anything. It wouldn't bring Horsa back. It wouldn't right any wrongs. It wouldn't make the pain, or the grief, or the anger go away.

'You saved my life in Siluria,' she said softly.

'If you're not here to kill me, then go away,' Ronan muttered. 'You talk too much.' His eyes were closing again.

'I am in your debt,' she went on.

'No, you're not.'

'Yes, I am. You saved my life, and I am bound by my oath to the goddess to try and save yours in return.'

His eyes flickered open again. He looked astonished and in truth, she had surprised herself.

'But I killed your brother.' Ronan began to cough, blood spewing between his teeth. Anya hauled him upright. She held fast to his shoulders, waiting for his choking to abate. He was bleeding internally, and she knew his chances of survival were slim.

'Go away,' he spluttered. 'There's nothing you can do. Leave me to die with some dignity, for God's sake.'

Anya froze, racked with indecision. She had a thousand reasons to hate this man, a thousand reasons to wish him dead

257

but, often when she least expected it, she had sensed a glimmer of virtue lurking beneath his casual cruelties. On the other hand, no-one expected her to help him. There would be no shame if she walked away and left him to die. No one would ever know.

But the goddess would know. The oath Anya had made in the sacred grove had been sealed with her own blood. She still bore the scar upon her wrist. She had sworn to heal and not to harm. She couldn't kill Ronan, and nor could she simply walk away, no matter how much she might want to.

She had reached a decision. She would do everything in her power to save Ronan's life. And then, whether Ronan lived or died, she would return to Dumnonia, to Silvanus. To the man she had loved forever.

'Save your strength, Ronan.' She eased him back onto the bed again. 'We have work to do.'

TWENTY FOUR

Rufus rode out of Aquae Sulis at dawn and followed the road towards Londinium. The country air smelled sweet and it made his throat itch, his nose run and his eyes stream. Alone, with only his dagger for protection, he had never felt more vulnerable or more afraid. Half expecting to be robbed, murdered and flung into the roadside ditch, he rode at a brisk pace, constantly glancing over his shoulder. But the Irish warbands had returned home to seal their grain pits and slaughter their pigs. To prepare for winter, for the lean time, the hungry time, the dying time.

The Dobunni were ploughing their fields, the slow monotonous plod of the oxen, the constant cries of the gulls overhead. No-one paid much attention to a lone rider, sitting awkwardly in his saddle like a perched crow. It was as if he was invisible, which he thought was ironic, for he had lived his life in Aquae Sulis in the shadows, as unnoticed as a cobweb.

He reined in at every village, asking for directions to the Saxons' camp. At first, he drew blank stares, but as he drew closer to Londinium, everyone knew of the battleground, directing him by way of lightning struck trees, crossroads, fords and inns.

'If you're looking to scavenge, you'd best be quick. It'll be picked clean by now,' one man told him, in an accent so thick Rufus could barely understand him.

'I am looking for the Saxon camp,' he repeated slowly, as if he was talking to an imbecile.

'Follow the smoke,' the man replied. 'And may the gods preserve you.'

Rufus was taken aback. Was he so far from civilisation that these savages had reverted to worshipping the old gods? As the man had suggested, the battlefield was not hard to find, the air thick with smoke from the funeral pyres. It stung his eyes and caught his throat and he sneezed repeatedly. It appeared the Saxons had given full funeral honours to their own dead, but left Vortigern's men unburied for the carrion crows. He could see human scavengers moving across the field too, stripping the corpses of weapons, jewels, even the clothes upon their backs. There were flies everywhere and the stench made his stomach heave.

Hengist's camp straddled the road a few miles further south, scores of hide tents with no obvious semblance of order. Camp fires burned, and the fatty aroma of boiled mutton pervaded the air.

Rufus dismounted, dragged a linen cloth from his sleeve and blew his sore nose again. He barely had time to push the sodden cloth back up his sleeve before he was surrounded by half a dozen yellow haired, blue eyed Saxon warriors. In a strangely disconcerting way, their colouring resembled God's angels in the Christian manuscripts, but these men were the very opposite of angelic. Huge, muscular and heavily armed, they were eyeing him with expressions of intense hostility.

Rufus straightened his shoulders, trying hard to disguise his abject terror.

'Take me to Hengist,' he demanded, in Latin. To his

chagrin, he realised his voice had a strong nasal quality. He badly needed to blow his nose again.

One man stepped forward. His scalp was shaved but his beard reached his chest, divided into three plaits, adorned with rings of gold. 'Maybe I kill you instead?' he said in the Saxon tongue.

Rufus didn't understand him, so he tried again. 'I am Vortigern's second in command. I must speak with Hengist.' His nose was itching and then, to his horror, he sneezed loudly, spraying mucus into the Saxon's face.

One of the men laughed, but the sound died in his throat as the warrior turned on him.

'Take this idiot to Hengist!' he snarled, wiping his face with the back of his hand.

Hengist stared into the flames of the struggling camp fire, lost in his thoughts. Although they had rarely seen eye to eye, now that his brother was gone, he mourned him. Under a full moon and bathed in brittle moonlight, they had retrieved Horsa's body from the battlefield, and sent him to meet his forefathers as befitting a great warrior. His funeral pyre had been hung about with shields and spears, so that he might prove his prowess to the warriors of Valhalla. The pyre had burnt until morning, its fierce flames lighting up the night sky.

They had found Vortigern's corpse surrounded by his fallen household guards, and Hengist had generously beckoned Cunedda to join him. The young boy had stepped forward, unsheathed his sword, and sliced Vortigern's head cleanly from his body. But rather than lifting the severed head jubilantly to the heavens, Cunedda had simply stared at Vortigern's mutilated corpse and then walked away, which made Hengist think the boy was sadly lacking in character.

261

He let out a heavy sigh. He was not given to introspection, but Horsa's death had left him feeling morose. Absently, he prodded the smoking fire with a twig. By the ancient code of kinship, he had no choice but to continue the blood vendetta and avenge his brother - which meant Ronan had to die. How fortuitous then, that vengeance and ambition were leading him down the same path - the path to Londinium. And then on to Aquae Sulis.

Hengist looked up. Two of his soldiers were dragging a puny man across the field. He looked vaguely familiar. Yes, he remembered now. It was Vortigern's scribe. What in the name of Odin was he doing here?

'Is he armed?'

'No, lord.'

'Then release him! Look at him. He hasn't the strength to harm a fly.'

'I am Rufus, Vortigern's second in command,' Rufus began. His nose was running and, surreptitiously, he wiped it on the sleeve of his cloak.

Hengist switched to Latin. 'I know who you are. What do you want, scribe? Only a fool walks into his enemy's camp alone.'

Rufus was trembling as if in the grip of fever, cold sweat beginning to trickle down his back. He felt intimidated and deeply unsettled by Hengist, his blue eyes so cold and pale they were almost transparent.

'I come to offer my allegiance,' he began again. To his mortification, his voice quavered like that of an adolescent boy.

Hengist's expression betrayed his surprise. 'I thought you were Vortigern's man?'

'Vortigern is dead. Your brother saw to that.'

'But I am told his son is still alive. Have you not offered your allegiance to him?'

'No,' Rufus croaked. He wanted to say more, but his throat was drying with fear.

'No loyalty at all? To anyone? What kind of a man are you?' Hengist asked sneeringly.

Rufus cleared his throat. 'I was loyal to Vortigern, but now he is dead, I would be loyal to you.'

'I don't need taxmen, I need warriors. And you are not a warrior. In fact, I'd wager you are most likely a spy. Perhaps I should hang you from that tree over there?'

Pure terror gripped Rufus. 'I swear on my mother's grave, I am no spy,' he stammered. 'I have come to serve you.'

'What can you possibly have that I need?'

'I can make you a wealthy man.'

'I'm already a wealthy man. Britannia is a treasure hoard without a dragon to guard it,' Hengist said dismissively, turning his attention to the fire again.

'I'm not talking about plunder and loot. I'm talking about tribute, grain supplies, trade routes, gold mines, silver, lead,' Rufus gabbled, painfully aware he was running out of time, painfully aware this was his last chance to right a lifetime of wrongs.

Hengist looked up at Rufus. There was such intensity in his gaze that Rufus felt as if he was being pierced by arrows. Finally Hengist gestured to the fire-side. 'Sit down.'

Rufus sat down, both terrified and exhilarated in equal measure, whilst Hengist continued to stare appraisingly at him.

'And what would you want in return?'

Rufus felt a sudden frisson of excitement. 'I want Aquae Sulis. I want to govern the city.'

He wanted to sit upon the dais in the council chamber. He

wanted his commands to be obeyed without question. He wanted everything Vortigern had enjoyed. He knew it was a twisted kind of revenge, but it was revenge none the less.

'That's it? You want to govern Aquae Sulis?'

'And Anya. I want her,' Rufus's voice wobbled, betraying his need, his hunger.

'My sister?' Hengist asked sharply. 'Why do you want her? She is worthless.'

'Then you can have no objection to giving her to me,' Rufus pressed. He watched Hengist bridle, and realised he had pushed too far. 'I apologise,' he said hurriedly. 'Your sister is newly widowed. Forgive me, I was insensitive.'

Hengist tipped his head back and began to laugh loudly. Bewildered and out of his depth, Rufus remained silent. But Hengist's laughter died as quickly as it had begun.

'Prove it, scribe. Prove your worth. Tell me something I don't already know about Vortigern's kingdom.'

'Er…' Rufus's mind went agonisingly blank. He had talked Vortigern out of nightmarish diplomatic situations many times, so why couldn't he find the words now, when it mattered to him? He wanted to weep with frustration.

Think! Think!

And it came to him then, in a flash of clarity.

'Vortigern was so arrogant he didn't believe anyone would dare to attack Aquae Sulis,' he said quickly. 'He hasn't repaired the walls for years. In parts, they need little more than a nudge to come tumbling down. I can show you where. I can draw a plan. And the south-west gate is rotten. It will melt like butter before a battering ram.'

Rufus couldn't breathe, his chest as tight as a drum. He had spoken truthfully but would the Saxon believe him? He felt his cheeks grow hot under Hengist's intense scrutiny, but he forced himself to match his gaze. He had studied Vortigern carefully over the years and learnt that warlords placed great store by eye contact. The silence stretched on. His eyes were sore and streaming but he was determined not to be the first to blink.

Finally, Hengist said, 'what are you doing here? What do you really want from me?'

'I've already told you. I want Aquae Sulis.'

'And you want to ride my sister, don't you, you sick bastard?'

'I would like to marry her,' Rufus said primly. Anya was not a whore. She deserved to be treated with respect.

And this time, Hengist laughed so loudly that rooks took flight from their roosts in the beech trees, sending a shower of red-tinged leaves drifting to the ground. Rufus had no idea what Hengist had found so amusing. He glanced nervously at the circling rooks, their ugly, jarring cries ringing in his ears. All about him, the leaves were falling from the trees. How had autumn arrived without him noticing it? This time of year always made him feel melancholy, a sense of things ending. And in the space of a few weeks, so many things had ended. He felt lost, adrift. But he had come this far, and he could not turn back now. He opened his mouth to speak, but Hengist had turned to Aelfric.

'Fetch the king of the Catuvellauni. I would like him to meet our guest.'

'Yes, lord.'

Aelfric got to his feet and strode away across the field. Ducking his head to enter a tent which bore the banner of a golden crown, he returned moments later with a tall, gangly youth. Rufus eyed the boy thoughtfully. Vortigern had killed Cunedda's father in battle several years since. He supposed it

265

should come as no surprise the youth had chosen to ally with Hengist.

'Ah, Cunedda, please, sit by me,' Hengist said courteously, in Latin. 'This is Rufus. He was Vortigern's scribe.'

Rufus tensed at the insult but chose to remain silent. Cunedda sat down beside Hengist, held out his hands towards the fire, and nodded curtly at Rufus.

'Cunedda's army fought bravely,' Hengist went on.

'I lost many good men.' Cunedda sounded angry, resentful. He brushed a strand of lanky hair from his eyes before returning his gaze to the fire.

Rufus noticed he had the long fingers of a musician, rather than a warrior.

'You lost most of your men,' Hengist corrected slyly. 'But their sacrifice will be remembered by the skalds. It was a great victory, and you should be proud of the part you played.'

Leaning towards Cunedda, he put a hand on his shoulder in what appeared to be a gesture of solidarity. Several moments passed before Rufus realised Hengist's dagger was now embedded in Cunedda's chest, and a stain of blood was spreading across the boy's tunic. Hengist continued to grip Cunedda's shoulder as the young man's hands fluttered ineffectually towards the dagger. His chest was heaving, his lips opening and closing, but the light was going from Cunedda's eyes.

Hengist wrenched the dagger from the boy's chest, watching dispassionately as Cunedda collapsed sideways into the flattened stubble, bright red arterial blood trickling from his teeth. His face was ashen grey. If he was still alive, he would not be for long. Hengist gestured to Aelfric, who quickly stepped forward and dragged Cunedda away.

Dizzy with shock, Rufus hoped he wasn't about to pass

266

out. To his dismay, he realised Hengist was eyeing him speculatively, an ugly, humourless smile playing on his lips.

'You are wondering why I did that.'

Rufus's terrified brain was curdling like five day old milk. He could find no words.

'I needed Cunedda to raise his army, such as it was,' Hengist said lightly. 'I needed him to fight for me, but I have no further use for him. And now, in the space of a heartbeat, his lands and his warriors are mine.' The smile broadened across Hengist's face. 'So, Rufus of the Dobunni, can you prove your worth to me, or will you share Cunedda's fate?'

'I have told you about the weak defences at Aquae Sulis,' Rufus stammered, his heart stuttering with terror.

'I can send out scouts to see such things. Tell me something else.'

Rufus's hands began to shake. He clasped them together in his lap. 'As I told you, I control tribute, taxes...'

'Yes, yes, but tell me about Londinium. Will Vortigern's garrison oppose me now their king is dead?'

Rufus was struggling to muster his terrified mind. When he was a child, the city of Londinium had filled him with a sense of wonder, as if he had arrived at the very centre of the world. Londinium had been one of the wealthiest cities in the Empire, levying a heavy tax on all trade conducted on its quays and within its walls. Sitting proudly on the northern bank of the Thamesis, its jetties had teemed with foreign ships and their exotic cargo. Carts had clogged the roads, bringing salt, oysters, eels from the coast; grain and vegetables from the countryside, and blooms of iron and baskets of pottery from the wealds. But gradually the traffic had ceased on the impressive wooden bridge and now it was rare for a ship to dock on the quays. Londinium's life-blood had been the merchants from the east carrying silks and spices, oils and wines. But they had long since begun to avoid Londinium, afraid of disease, of plague, of Saxons.

And then, Vortigern had marched his army to the city's gates. The inhabitants' refusal to surrender had resulted in a bloodbath. In retribution for their futile stand against him, Vortigern had ordered his army to conscript Londinium's men, rape the women, and slaughter the children. The city was no longer glorious, no longer the centre of anyone's world. Collecting taxes in Londinium had become a dangerous affair, even when protected by burly bodyguards.

'The garrison are half-starved conscripts. Once they hear Vortigern is dead, I believe they will surrender without a fight,' Rufus replied honestly. 'And the citizens have been sorely treated. I assure you, they have no loyalty to the Dobunni.'

Hengist stared at him for a long moment. 'If your intelligence proves correct, if you prove your worth, then we will talk again. Now go away, before I change my mind.'

Dumbfounded with both shock and relief, Rufus stood up too quickly and his world began to swim.

'Thank you. You won't regret -' he began, but Hengist was looking over his shoulder at Aelfric.

'Don't let this runt out of your sight,' he said in his own tongue. 'If he tries to leave the camp, kill him.'

TWENTY FIVE

Tintagel, kingdom of Dumnonia

It was stiflingly hot in the great hall. Silvanus, at the head of the long oak table, was struggling not to yawn. His councillors sat on his right, and on his left, sat the plaintiffs and defendants. The court had been in session all day, a special court, convened for cases which had not reached resolution at the moot hearings. Silvanus's head was throbbing; he felt as if he was drowning in other men's troubles.

This latest case involved a contested will. A recently deceased farmer had left his entire estate to his son by his first wife, leaving nothing to his current spouse. Seated on Silvanus's left, she was sobbing pitifully, her eyes bloodshot, her cheeks mottled with distress. Her step-son, a scrawny youth of no more than sixteen years of age was studiously ignoring her misery.

'My father's will is clear, and no one disputes its authenticity. He left me the estate. I am under no obligation to offer a home to his wife,' the boy pronounced coldly.

'You would see your own step-mother cast out to starve?' Silvanus asked levelly. 'Did she not toil in the fields beside you? Did she not build a home for you and care for you?'

'My father hated her. We all hated her.'

'And yet your step-mother has provided ten witnesses who swear she was a good wife and step-mother,' Silvanus replied calmly, although he wanted to box the youth about the ears. Enough time had been spent on this. It was time to make a decision. He looked first at the weeping woman and then at the indifferent youth at her side. He knew why this case had failed to reach resolution at the moot courts. Dumnonia's peace and stability depended on maintaining the letter of the law, but in this instance, the law was an ass.

And so, as always, he wondered what Anya would advise. In the silence that followed, Evric dragged the jug of watered wine across the table and filled his cup. Taliesin's chin dropped onto his chest and wisps of his long, grey hair fell across his face like cobwebs. A snore rumbled in the old priest's throat and Silvanus surreptitiously nudged him beneath the table. Taliesin awoke with a start and Gorran and Boult exchanged furtive grins.

Silvanus's expression however, remained resolutely solemn. 'I have reached a decision, and the decision of the high king is final and irreversible,' he declared, turning first to the son. 'You will inherit your father's estate in its entirety.'

A smug smile spread across the youth's face but Silvanus had not finished. 'Your step-mother will live in your house for the rest of her days. She will be treated with the respect and kindness owed to her position as your late father's legal wife. And if it comes to my attention that you have not followed my judgement then you will forfeit your father's estate in its entirety and with immediate effect.'

The youth opened his mouth then closed it again, like a floundering fish.

'Thank you, lord,' his step-mother stammered.

Tears were still streaming down the woman's face and Silvanus was tempted to put a comforting hand on her arm, but Etar had taught him kingship demanded a certain level of decorum, of separation. And so he simply stood up and announced, 'this court is adjourned. Refreshments will be served shortly.'

He kept his head down as he left the hall, avoiding all eye contact. His stomach was rumbling with hunger but he could not eat with the scores of plaintiffs and defendants still awaiting their hearing. From past experience he knew they would try to bend his ear, plead their special case.

After the suffocating heat of the hall, it felt cold outside. He walked briskly towards the low wall at the cliff edge, hoping the fierce wind might calm his aching head, but instead his thoughts began to accelerate. Almost a year had passed since he had last seen Anya. In that time he had lost his father and ascended the throne. But instead of making his mark on Dumnonia, he had procrastinated. Decision making had never been easy and now, when so much depended on him, he found it harder still. Despite the council calling for Lucan's death, his half-brother still languished under close guard at the top of the watch tower, unpunished.

Silvanus looked down at the beach far below him, remembering the times he had walked with Anya there. She had believed in him, assured him he was no better or worse than any other man. She had told him to trust his instincts, told him to start at the beginning and the rest would follow. But here he was, still at the start line, like a frightened horse that refused to run.

If Anya were to return to Dumnonia now, she would think him a coward, a failure.

He kicked the wall in self-disgust.

'The wall has offended you in some way, lord?'

Silvanus spun around. Jago was eyeing him curiously, a half smile on his lips.

'What do you want?' Silvanus growled.

Jago's smile vanished. 'A messenger has arrived, lord. There has been a great battle between Vortigern's forces and a Saxon army led by Hengist. Vortigern is slain, so too is Horsa. The Saxons claimed the field. They have taken the city of Londinium.'

Silvanus stared open mouthed at Jago, his mind spinning like a swarm of blackflies.

Vortigern was dead.

Hengist had taken Londinium.

Horsa, Anya's beloved brother, slain.

Silvanus's mind raced back full circle.

Vortigern was dead. Anya was free. She was free to return to Dumnonia, she was free to return to him. But where was she? Did she even know her husband was dead?

'Who has succeeded Vortigern as ruler of the Dobunni?'

'It is uncertain. Ronan is badly wounded. He is expected to die, but -' Jago broke off, unwilling to look Silvanus in the eye.

'Go on.'

'Ronan is expected to die but... but...' Jago faltered. He looked as if he hoped the earth might open and swallow him up. 'Anya is in Aquae Sulis. She is attempting to save his life,' he said at last.

Silvanus felt disorientated, weightless, as if he was falling from the clifftop towards the deadly rocks below. Why, after escaping from Vortigern's clutches all those months ago, had Anya chosen to go back to Aquae Sulis? Why had she not returned to Tintagel? There was a cold feeling in his stomach. He recognised it as betrayal, and it felt as bitter as bile.

272

He turned away from Jago, his emotions scattering.

'At least we now know for certain Anya is alive,' Jago began but Silvanus cut him off.

'Leave me!'

Clearing his throat, Jago ignored his king's command and said evenly, 'I believe there is a simple explanation for Anya's return to Aquae Sulis. She was held captive in Siluria. Ronan mounted a rescue. She -'

But Silvanus was no longer listening. The feeling of betrayal was building inside him and it felt cold, heavy, ugly. 'I will hear no more petty petitions today. Tell them all to leave. And then bring me Lucan's death warrant.'

Jago's expression darkened for a fraction of a heartbeat before he gave a small bow and hurried away.

Silvanus turned back to the sea. It was grey and angry, white foamed waves booming like thunder against the sheer cliff face. The sea's fury matched his mood. In Epona's circle, Anya had told him she loved him. Had she meant any of it?

The strong westerly wind was cold and raw across Silvanus's cheeks. It tore through his cloak, his tunic, his skin. He wondered if this was now death felt, the terrible icy chill, the realisation that nothing mattered any more. Turning on his heel, he strode back to the great hall.

As he had instructed, the hall was now empty save for Jago, Taliesin, Evric, Boult and Gorran. Seated at the table, they were unusually quiet, the air thick with tension.

'It is prepared, lord.' Jago tapped the parchment before him.

In truth, the document had been prepared for a very long time. All it needed was Silvanus's seal. He sat down, pulled the parchment towards him and quickly scanned the neat script, although he already knew the words by heart. He had read the

273

document countless times since Lucan's death sentence had been ratified by the council.

Picking up the stub of sealing wax, he placed it in the candle flame. From years of practice, he knew the precise moment to remove it, so the wax did not drip across the table, but fell in a shiny quivering pool on the parchment. Next, he picked up the silver seal of Dumnonia.

The hall fell silent. No sparrows flitted between the rafters, no mice scurried through the rushes. Silvanus hesitated, frozen with sudden, paralysing doubt. Should he show mercy? Or should he bow to the wishes of the council and seal the warrant? Whichever choice he made, he knew there would be consequences, and who could say how they might reverberate through the years to come?

His thoughts turned to Anya. What would she do? She had always been such a strong advocate for peace, for negotiation, for forgiveness. But Anya was not here. Anya was in Aquae Sulis, with Vortigern's son, with Ronan, the man who had killed her own brother. She had turned her back on Dumnonia. She had turned her back on him.

Silvanus brought the seal down hard into the wax, watched it squelch and hiss as if affronted. He held the seal firm for several moments then carefully rolled it off. It was a clean mark, the dragon of the banner of Dumnonia clearly imprinted in the wax. The deed was done. A decision had been made. Whether it was the right decision, or whether it would torment him for the rest of his days, only time would tell.

Taliesin leant across the table and took the parchment from him. Silvanus realised he had forgotten to breathe. He drew a long, ragged breath and looked around at the sombre faces of his brothers in arms. The compassion in Jago's eyes was

274

almost his undoing, and he was tempted to snatch the parchment back from Taliesin. Perhaps sensing Silvanus's wavering resolve, the old priest quickly rolled up the parchment and dropped it into the leather bag slung across his chest.

Silvanus opened his mouth then closed it again. Numb with grief, he could find no words. He stood up slowly and walked out of the hall. His body felt unbearably heavy, as if his limbs had turned to stone. Evric made to follow him but Taliesin put a hand on his shoulder.

'Let him be,' he said quietly. 'Let him be.'

Silvanus awoke the next morning with a furred mouth and a thundering headache. He rolled onto his back and groaned loudly. And it came back to him then, in a horrible, sickening flash, why he had such a terrible hangover. He had drunk an entire amphora of wine last night in the hope he might forget he had signed Lucan's death warrant.

But he remembered all too clearly now. He remembered banging the seal down, the hot wax hissing at him like a vengeful demon of the underworld. Without warning, a massive wave of self-reproach crashed over him. The gods would never forgive him for sentencing his own flesh and blood to death. And he would never forgive himself either.

But it was not too late to rectify this terrible lapse of judgement. He would throw Lucan's death warrant into the fire, and this shameful incident would never be spoken of again. Lucan, the little baby with the jet black curls he had held in his arms all those years ago, would live.

Silvanus stumbled from his bed. He did not open the shutters, knowing full well the bright sunlight would burn his dry, aching eyes. Instead he crashed blindly about the chamber in semi-darkness, his head throbbing fiercely every time he bent down to retrieve clothes he had abandoned the night before.

His legs felt wooden and unresponsive and in his haste, he stumbled down the last few steps of the spiral staircase, and half fell into the hall.

There was no sign of Taliesin but Jago, Evric, Boult and Gorran were seated at the table, giving the appearance they had not moved since the previous day.

'Lord, will you take a cup of wine?' Evric asked courteously.

'No. Is that Lucan's death warrant?' Silvanus pointed at the furled parchment on the table. 'Give it to me.'

Jago, Evric Boult and Gorran eyed one another warily.

'Why are you looking at each other like that?' Silvanus demanded, his head throbbing like a wound.

After a long, awkward silence, Jago finally spoke. 'Yes, it is Lucan's death warrant.'

Snatching the warrant from the table, Silvanus strode to the hearth and threw the parchment into the fire. He watched it spit and hiss, writhing in the flames as if fighting against its own demise.

And then he turned around.

'The death sentence is rescinded. By the king's prerogative, Lucan is to remain under house arrest indefinitely,' he announced. He felt suddenly, brutally sober.

No-one said a word, but his men's horrified expressions made Silvanus's blood run cold.

'What is it? What's happened?'

Evric stood up and walked towards his oldest friend.

'Lucan is dead, lord.'

'What did you say?'

'The sentence has already been carried out.'

276

Silvanus stared, dumbfounded at Evric. He felt as if his heart had been shattered into a thousand bloody shards.

'By whose command?' he asked fiercely, but he already knew the answer.

The laws of Dumnonia decreed that once a death warrant had been signed by the king, it was the high priest's responsibility to choose the manner of execution, and to carry out the sentence.

'By Taliesin's command, Lucan was thrown from the cliffs at dawn,' Evric replied.

TWENTY SIX

Aquae Sulis, kingdom of the Dobunni

Anya sat down on the delicately carved chair at Ronan's bedside. He was fast asleep. She put her head back against the wall and closed her eyes, drifting on a haze of exhaustion. And in her half dreams, the sword, her sword, was rising above the chaos and devastation and death. It felt like a beacon to brighten a winter's night. It felt like hope.

Ronan mumbled something and she opened one eye. He often talked in his sleep, but she could rarely make any sense of it. At first, she had felt certain she would not be able to save him. His wound was deep, the surrounding skin mottled and distended, a sure sign of internal bleeding.

But with Maud's help, she had stripped away Ronan's filthy clothes and bathed his bloodied and bruised skin. She had packed the wound with cobwebs and applied nettle compresses then sage, then honey, but still the wound wept and suppurated. She had given him tinctures of bilberry and common oak for the internal bleeding, but the mottling had worsened as he continued to bleed. And so she had resorted to yarrow, the gift of the moon goddess, and slowly, slowly, she began to dare to hope.

Maud, practical as ever, had tidied Ronan's room. In one of his lucid moments, he had opened his eyes and protested loudly, 'leave it all where it is! I won't be able to find anything if you tidy it away!'

'We can't work in this mess,' Anya had replied firmly, but not before she noticed Maud physically flinch at the sound of Ronan's voice.

His breathing was changing, quickening, and then he opened his eyes. 'God's teeth, are you still here?'

Anya ignored his sarcasm. Helping him upright, she put a beaker to his lips whilst he drank. He pulled a face, grimacing as he swallowed the bitter infusion.

'What is that? Poison? It tastes worse than yesterday's brew.'

Anya tipped the remaining brown liquid down his throat.

'Believe me, if I had wanted to poison you, you would be dead by now.'

Taking meticulous care, she wiped her hands on a cloth soaked in juniper oil, then removed the linen from his wound and wiped away the old compress. He winced with pain as she applied a fresh honey-based poultice. Ronan's eyes were closing again. He was still very weak.

Every single day, she wondered if she had been right to save him, this man who had slaughtered her beloved brother. Every single day, there were moments when she regretted her decision. Only time would tell if she had made the right choice. Only time would tell which road to kingship he would choose. Would it be Vortigern's choice - the easy, well paved road to intimidation and terror? Or would he dare to forge his own way? Would he have the courage to choose the difficult road - the narrow, winding, overgrown path to peace?

Anya wiped her hands on the cloth again. Her exhaustion

was making her melancholy. She had awoken in the dead of night some three weeks since, and her vision had been sharp and clear. Moonlight. A funeral pyre ablaze, and Horsa's soul rising with the smoke towards the star filled sky. He had died in battle, and the warriors of Valhalla would welcome him. It was a small comfort that he was with his ancestors now, reunited with Eown, with Elsbet.

But there had been no funeral honours for Vortigern.

'Your men left your father's body unburied on the battlefield. Do you grieve for his fate?' she said.

Ronan's eyes shot open. 'It grieves me that you ask so many questions. My father is dead. You will not speak his name again. I am the high king of the Dobunni now.' He scowled at her, as if daring her to challenge him, but for all his bravado, she could see strong emotions reflected in his eyes. No matter how vehemently he denied it, he was grieving for his father. She turned away, making a show of sorting her medicine box, and a heavy silence fell.

'Why are you still here?' he asked at last.

It was a good question. The plague had abated. There had been no new outbreaks for weeks. Ronan was still weak, but as the days passed, she had grown more was confident he was going to live. Her debt was paid. There was no reason for her to remain in Aquae Sulis now. It was time for her to return to Dumnonia. The thought of seeing Silvanus again made her cheeks flush with delicious anticipation.

'No answer for me?' Ronan needled. 'Let's try another question. Why did my father trust your brothers? Why did he invite Saxon wolves into the sheep pen?'

'Because he under-estimated them?' she replied cautiously.

'Like I under-estimate you? Will you sink that beautiful sword of yours between my ribs whilst I sleep?'

Anya sighed wearily. 'Your wound was infected, your blood was poisoned. If I had wanted you dead, I would have simply walked away.'

'So, why didn't you?'

Because I sensed goodness in you', she thought to herself.

'I told you why. You saved my life. I was in your debt.'

'Enough!' Ronan waved his hand irritably. 'I have more important matters to consider. This morning, whilst you were brewing your potions - or whatever it is you do - my spies brought news. Rufus has sworn allegiance to your brother. I always did hate that wretched, stinking turd of a scribe.'

Anya's eyes widened with shock. She had often wondered how Rufus might seek revenge for a lifetime of humiliation, if given the opportunity, but she had never dreamed he would choose to betray his own people.

'Your brother's hold over this island is growing stronger by the day,' Ronan said bitterly. 'Today I learnt he has taken Londinium. Apparently, he marched to the gates, held up my father's severed head and swore if the garrison commander did not surrender immediately, every man woman and child within the city would share Vortigern's fate. They tell me Hengist will march on Aquae Sulis before winter. Your brother is coming to kill me. The never ending wheel of vengeance just keeps on turning. What do you say to that?'

Anya stared at Ronan, horrified. 'But you have lost so many men, how can you hope to defend the city?' she asked faintly.

'Why should you care? Horsa has already killed my father. And here you are, ready to open the gates of Aquae Sulis and let your other brother in. I believe it's the only reason you have stayed in Aquae Sulis – to betray me. To betray us all.'

'No!' Anya exclaimed, aghast. 'I would never help Hengist take this city!'

'Why not? He is your brother after all, your blood, your kin.' Ronan was eyeing her thoughtfully. 'My father believed you had cursed him. He told everyone you were a witch.'

'I heal people. I don't curse them!'

But Ronan wasn't listening. 'Vortigern wanted you to burn. Perhaps I should grant him his last wish, because you are far too dangerous to be allowed to live.'

A shudder of fear flickered down Anya's spine. 'I saved your life, doesn't than mean anything to you? I want peace, not war - you have to believe me.'

'Your brothers are oath-breaking heathens. Give me one good reason why I should believe you?'

'Where were your Christian priests when I was risking my life to help the sick? They locked themselves in the basilica, too afraid to venture out. I care about your people, Ronan!'

But Ronan was closing his eyes. 'Go away,' he said dully. 'Let me rest.'

'No, listen to me!'

Ronan opened one eye, his expression resigned. 'I can't move from this bed, and you won't go away, so it seems I have no choice.'

'You've lost too many men. You can't hope to defend the city alone. Your only realistic option is to call for aid.'

'Is that your grand plan?' Ronan scoffed. 'I have already sent word to the Coritani, demanding they provide five hundred spears. But they say the plague has decimated their kingdom and they have none to send.'

'Do you believe them?'

'No, of course I don't. Aquila, their boy king, is building an army to march against me. Sons avenge their fathers. It is the way of the world.'

Their eyes met for a moment, and Anya knew he was

remembering the killing ground before the walls of Londinium. She willed herself to stay focussed.

'The kingdom of the Atrebates pays tribute to you. Have you sent word to them?'

'The cities of Venta and Calleva have mustered barely three hundred men between them - shopkeepers, not warriors. As for the villages - Vortigern took their farm boys, only for them to fall in the battle for Londinium. And I dare not take the garrisons. Cerdic has retreated to Heytesbury Head, but if he were to hear our cities were undefended -'

'Perhaps the Durotriges will come,' Anya went on resolutely, remembering the kingdom that stood like a shield wall between the Dobunni and Silvanus's kingdom.

'No, they won't. Vortigern has sucked them dry. If they were forced to choose, I suspect they would side with Hengist.' Ronan fell silent, his eyes darting back and forth, a sure sign he was thinking hard. 'Dumnonia!' he exclaimed. 'It's one of the few kingdoms my father didn't alienate. They say Etar's son has raised an army a thousand strong. They say he has transformed fishermen and farmers into warriors. He may be willing to send aid.'

'No!' Anya gasped, appalled. The idea was abhorrent. Unthinkable.

'Why not?'

'Because...' Her voice trailed away.

Because she could not bear to think of Silvanus upon a battlefield. Because she could not bear to imagine him in danger. She tried desperately to gather her wits. 'Because you'd be wasting your time. Why should Dumnonia come to the aid of the Dobunni?'

'They'd fight if they believed their own kingdom was in danger, which it would be, if Aquae Sulis fell.'

Anya's heart was gripped by ice. There was logic in Ronan's argument, for Rufus now sat at Hengist's side, whispering in his ear. Rufus may not have the strength to wield a sword, but he could be dangerous in countless other ways. He knew Aquae Sulis like the back of his hand, the culverts beneath the city walls, the weak points in its defences. And he knew all about Dumnonia, about the rich seams of copper and tin that had brought prosperity to Silvanus's kingdom since time began.

Anya sighed despairingly. She had returned to Vortigern for one reason only - to spare Dumnonia and its people from bloodshed and suffering. Had it all been for nothing?

She thought of her years in the sacred grove in Germania. How simple life had been then. In her childish innocence, she had heard the wind chimes murmur messages of harmony and balance and peace, but whispering wind chimes were no defence against an army of a thousand spears, and she had been naive to believe they ever could be. In times of great peril, the high priests had not been afraid to speak for war. They had understood that sometimes there was no other way.

She could feel a cold, pervasive sense of dread creeping across her skin. 'Are you certain Silvanus has raised an army?'

'Yes, I am certain of it. Old King Etar trusted in the ancient gods of the land to protect his kingdom, or some such pagan nonsense, but it seems his son has more sense.'

Anya nodded mutely. She knew Silvanus's small warband was fiercely loyal to him; she knew his warriors would die for him. She had no doubt the fishermen and farmers of his kingdom would also die for him, if he asked it of them. The thought tore her heart, but what choice did she have?

'Silvanus is a good man,' she said, her throat tightening with emotion. 'He won't stand by and watch a neighbour fall. I'll

284

ride to Dumnonia. I will act as emissary.'

'No, you won't!' Ronan exploded. 'I'm not putting the defence of my kingdom in the hands of a Saxon girl!'

'Why not? Your life has been in my hands for the last few weeks.'

'If I let you out of my sight, what's to stop you running back to your brother and betraying me?'

Anya let out an exasperated sigh. 'I hate my brother,' she said slowly, as she was talking to a small child. 'And he hates me.'

Ronan raised an eyebrow, sceptical.

'If I set foot in his camp, he will hang me, or drown me, or have me ripped apart by dogs.' Anya's voice was little more than a whisper.

Ronan's expression faltered. 'Savages,' he muttered.

'Silvanus gave me shelter for several months,' Anya continued. 'He knows me. He'll listen to what I have to say.'

'I bet he will,' Ronan interrupted nastily. 'Rufus once hinted that he suspected Silvanus took you to his bed.'

'Rufus knows much of taxes but nothing of affairs of the heart,' Anya replied, her casual tone masking her unease. 'I swear to you, by the sacred goddess, I will ask Silvanus to fight for you.'

Ronan stared at her for a long moment. Anya could almost see his mind working; measuring the odds, weighing the consequences, just as Vortigern had so often done.

'You can go to Dumnonia,' he said at last, casually, as if it meant nothing. 'But you will be accompanied by emissaries of my choice, and you will not leave until I'm fully healed.'

He sank back against the cushions and closed his eyes, as if the matter was resolved.

Anya's heart was pounding. 'You are out of danger and so I

will go now,' she said briskly. 'There is no time to lose.'

Ronan opened one eye. 'It would have been so much easier just to burn you. Now leave me alone for God's sake.'

Anya stood up shakily. Her life had come full circle. In all the long months she had been parted from Silvanus, he had never been far from her thoughts. She had thought of him in snatched, precious moments during a busy day or in the long, silent hours of the night when sleep eluded her. But in all that time, she had never once imagined she would return to Dumnonia to ask him to lead his people to war.

A chill easterly wind was racing across the forum, shepherding a flock of fallen leaves across the cracked flag stones. Anya shivered. She had been so preoccupied with healing Ronan, she had not noticed autumn settle upon Britannia. Ronan had risen from his bed to bid her farewell but the walk from his chamber had proved too much for him. He stood at the foot of the basilica steps, beads of sweat standing out on his forehead, his face pale and strained.

He had chosen ten warriors to accompany Anya, and their commander stepped forward to greet her. Tall and broad, he wore the close cropped hair style favoured by all Vortigern's men. It lent him the menacing appearance of a back street thug, but his tone was surprisingly measured and courteous.

'Lady Anya, I am Petilius Cerialis and it will be my honour to escort you to Dumnonia. May God grant us a safe journey.'

Anya merely smiled. The Christian god was favoured by Ronan's men, but it would be Lugh the sun god who watched over them during the daylight hours, and Luna, the virgin goddess of the moon, who kept them safe by night.

Petilius helped her mount up. Anya was not an accomplished horsewoman, and the mare, sensing her uncertainty, jittered and fretted. She had not ridden for several months, not since the battle before Londinium, not since Ronan had driven his sword into Horsa's heart. She felt grief begin to overwhelm her again, and she swallowed hard.

'Are you sure you can ride?' Ronan raised a querulous eyebrow.

Anya nodded curtly, shortening the reins and then a thought occurred to her. Kicking the mare's flanks, she guided the horse to the foot of the steps and said under her breath, so only Ronan could hear, 'swear to me you will not touch Maud while I am away.'

'Who is Maud for God's sake?' Ronan asked fractiously.

'The slave girl who helped me save your life.'

'Oh – her,' he said dismissively.

'Yes, her. And I mean it, Ronan.'

'You have no right to make demands upon me. You are nothing now. You are no longer a priestess, nor a princess of Saxony, nor the wife of the high king of the Dobunni.'

'I saved your life,' Anya replied coolly. 'And so I will ask one more thing from you before I leave.'

Ronan snorted dismissively, but Anya spoke over him.

'Vortigern gave Hengist land at Corinium in exchange for military service. I am told Hengist has created a thriving settlement there, a farming community, not a military fortress. You must swear you will not destroy the village. You must swear the Saxons are allowed to live in peace.'

'Why would I do that?'

'If for no other reason than because Elsbet, Horsa's betrothed, lived there for several months before she was taken as hostage by your father. Nothing you do can bring Elsbet back, but if you were to spare the village, it would be reparation of a kind.'

287

'You must be mad,' Ronan said scathingly. A trickle of sweat ran down his forehead. He quickly wiped it away, turned his back on her, and began to climb the steps.

'Please?' Anya called after him.

Ronan came to a halt. He stood motionless for a long time. At last, he turned around, his expression impenetrable.

'I will spare the village,' he said curtly. And then he glanced at Petilius.

'You know the urgency of the situation. Make haste. Ride hard.'

The journey to Dumnonia was difficult and uncomfortable. The wind buffeted and howled, stripping the leaves from the trees until the old Roman road was swathed with vivid russets and oranges, as if a Byzantine cloth of gold had been laid out before them. They passed no-one on the road. The countryside was seemingly deserted save for rooks perched in the trees, watching them with black, malevolent eyes.

Anya's emotions were in turmoil. At times she felt sheer joy at the thought of seeing Silvanus again. At other times she was filled with suffocating fear. As high king, the council would be pressing him to take a wife and provide an heir. What if another woman was sitting at his side in the great hall of Tintagel, lying in his arms at night, carrying his son in her belly? The thought of it made her feel angry, bereft.

More worrying still, her dreams of Dumnonia featured suffering and death, of the great hall smothered beneath rotting vines and malignant gore. She tried to tell herself they were nightmares, not premonitions, but the feeling of dread remained.

By night, Anya and her bodyguards took shelter in roadside settlements, offering ancient silver coins to strangers in exchange for a place at their fireside. Despite the unease in the villagers' eyes, no-one turned them away, perhaps in awe of the black boar upon the warriors' shields, or perhaps reassured by the bite of solid silver against their teeth. The country folk were hungry for news of the outside world, but Anya noticed Petilius's vague monosyllabic answers gave little away. She supposed there must be spies everywhere, lurking unnoticed, like cobwebs in the rafters.

They entered the forest of Selwood on the third day. It smelled of the earth, of leaf mould, mushrooms and pine. There were other baser scents too: stagnant water, the musty tang of badgers' lairs, the carcass of a deer taken down by wolves. The trees closed up, blocking out the sky and in the half-light, it was as if twilight had fallen. It had been cold on the open road but in the forest, it felt colder still and the damp air settled oppressively upon them. The horses' hooves were deadened by a thick layer of fallen leaves, the eerie silence broken only by the sound of raindrops falling from the skeletal branches overhead.

Anya could sense the warriors' unease. She had heard it said that Selwood filled even the bravest men with terror, for it was not unusual for men to enter there and never return. Even in summertime, it was a place full of dangers and evil spirits, of bears and wolves and outlaws. The soldiers rode in close formation and she felt comforted by their presence. She had not always been afraid of the forest. In Germania, the woods had been her medicine chest, a hunting ground for roots and plants. But that was before she had come to Britannia, before the Irish had charged from the tree line on the road to Aquae Sulis, slaughtered her guards and sent her running for her life.

By the third day they had left the forest behind, and by

289

midday on the fourth, they reached the borderlands of Dumnonia. Anya reined in, marvelling at the sweeping expanse of moorland, dusted with crisp frost, and relishing the sharp, salty tang of the sea. After the stinking overcrowded, streets of Aquae Sulis, she felt as if they had reached the top of the world.

They rode on, drawing steadily closer to the granite walls of Tintagel, looming dark against the pale blue sky. Remembering her dreams, Anya's chest tightened with trepidation. As they approached the gates, a guard on the parapet called down to them in the familiar, lilting tongue of the Dumnonii.

'Who are you, and what is your business?'

Anya flung back the hood of her cloak. She had learnt enough of the language of Dumnonia to reply, 'I am Anya. Do you remember me?'

She saw a flicker of recognition in the man's eyes. 'Yes, I remember you.'

'I must speak to Silvanus. Open the gates.'

She realised the guard was eyeing her warriors warily.

'These men are my bodyguards. I will vouch for them.'

'Wait there.' The guard hesitated for a moment longer, uncertain, before disappearing from view.

Anya gripped the mare's reins, struggling to appear composed but her mind was reeling with fear and dread. It seemed an age before the gates finally began to swing open. She kicked her heels and rode into the cobbled courtyard. Her warriors stayed close, scanning their surroundings, their hands on the grips of their swords.

To her enormous relief, Tintagel appeared unchanged. A market was huddled in the lee of the walls, its stalls buffeted by the ever-present wind. Women were hauling carts laden with freshly caught fish towards the kitchens. Somewhere in the distance she could hear the steady clash of a hammer striking an anvil, the sound of laughter, and children playing. High above her, gulls were circling, filling the air with their haunting cries.

Anya dismounted, waiting impatiently whilst her men disarmed and handed their weapons to Silvanus's guards. She noticed they bore the emblem of a red dragon upon their cuirasses. She did not remember seeing Silvanus's men in any kind of livery before.

'Lady, your sword?'

The guard held out his hand expectantly, but Anya's fingers tightened about the pommel. She had made Ceinwin a promise and she knew she could not let the sword out of her sight again.

Looking the guard squarely in the eyes, she said, 'the sword stays with me.'

He appeared taken aback but then to her amazement, he lowered his gaze in acquiescence.

Gesturing for her bodyguards to follow, Anya walked towards the great hall. Her stomach was in knots. She had ridden away from Dumnonia more than a little in love with Silvanus and in the long months they had been apart, he had never been far from her thoughts. But how would she feel when she saw him again? Had any of it been real, or had she merely imagined her love for him, to ease the long, dark hours before dawn?

TWENTY SEVEN

The doors of the hall were open. Tense with anticipation, her heart beating out a frantic rhythm, Anya stepped inside. There were no rotting vines, or decayed corpses. All was as she remembered it: the soaring roof posts, intricately carved with tiny horses, racing in spirals towards the rafters. The walls adorned with sumptuous Byzantine tapestries in the rich colours of autumn. Hounds asleep by the hearth. The warm, sweet scent of lavender in the rushes, the rich aroma of a meat stew.

Silvanus and Evric were seated side by side at the long table, talking earnestly to one another. They turned in unison and she saw their conversation die on their lips. Silvanus was on his feet in an instant, staring at her as if he was seeing a ghost.

And Anya stared back at him, mesmerised. She felt like a mariner, catching sight of uncharted land after many months at sea. The great hall faded around her, the sights, the sounds, the scents. Silvanus however, remained vividly in focus and she stood, transfixed, drinking him in.

As the long months had passed, her memories of him had become idealised, made of flimsy hopes and dreams. It was almost impossible to comprehend that he was standing before her now, real flesh and blood. She had forgotten quite how breathtakingly handsome he was.

For a long moment, no-one spoke and then Silvanus, as if suddenly remembering what was expected of him, hurried towards her. She found herself revelling in the intensity of his gaze. It felt like a caress.

'We were not expecting you.'

Too late, she realised his arms were outstretched in greeting. When she did not respond, he quickly lowered them again, his face full of confusion. Flustered, Anya hurriedly reached out for him, but the moment had passed and they stood in awkward silence, still staring at one another, unable to look away.

Anya heard a clatter of wood across stone. Evric had left his chair and was striding towards them.

'No doubt you and Anya have matters of state to discuss, lord. Perhaps you would be more comfortable in the small council chamber, whilst I offer hospitality to Anya's men here in the hall?'

Anya read the brief look that passed between them. Compassion on Evric's part, gratitude on Silvanus's.

Petilius was at Anya's side in an instant. 'I will accompany you, my lady.'

'Thank you, but that won't necessary.'

Petilius frowned, uncertain, but Anya's expression brooked no argument.

'As you wish, my lady.'

Somewhat belatedly, Silvanus gathered his wits.

'Welcome to Tintagel, gentlemen. Please, sit down, make yourselves comfortable. Evric will see you are well looked after.'

And then, putting a hand lightly on the small of Anya's

back, Silvanus began to guide her across the hall. Despite the thickness of her cloak, she was aware of his touch, a thousand tiny shivers skimming across her skin.

'Come, gentlemen,' Evric said brightly. 'You must be hungry and thirsty after your long journey. We have a cellar of Frankia's finest wines. I wager my sword you will not be disappointed!'

'Very well,' Petilius replied, casting a final uneasy glance at Anya's departing back.

Silvanus led Anya to the council chamber and closed the doors behind them. She looked about. The room was cold and uninviting. The only furniture was a long, oak table surrounded by twelve, tall, straight-backed chairs. A faint trace of beeswax polish lingered in the icy air. The high windows were paned with opaque glass which cast a greenish tinge across the plain, white-washed walls.

Anya was aware of Silvanus's eyes upon her but, for some inexplicable reason, she felt shy. What was the matter with her? She had known Silvanus forever, through all the ages of men. Her memories of those different lifetimes had blurred by the passing of the centuries, but nevertheless, they were a part of her. Then, they had been lovers. But in this life, she had known him for just one, brief summer. They had talked and laughed and she had fallen in love, but she had not gone to his bed.

'Are you well, Anya?' Silvanus asked gently, breaking the silence. His voice sounded like an echo in the unadorned room.

'Yes, thank you.' She realised her voice sounded cold, stilted.

'I was sorry to learn you lost your husband.'

The mention of Vortigern touched a raw nerve and she felt

herself tense. 'I do not mourn for him,' she replied, her expression closed, guarded.

She saw Silvanus frown. She could sense his frustration and his unease, but she didn't know what else to say. How could she begin to find the words to tell him about Vortigern, about all the suffering he had caused?

'When I heard of Vortigern's death, I hoped you might return to us. Why did you wait so long?'

His expression was vulnerable, like a wounded animal, and Anya felt deeply ashamed.

'There were things I had to do,' she replied lamely.

'I see.'

It tore her apart to see the hurt in his eyes. She ached to tell him he had never been far from her thoughts. But if he had taken a wife, she had no right to say such things. Did his heart belong to another now? She longed to know the answer, but she couldn't bring herself to ask the question. Strong, painful emotions were firmly trapped inside her heart. If they were to escape, she was very afraid she would never be able to bottle them up again.

Silvanus stepped away from her, and she hated the sudden distance between them. She badly wanted to pull him into her arms.

'I'm forgetting my manners. You must be tired and hungry after your long journey,' he said, his tone polite, distant.

Anya nodded mutely, stung by his impeccable formality. She watched him open the door and call for a serving girl to bring food and drink. She had forgotten how languidly he moved. He was at ease in his own body, the unmistakeable mark of a warrior. She wondered if he was no longer tortured by self-doubt, if the day-to-day duties and responsibilities of kingship rested more easily on his shoulders now.

He gestured towards the table, and they sat down together, side by side. He was smiling at her, and shyly, she returned his smile. She caught the familiar scent of him: horses, leather and sandalwood and something else, something indefinable, his own unique scent. He leant towards her a fraction and, unconsciously, she mirrored him.

There was a knock on the door. They both jumped, and quickly moved apart. A serving girl came in, carrying a tray bearing slices of bread and beef, a large slab of cheese and a jug of wine. She placed it on the table then quickly left again.

Anya did not touch the food. She was too on edge to eat, too distracted by Silvanus. He was so close, so intoxicatingly close. Instead, she took a sip of Lucius's wine. It was rich and smooth, tasting of far-away hillsides baking beneath a hot sun.

'I heard you ran away from Vortigern,' Silvanus said. 'But I had no way of knowing if it was true.'

'It was true. I went to Siluria, to the home of my mother's kin.'

Silvanus raised his eyebrows in astonishment. 'You travelled alone?'

Anya nodded, remembering the deep snow, the bitter cold, the terrible feeling of isolation.

'It was a difficult time,' she said quietly.

Silvanus laughed. 'You always were the master of understatement!'

She returned his smile and looked into his eyes, those gentle, familiar eyes, and she felt her pulse quicken.

'I found my grandfather,' she said hastily. 'He's a sheep farmer. In the winter, my kin struggle to survive. They have so little, but they made me welcome, shared what little they had. They are such warm, generous people. They know who they are, and how they came to be.'

'You sound as if you envy them.'

'I do.'

'Why? Their blood flows in your veins. You are one of them.'

'I hoped I might be one of them. I turned their quern stones, and I healed their sick but in my heart, I knew I wasn't meant to stay there forever. But you - you know where you belong. Your roots are here, in the soil of Dumnonia. I envy you that certainty.'

'There are days when it feels like a blessing, and days when it feels like a curse,' Silvanus said dourly, staring at the brightly polished table top. 'I don't mean to sound ungrateful. It's just you -' he was struggling to find the right words. 'You are one of the few people I can be myself with, one of the few people I can be entirely honest with -' he broke off, embarrassed.

Anya was lost for words. Did he have any right to say such things to her? She wanted to ask if he was a married man but the question refused to form on her lips. Instead she said, 'I'm sorry your father has passed through the veil.'

Silvanus nodded, his expression shadowed with sadness.

'There's not a day goes by when I don't miss him.'

'And now you are king.'

'And now I am king,' he repeated flatly.

'Is it as bad as you feared?'

'Worse!' A hint of a smile played at the corners of his mouth.

Anya grinned. She could feel the stilted formality between them beginning to crumble at last.

Silvanus let out a deep sigh. 'I have an army now, cavalry and foot-soldiers, but it's sorely untried and untested. We drive the Irish raiders back to the sea, but against a Saxon horde?' He shrugged his shoulders, his eyes troubled. 'I don't know. Etar always said the goddess would protect us and I can only pray he was right.'

Anya's brief sense of wellbeing vanished. She knew full well Silvanus's novice soldiers would be lambs to the slaughter against the might of Hengist's army.

'Lucan is dead,' Silvanus said, his voice monotone. 'The council found him guilty of treason. He was thrown from the cliffs at dawn.' Deeply ashamed, he stared at the table top, unable to bring himself to look at her.

'He was your brother, your kin, and so I am sorry,' Anya replied, but in her mind's eye she could see Tristan's tiny body falling, hitting the beach far below like a splayed starfish. Lucan was a child murderer. He deserved to die, and his punishment was a suitably fitting end.

Silvanus sighed deeply again then pointedly changed the subject. 'What happened in Siluria? Jago said you were taken prisoner?'

But Anya was still thinking about Lucan. She was remembering her dream. Tintagel's great hall filled with rotting corpses. Mairi holding a child aloft, proclaiming the prophecy of Epona.

'Anya? Are you unwell?'

She shook her head, pushing the image of Mairi from her mind. 'I was taken by slavers. Tewdric's men,' she replied dully.

'By all the gods!' Silvanus exclaimed. 'Did they mistreat you? Did they hurt you?'

Anya hesitated. Part of her didn't want to talk about it, didn't want to remember the terrible sense of helplessness, humiliation and despair. But Silvanus's expression was so full of compassion that she found herself telling him of the neck rings that had linked her kin in a pitiful human chain. And the pit with sharp stakes beneath the high palisades, and the infected wound that had almost killed her. She was about to tell him of Ronan and Horsa, circling each other in a field of stubble, how heavy Horsa had felt lying in her arms as his life blood pulsed into the earth, but suddenly, Silvanus clasped her hands in his.

His touch was so unexpected she immediately lost her train of thought. The question slid from her lips, and lay, naked and exposed, between them:

'Have you taken a wife?'

'No, of course not!'

'Why not?' she breathed, deliciously aware of his warm hands encasing her cold fingers.

'Do you really need to ask that question?' That hint of a smile was playing at the corners of his mouth again.

Quite suddenly, Anya felt as if a huge weight had been lifted from her shoulders, her heart as light and shiny as a soap bubble. 'I've missed you so much,' she whispered.

'I've missed you too. More than you'll ever know. When you didn't come back, I thought... I couldn't bear it...' He was visibly struggling to control his emotions. 'But you're here now, and I'll never let you go again.' He planted a tender kiss upon her cheek, his lips warm and soft against her skin.

Their need for each other flared and ignited. They stood up in unison, and fell into each other's arms. Anya ran her fingers through his hair, down the nape of his neck, across his broad shoulders. She had waited so long to be in his embrace again. His kisses were trailing across her jawline and then his lips found hers, tentative and achingly gentle at first but then, as if sensing her need, more urgent. And she clung to him, revelling in his touch, his scent. No longer aware of her surroundings, she saw only him, felt only him. She was utterly lost and hoping never to be found, the sensation of his body pressed against hers driving all rational thought from her mind.

And so she forgot all about her promise to Ronan, forgot Hengist's army mustering in Londinium and forgot the defenceless citizens of Aquae Sulis.

It was a long time before either Silvanus or Anya became aware someone was knocking on the door but, even then, they both chose to ignore it. Eventually the knocking became so persistent that, with the greatest of reluctance, they drew apart.

Silvanus's breathing was erratic. Anya's entire body felt exquisitely sensitive, as if a thousand feathers were skimming across her skin. Although she was no longer touching Silvanus, she still felt bound to him, fettered like Fenrir the wolf until the end of time.

'Who is it?' Silvanus asked, not taking his eyes from her.

'Evric, lord.'

'Can it wait?'

But Evric had already opened the door a fraction and peered inside.

'The evening meal is served, lord.'

Embarrassed, Anya made a furtive attempt to tidy her hair and straighten her gown.

Under his breath, Evric added, 'I thought perhaps you might need to come up for air?'

'Cheeky bastard,' Silvanus grinned.

Anya heard Evric chuckle as he closed the door again. She realised she felt happy, and she had not felt happy for such a long time. It was a strange, unfamiliar feeling, a glorious, light-as-air sensation.

'Are you hungry?' Silvanus took her hand, turned it over

and kissed her palm. The touch of his lips sent a quiver of pleasure down her spine.

'Yes, I suppose so,' she said reluctantly. She did not want to leave this small, cold chamber. She did not want to face the world ever again.

Silvanus let go of her hand and together they walked out into the great hall. The benches at the long table were crowded with people now, but the hum of laughter and conversation died away instantly as many pairs of curious eyes turned in their direction.

'I'm sure you all remember Anya,' Silvanus said warmly. 'She will be dining with us tonight.'

They sat down side by side but Anya shifted in her seat, uncomfortable in the face of such intense scrutiny. When she had first come to Dumnonia, many had seen her as the enemy, the Saxon spy in their midst. Did they still feel the same way now? As if sensing her discomfort, Silvanus's fingers entwined with hers beneath the table, like a love knot made of flesh.

Collectively remembering their manners, Silvanus's guests quickly picked up where they had left off and within moments, the hall was filled with the hubbub of conversation once again.

Anya took a cup of wine and looked about the hall. It was all as she remembered it. Unlike Germania, there was no high table. Silvanus still sat amongst his people, sharing their bread and meat.

And yet, despite the lack of ceremony, Tintagel still exuded the same air of wealth and luxury. Firelight danced upon the gold thread in the fine tapestries and silk cushions. The table was dressed with gold rimmed drinking cups, delicate glassware and embossed silver platters. But for all the luxury,

301

this was also Silvanus's home. His hounds were asleep by the hearth, his cloak thrown carelessly across a nearby stool, rolls of parchments strewn across a side table.

Anya smiled to herself. As the months had passed, she had begun to doubt she would ever see Dumnonia again. And yet, the wheel had come full circle. The goddess had led her back to Silvanus's hall, but why? For what purpose? Was it to grow old at Silvanus's side, for wasn't that what she wanted, more than anything else in the world?

Or was it to ask him to lead his men to war, to risk their lives in a conflict not of their making? Anya pushed her dark thoughts aside, and took a mouthful of pork. It tasted delicious and she realised she could not remember the last time she had eaten. She glanced about again. There were so many familiar faces at the table. Her bodyguards, relaxed now, oiled with good food and wine. Silvanus's brothers in arms, Evric, Gorran, Boult and Jago, full of banter and good humour.

But Lucan was not amongst them, nor was Mairi.

Anya turned to Silvanus. 'Mairi was with child when I left. Was she safely delivered?'

'Yes. A boy, given the name of Mordred. Mairi is under house arrest. The babe with her.' Silvanus lowered his voice. 'Taliesin would have me put them to death. He says they are too dangerous to be allowed to live.'

'He's right,' Anya said before she could stop herself.

'You would have me murder a woman and a child?' Silvanus asked, stunned. 'The babe is my kin.'

'Forgive me, I spoke out of turn,' she said quickly.

'No, you said it for a reason. Tell me, what have you seen in your dream paths?'

In her mind's eye, Anya could see her dream all too clearly.

Mairi surrounded by corpses, holding the child aloft, her voice magnified as she recited the prophecy. 'And he will bring new life and new hope to a new golden age.'

'Anya?' Silvanus asked sharply. 'What is it? What have you seen?'

She hesitated, torn with indecision. Mairi had poisoned Etar, slowly, with calculated precision, and she had done nothing to prevent her husband murdering the young kitchen boy. Mairi was without doubt, an evil, dangerous woman. And yet how could she condemn her for an atrocity she had yet to commit, for an atrocity she might never commit? Where was the justice in that?

'Where's Taliesin?' she asked, changing the subject.

'Anya?' Silvanus stared hard at her, but Anya simply stared back. Eventually, he raised his hands in a gesture of frustration and defeat. 'The years are taking their toll on Taliesin. He prefers his own fireside these days.'

'I should very much like to see him.'

'And he would very much like to see you.'

'And Breg? Where is he?' she asked, remembering Silvanus's favourite hound.

'Over there, by the fireside. But I should warn you - if you thought he smelled bad a year ago...'

Anya giggled.

'I've missed your laugh,' Silvanus whispered.

'Anya!' Jago called down the table. 'It's good to have you with us again.' His wife Eloise was at his side, heavy with child.

Anya smiled warmly. 'Congratulations to you both.'

Jago and Eloise beamed adoringly at one another.

'I want a wife,' Boult complained miserably, his mouth stuffed full of pork.

'You should try eating less, you fat bastard,' Gorran grinned. 'What woman in her right mind would want to spend the rest of her days keeping you fed and watered?'

'I'm not fat. This is pure muscle!' Boult snorted indignantly, patting his belly with one hand whilst stuffing two more slices of pork into his mouth with the other. 'I have a healthy appetite, and there's nothing wrong with that.'

Evric rolled his eyes, as if he had heard all this before, and then his expression became serious. 'What news from the world beyond our borders, Anya?'

'Er…' Anya stalled.

Where to begin? In her mind's eye she could see Hengist building a great army, preparing to march on Aquae Sulis, preparing to seek vengeance for Horsa's death. And she could see Ronan, the man who had slaughtered her beloved brother. The man she had, inexplicably, decided to nurse back to health.

And then she remembered the oath she had made to Ronan and the army she had promised him. She bit her lip despairingly. She loved Silvanus. She had always loved him. Every choice she had made since coming to Britannia had been to protect him and keep him safe. So how could she ask him to lead his people to war?

'Forgive me,' she said. 'I find it difficult. I lost my brother…'

Evric was mortified. 'No, no. It is I who must apologise for being so tactless.'

And the conversation moved on, quickly and kindly. Anya sank back in her chair. Silvanus was watching her, his expression baffled and concerned in equal measure, and she felt a sharp pang of guilt. There was so much she wanted to tell him, but not here. Not with so many prying eyes.

Perhaps sensing her anguish, Silvanus squeezed her hand beneath the table.

'You must be weary. Would you like to rest now?'

She nodded gratefully. 'Thank you, yes. It's been a long day.'

Silvanus stood up. 'I will show Anya to her room.'

Petilius was on his feet in an instant and Anya realised Ronan had been right to trust him. Despite the lure of Lucius's fine wine, he was still sober enough to be mindful of his duty.

'I am safe here,' she mouthed and Petilius sat down again.

'I wonder what your people think of me,' Anya asked as Silvanus led her out of the hall. 'The last time I was here, half of them believed I was a goddess, but the rest believed I was a spy or a witch, or both.'

Silvanus grimaced. Lucan had done his best to turn the people of Tintagel against Anya. An image of his brother falling to his death flashed unbidden into his head. He had not asked which man had physically thrown his brother from the cliff-top, because he did not want to know. He felt a sudden stab of anguish, so acute he drew a sharp intake of breath.

'My people love you, just as I love you,' he said quietly. 'They haven't forgotten how you worked alongside Taliesin. They haven't forgotten all the babies you held up to the light, and all the lives you saved.' He paused for a moment. 'Taliesin is so frail. He needs you. He'll be delighted you're back.'

Anya felt herself tense. Silvanus was expecting her to remain in Dumnonia. And she wanted to stay here, more than she had ever wanted anything in her life. She wanted to lie beside Silvanus each night and work alongside Taliesin each day. But could she turn her back on the people of Aquae Sulis? Could she abandon them to their fate?

Silvanus took her hand and led her up the watchtower stairs, towards her old room. With bare walls and no fire in the hearth, Anya remembered it had always been bitterly cold.

'I've asked for a fire to be lit,' he said, as if reading her thoughts.

Anya felt a sudden, intense pang of disappointment. In the long months they had been apart, she had often dreamed of being with Silvanus again, but none of her dreams had featured spending the night alone in the cold watchtower room. She glanced shyly at him. They had been lovers once, many lifetimes ago. Perhaps in those distant times she would have known how to make him understand her need for him, but in this life, she felt inexperienced and painfully awkward.

They had reached the small landing.

'I will bid you goodnight. Unless,' Silvanus's voice was infinitely gentle.

Their eyes met and held. 'Yes?' she asked, hopefully.

'Unless you...' his voice trailed away, his expression hesitant.

She opened her mouth then closed it again, her courage failing her.

'Of course,' Silvanus said quickly. 'Goodnight.'

He released her hand and turned around.

'I don't want to be alone tonight,' she whispered.

He turned to face her again. His eyes were molten.

'I don't either.'

He reached out and touched her cheek. His fingertips against her skin felt like a spark from a flint, so intense it made her gasp. Clasping her hand, Silvanus turned on his heel and led her back down the stairs. He took her along a series of cold, dark passageways lit only by guttering torches until they came at last to an ornately carved, oak door. Opening it, he stood aside to let her pass. 'My room. If I'd known, I would have tidied.' He sounded apologetic.

Anya had waited so long for this moment that her entire body was trembling with nervous anticipation. She looked about. His chamber was lit by a fiercely burning fire and several tiny oil lamps suffused with the scent of citrus, cinnamon and cloves. A huge bed dominated the room, its oak bedhead carved with intertwining vines and foliage. The walls were lined with identical oak panelling and adorned with tapestries.

A small table stood against the far wall. Upon it, sat a portrait of a lady with kind eyes, surrounded by a scatter of furled parchments, coins, knives, daggers and scabbards. A heap of breeches, shirts and tunics were piled upon a chair. There were so many personal belongings, she felt as if she was intruding.

Silvanus put a hand lightly on her shoulders and turned her around to face him.

'You are so beautiful,' he murmured.

Bending his head, he kissed her tenderly. She closed her eyes. Delicious tremors were flickering across her skin and she felt as if her very bones were melting.

'Come to bed,' he whispered in her ear.

He drew away fractionally, searching her eyes for her answer. She nodded, breathless, her heart beating out a frantic rhythm. But then her gaze fell upon Silvanus's bed, and she tensed.

'What's the matter? Are you alright?' he asked anxiously.

She couldn't look at him. She loved him so much, and she wanted him so much, but memories of her wedding night were invading her head and no matter how hard she tried, she couldn't hold them back.

'I have to tell you something.' Her voice wobbled as she spoke.

'Yes?' Silvanus asked warily.

She stared fixedly at the floor. How could she tell him she was very afraid she might run screaming from his bed, tormented by painful memories she could not control?

'I've never... I'm...'

'What are you trying to tell me?' Silvanus asked gently.

And still she could not look at him.

'I'm a virgin,' she whispered. It was the truth. There was more to tell, much more, but she couldn't find the words.

Silvanus looked dumbfounded. He did not ask how it was possible she had never lain with her husband. Instead, he took a step away from her, utterly mortified.

'By all the gods, I've behaved like an ignorant savage. I'm so sorry!'

'No! I - what do you mean?' Anya stammered in confusion.

Silvanus was full of remorse. 'You're a priestess, promised to the goddess. I should have realised. I'm so sorry. Can you ever forgive me?'

His words were like a balm upon a raw wound. She looked up, into his kind, gentle eyes. Silvanus was a good man, an honourable man. And she knew then, with absolute certainty, there was no need to be afraid, and all would be well.

'There's nothing to forgive,' she whispered. 'That's not what I meant. I just wanted you to know that you are the first.' She framed his face with her hands. And as she looked at him, the memories of her wedding night, all the humiliation and fear and pain, simply faded away.

'I love you,' she whispered.

'And I love you.' Fierce emotions burned in Silvanus's eyes. 'But what about your oath to your goddess?'

'I am at peace with my goddess.'

But then, to her intense disappointment, Silvanus stepped back a pace.

Anya's hands fell to her sides. They felt empty, achingly empty, without him.

'Are you quite sure this is what you want?' he asked hesitantly.

'I want you,' she said. 'I have always wanted you.'

Down the ages, through the constantly rolling years, lifetime upon lifetime, there had been no other.

Silvanus nodded mutely. He pulled her into his arms again, holding her tightly, as if afraid he might lose her all over again. His kisses were feather light upon her lips, her throat, her collarbone and this time, when he whispered, 'come to bed', she did not hesitate.

TWENTY EIGHT

Much later, Anya lay beneath the rugs of Silvanus's bed, her body entwined with his, drifting in a haze of warm contentment. Resting her head on his chest, she listened to his strong, steady heartbeat.

'Was I... did I hurt you?' he asked tentatively, his voice full of concern.

'It was perfect. You are perfect,' she replied.

'You have too high an opinion of me.'

'No, I truly don't. If you had seen...' but her voice trailed away.

She felt his body tense. 'What? Seen what?'

'Nothing.'

'Tell me,' he persisted, and there was an edge to his tone now.

Anya sighed. 'I left Germania as an innocent child. I didn't understand the ways of the world.'

'And now you do?'

'I'm beginning to, yes.' She said nothing further. She was too warm, too safe and too contented to talk of betrayal, war and death.

As if sensing her reluctance, Silvanus kissed the top of her head and changed the subject. 'Are you hungry?'

'Not really.' She had no idea what time it was but strips of daylight were visible between the shutters at the window. She didn't want to leave the warmth of the bed and the comfort of his embrace, although her empty stomach was rumbling loudly. 'But perhaps we should get up, before Evric begins to wonder where you are,' she conceded reluctantly.

'I think Evric has a pretty good idea where I am,' Silvanus laughed.

He kissed her again then extricated himself from her arms. Flinging back the rugs, he stepped naked from the bed. Anya watched him as he strode about the room, retrieving his abandoned clothes from the floor. Aware of her appreciative gaze, he picked up a cushion and launched it at her.

'Come on,' he said, grinning broadly. 'I'm starving. Let's find some food.'

They went to the kitchens for bread and cheese and carried their simple meal down to the beach. He took her hand as they descended the steep cliff path, for recent rain had rendered it slippery underfoot. Anya jumped the last few feet, her boots sinking into the soft, wet sand. The beach beneath the fortress was just as she remembered it, a wide expanse of sand that stretched for miles, protected by the high cliffs of Tintagel. It was deserted, save for fishing boats with their nets cast wide beyond the breaking waves.

She turned full circle, entranced. She could taste the sea on her tongue; salt and fish and seaweed. The retreating ebb and flow of the tide had carved the beach into wave after wave of soft ridges, as if serpents writhed beneath the sand. Black rocks, shiny with seaweed, sat like a colony of seals turned to stone, each one surrounded by a rock pool, a bustling ocean in miniature. Every now and then, the weak October sun slipped from behind a cloud, and the sea danced and sparkled with

311

light. Anya turned her face to its welcome warmth. 'Tintagel is so beautiful. You are so blessed this is your home.'

'It can be your home now too.'

His words were like a shard of reality piercing her dreamlike state. She yearned to stay in Tintagel but her mind was filled with images of the people of Aquae Sulis, living side by side in the overcrowded, stinking city, and dying side by side from starvation and disease.

'What's the matter?' Silvanus asked apprehensively.

She did not reply immediately. Instead, she took his hand and led him to the flat topped rock she remembered from her previous visits to this beach. Crouching down, she found his initials, and Evric's, carved into the stone.

'Your rock, if I remember rightly?' she asked, looking up at him.

'I'll share it with you,' he smiled although there was anxiety in his eyes.

They sat down together, and Anya began at the beginning. She told him of Vortigern's attempted rape, how he had failed to consummate their marriage, how she had fled to Siluria. She told him of Rhys lost to the slave traders, and of Elsbet, her body lying in an unmarked plague pit. And then, finally, she spoke of Ronan. 'He led a warband to Tewdric's stronghold. I would have died but for him. But then, he killed Horsa,' her voice was trembling now. 'I held my brother in my arms, and I watched him die.'

Silvanus clasped her hands in his, squeezed them tightly.

'I'm so sorry, Anya.'

'Nerthus, my goddess, wants something from me, but I cannot see the path she would have me take.' Anya's voice was as faint as an echo.

'No doubt you will do her bidding, when the time is right,'

Silvanus said reassuringly but his expression was tormented. 'This is all my fault. I should never have let you go back to Vortigern. I should have kept you safe.'

'It was Etar's decision to send me back to Vortigern, not yours,' Anya replied. 'He was your father, your king. You had no choice but to accept his decision. But ultimately, the gods decide our fates. We are as flimsy as chaff in their hands.'

Silvanus put an arm around her shoulders. 'Well, I thank the gods you're safe now. I swear as long as I have breath left in my body, no-one will ever hurt you again.'

Anya stiffened. She felt as if something cold and heavy had fallen into the pit of her stomach. Now was the time to tell him of the oath she had made to Ronan, but she could not find the words. Silvanus was watching her intently, his expression wary. For a long moment, neither of them spoke. Finally, he gestured to the sword and scabbard at her belt.

'You never used to carry a sword.' His jovial tone sounded strangely forced. 'It looks very old. Where did you get it?'

Her fingers tightened possessively around the hilt. 'Siluria. I told you, my kin are descended from ancient kings.' She knew she sounded defensive, but she couldn't help it.

Silvanus looked mystified. He waited a moment before continuing in the same cheerful tone. 'Taliesin will be so pleased to see you again. He has finally taken an apprentice, but he doesn't have a good word to say about the boy.'

Anya stared fixedly at the sand and did not reply. Silvanus's expression darkened and, finally, his patience ran out.

'Anya, please tell me whatever it is you've been afraid to tell me from the moment you walked into the great hall.'

She let out a groan, and put her head in her hands. There were two roads before her. One led to Silvanus, to a home, a hearth, and family. The other led to war. Her thoughts were

313

spinning. A thousand images flashed behind her eyes, but one persistently rose to the surface: the pale, hungry children of Aquae Sulis scavenging for food amongst the rubbish heaps. She lowered her hands and looked up at him.

'Hengist has gathered a huge army. He has men from the northern tribes, and the Catuvellauni, and reinforcements from Saxony. He intends to march on Aquae Sulis.'

Silvanus was frowning and for a moment her resolve wavered. She took a deep breath before continuing. 'The army of the Dobunni has been virtually wiped out in the last few months, firstly at Venta, and then at Londinium. We'll be hugely outnumbered.'

'We?' Silvanus repeated questioningly.

Anya dug her fingernails into her palms and willed herself to go on.

'Hengist is driven by his ambition and a thirst for power. He won't stop until he's high king of all Britannia. We can't allow that to happen.'

'When you say 'we', are you referring to Ronan and yourself?' Silvanus's expression was thunderous now.

Anya looked into his eyes and felt suddenly ashamed. He was jealous. How could she have been so selfish, so naïve, not to realise that? 'Ronan killed my brother, and I can never forgive him for it. He means nothing to me,' she said emphatically. 'But nor will I leave him and his people to die.'

Silvanus's mouth fell open and he stared at her, stunned.

'So this is why you didn't return to Dumnonia?'

'Vortigern brutally suppressed his client-kingdoms. He turned them against him, and Britannia is sinking into civil war,' she went on breathlessly. 'The tribes fight against each other, when they should be uniting against my brother.'

'I thought Vortigern gave your brothers a generous gift of

land? Isn't that enough for them?' Silvanus sounded confused, bewildered.

'It would have been enough for Horsa. All he ever wanted was Elsbet, to grow old at her side. But Hengist is cut from very different cloth. In his eyes, our father shamed him by sending him away to serve as a common mercenary. Hengist won't rest until he has more land and more wealth and more power than our father has ever dreamed of.'

'I'm ambitious too, Anya, but for my kingdom, my people. I want good harvests. I want the seas to teem with herrings. I want to keep our trade routes open, so I don't have to tax my people until they bleed.' Silvanus paused, as if a thought had suddenly occurred to him.

'You're going back to Aquae Sulis, aren't you?'

Anya felt as if she was no longer secure upon the rock but drifting away into deep waters. 'Vortigern was a fool. He made enemies, not allies. There's no one Ronan can turn to. He's utterly alone.'

Dismay spread across Silvanus's face. 'You didn't answer my question.'

'Yes, I'm going back to Aquae Sulis - with, or without you.'

Hurt bloomed in his eyes. 'Why? The Silures are your people. The Saxons are your people. But the Dobunni are nothing to you, nothing at all.'

'That's true, but they are good people,' she said helplessly. 'And they have suffered so much already.'

She watched realisation dawn in his eyes.

'You're asking me to raise an army to defend them,' he said incredulously. 'That is what you're asking me, isn't it?'

Anya couldn't look at him. She felt wretched, and racked with guilt. This was all wrong, so terribly, terribly wrong.

'You're asking me to fight against Hengist, your brother,

your own flesh and blood, your kin?' Silvanus sounded angry now.

Anya let out a cry of anguish.

'I'm an exile. I don't belong anywhere now! Not in Germania. Not in Siluria. I probably don't even belong on this god-forsaken island at all. But I do know that I can't stand by and watch Hengist destroy it. I will not believe, I cannot believe, that he's meant to have dominion over Britannia. He is not a moral man. There has to be another way, a better way.'

Silvanus was staring into her eyes, as if he was looking for something, as if he was willing it to be there.

'I had hoped you belonged in Dumnonia,' he said at last, his voice hollow.

'I should like to,' she replied. 'More than you will ever know.'

She felt as if her heart was about to break open and drown her in misery. She wanted to stay in Dumnonia, more than she had ever wanted anything in her life. She wanted to stay with him, bear his children and grow old at his side.

The muscles at Silvanus's jaw line were working furiously.

'You're asking a great deal of me.'

'I'm asking too much of you, far, far too much. But wouldn't it be better to ride out and meet Hengist from a position of strength, rather than wait for him to rape your women and burn your villages, and steal your crops?'

'You've changed,' he said soberly.

'Yes, I have. Like I said before, I think I'm finally beginning to understand how the world works.'

A tear trickled down her cold cheek.

Silvanus watched its progress for a moment then swept it away with his thumb. He pulled her close again, holding her tightly. She rested her cheek against his cloak, revelling in the warmth of him, the scent of him. They stayed like that for a long time. Eventually he put a finger beneath her chin and tipped her face to his.

'I can't do it, Anya. I can't ask it of my people.'

Anya realised she had been holding her breath. There. He had said it, just as she had always secretly hoped he would.

'I understand,' she whispered.

'I'm proud of the army I've built.' His tone was measured, controlled. 'The men of Dumnonia will fight, and die if necessary, to protect their kingdom. But I can't ask them to die for someone else's kingdom.'

'I understand,' she repeated, but in her mind's eye, she could see Hengist's army marching across the moors of Dumnonia, the banner of the white wolf flying high against a cold, blue sky. She knew with absolute certainty Hengist would come, just as she knew he would burn and rape and kill. Silvanus was only delaying the inevitable, and by a few months at most.

'I love you,' she said softly. 'I will always love you.'

'And I love you. Without you, I am nothing.'

She saw the frustration and the anguish in his eyes, the internal battle still raging.

'It's alright,' she whispered, her tears falling freely now. 'It's alright.'

She put her hands to his face, kissed him tenderly, and then she stood up. Away from Silvanus's sheltering warmth, the wind felt bitterly cold. 'I'm going to see Taliesin now.'

He nodded, his jaw clenched with suppressed emotion. 'I'll come with you. The path is treacherous.' He got to his feet wearily, as if shouldering a heavy burden. 'Forgive me, Anya.'

'There is nothing to forgive,' she replied.

317

They walked across the beach and up the cliff path in silence. Occasionally, when her feet threatened to go from under her, he steadied her with a hand at her elbow, but she was aware of a distance between them now, as if someone was wrenching hard on Fenrir's chains.

'Shall I go with you?' Silvanus asked as they reached the top of the cliff.

His tone was polite, but its bleakness made her want to weep all over again. 'I'll go alone. Taliesin and I will have much to talk about.'

'As you wish.'

And so they parted. Silvanus turned towards the great hall and she took the cliff top path towards Taliesin's home. After a dozen or so steps, she stopped and looked over her shoulder. He too had turned. He was gazing at her and his expression was immeasurably sad. She raised a hand in farewell. He mirrored her gesture then turned and walked away.

Taliesin's turf-walled hut stood within the walls of Tintagel, surrounded by herbs and medicinal plants. Last summer, Anya had spent many hours weeding the small garden, but it was overgrown with nettles, mare's tail and convolvulus once again. The narrow path to his door was made up of shards of broken amphorae and they crunched loudly beneath her feet. She had always suspected this was a deliberate ploy on Taliesin's part, giving him advance warning of visitors.

She knocked loudly. A boy, perhaps fourteen summers old, opened the door. Large, startlingly blue eyes peered at her from beneath an untidy mop of sandy-brown hair. Pale, tall and gangly, he reminded her of an overcrowded bean stalk struggling towards the light.

'Taliesin is resting,' he said politely. 'Could you come back tomorrow? Unless you're very sick – in which case, I'll try to help.'

'I'm not sick,' she smiled.

There was a scuffling in the darkness behind the boy, and then the youth was pushed aside with surprising force and Taliesin appeared in the doorway.

'Anya! By the goddess! Come in! Come in!' The old priest's skeletal face lit up like a turnip lantern.

She stepped inside and swept him into an embrace. It was like hugging a sack of bones, but at least he didn't stink of piss. The boy was obviously looking after him.

'It's so good to see you!' she beamed, finally letting him go.

'Yes, yes.' Taliesin seemed distracted. And then he turned to the youth. 'Foolish boy!' he scolded. 'How dare you try and turn the lady Anya away?'

'I'm sorry, I didn't realise,' the boy muttered, shamefaced.

'It's alright,' Anya said, touching Taliesin's arm. 'No harm done.'

'Yes, well, that may be,' the old priest grumbled, and then he rounded on the boy again. 'Make us an infusion, rose hip, not too strong. Quickly now!'

The boy slunk away like a beaten dog.

'My dear, come and sit with me.' Taliesin was all gentleness again. Taking her arm, he led her to the fireside. It saddened her to see how slowly he moved and how he winced with pain as he eased himself into his chair.

'Garth has promise,' he conceded, rubbing his right knee cap absently. 'But he's not you. No, he's not you.'

'He's very young. Give him time,' Anya replied, surreptitiously glancing about. In the months she had spent at Tintagel, she had worked hard to transform Taliesin's home

319

from a fetid hovel of flea infested bed rugs and dirty rushes, to a sweet smelling place of healing. She had laundered Taliesin's clothes and encouraged him to take a bath, and to her immense relief, it seemed Garth was doing much the same. Taliesin's hair smelled clean, his long, white gown was stain-free. The floor rushes were fresh, the ink pots filled, the wooden shelves neatly stacked with baskets of dried herbs, medicine bottles, and wax-sealed jars.

'He works hard,' she added.

'Yes, yes, I suppose he does. But he's not you,' Taliesin repeated petulantly.

Anya smiled at his grumpiness. 'It is so good to see you again.'

It was not a courtesy. She meant it. Taliesin understood her world. Or rather the world she had left behind, the world of the sacred grove, of priestly rituals and healing hands.

'Yes, yes, but I knew you'd come back. Didn't I say you'd come back to us?'

Before she could reply, the old priest sat bolt upright in his chair. His distracted air had vanished. He was utterly focussed now.

'I see you found the sword.'

Her fingers curled protectively about its grip.

'Tell me, Anya, where was it?'

'In Siluria, in the home of my mother's kin.' She sounded defensive, but she couldn't help herself.

'Siluria! Of course! That makes perfect sense.'

'Does it?'

'Yes, my dear, it does. May I see it? May I hold it?' He held out a bony hand. His finger joints were as red and shiny as rosehips.

Anya didn't want to take the sword from her belt. She had

promised Ceinwin she would keep it safe, protect it with her life. But then she noticed the sleeves of Taliesin's gown had slipped back to his elbows, revealing his ancient, faded tattoos, one for each year of his service to the gods. It was Taliesin who had led her to the cave of fires. It was Taliesin who understood the power of dream paths. Without him, she would never have found the sword.

Reassured, she unclipped the sword from her belt and handed it to him. The moment it left her grasp, she felt both afraid and full of remorse, as if she had committed an unforgiveable crime. Taliesin's gnarled fingers skimmed across the scabbard's bronze front plate and lingered over the insets of red glass.

'Blood,' he said quietly, 'the blood of your enemies.'

Anya jolted. Ceinwin had said the exact same words.

With infinite care, Taliesin withdrew the sword from its scabbard. He held it lightly, reverently, as if touching something sacred.

'A thing of beauty,' he marvelled, turning it this way then that until the firelight caught the intricate, intertwining spirals of the pattern welded blade. 'And a thing of immense strength and power.'

Anya's fingers were knotting frantically in her lap. She felt painfully on edge.

'I'm supposed to keep it safe,' she said, failing to keep the panic from her voice.

Taliesin's expression was mild, benign. 'I understand,' he replied, and she sensed he did.

He held the sword out to her and, with a great sense of relief, she quickly returned it to her belt. She felt as if she had narrowly escaped something truly terrible. What on earth was the matter with her?

Garth brought them two cups of steaming rose hip infusion and then retreated to the preparation table. Taliesin took a sip and wrinkled his nose in distaste.

'It tastes bitter. It's too strong!' he complained, without bothering to turn around.

Garth looked up from his pestle and mortar. His eyes met Anya's and they shared a brief, secret smile.

'Oh yes,' she thought. '*The boy will do very well indeed.*'

Taliesin put his cup on the floor beside his chair, the steaming infusion untouched. Anya stifled another smile; old age was making the priest stubborn.

'I want to ask you about Mairi,' she began.

Taliesin rolled his eyes and rubbed his forehead, as if the very thought of Lucan's wife was enough to bring on a serious headache.

'Since Lucan was put to death, she has been begging to be released from house arrest. She is claiming she is innocent of all charges and that Lucan forced her to poison Etar. She also claims that Mordred, her son, is Epona.'

A sudden, searing pain jarred through Anya's head. She cried out, gripping the chair arms for support. The pain vanished as quickly as it had come, leaving her with an unsettling sense of foreboding, of evil.

'Anya? What did you see?'

'I didn't *see* anything,' she replied truthfully.

Taliesin pursed his lips. 'The babe has a club foot. And Mairi will not be able to hide it for much longer.'

'Oh! Well, perhaps that explains…' but her voice trailed off because it wasn't a physical deformity she had sensed.

Taliesin coughed and his chest rattled as if it were full of dry leaves.

And then, as always, he appeared to read her thoughts.

'You are not mistaken,' he replied, his expression sombre. 'I too have sensed darkness in the child. Let us pray we can guide him towards the light.'

Anya felt sadness wash over her. There could be no 'we'.

Taliesin grasped her arm. 'You are Epona, my dear. I have always known it. And you know it too, in your heart. Epona, the chosen one, come from the sea to bring new life and new hope.'

Anya stared hard at the old priest, her cup of rosehip infusion entirely forgotten. She wished she shared Taliesin's certainty, his unyielding belief in an ancient prophecy. The only certainty in her life now was Silvanus. And soon, too soon, she would have to leave him again and return to Ronan, to suffering and to war.

'I can't stay here. I have to go back to Aquae Sulis.' The words stuck in her throat, as bitter as rue.

Taliesin said nothing, but she felt his pale, watery eyes bore into her skull and skitter across her memories like a flat pebble across a lake: *The stake pit in Tewdric's stronghold. Ronan carrying her in his arms, running full pelt across the open fields, tipping the vial of fermented grain down her throat in Aquae Sulis.* Taliesin was going deeper now: *Vortigern's bedchamber, the shame of her wedding night.* She wanted him to stop. She felt vulnerable, naked and exposed. She put a hand to her temple and felt the pain building behind her eyes.

'Enough! Enough!' Had she spoken the words out loud or screamed them inside her head?

She felt him release her and she sank back into the chair, her breath coming in ragged gasps. She had used her own gift of mind-seeking many times before, on many different people, but she had never once stopped to imagine how intrusive, how painful it felt. She realised Taliesin had turned away from

323

her and was staring into the flames. She felt a flare of anger. He had laid her bare, stripped her to the bone and, irrationally, she wanted an apology but instead, he was simply ignoring her.

Finally, Taliesin asked flatly, 'I take it you have feelings for Ronan?'

'No! He killed my brother. I do not have feelings for him. I will never have feelings for him,' she replied indignantly.

'But nevertheless, you asked Silvanus to fight for him.'

His words hurt, like a physical pain. 'It was an impossible choice.'

'And yet, you made that choice, Anya.'

'You believe I was wrong?'

Taliesin was still staring into the flames. 'That is not for me to say.'

'But you always have an opinion on everything.'

'I see only what the gods allow me to see. All I know for certain is that you are Epona and that one day, you will return to us again.'

She felt a sudden flicker of irritation at his unwavering conviction. 'Silvanus isn't going to help the people of Aquae Sulis,' she said quietly.

'You ask too much of him, Anya.'

She let out a deep sigh and put her head in her hands. 'I shouldn't have come back. All I ever wanted was to keep Dumnonia safe. If I am honest, I was glad when he refused.'

'Tell me, my child,' there was the merest hint of compassion in Taliesin's voice now, 'what does the goddess want of you?'

'I wish I knew,' she replied wearily.

'Think!'

She sat up, startled by the sharpness of his tone.

Her fingers tightened instinctively around the grip of the sword and the old priest nodded. 'Yes, Anya.'

'But I can barely lift it. I don't know how to fight,' she said helplessly. 'I don't understand what I'm supposed to do.'

'Just keep it safe.' Taliesin patted her arm absently, and then his expression brightened. 'Wait a moment. I have something for you.'

He stood up but his legs gave way beneath him and he stumbled. Anya caught him before he fell into the fire. He shook her off as if she was making a fuss and tottered towards the well-stocked shelves. Moments later, he returned with a small basket.

'Hold out your hand.'

Anya did as she was bid.

'Elf shot,' he said triumphantly, tipping the tiny stone arrow-heads into her palm. 'For the battle to come. They are one of the goddess's most powerful protectors.'

Anya walked back along the cliff path towards the great hall, deep in thought. As usual, Taliesin had offered reassurance and hope, but as usual he spoke in riddles wrapped in blind faith. She yearned for certainty in her life, for black and white rather than a thousand shades of grey. Frustrated, she looked up at the sky. The wind had changed direction. Blowing in from the south, it was surprisingly warm, tinged with faint, exotic traces of distant, sand-covered kingdoms.

She sighed heavily. Much as her heart yearned to remain with Silvanus, her head knew she should return to Aquae Sulis. And there was no time to lose. What if Hengist had already begun the long march towards the city? Perhaps she could ride out and meet him and broker for peace? But why would he listen to her, the half-sister he had always despised?

Anya turned the corner into the stable yard. Evric was unsaddling his horse. 'Where's Silvanus?' she asked.

'He's not back yet. He rides out for hours. He says it helps him think.'

'And he has much to think about,' Anya thought miserably.

Evric passed the saddle to a stable boy then turned to her.

'I need a drink. Keep me company?'

He blasted her with the full force of his infectious grin and despite her sadness, she felt her spirits lift. There was something immensely likeable about Silvanus's quick witted, exuberant brother in arms.

'So, where've you been?' he asked as they walked towards the great hall.

'I've been to see Taliesin.'

'Ah! I tell you, Anya, I pity his new apprentice. Taliesin treats him little better than a slave.'

'Garth has the measure of him.'

'Well, I'm glad to hear it. So, what shall we drink?'

Evric opened the door of the hall. Comforting, familiar scents drew her in, enveloping her and, quite suddenly, she knew she had to leave now, before it was too late, before Tintagel's magic ensnared her forever.

Her guards stood up respectfully as she approached the table.

'We leave within the hour,' she announced abruptly. 'I will meet you in the stable courtyard.'

Petilius nodded, unperturbed. 'Everything will be ready for you, my lady.'

But Evric was aghast. 'Anya? Why now? Why so soon?'

'I'm sorry, Evric. There's something I have to do. It's complicated. Silvanus will explain. But I pray to the goddess that I will return to you all one day.'

Evric looked stunned. 'Does Silvanus know you're leaving?'

'No.' She felt her voice waver.

'Won't you wait until he returns?'

'I can't.' She knew if she laid eyes on Silvanus again, she wouldn't have the strength to walk away. 'Look after him for me,' she whispered.

Evric's handsome, boyish face was suddenly grave.

'Yes, of course. Always.'

Silvanus's room was just as they had left it that morning. The bed was unmade, rugs tumbling towards the floor. Memories of the previous night flooded back. She had felt so safe, so cherished in his arms. Wrenching her gaze from the bed, she sat down at the small table, unfurled a piece of unused parchment, dipped a quill into the ink pot, and began to write.

Forgive me, but I have endured too many good-byes. I understand why you said no, just as I hope you understand why I had to ask. I'm glad you refused, because all I've ever wanted was to keep Dumnonia safe, to keep you safe.

Taliesin is certain I will return to you one day. I pray he is right because I want nothing more than to be at your side. But if we are not meant to find happiness in this lifetime, then I pray the goddess may grant us the chance to grow old together in the next.

I love you. I will always love you,

Anya.'

TWENTY NINE

'Are you unwell? Shall we stop?' Petilius asked solicitously.

Anya shook her head mutely. Riding at his side, she maintained a morose silence as the moors of Dumnonia receded into the distance behind them. From time to time, she sensed his watchful gaze, and she wondered if he guessed she had gone to Silvanus's bed. Fear shot through her before she remembered Vortigern was dead and her life was no longer in his hands. She was free. Free to remain with Silvanus. And yet here she was, riding away from him. What kind of madness was that?

The journey felt interminable; long days in the saddle with only her guilt and remorse for company, followed by long, sleepless nights beside strangers' hearths. When Aquae Sulis finally came into view at twilight on the fourth day, she felt strangely numb, both her mind and body leaden with exhaustion and regret. In the distance, the land glowed blood-red with countless bonfires. She glanced at the eastern horizon, at the myriad constellations, at Orion the hunter striding above the tree line, and did a quick mental calculation.

It was Samhain. The veil between this life and the next was drawing back and spirits were walking abroad. Petilius eyed the fires and made a show of crossing himself in the Christian way. Anya merely closed her eyes and said a brief, silent prayer, asking the shades of long dead ancestors to let them pass without harm. And then she opened her eyes again and drew a crumb of comfort - in an allegedly Christian land, the old ways were not entirely forgotten.

Dismounting in the forum, Anya's world swayed as her feet hit the flag stones. She closed her eyes for a moment, filled with a deep sense of unease. She had ridden to Dumnonia as Ronan's emissary, seeking an alliance, but she had come away empty handed. She had failed him. He would be less inclined than ever to trust her now.

Petilius kept pace with her as she walked across the vast basilica hall and they entered the council chamber side by side. Ronan was seated on the raised dais, alone and lost in his thoughts. His calculating expression reminded her of Vortigern and she felt herself falter, as if an iron fist had closed about her heart.

'I've made a mistake. I shouldn't have come back', she thought wretchedly.

Ronan looked up in surprise. 'Anya! I didn't expect I would ever see you again.'

'I keep my promises,' she replied, glancing apprehensively around the council chamber. She found it hard to breathe in these cities of stone - too much brick, too much tile, too much marble.

'Unlike your brothers,' Ronan replied.

Anya thought of the strand of red hair escaping from beneath Horsa's helmet, the moment she had known Ronan was about to kill her brother. What was she doing in this cold, soulless place? Why had she chosen to ally herself to this man?

Ronan was climbing down the steps. He dismissed Petilius with a curt flick of the hand, and waited until they were alone.

And then he leant forward, burrowed his nose between her breasts and sniffed. 'You smell of sex.'

Anya pushed him away angrily. 'Don't be crude. What's the matter with you?'

But Ronan merely smirked. 'I always suspected you went to Silvanus's bed, and I was right, wasn't I.'

'As long as your father lived, I was faithful to him,' she replied carefully.

'And when he no longer lived?'

She forced herself to match his gaze. 'I'm not answerable to you, Ronan.'

'Yes, you are. You are my late father's wife. According to Roman law, I could marry you, or fuck you, or kill you, as my father planned to do.'

Anya felt a jolt of fear. 'You don't like women very much, do you?'

'Women are good for just one thing, and until recently, I assumed you were useless at it. But I was wrong, wasn't I?' He smiled slyly at her.

'Was I so wrong about you?' Anya retorted. 'I hoped you were better than this. We haven't much time. Let's not waste it on foolishness.'

'I am no fool, Anya. The security of my kingdom is my sole concern.' He was eyeing her intently now, eyes narrowed. 'You ride to Dumnonia, you go to Silvanus's bed, and yet you return without him. What am I to make of that? Are you in league with him? Are you plotting against me?'

'There is no plot!' Anya exclaimed, exasperated.

'For God's sake, what are you doing here then? Did you come back to open the gates of the city for Hengist? Is that still your plan?'

'That was never my plan! Whilst you and your father were

slaughtering Saxons at Venta, I was trying to save the people of Aquae Sulis.'

'But you couldn't, could you? They still died in their hundreds. Your medicines were useless. You were useless!'

Anya bit her lip. He had hit a raw nerve. She had not been able to save them.

'The plague has returned,' Ronan said flatly.

Anya felt her heart stutter. 'How many cases?'

'Enough to know it's going to spread. People blame the Saxons for it.'

'They seek a scapegoat,' she replied dismissively, but her mind was racing. Her medical supplies were sorely depleted and it would be difficult to replenish them in winter. It would be months before stitchwort and wood anemone, the earliest spring flowers, began to bloom.

'So, did you persuade Silvanus to ride to my aid?'

Momentarily thrown by his abrupt change of subject, she faltered. 'No, he -'

Ronan laughed, an unpleasant sound, devoid of compassion. 'So you went to his bed, and you still couldn't persuade him? You truly are useless, aren't you?'

Without thinking, Anya slapped him, hard.

'Don't speak to me like that!' she hissed.

A look of utter incredulity crossed Ronan's face. She watched him raise his right hand, watched him move to strike her back. A small voice inside her head was telling her to retreat, but a louder voice urged her to stand her ground. Their eyes locked and held. At last, Ronan lowered his hand to his side.

'I could have you put to death for striking your high king.' He was breathing heavily, his rage palpable.

Anya opened her mouth then closed it again, astonished by

her own recklessness. She had not intended to strike Ronan but he had goaded her, as he goaded everyone, like a spear probing for weaknesses in a shield wall.

'Tread carefully', she warned herself. *'He has much of his father in him, no matter how much you yearn to believe he has not.'*

'Nothing to say now, Anya?' he asked, his tone threatening.

Taking a deep breath, she said, 'your father was the most powerful warlord in Britannia and yet you are within days of losing his kingdom. Your army is depleted. You stand alone. You have no allies. What are you going to do?'

'Your brother is marching against me. Do you honestly think I would be willing to share my battle strategies with you?'

'Hengist is my kin, and I would not see him dead, but nor do I want him to be high king of Britannia,' Anya replied, adopting an air of composure she did not feel. 'The people of this island deserve better.'

'So just who do you see as high king of Britannia?' Ronan asked sarcastically.

'I have no idea.'

'Not me, then?'

'I cannot see the future,' Anya replied evasively.

'I thought witches could see the future?'

Anya pulled a face. He was deliberately provoking her again. 'We're wasting time, Ronan. Tell me, does Rufus still serve Hengist?'

'My spies say he never leaves his side.' Ronan's expression betrayed his bitterness.

'Then Hengist will know everything there is to know about Aquae Sulis,' Anya said grimly. 'Have you replaced the rotten wood in the south-west gate?'

'Yes, of course,' Ronan replied brusquely.

'And have you sealed the culvert by the baths of Sul?'

'The culvert?'

'It runs beneath the city wall and out into the ditch beyond. It's large enough to crawl through.'

'How do you know this?' Ronan asked suspiciously.

Anya hesitated. She had hidden in the culvert during her escape from the snow covered city, a year since.

Avoiding his question, she said airily, 'there's bound to be more than one culvert beneath the walls. You'll need to find the others and block them up too.'

'Lord!'

They turned in unison. Julianus was striding towards them, his face set hard. 'Our scouts report Hengist is fifty miles away. He marches on the old Roman road.'

Ronan sidestepped to avoid the strand of spittle which flew from Julianus's misshapen mouth. 'Numbers?' he demanded.

'Initial estimates - a thousand men.'

Ronan flinched as if he had been struck and the colour drained from his face.

Anya drew a sharp intake of breath. A thousand men? Surely no one could defeat such an army. 'Let me ride out and meet him, let me broker for peace,' she began desperately but Ronan turned on her.

'Are you insane? Do you really think I'd let you anywhere near him!'

'He will listen to me. I might persuade him -' but he interrupted her again.

'Persuade him to do what? To leave Britannia? Don't be naïve Anya. Your brother isn't going anywhere. If I offer him silver, he will most likely use it to recruit more men.'

The mists of vision were drawing across Anya's eyes, the pain building inside her head. She could hear the sound of a battering ram pounding against the south-west gate and rising above it, she could hear the screams of the dying.

'What's the matter with you?' Ronan's voice was as sharp as a sword blade. She looked about, disorientated.

'Your city will fall,' she whispered.

'Not while I live and breathe. The walls of Aquae Sulis are strong and high. They were built by the Roman legions. They can easily repel a hoard of unwashed barbarians.'

Anya glanced at him, surprised by the conviction in his voice. 'Then tell me what I can do to help.'

The temple to Sulis Minerva dominated the precinct of the great baths, its tall pillars and soaring pediment a mighty monument to the fading empire of Rome. Within its inner sanctum, Anya and Maud had worked tirelessly, supervising the cutting of linen sheets into bandages and the preparation of makeshift pallets for the wounded. They had many willing helpers but Anya mixed the medicines herself, eking out what little remained of the juniper oil, the tinctures of bilberry and the poultices of yarrow and honey.

Oil lamps illuminated the frightened faces of the old men, women and children who had chosen to take refuge in the temple's dark sanctuary, watched over by the towering bronze statue of the goddess. Minerva stared serenely into space, neat curls framing her vacant face, her gown highlighting the feminine curves of her bronze body; a Roman goddess, adorned in ancient Roman fashion.

Anya put down her pestle and mortar and looked around. She had no idea how to comfort these people, no idea what to say to them. In truth, she shared their fear. It seemed highly likely that Hengist would take the city. She stood up wearily and stretched her aching back.

'I'm going to get some air.'

Maud nodded, tearing a strip of linen between her teeth.

'You're getting good at that,' Anya smiled.

Outside, dawn was breaking over the city. Anya stood on the portico between the two rows of columns and watched the sun smear the sky blood red. It was a bad omen. The soldiers chosen to guard the temple were gathered around a brazier at the foot of the steps, talking quietly amongst themselves. They were a mixed bunch. A handful of Ronan's warriors clad in mail with swords at their belts. A handful of new recruits - youths from the outlying villages, clutching the spears they used for hunting boar in the forest, their swaggering attitude not reaching their frightened eyes. And a handful of boys, their slender bodies barely out of childhood. They looked so bewildered that pity tugged Anya's heart.

She climbed down the temple steps and stood at the stone altar in the centre of the precinct. The carved inscription, already over three hundred years old, was beginning to fade after centuries of exposure to wind, rain and snow. Taking the tiny wooden runes from the leather pouch at her belt, she tipped them onto the altar. Then she closed her eyes and prayed for the people of Aquae Sulis.

She prayed to Sul, the water god of the healing springs. She prayed to Nerthus, her own goddess, the protector of the people of Saxony. She prayed to Taranis, god of the storm, and Andraste, goddess of the flames of war. Her hands hovered above the tiny wooden blocks, and she felt the power of the runes surging through the cold, still air. And then her hands dropped abruptly onto the altar, her fingers trembling.

'Are we safe now?' one of the boy-soldiers asked in awe.

'Nothing will harm you now,' Anya replied, but her stomach was in knots. Her prayers might give solace to the

335

men responsible for guarding the temple, but she sincerely doubted they had the power to protect the entire city from an army of one thousand spears. Gathering up the runes, she returned them to her leather pouch.

Ronan had ordered her to stay at the temple, but she was being drawn to the battlements of the city. If Hengist's army was upon them, she wanted to see it with her own eyes. With a final glance back at the temple, Anya set off towards the south-west gate. Ronan had ordered it to be repaired but Rufus couldn't know that. She felt certain he had advised Hengist to concentrate his initial attack there.

There were soldiers and civilians at every well she passed, toiling to fill buckets and cooking pots. She suspected they were wasting their time. The forum, basilica and temples were built of stone, but away from the centre of the city, the homes of the poor were wood and thatch. They would burn quickly under an attack of fire arrows, and a cooking pot filled with water would be useless against a rapidly spreading fire.

Shouts rang out above her head and she looked up at the battlements. Men were wheeling a massive wooden catapult into position on a wide bastion. She stared at the machine in awe; it was the height of at least two men. She had heard the merchants speak of these marvels of Roman engineering, but she had never seen one until today. She suspected it must be very old. Did Ronan really hope to fire it in anger?

A group of thirty or more soldiers were drawn up in close formation before the south-west gate. Battle hardened warriors, they had evidently been chosen as the city's first line of defence if the gate was breached. Further on, a line of soldiers ran up the steps and onto the battlements, passing missiles for the catapult from one man to the next. The soldiers, their arms full of masonry and broken roof tiles, halted their work to let her pass. At the top of the battlements, Anya raised a hand to shield her eyes from the glare of the rising sun. Beyond the city walls, the once tranquil water meadows were filled with row upon row of hide tents. Hengist's army had come, and it was vast. Men were unloading supplies from a column of covered wagons. She had once marched with her brother's army, and she knew exactly what the wagons held - salted meat, caskets of wine, sacks of grain, sheaves of arrows and iron tipped spears.

And then she saw the battering ram, and her blood ran cold. It was hewn from the trunk of a single giant oak, supported upon a large cart-like frame. How long could any gate withstand such a weapon? Images of the battle for Londinium sprang into her head, the carnage of the shield wall, Horsa dying in her arms. She dug her fingernails into the palms of her hands. Yet again, she was facing the prospect of watching her kin fall.

Seeking comfort, she closed her eyes and sought her goddess. For a fleeting heartbeat, she saw the sacred grove and heard the wind chimes, but then Ronan's voice, loud and authoritative, cut across her prayers. She opened her eyes. He was striding along the battlements, issuing orders to the men stacking arrows, javelins and sling shot at regular intervals along the wall.

Catching sight of her, he said roughly, 'what are you doing up here? Are you insane?'

'I wanted to see -' but he interrupted her, shaking his head angrily. 'I told you to stay at the temple. It's not safe up here. It will be bad for morale if one of Hengist's snipers puts an arrow through your heart.'

'They're out of range -' she began but he cut her off again.

'The ones you can see are out of range!'

337

Anya peered nervously over the battlements. It had not occurred to her Hengist's bowmen may be crouched behind hedges, or perched unseen in the branches of trees.

'Is everything ready at the temple?' Ronan demanded.

She nodded, but in reality she had few bandages and even less medicine. She would not be able to offer much comfort to the injured or dying.

'Then go there, and stay there.' Ronan put a hand on her shoulder. 'And be safe.'

Anya was taken aback by the compassion in his voice.

'You too,' she replied.

She walked back down the steps. In the street below, soldiers were dragging blankets and rugs from houses and piling them up on the cobbles. She presumed they were intended to beat out fires.

She looked up at the battlements again, at the stacks of javelins and arrows, and the heaps of stones, ready to crush the skulls of Saxon men, her own kin, and her heart felt unbearably heavy. She was a healer. It was her duty to save life, not take it. But if her own life depended on it, if it came down to a question of kill or be killed, could she do it? She prayed she would never have to find out.

She did not return to the temple. She went to the baths instead. Ronan was not exaggerating when he said the plague had taken hold again. The sick and dying were gathering beside the steaming waters of Sul and the stench was overpowering, the terrible, familiar reek of suppurating flesh, decay and death. A thin, middle-aged man hurried over to her. Like all the citizens of Aquae Sulis, he was thin and pale, but he had no obvious signs of sickness.

'You have to help us. They're taking them away! Please, I beg you, come with me!'

338

Taking Anya's arm, he led her into a side room. Its walls were painted with scantily clad gymnasts, their lithe bodies ghost-like now after centuries of exposure to warm, damp air. The corpses of plague victims, men, women and children, lay side by side on the dirty floor tiles. The foul black swellings at their necks, underarms and groin had exploded like over-ripe fruit, and their soiled garments reeked of putrefying decay.

The doors at the opposite end of the room were open, providing a welcome draught of clean air. Soldiers, wearing makeshift masks over their nose and mouth, were dragging the corpses out into the courtyard then loading them onto carts. Anya could not understand why the man was so distressed. 'Are they taking them for burial?' she asked.

'Ask them.' The man's face was rigid with rage. 'Ask them where they're taking the bodies.'

Anya tapped one of the soldiers on the shoulder. 'What's going on here?'

The soldier pulled down his mask. 'We're taking them for the catapult, on the orders of the king.'

Anya ran all the way back to the gate, her sense of outrage giving her wings. Beyond the walls she could hear the blare of battle horns and the boom of drums. She came to a ragged halt before the unit of men guarding the gate.

'Where is he? Where's Ronan?' she gasped.

'On the battlements, but you mustn't go up there. It's too dangerous.'

Anya heard Hengist's fire arrows before she saw them; the sound of a breeze through leaves then louder, like an approaching storm. A trail of light blazed through the air, as if a hundred comets were hurtling across the sky. She watched open-mouthed as the men guarding the gate raised their

339

shields, bracing for impact as flaming arrows hit linden wood. Not all the arrows found shields. Some skittered harmlessly across the cobbled road, some struck door lintels or thatch, but others found flesh and bone, and the first casualties fell, screaming, their clothes alight.

'Attend to them!' someone yelled, and men ran forward to douse burning flesh with blankets and rugs, then carry the wounded to safety.

'You should go to the temple. The wounded will have need of you.'

Anya swung around. It was Petilius.

'I will, but first I have to speak to Ronan,' she replied.

With Petilius's protests ringing in her ears, she pushed past him, taking the steps up to the battlements two at a time. The sight that greeted her beyond the walls was more terrible than she could ever have imagined. Hengist's army had surrounded Aquae Sulis, like a noose around the city's neck. The noise of the battle horns and the beating drums was so deafening it echoed inside her ribcage. Hundreds of braziers glowed red hot as Hengist's archers continued to shoot fire arrows into the city. All around her, Ronan's officers were barking orders whilst sweat-drenched men pounded the enemy below with spears, arrows and pieces of masonry.

'Anya!'

She turned at the sound of her name. Ronan was running towards her in full battle dress - chain mail and helmet, shield and sword. 'Why did you come back? Why did you disobey my order?'

'Is it true you're using corpses for the catapult?'

Ronan stopped in his tracks as an arrow whistled past him, missing his shoulder by a hair's breadth. And then he was on the move again, grabbing her shoulder and pushing her to her knees behind the parapet. Crouching down beside her, he snarled, 'what better way to spread terror amongst the enemy than airborne plague?'

'You can't dishonour the dead like that!' she spluttered.

'They're past caring, Anya.'

'But -'

The battering ram hit the gate with a sound like thunder, and although most of Ronan's face was hidden beneath his helmet, she saw the flash of fear in his eyes. And then he let go of her and leapt to his feet, striding towards his men.

'Catapult!' he bellowed. 'Catapult! Now!'

Anya watched the first corpse fly from the powerful arm of the Roman contraption. The body sailed through the air, its limbs flailing like a broken starfish. Still on her knees, she did not see the corpse land amidst Hengist's men, but she heard their response.

They screamed.

And then she heard Ronan's voice above the tumult of noise. 'Again!'

Shakily, she stood up. Below her she could see the broken, bloated corpse, its unnaturally splayed limbs covered in foul green discharge. Hengist's men were already backing away from it when the second corpse landed close by. More men scattered, but the battle horns sounded again and the battering ram did not falter.

It was protected by a unit of men in close formation holding their shields above their heads. She had heard the bards speak of such a thing. The Romans had called it *testudo*, the tortoise shell. The impact of the ram was reverberating through the gate and along the battlements. She could feel it in the soles of her feet and it felt as strong as a heartbeat. Once it stopped beating and the gate fell, the city would die.

341

A fire arrow whistled overhead, close, too close. She could smell the burning pitch, and feel its heat. Ronan's men were pummelling the *testudo* with masonry and rocks, but most of their makeshift missiles were bouncing harmlessly off the Saxon shields. Anya felt overcome with despair. There was nothing she could do. It was hopeless. The citizens of Aquae Sulis were all going to die, either from the plague, or at the end of a Saxon sword.

She glanced along the battlements. Four soldiers were bearing the weight of a huge cauldron supported by staves running through thick metal rings. Under Ronan's guidance, they manoeuvred it into position over the parapet. Two of the soldiers bore down on the front staves, the cauldron tilted, and boiling pitch fell thickly onto the *testudo* below. Men screamed as the pitch found its mark and the ram came to a sudden halt. All around her, Ronan's men shouted in triumph.

Anya put a hand over her mouth and fought a strong desire to retch. She could only imagine the agony of skin flayed by boiling pitch. She turned and stumbled back down the steps, running her hand along the stone wall as she went. It felt reassuringly solid when everything else around her seemed to be crumbling. The soldiers guarding the gate were celebrating the small victory but she couldn't share their jubilation. She knew her brother would order more men to the ram. This was only a temporary reprieve.

She hesitated for a moment. Ronan was right. She was only a hindrance on the battlements, a target for an opportunist sniper. At the temple of Sul, at least she could help the injured. Tugging her cloak about her, she turned east. A storm of Hengist's fire arrows flew over her head. Several landed on a house close by. The thatch smoked like damp kindling then flared into life, flames licking towards the sky. After the stillness of the morning, a wind had sprung up, bringing scudding clouds from the north. Even as she watched, the wind caught the flames of the burning thatch and jumped to the next roof like a cat pouncing on its prey.

At the next crossroads, Anya stopped and looked about. She wasn't far from the temple now but the buildings were ablaze up ahead. The street was deserted. No-one was attempting to fight the fire. Perhaps they had taken heed of Ronan's decree and sought refuge in the stone-built buildings in the centre of the city. All around, she could hear burning timbers groaning and splintering, the roar and crackle of the fire. It was spreading rapidly, spewing like a raging dragon, destroying everything in its path. A pall of black smoke was rising over Aquae Sulis and the air smelled like a smithy.

Gripped by fear, Anya broke into a run.

The cries were so faint above the roar of the flames that at first she thought she was imagining them. She ran on a few paces then stopped and turned around, listening intently. It seemed not everyone had taken heed of Ronan's decree.

She could definitely hear a voice, high pitched and desperate. A child.

The house looked like a turnip lantern, its unglazed windows lit up by the fire that raged within. Anya eyed the door handle. It was made of iron. In all likelihood it would be red hot. Wrapping the edge of her cloak around her left hand in a makeshift glove, she turned the handle. It was hot; she could feel it burning her palm through the woollen fabric.

The moment she opened the door, the heat hit her, so intense it took her breath away. The house was filled with acrid smoke and instantly she began to cough. Pressing her cloak to her nose and mouth, she stepped inside. The fire was like a living creature, a monster engulfing the walls with its rippling, flaming limbs. 'Hello?' she shouted. 'Is anyone here?'

'Help us!'

Anya narrowed her eyes against the smoke. The roof had partially collapsed; the floor was a maze of fallen joists. Two children were huddled beside a woman, her torso crushed beneath a broad beam. Cautiously, Anya navigated her way around the fallen timbers. Her cloak was an ineffective shield and the smoke was making her eyes sting. With every step, it became harder to see where she was going. She knelt beside the trapped woman. There was blood and brain matter in her hair. Anya felt for a pulse, but found none. She closed the woman's vacant eyes then turned to the children.

'We have to get out of here. You have to come with me.'

The smallest child huddled closer to her mother's body. The older girl shook her head vehemently. 'We can't leave her.'

'You must,' Anya said firmly and took her hand. 'Trust me, she wouldn't want you to die here.'

'No!' The girl snatched her hand away.

There was a sudden, deafening crack and another roof beam crashed to the ground in a fury of sparks and burning thatch.

'We have to go. Now! Come on!'

Anya grabbed the older girl's hand and swept the younger child onto her hip. The little girl buried her face in Anya's neck, her tiny chest heaving as she struggled to breathe. Coughing violently, Anya steered a cautious path back the way she had come. Wisps of burning thatch were drifting down, illuminating the smoky air with tendrils of orange light. She tried to swerve around them but a flaming stalk landed on the little girl's arm and she yelped with pain, coughing and writhing in Anya's arms.

344

Anya's eyes were streaming from the smoke. The heat was like a furnace, so vicious she could feel it through her cloak. With the children clinging to her, her progress was slow. If another roof beam fell, she doubted she could move quickly enough to avoid it. But she could see the doorway; it was tantalisingly close. With a silent prayer to the goddess, she kept going. Above the sound of the flames, she heard the house shift and groan as the fire devoured its wooden walls. She suspected the building was close to collapsing.

'We're nearly there,' she croaked, her throat as raw as a wound.

The intense heat vanished the moment they stumbled out into the street. Anya put the little girl down then dropped onto all fours, coughing violently. It was some time before she was able to sit up. The children were clinging to one another. Beneath the soot and grime, their faces were blank with shock and deathly white. In stark contrast, the burn on the younger girl's arm was vivid red, the skin puckering. Anya knew how easily it could become infected, how easily it could prove fatal. She stood up unsteadily.

'Let's get some water to bathe your arm.' It hurt to talk, and it hurt to breathe.

Taking the girls' hands, she led them to the well at the end of the street. It was surrounded by buckets of water to fight the flames. But the soldiers had been ordered to the battlements and there was no-one to stop the fire spreading now.

'Drink some water. Drink as much as you can.'

Obediently, the girls cupped their hands and took long grateful gulps. When they had drunk their fill, Anya submerged the little girl's injured arm in a bucket of water. She smiled encouragingly, but half her mind was on the burning buildings all about them. It would be best to keep the burn under water for a long time, but she knew they should not linger here.

'You can take your arm out now.'

Anya quickly tore a strip of linen from her under-skirt. Soaking it in the cold, clean water, she tied it tightly around the little girl's wound.

'We have to go now. Come on.'

'Where are we going?' the older girl asked, her eyes glazed with shock.

'To the temple of Sul. It's built of stone, it won't burn. You'll be safe there.'

They had taken no more than three steps when they heard the south-west gate fall. The initial sound was like lightning, an intense, sharp crack as the oak splintered. The entire city seemed to pause, as if waiting for the storm to follow. And sure enough, a heartbeat later, the gate crashed to the ground, as if Taranis himself had felled it with a thunderbolt.

The little girls looked terrified. It was obvious they understood what the sound meant, just as Anya understood the noises that quickly followed: the grunting, clashing savagery of hand to hand combat.

The city was breached.

Grabbing the girls' hands, she broke into a run. Her damaged lungs quickly rebelled and, coughing violently, she was forced to slow her pace. At the end of the street she looked left then right. The fire had spread to this part of the city too. The air felt dangerously hot, filled with billowing black smoke. Looking up, she caught sight of the soaring temple of Sul and the distinctive domed roofs of the baths, rising defiantly above the burning city.

'This way, quickly!'

The younger child stumbled and fell. Anya swept her into her arms again and ran on. She kept to the widest streets, for the narrow alleyways that criss-crossed the city were tunnels of fire now, belching their flames into the streets as if stoked by a smith's bellows. At the next well, she stopped again. Above the roar of the fire, she could hear other noises now: desperate cries of alarm, and frantic screams. Hengist's army had fought its way into the city. May the gods preserve the people of Aquae Sulis.

'Not far now, but we need to drench ourselves with water, it will protect us against the fire,' Anya explained, liberally splashing their soot-covered dresses. Removing her own cloak, she plunged it into a barrel of water then swung it around her shoulders again. The drenched wool felt heavy and cold against her over-heated skin.

'Is your father in the city?' she asked.

'Our father is dead.'

'I'm sorry.' Anya wondered what would become of these two orphaned children if the city fell to Hengist. She suspected they would be destined for the slave markets of Gaul.

'Come,' she said, taking their hands. 'We must make haste.'

'You there!' The voice was loud and harsh, spoken in the Saxon tongue.

Anya spun on her heel. Six men were swaggering down the street, swords drawn, each bearing the white wolf upon their shields. Hurriedly, Anya crouched down before the girls and whispered urgently, 'the temple of Sul is just there.' Surreptitiously, she pointed to her left. 'See the round roofs? Don't stop until you get there. My friend Maud will be waiting for you. She'll look after you. Now run! Run!'

The older girl nodded gravely and took her sister's hand.

Only when they were safely through the gates of the temple precinct did Anya turn back to face the Saxon warriors.

'I thought you were ignoring me, whore!'

'I am no whore,' she replied, in Saxon.

She rarely spoke the language of her homeland now and it felt strange on her tongue.

The warrior looked surprised but quickly gathered his wits. 'Your hair's the colour of fire. Is this inferno your doing, witch?'

'The inferno is your doing, your fire-arrows are destroying the city,' Anya replied, edging backwards, one step at a time.

'You have a sharp tongue,' the Saxon replied, affronted. 'Where do you think you're going? We want some entertainment.'

They were just yards away from her now. There was blood on their leather cuirasses, the white wolf streaked with gore, blood on their hands, and the blades of the swords. And there was lust in their battle-hardened eyes. She wondered if this was how all men acted when gripped by battle fever? But she couldn't imagine Horsa behaving like this, or Silvanus, or any of his men.

She looked them up and down, struggling to control her fear, struggling to think. They were burdened with heavy mail. Could she outrun them? Perhaps, but not today, not with her swollen throat, and smoke filled lungs.

'I am of noble birth. My hair is the colour of fire because I am favoured by Andraste, goddess of war. And I am not afraid of you.' She was lying. She was afraid. She was very afraid indeed.

'Well, you should be, princess, because I fancy a taste of you.'

Anya took a shallow, painful breath and withdrew her

348

sword from its scabbard. It felt heavy, but she tried hard not to show it.

'Mind you don't cut yourself with that, princess,' the Saxon taunted.

Anya's mind was roiling with panic. Was this the day Ceinwin had spoken of? Was this the moment the sword had been waiting for? She wished she felt brave, but her heart was pounding frantically.

'I am Wulfstan, lord of Seourland, and I will take you first. And when I am done with you, my men can have their turn,' the Saxon declared, prowling around her like a wolf preparing to leap upon its prey. She turned on her heel, keeping him in her sights but terror was gripping her damaged, aching lungs. She rubbed her stinging eyes and tried to take a deeper breath, but quickly succumbed to another bout of coughing.

She heard one of the Saxons say, 'Odin's balls, does she have the plague?'

Wulfdan looked her up and down. 'No. You've been too close to the fire, haven't you, princess.' He was still prowling around her. With each step he lessened the distance between them.

From beyond the city walls, Hengist's battle horns sounded once more. Three short blasts then a pause, repeated over and over again. Anya didn't recognise the pattern.

'In the name of Odin, what's happening out there?' Wulfdan's eyes darted in the direction of the south-west gate.

Taking advantage of the Saxon's momentary lapse in concentration, Anya made a run for it. She didn't get far. One of Wulfdan's men grabbed her forearm and dragged her back, laughing as if this was a game played in a summer meadow.

'Come here. We've not even started yet.'

'Lord!' A soldier was hurtling towards them down the

349

smoke filled street. 'The army of the red dragon rode out of Selwood,' he gabbled breathlessly, 'a great army, horsemen and foot-soldiers. The battle is lost.'

'What?' Wulfdan sounded confused. 'No, the city is breached, the battle is won!'

But the soldier shook his head. 'Our shield wall has broken. Our army is in retreat. You must make haste, lord, or you will find yourself trapped inside the city.'

Anya stared at the soldier in astonishment. In Tintagel, Silvanus's guards had worn the emblem of a red dragon upon their cuirasses. *Was it possible?*

Wulfstan's men were all shouting at once.

'Is Hengist still alive?'

'We should make for the basilica. Rufus said there's gold and silver there.'

'Forget the basilica. We need to get out of the city.'

'I'm not going anywhere yet,' Wulfdan's voice rang out.

Anya felt her heart lurch. The Saxon was staring at her again.

'Don't be a fool, brother. She's not worth it.'

'Go then, Athelstan. All of you, go. This won't take long. I will catch you up.'

Shaking their heads in disbelief, his warriors moved off down the street. Only Wulfdan remained, his gaze fixed upon Anya. She tightened her grip on the sword. It felt unbearably heavy now, her muscles protesting violently.

'That's a beautiful sword,' Wulfdan said. 'Who did you steal it from?'

'It belongs to me.'

'And who taught you to speak the Saxon tongue, whore?'

'I told you, I am a Saxon by birth. I am no whore.'

Wulfdan laughed loudly and then, without warning, his

sword blade lashed out like an adder's tongue. She heard it rip through her cloak, felt it slice through the flesh of her upper arm. The pain that followed was so intense she almost dropped the sword.

'You don't like to be tickled, my sweet? You prefer it rough then?' and he laughed again.

Anya gritted her teeth and held her ground. The burning city and the bloodshed within its walls were fading away. Her vision was focussing, as if a bright light shone upon the prowling Saxon. She felt her anger spill over into her veins and surge to her finger-tips.

Blood was running down her arm and onto the grip of the sword, making it slippery and difficult to hold but, quite suddenly, the grip burned white hot in her hand. Intense heat pulsed down the entire length of the blade as if it was being forged in fire.

She did not move an inch, but Wulfdan collapsed to the ground, writhing in agony and clutching his throat. His body was contorting as if his very life blood was boiling in his veins. Anya stared in horror as his body continued to convulse and his face turned a deadly shade of blue.

And then, finally, Wulfdan lay still.

Anya sank to her knees, paralysed with shock. What had just happened? Surely it wasn't possible to kill a man without laying so much as a finger upon him? Turning to one side, she retched onto the cobble stones. She let go of her sword and it slid from her lap and clattered to the ground. She didn't want it anymore. Whatever hold it had once exerted over her, had vanished the moment the life had gone from Wulfdan's eyes. Ceinwin had been mistaken. The sword was never meant to come to her.

She closed her eyes, her body shuddering so violently she

felt as if the plague had taken hold. She had no idea how long she remained kneeling in the mud. Images were unfolding inside her head, a never ending stream of death: Emma murdered in the sacred grove; Horsa dying in the stubble field; Elsbet's body in an unmarked pit; Wulfdan the Saxon convulsing in his death throes.

Drenched in water from the well, she did not notice the first drops of rain falling on the burning city. It was not until they began to land more heavily that she opened her eyes and looked up at the sky. Dark storm clouds loured over Aquae Sulis. Lightning lit up the black sky, a crack of thunder exploded overhead, and the clouds burst in a torrential downpour.

She made no attempt to get up. Instead, she tipped her head back, relishing the feel of rain pouring down her face and into her scorched throat. Taranis, god of the storm had finally listened to her prayers, for the torrential rain did not lessen. It continued to beat down, extinguishing the fires that raged throughout the city.

'Anya?'

She recognised that voice.

Silvanus was walking towards her. Over his mail, he wore a cuirass bearing the emblem of the red dragon. His shield was slung over his back, his sword was sheathed and he carried his helmet under his arm. He was soaked to the skin, his short brown hair plastered to his scalp. For a moment she thought she must be dreaming. Or perhaps she was imagining him. Imagining the one person she most wanted to see.

She wiped the rain from her sore, streaming eyes then looked again. He was standing in front of her now. He put down his helmet, clasped her hands and pulled her to her feet, but still she refused to believe it. If she closed her eyes even for a moment, would he simply disappear? His hands were encasing hers and she felt their reassuring warmth. And then she looked into his eyes, those gentle, familiar eyes. She was not imagining him. He was real.

She fell against him, rested her head against his chest and felt his arms envelop her, felt the small, overlapping iron plates of his armour dig into her cheek. He smelled of battle: of sweat, filth, blood, horses, leather and smoke. But underneath all that, she caught a trace of his own unique scent, and it felt like a balm.

'You came. Why?' she breathed, looking up at him.

He brushed strands of wet hair from her face. 'Because I knew you would fight, and most probably die, with that extraordinary sword in your hand, and I couldn't bear it, Anya. I couldn't bear it.'

'You risked the lives of your people for me?'

He shrugged and a smile twitched at the corners of his mouth. 'For you, for Dumnonia, for Britannia.'

'That's less romantic!' But her smile faded as quickly as it had come. 'The battle is won?' she asked anxiously.

'The city is saved, for now,' Silvanus replied, his expression solemn.

'My brother,' she asked tentatively. 'Is he dead?'

'He lives.'

'Oh…' her voice trailed away. She felt relieved and yet at the same time, disappointed. She frowned, conflicted and ashamed.

'How is it that he survived? Is he held captive?'

'No. We broke their shield wall, and they fled in disarray. We pursued and we killed, but Hengist retreated to the old fort atop Badon Hill. Initial estimates suggest he has lost half his men. Even so, his army is still a formidable force. He now holds the high ground, and Ronan tells me the fort's defences are sound.'

Anya stared at Silvanus in dismay. More than half of Hengist's men had lost their lives before the walls of Aquae Sulis. For what? For Hengist's empty promises of gold and glory? Their blood was on her brother's hands.

'How many men did you lose?'

'Thirty seven,' he replied grimly. 'And at least five more will not last the night.'

'I'm so sorry,' she whispered, unable to look him in the eye. 'It's my fault your men are dead. If I had not asked you to -'

He put a hand beneath her chin and lifted her face to his again. 'None of this is your fault.'

She could tell he meant it, and perhaps he was right. But nevertheless, her guilt felt cold and heavy. She stared up at him, searching for answers. But in her heart, she already knew the answer she was seeking. Somewhere deep inside, she had always known.

Crouching down, she picked up her sword, weighing it in her hands. It felt so heavy, so utterly wrong. If she was honest with herself, it had never felt right.

Silvanus caught sight of the trail of blood running down her arm. 'You're hurt!'

'It's nothing.' She shrugged away his concern and held out the sword to him. 'This belongs to you.'

He looked nonplussed. 'No, it doesn't.'

'The goddess led me to Siluria. She wanted me to find the sword, but it's not meant for me. It's meant for you.'

'What makes you think that?' Silvanus asked, astonished.

'Trust me,' she whispered. 'It's yours.'

There had been so many dreams of mountains running with blood, of villages drowning in gore. So many dreams about the sword, held aloft, holding back the tide of death. Only rarely had she caught a glimpse of the man who held the sword. But she had always turned away, unwilling to acknowledge the truth.

Until now. Until this moment.

She held out the sword again, and saw the bewilderment growing in Silvanus's eyes.

'Please, take it.'

His fingers curled around the grip. She stepped back, watching him swing the sword to and fro, watching his smile grow as he appreciated its perfect balance.

Quite suddenly, she felt as if the greatest of weights had been lifted from her shoulders.

'It's a good sword,' he said. 'A beautiful sword.'

THIRTY

Silvanus had always believed the great hall of Tintagel to be the most splendid in Britannia, but the basilica of Aquae Sulis dwarfed it by comparison. Sitting beside Ronan in the vast council chamber he could not help but feel intimidated. Etar had nurtured his kingdom's isolation as a barrier against the world, and until a few days ago, Silvanus had never ventured beyond the borders of Dumnonia. But here he was, at the very centre of the most powerful kingdom in Britannia, surrounded by the last vestiges of Rome's wealth and grandeur.

'I trust you have been offered refreshment?' Ronan enquired, a hint of frost in his tone.

'I have, and I thank you for your hospitality,' Silvanus replied, although he had not expected to be the one offering thanks. Three days had passed since the battle for Aquae Sulis. Surely it should be Ronan thanking him? He had been warned Vortigern's son was an arrogant bastard, and it seemed his intelligence was correct.

Tearing his gaze from the opulence of the room, Silvanus eyed Ronan speculatively. Vortigern's son had inherited a vast kingdom of unimaginable wealth and power, but he did not give the impression of a powerful man. It was hard to believe this diffident youth had killed Pascent of the Coritani in battle, led the valiant defence of Aquae Sulis, and mounted a successful rescue mission into Siluria, risking his own life to save Anya's.

Silvanus's expression hinted at his inner turmoil. It was difficult to accept he owed Ronan a debt of gratitude he doubted he could ever fully repay. And it was even harder to accept that Anya had chosen to nurse Ronan back to health, despite Vortigern, despite Horsa, despite the terrible cycle of the blood vendetta.

Ronan was fidgeting now, picking at the torn skin around the fingers nails. Silvanus, his emotions in disarray, felt a sudden, entirely unexpected, flash of pity for the boy. Vortigern's son looked very young, tiredness etched beneath his eyes. Perhaps the burdens of kingship were weighing heavily on him too.

Much as Silvanus was loath to admit it, he realised they had much in common. They were both the sons of kings who had wielded great power but who had turned their backs on diplomacy. Kings who had taught their sons how to kill, but had failed to teach them how to rule.

Ronan looked up from his finger nails, but still did not make eye contact with Silvanus. 'Thank you. I am in your debt. The people of Aquae Sulis are in your debt.' There was a pinched expression on his face, as if the words tasted bitter on his tongue.

Silvanus glanced at Ronan in surprise. '*Better late, than never,*' he thought to himself.

Out loud, he said, 'you must be aware my actions were not entirely altruistic. Ultimately, I fought to protect my own people. And to that end, I will speak plainly. My father chose to rule in isolation. I believe your father also cared little for alliances. But if we are to defeat the Saxon threat, the kingdoms of Britannia must unite.'

'You wish to form an alliance?' Ronan sounded incredulous. 'Tell me, why should I make an ally of the kingdom that harboured my father's runaway wife for more than six months?'

Silvanus gritted his teeth. He had set out to be civil and statesmanlike, but Ronan was deliberately baiting him. He forced himself to remain calm.

'We did not know Anya's true identity. As soon as we learnt she was your father's betrothed, we arranged for her to be returned to him. But you already know this.'

A contemptuous grunt issued from Ronan's throat and, despite his best intentions, Silvanus felt his anger flare. 'My men died for you,' he said, and there was an edge to his voice now. 'That should be enough to prove my sincerity.'

Ronan gave Silvanus a long, hard stare. At length, he looked down at his nails and said guardedly, 'I can see the advantage of an alliance.'

Silvanus had not expected the boy to capitulate so easily. Suspecting a trap, he chose his next words with care. 'If we are to become allies, I suggest we draw up a written treaty.'

'Why? Are you insinuating you don't trust my word?' Ronan asked bluntly.

Of course he didn't trust him. How could anyone trust the son of Vortigern, a high king who made war against his own people? 'Is there any reason why I shouldn't trust you?' Silvanus asked levelly.

'There is not,' Ronan replied, holding his gaze.

The boy is learning to deceive before my very eyes,' Silvanus mused. In truth, he felt weary to his bones. This was all a waste of time. This treaty would not be worth the parchment it was written on. Ronan was Vortigern's son. Treachery and betrayal ran through his veins.

Frustrated, Silvanus's gaze swept across the council chamber before coming to rest on the mosaic floor. He had never seen anything like it before, so bizarre, so cold, so alien. It made him yearn for the great hall of Tintagel, for the camaraderie, the warm familiarity of the place. And then a thought struck him. For some inexplicable reason, Anya trusted Ronan, or she would not have asked him to ride to Aquae Sulis, to risk the lives of his men.

He turned to Ronan again. 'Anya tells me you saved her life in Siluria.'

Ronan leant back in his chair and exhaled deeply. 'Anya. It all comes back to Anya, doesn't it?'

'Does it?' Silvanus queried, taken aback.

'Of course it does. Without her intervention, you wouldn't be sitting here, would you? She's at the centre of everything, isn't she? The hub around which we all turn.'

Silvanus did not know how to reply to that.

'You love her,' Ronan stated flatly, with no discernible trace of malice or accusation in his tone. 'That's why you risked everything to come here.'

Stunned, Silvanus wondered if he should lie to protect Anya, but he could see no reason for pretence now.

'Yes. I love her.'

'I thought so.'

Silvanus saw a shadow cross Ronan's face, gone as quickly as it had come. He remembered his last conversation with Anya on the beach. She had spoken about Ronan.

We'll be hugely outnumbered…'

We can't allow that to happen…'

We…'

The question slipped from his lips before he could stop it.

'And what about you? Do you have feelings for Anya?'

'No! I'm not so desperate I'd want to fuck my father's wife.'

Silvanus's expression faltered. He took no offence at Ronan's coarseness, but he didn't like to be reminded Anya had once belonged to Vortigern.

Ronan was momentarily disconcerted. 'Forgive me. I shouldn't have said that, but Anya...' He attempted to find something tactful to say but quickly gave up. 'My father thought she was a witch,' he said baldly.

'She is a healer! She is not a witch!' Silvanus exploded furiously.

'If you say so, but your brother was convinced Anya had ensnared my father with her pagan devilry. Yes, I have met your brother,' Ronan went on smugly. 'He came to Aquae Sulis. He wanted Vortigern to help him take your throne, but my father would not countenance such underhand dealings.'

'You tell me nothing I do not already know,' Silvanus retorted sharply. 'My half-brother Lucan was executed for treason a month since.' He met Ronan's gaze steadily but the mention of Lucan's name had unsettled him. He could feel his self-control beginning to slip away.

'A good decision, I am sure,' Ronan said, as lightly as if they were choosing which wine to have with venison. 'I am fortunate I do not have brothers to plot against me. But whilst we are on the subject of siblings, perhaps it is time we discussed what to do about Anya's brother, encamped on Badon Hill?'

By a powerful effort of will, Silvanus pushed all thoughts of Lucan from his mind and asked dispassionately, 'you sent an emissary to negotiate peace?'

Ronan shot him a withering glance. 'Anya assured me

360

Hengist would return to Londinium if I offered him enough silver, so I sent one of my best men. He returned at sunset, strapped to his horse and minus his head.'

Silvanus grimaced.

'So much for attempting diplomacy with pagan savages,' Ronan grunted. 'And it serves me right for listening to the counsel of a woman.'

Anya had requisitioned the dining chamber of the basilica and fashioned a makeshift place of healing. She had recruited Maud as her assistant and the slave girl had proved to have the makings of a fine healer. Together they had worked through the night, polishing the table with beeswax and scrubbing the floor with hot water infused with juniper. They had raided the laundry for clean linen, and the store rooms for honey and herbs. They had removed the silver platters from the dining table and replaced them with baskets of linen, suture dishes, pestles and mortars, and what little remained of her ointments and poultices. Suspended above braziers, infusions of chicory and feverfew simmered in three large cooking pots.

The room was strongly scented with oil burners of fennel and lavender, but it barely masked the stench of suffering, putrefaction and death. Anya knelt beside a barely conscious soldier. His skin was the colour of ash, his skin pinpricked with sweat. There were downy hairs on his cheek; he was scarcely more than a boy.

Surely he had fought for Ronan? Surely Silvanus would not send a child into battle? She knew for a fact he was not a Saxon, for Ronan had taken no prisoners. After the battle, he had ordered his men to search the field and dispatch the wounded and dying enemy troops with a quick sword thrust through the heart. *'They are mouths we cannot feed,'* he had

361

explained later, but his callous, cold-hearted logic had done nothing to dispel Anya's rage and grief.

The boy cried out incoherently. Anya put a hand on his forehead. He was burning hot; his fever had not abated. Removing the linen dressing from his abdomen, she grimaced at the sight of the wound. Despite her best efforts, it was still badly infected. As she cleaned the wound and dressed it, her stomach rumbled loudly. She could not remember the last time she had eaten. Standing up, she caught Maud's eye.

'I'm going to fetch us something to eat. I will be back shortly.'

The quickest route to the kitchens was through the council chamber. The chairs on top of the dais were empty; there was no sign of Ronan. She walked quickly, lost in her thoughts. Her poultices were not proving as beneficial as she had hoped. She blamed Ronan for catapulting the corpses of plague victims over the wall, for releasing disease and putrefaction into the air. There were so many seriously injured men, so many badly infected wounds. So many men crying out for relief and she had only ground willow bark to offer them now. She had used the last of the poppy milk syrup two days since.

Panic was building inside her chest. Coming to an abrupt halt, she put her hands on her knees and tried to catch her breath. She found herself staring at the floor. She had scarcely noticed the mosaic before, because Vortigern's presence had dominated this echoing room for so long, eradicating all else.

In each corner of the mosaic, four roundels depicted the seasons. The personification of winter wore a heavy cloak. His sombre, mysterious face with dark, staring eyes, peered from beneath his hood. Kneeling down, she ran her fingers across the small cubes of marble, terracotta and glass. It was hard to believe the rulers of Aquae Sulis had once found the time and the money to commission such painstaking craftsmanship. They were relics of a lost age, an age of art and sculpture and literature and music.

The Britannia she knew was very different, stripped bare of everything but disease and war. The torrential rain had extinguished the fires, but much of Aquae Sulis lay in smouldering ruins, and a pall of smoke lingered above the rooftops. So many men had died, both Saxons and Britons alike. She was not surprised when they did not find Rufus among the dead. He was not a soldier; he would not have been on the battlefield. But he would surely have been in the camp close by, and she wondered what he had felt when he saw his city burning. And then she thought of Ronan's emissary. His brutal, pointless death was on her hands, and she felt sick to her stomach. How naïve, how foolish she had been to hope Hengist would negotiate.

'Anya! There you are. You weren't in the place of healing. I've been looking for you.' Silvanus crouched down beside her and stared, fascinated, at the perfectly executed mosaic. 'These floors are so ugly, and yet the craftsmanship is extraordinary, don't you think?'

Anya shrugged. 'They're incredible but irrelevant. Our world has no use for such things.' She leant into him, resting her cheek against his cuirass and breathed him in.

'Are you alright?' he asked.

'No, I'm not alright. I have this rage inside me. It's like a scream struggling to get out and I don't know what to do.'

He was silent for a moment and she wondered if she had shocked him.

'I'm here now. I won't ever let you go again.' He put his arms around her and she stifled a wince. The wound Wulfdan had inflicted on her upper arm was bandaged and smeared with a honey poultice but it still hurt. 'Sorry,' he said, hurriedly lessening his hold.

'Don't let go,' she whispered.

'Never.' He kissed the top of her head, but she sensed a sudden wariness about him, as if he was holding something back.

'What is it?' she asked.

'Ronan has accepted my offer of an alliance. I've told him my army will not be returning to Dumnonia just yet.'

Anya pulled away from him. 'No! You've done enough. This isn't your land. These aren't your people.'

He had survived one battle. She couldn't bear to think of him risking his life in another.

'I have no choice, Anya. Ronan is too powerful a man to have as my enemy. I swore an oath of allegiance to protect Dumnonia, but as long as there's war in Britannia, my people will never be safe. There is unfinished business here, and I want your blessing. I need your blessing.'

Anya felt chilled to her bones, as if a chasm was opening beneath her feet, and wraiths were trying to pull her down into its cold, black depths. Her heart was telling her Silvanus was wrong, but her head knew he was right.

'Of course you have my blessing,' she replied at last. 'But I should warn you, Ronan's volatile and he doesn't know his own mind. He could tip either way.'

Silvanus nodded, his expression grave. 'Then let's pray we can find a way to tip the scales in our favour.'

THIRTY ONE

Badon Hill, kingdom of the Dobunni

Rufus awoke to find the girl's naked body entwined with his. He had drunk a great deal the previous night. In the darkness, he had almost managed to convince himself this girl's warm body belonged to Anya. But in the cold light of day, he could see that her hair was not the colour of amber, but a dull mousy brown. And her skin was not peach-soft and clear, but as pock marked as a scabbed apple.

The sight of the girl's naked flesh revolted him now. Disentangling himself, he pushed her from his bed. Bleary eyed, she picked up her clothes and fled. Rufus did not make a habit of taking women to his bed because the fleeting moment of pleasure was invariably followed by self-loathing and shame. But with Anya, he knew it would be different. With Anya it would be perfect and pure. She was the daughter of a king. She was noble, beautiful and refined. And he knew she loved him because he had seen it in her eyes.

Rufus sat up, goose pimples rising on his pale flesh. As Hengist's chief advisor, he had commandeered the second largest round-house, but it was a cold and squalid hovel in comparison to the basilica. Disappointment and frustration coursed through him. He should be the governor of the city now, sitting on the raised dais in the council chamber with Anya at his side, not hiding on this hilltop like a common outlaw.

The failure to take Aquae Sulis had been a bitter blow for him. From the safety of the supply camp, he had watched the gate fall, and his spirits had soared. But then Silvanus of the Dumnonii had ridden out of Selwood, and his cavalry had scattered Hengist's army to the four winds. Rufus had run for his life, chasing after the banner of the white wolf as Hengist fled to Badon Hill.

With their peaceful hilltop overrun by an army in the grip of battle fever, the inhabitants of the old fort had chosen slavery over death and quickly surrendered, offering up their homes, their livestock and their grain pits.

Rufus caught sight of his clothes strewn across the floor, abandoned in haste the previous night. He scowled. He didn't like anything out of place; it made him feel on edge. Rolling off the low pallet, he began to pick them up. It was then he noticed a bite mark on his thigh. He remembered the girl's mouth on him and he shuddered with disgust. He felt dirty, unclean, and he badly needed to take a bath. Opening the door, he yelled, 'bring me hot water. I must bathe.'

An hour later, having been offered just one bucket of tepid water, Rufus still felt unclean. He walked slowly through the hilltop settlement, weighed down by a debilitating sense of trepidation. He had failed Hengist. His counsel had not led to the capture of Aquae Sulis, and he was acutely aware his life was balanced on a knife edge now.

Pulling his cloak tightly about his thin frame, he forced himself to concentrate, looking about with a taxman's keen eye, looking about for an opportunity to prove his worth. The top of the hill was as flat as a bread cake, an untidy, stinking maze of round-houses, workshops, barns and animal pens. In the desperate flight from the battlefield, Hengist had been forced to abandon the supply wagons. Rufus wondered how long the villagers' meagre grain stores would feed an army of five hundred men, and what he might suggest to eke out their supplies.

Not all of Hengist's army had followed him to Badon Hill. The Picts, seeing their promise of spoils fading, had vanished into the forests to begin the long journey back to their lands beyond the wall. Likewise, the Catuvellauni had chosen to abandon Hengist and flee to their estates north of Londinium. The warriors who remained were predominantly Saxons, and they scowled at Rufus with disdain as he passed by. In turn, Rufus thought them ugly barbarians with their unkempt yellow hair and long, ring-plaited beards, as garish as whores with their brightly bejewelled clasps, buckles and belts.

Unnerved, he let his gaze sweep across the hill. He had played here as a child. In the summer, bird's foot trefoil, vetches and orchids covered the limestone grasslands, moths and butterflies darted across its juniper bushes, and skylarks warbled their trilling songs.

But autumn had come to the lands of the Dobunni, and the leaves were turning red and gold as if a forest fire, fanned by easterly winds, was blazing across the land. The hill top afforded an impressive view of Aquae Sulis, and Rufus stared at the city with hungry eyes. Anya was behind those walls. She was so close now he could almost taste her.

Hengist had requisitioned the largest round-house, centrally placed at the summit of the hill. Two guards stood outside the door and they studiously ignored Rufus as he went inside. The round-house was dark and gloomy, and smelled of rotting

367

timbers and mouldy thatch. Hengist was sitting at a small table, with Aelfric at his side. Aelfric was carving something into the table top with his dagger, fine slivers of wood skittering across its crumb-strewn surface. Rufus thought he must be carving runes, the crude, angular symbols which passed as the written word for these illiterate savages.

Hengist was eating an enormous heap of scrambled eggs from a wooden platter. Tearing off a chunk of rye bread, he stuffed it into his mouth alongside the egg. Rufus noted with disgust there were specks of food lodged in Hengist's beard.

A low moan emanated from the shadows and Rufus turned nervously. The village chieftain was on his knees, his hands bound behind his back, his head lolling onto his chest. He had been badly beaten, his face a mass of blood and bruises. His wife, a wrinkled grey ghost of a creature, was stirring the cooking pot, whilst his daughters filled Hengist and Aelfric's cups with wine. They moved like timid mice.

Fear dried Rufus's throat. He could still picture Cunedda of the Catuvellauni gasping his last breaths beside the smoking camp fire.

Would he soon share the same fate?

'What is the matter with you, scribe?' Hengist asked with his mouth full. 'Was that girl you took to your bed a disappointment? Did you fail to get it up, eh?' Hengist winked at Aelfric, who smiled vaguely but did not look up, still intent on the runes.

Rufus flinched at the insult to his manhood, which was closer to the truth that he cared to think about.

'I can't hear you, scribe!' Hengist crowed. 'Speak up!'

Rufus glared at Hengist. He had betrayed his own people to escape a lifetime of scorn and humiliation, and for what? To endure more of the same from an ignorant heathen?

368

'When do we march on Aquae Sulis again, lord?' he asked. He realised he had failed to disguise his fear, for his voice trembled as he spoke.

'Still thinking of my sister, you sick bastard?'

'No, lord,' Rufus lied.

He was thinking of the oath Hengist had sworn, that he would govern Aquae Sulis, with Anya at his side. But that was before Silvanus had ridden out of Selwood and ruined everything. An image of Anya's face, those deep green eyes, shot into his head. No matter how afraid he felt, he couldn't give up on her. He had to find the strength to keep going, for her sake.

Rufus cleared his throat. 'You should make haste, lord. You should attack Aquae Sulis again, before Ronan has time to call for reinforcements.'

The wooden spoon stopped an inch from Hengist's open mouth.

'Reinforcements? You assured me Ronan has no allies, so just who is he supposed to call upon?'

'The Coritani are under his dominion, so too are the Atrebates.'

'I have marched through the lands of the Atrebates. They are farmers not warriors. Their villages are abandoned, their fields are fallow. He will find no spears there,' Hengist said dismissively.

In addition to the food caught in his beard, a sliver of scrambled egg was clinging to Hengist's pale lips. Rufus stifled a shudder of revulsion and tried a different tack. 'The gate fell under your ram, lord. It will take days to rebuild it. The city is yours for the taking. As I told you before, there are culverts beneath the city walls, large enough for men to crawl through. Under cover of darkness, it would be easy -'

369

'Enough!' The scribe's whining voice was beginning to get on Hengist's nerves. 'I have listened to your counsel, but it has proved worthless. I have no further use for you.'

Rufus turned deathly cold. Hengist had used the same words to describe Cunedda, moments after he had plunged his dagger into the boy's chest.

Hengist shoved another chunk of bread into his mouth and chewed it vigorously, watching Rufus with narrowed eyes. The scrawny little man was squirming like a trout on a hook. He was sorely tempted to kill him because weak men had no place in this world. But the scribe was renowned for extracting taxes from a stone. He might still prove useful.

'My men are bloodied and battle weary,' he said, almost to himself. 'They need to rest and regain their strength. We are fortunate the gods brought us to this place. The defences are sound, the grain pits are full, and the well is clean. But make no mistake, before the last leaf falls, I will take Aquae Sulis.' He waved his spoon at Rufus, summarily dismissing him.

Rufus stumbled outside, his heart thudding with relief and disbelief in equal measure. He had been given a reprieve. He lifted his gaze heavenward and said a silent prayer of thanks to the Christian God, a god he had previously regarded with profound scepticism. Walking back to his damp round-house he held his head a little higher.

There was still hope.

Hengist turned his attention to his platter of scrambled eggs again. Quite unexpectedly, an image of Anya's face darted across his mind and he felt a sharp stab of anger, of hatred. Instinctively, he touched Taranis's hammer, the amulet he wore about his neck. Anya had betrayed him, betrayed her own kin, betrayed the gods. She had laid charms of protection about the walls of Aquae Sulis. She was responsible for his failure to take the city. She was responsible for the deaths of his men. For that, and for so many other reasons, he wanted her dead, the last of Eown's monstrous, red haired, green-eyed brood.

He took a draught of wine. It tasted sour and he spat it out onto the rushes.

'By Odin, this tastes like piss!' he bellowed. Grabbing the older daughter's hair, he slammed her head down hard on the table. 'Bring me more wine, do you hear, and it had better be drinkable, or I'll flog the skin off your bones!'

The girl fled, clutching her cheek, her eyes bright with tears.

A tower of frustration was building inside Hengist. He was wasting time on this hill-top when there was so much to be done. He glanced at Aelfric. He was still carving runes, and the man's quiet concentration irritated him beyond measure. Aelfric was his right-hand man, a fierce warrior not a placid wood-smith.

Snatching the dagger from Aelfric's hand he embedded it, point down, in the table top. Aelfric remained utterly still for several heartbeats and then he stood up, his expression carefully composed.

Bowing from the waist, he said, 'lord, if you will excuse me, I must go and check on the men.'

Hengist scarcely noticed Aelfric fasten his sword to his belt and stride out the door, for his thoughts had turned to more pressing matters. Once he had taken Aquae Sulis, and displayed the boy-king's head over the gate, he would send word to Saxony. He would inform Athelwald that his unwanted fourth son was no longer a mercenary for hire, but the most powerful warlord in Britannia.

Next, he would march to Dumnonia, kill Silvanus, burn his

stronghold, and take his men, women and children for slaves. And finally, he would send Anya to meet her goddess. He had not yet decided on the manner of her execution. There were so many tantalising possibilities to choose from: impaled at the bottom of a stake pit, drowned beneath hurdles in a stinking mire, or strung up from a sacred oak.

Only when Anya was dead would he afford himself the luxury of a warm fire and a winter spent planning his final offensive - the total conquest of Britannia.

It was his birth-right, ordained by the gods, and he would not allow his half-bred sister, or Ronan, or Silvanus, or any of the pirates and chancers flooding into Britannia, to stand in his way.

THIRTY TWO

The council of war for the combined armies of the Dobunni and the Dumnonii took place in the council chamber of Aquae Sulis. There was a general air of despondency among the assembled commanders, for they all knew the Saxons had seized the advantage of the higher ground. There was no fire burning in the makeshift hearth and the chamber felt cold and damp.

Doubts and recriminations were swirling around Anya's head. She had persuaded Silvanus to become embroiled in the affairs of Britannia. She had brought him to this moment. She should have left him in peace, protected by the dense forest of Selwood and the seemingly endless, heather-clad moors of Dumnonia. At night, her dreams were growing darker, riddled with images of young kings put to sleep by the sword, and of ravens glutting upon the dead. Would Silvanus be among them?

'With respect, lord, I believe we should remain within the walls of Aquae Sulis. We should not engage. For all we know Hengist means to winter on Badon Hill. Why risk our men's lives when he is no direct threat to us?' Julianus was rubbing his oversized forehead with a huge, bear-paw hand, as if fighting a ferocious headache.

Anya was intrigued by his comment. Julianus had served Vortigern with blind obedience, and she had rarely heard him offer an opinion on anything.

'Hengist is camped barely a mile from Aquae Sulis,' Ronan replied. 'His very presence is a threat. And the longer he remains here, more men will join him.'

'I agree with Ronan,' Silvanus said, steam rising from his beaker of warm honey mead. 'Hengist's army is depleted. We all saw the Picts and the Catuvellauni vanishing into the forest. We should attack now, before he has time to call for aid.'

'How can he call for aid? We have guards set around the base of the hill. They are trapped on that hilltop like pigeons in a net,' Julianus objected.

'I suspect a messenger could still get out, under cover of darkness. Hengist will send for reinforcements,' Ronan contradicted dourly.

Silvanus turned to Anya. 'He is your brother. Out of all of us, you know him best. What do you think he intends to do? Will he winter on Badon Hill, or will he attempt to take the city again before the first snowfall? Or will he retreat to Londinium?'

Ronan gave a disparaging snort. 'Anya does not deserve a voice in this counsel, considering the last piece of advice she offered ended in the death of one of my best men.'

Silvanus watched Anya's expression falter, and he saw the anguish and regret in her eyes. In all the months they had been apart he had begun to believe she was the strong one, the invincible one, the one with all the answers. But then she had returned to Tintagel and in those brief, precious hours, she had shared her hopes and fears, opened her heart to him and shown him she was only human, as vulnerable and breakable as the next person.

And, if it were possible, he loved her even more deeply because of it. Her vulnerability had awakened a fierce desire to protect her, to keep her safe. He turned to Ronan.

'I would have offered the same counsel,' he said emphatically. 'Negotiation was the correct course of action.'

'Then you would both have been wrong, because it failed,' Ronan responded curtly.

Silvanus was utterly determined to stand his ground, for Anya's sake. 'We are civilised men. If there is the slightest chance negotiation might succeed then we must never be afraid to attempt it, whatever the circumstances.'

Ronan muttered something under his breath. Silvanus didn't catch his words but his tone was unmistakeably derisory. A heavy silence descended. Anya and Silvanus's eyes met and an unspoken exchange passed between them: compassion on his part, gratitude on hers.

Finally, Silvanus broke the silence. 'So, to return to the matter in hand. What does your brother intend to do, Anya?'

Anya opened her mouth then closed it again. She knew exactly what her brother intended to do, because she knew exactly how his cold, ruthless mind worked. But despite everything Hengist had already done, and everything he still planned to do, he was still her kin, her flesh and blood. She swallowed hard, restraining a strong desire to put her head in her hands and weep. How was she supposed to make sense of any of this?

Ten pairs of eyes were fixed upon her, awaiting her reply. She wanted to stand up and run from the council chamber and keeping running until she was far away. But it was as if Fenrir's chains were binding her, and holding her fast.

She glanced at Silvanus. The chains were binding her to him, just as they had always done, through countless lifetimes.

'May the goddess forgive me,' she thought.

'My brother is an ambitious man and he believes the gods are with him,' she began. 'He is also an impatient man. He will not want to spend the long winter months trapped on Badon Hill. I believe he will make a second attempt to take Aquae Sulis as soon as his men are rested.'

A murmur of dismay ran around the chamber.

Ronan's first instinct was to shout Anya down, for what kind of fool paid heed to the counsel of a girl, and a Saxon girl at that? And yet, a small persistent voice inside his head was telling him her reasoning was sound. Even so, he didn't want to listen to it.

Vortigern had ruled by gut instinct; he would have known instinctively what to do. But Vortigern was no longer here. Paralysed with indecision, Ronan looked around at his men. They gazed back at him, their expressions neutral, impassive. All except Petilius who, almost imperceptibly, nodded his head. Ronan glanced at his finger nails, bitten to the quick in the long dark hours before dawn when the heavy weight of kingship bore down all around him. And then he looked up again, and leapt into the unknown.

'Perhaps we should consider taking Badon Hill, before Hengist attacks our city again.'

To his surprise and chagrin, his suggestion was met with a marked lack of enthusiasm, with raised eyebrows and furtive, sidelong glances.

Sensing the general air of despondency in the chamber was deepening still further, Silvanus straightened his shoulders.

'We should treat this situation as a god-given opportunity,' he said adamantly. 'They have chosen to hide on a hilltop, which puts them on the defensive. In turn, this allows us to fight offensively. We can attack on our own terms.'

'It worked for the Romans, all those years ago,' Evric agreed. 'The tribes of Britannia hid on their hill tops, but the legions dislodged them as easily as stoning crows.'

'The Romans had vastly superior numbers, and vastly superior weaponry – siege engines and ballista, against men armed with little more than slingshot,' Jago countered. 'We have but one decrepit catapult. And if our estimates are correct, Hengist still outnumbers us. I fear it will be a massacre.'

Julianus nodded grimly. 'Badon has a rampart of dry stone walls twelve feet high and, in parts, twenty feet across. How are we to breach it?'

'It could be worse,' Silvanus replied doggedly. 'There are weak spots in their defences. Badon has just one ring of ramparts, and there are places where the stones have tumbled.'

'Absolutely right,' Evric concurred enthusiastically. 'I have seen it with my own eyes.'

Anya smiled to herself. Evric, Silvanus's ever loyal brother-in-arms.

'But surely those are the places Hengist will defend most strongly?' Jago persisted.

The mood in the chamber was deteriorating still further. Anya glanced at Silvanus and saw the plea in his eyes as clearly as if he had spoken it. Much as she yearned to play no part in any of this, he was asking for her help.

She took a deep breath. 'The ramparts are irrelevant. My brother remains on top of the hill simply because it offers protection in a hostile land, but if we were to march out in force from Aquae Sulis, I believe he would come down from the hilltop and face us.'

'How can you know that?' Jago asked.

'Because I understand how his mind works.'

'But why would Hengist choose to give up his advantage?' Ronan demanded.

'Because he is a warrior, and his seat in Valhalla depends on his valour in battle. There is nothing heroic about hiding on Badon Hill. It will not win him his place in the feasting halls of the gods.'

'You are certain of this?' Ronan pressed.

'Yes, I am,' Anya lied. She was not at all certain her brother would be so reckless as to give up the advantage of higher ground, but to delay would only strengthen Hengist's hand. She looked around at the men's sombre faces. 'Don't waste time planning an attack on the hilltop. Assemble the army on firm ground at the foot of the hill. If you goad Hengist and his warriors with taunts of cowardice, they will fall over themselves in their haste to be the first to come down and look you in the eye.'

Ronan's warriors were shaking their heads incredulously, but Silvanus seized upon her words.

'We should pay heed to Anya's counsel. Do not forget she is the daughter of a high king. Her advice is sound. We should not sit idly by with a Saxon army camped at our heels. We should form our battle lines at the foot of the hill, we should beat our shields, and we should demand they face us, man to man.'

Anya watched Ronan's men turn towards him, their heads bent, deliberating in low voices. Silvanus's men on the other hand, remained silent. They had accepted his final judgement without question; nevertheless, she noticed Jago's brow was furrowed with concern.

At length, Ronan's warriors moved apart. A decision had been made. Their dispirited air had evaporated, replaced with a palpable sense of purpose and of hope. Anya wished she could share it. Instead, she felt utterly wretched.

Silvanus looked at each warrior in turn. 'So, we are in agreement?'

Jago and Julianus hesitated for longer than the rest, but eventually each man gave their assent, save for Ronan. He remained perfectly still, but his eyes were darting back and forth. Anya had come to recognise this quirk; it meant he was deep in thought. Finally, his gaze focussed and he gave a quick nod.

'We are in agreement.'

'So be it,' Silvanus decreed. 'At dawn tomorrow, we fight. May the gods be with us.'

'May God be with us,' Ronan corrected him. 'The one true God.'

'Yes,' Silvanus replied. 'Him too.'

As the commanders filed out of the chamber, Silvanus took Anya to one side.

'Are you certain this will work?'

'Yes, I believe so.'

Her throat was tight with emotion and she could not bring herself to speak further. Perhaps he understood, for he pulled her into his arms.

'What did you tell me, all those months ago?' he whispered. 'Whether or not it is clear to you, no doubt the universe is unfolding as it should.'

She nodded absently. The priests of the sacred grove had taught her those words, but today they brought her no comfort. She did not feel as if the universe was unfolding as it should. Instead she felt as if it was hurtling, out of control, towards *Ragnarok,* the end of days, when Fenrir the wolf will break free from his fetters and devour the sun and the moon, and eternal darkness will fall upon the earth.

That evening, Anya slipped out of the city as dusk fell. The bulk of Silvanus's army had made camp outside the walls, their squat leather tents like autumn mushrooms clustered around a mighty oak. Men gathered at camp fires, talking in low voices. Some sat upon their shields to prevent the chill of the earth from reaching their bones, others used them as makeshift tables to eat their evening meal upon, or to play a game of dice.

No-one noticed her as she hurried away, her distinctive hair hidden beneath the hood of her cloak. The evening was cold, as if a death shroud had fallen across the low lying lands around Aquae Sulis. Tomorrow, Ronan's priests would bless his men with the Christian cross, but the army of Dumnonia would expect Anya's prayers. She needed mistletoe, the most sacred and powerful protector of all.

She quickened her pace along the drovers' track. The sun was setting, a blood red gash across the far horizon. It spoke of a cloudless day to come. Tomorrow, Britons and Saxons alike would die with weak autumn sunshine on their shoulders. The track through the forest was utterly silent. Yellow leaves drifted to the ground. There was not a breath of wind, the sounds of the woodland deadened by low-lying mist. Anya took the small dagger from the scabbard at her belt, and began to cut shiny red hips from the wild roses that grew in the hedgerow.

Leaves rustled and she turned fearfully. The young deer stared at her for a moment then vanished into the undergrowth with a graceful gait. Anya climbed up the steep bank of the trackway and into the woods, her boots sinking into the freshly fallen leaves. This place reminded her of the forests in Saxony; this place reminded her of home.

She quickly found what she was looking for, a perfect sphere of mistletoe hanging from the branches of an oak tree. Its deep green leaves were dotted with white berries, like stars hanging in a firmament. But even on tiptoes, arms outstretched, she couldn't reach them. There was nothing for it, she was going to have to climb the tree. Hitching her cloak into her belt, she grabbed the lowest branch for leverage. A twig cracked, loud in the silence and she spun around, expecting to see the deer again.

'I thought I might find you here.'

It was Rufus.

Anya stared at him, dumbfounded. He belonged in Aquae Sulis, skulking in Vortigern's shadow, not here in the damp stillness of the forest. She noticed his tunic, usually so pristine, was stained and crumpled. He looked tired and drawn, and thinner than she remembered. Perhaps life with Hengist was proving more difficult than he had hoped. And then she noticed the look in his eyes. It was not gentle or kind but needy, hungry, desperate. Fear shot through her.

'You cannot harm me,' she said, slowly backing away from him. 'If enemies meet beneath mistletoe, they must lay down their arms, and maintain a truce until the break of dawn.'

Rufus closed the distance between them. 'I am not your enemy, Anya. It saddens me you would think I am. I would never harm you. From the first moment I saw you at the gates of Calleva, I have only ever wanted to protect you.'

Anya's eyes widened. 'I don't need protecting. You should go back to Hengist, and leave me be.'

'I can't.' Rufus's eyes were glittering. 'Now I have found you, I will never let you go again. Do you have any idea how painful it was for me to watch Vortigern claim you? He was a brute of a man. But I will be considerate, loving.'

Anya frowned. 'I am not yours to claim, Rufus. I am a free woman.'

'You fool yourself, Anya. You are not a free woman. All your life, you have belonged to one man after another, beginning with your father. With Vortigern dead, you belong to Hengist again, and he has sworn to make you my wife. I will govern Aquae Sulis, and you will sit at my side.'

Anya could see the excitement, the anticipation, in Rufus's eyes, but she knew he was fooling himself. If Hengist was victorious in the battle to come, he would not permit a tax collector to rule Aquae Sulis. Nor would he allow Rufus to take her as his wife. It was far more likely Hengist would sacrifice her to the gods, in the most agonising manner his priest could devise.

A cold shudder of fear ran across Anya's skin. What should she do now? Should she turn and run? Or should she stand and fight? Her left hand reached for her sword, but then she remembered it belonged to Silvanus now. She reached for her dagger instead, her fingers closing around the grip, but then an image sprang into her head:

Wulfdan writhing in agony, his hands clawing at his throat as he slowly choked to death. Somehow, she had done that to him. She had taken one life and she had no desire to take another. There had to be another way.

'If I am to be your wife, as Hengist has promised, then there is no need for haste,' she said quietly. 'There will be a proper time and a proper place for our betrothal, and our marriage vows in the sight of your Christian God. Let me pass now Rufus and we will meet again, after the battle is won.'

'No, no, no,' Rufus tutted fussily, as if she had spilled milk on his tunic. 'Vortigern always said you talked too much. He said words were your only weapon, because you were a weak

382

and feeble woman. But I don't believe that. You are not weak or feeble. You are strong and kind and clever, and that is why I love you.'

'You love me?' Anya echoed faintly.

'Yes, I love you, and I swear I will make you happy.'

Anya stared at him in bewilderment. She had always believed Rufus to be a shrewd, intelligent man. How could he be so deluded about Hengist, about her, about everything?

'You can never make me happy, Rufus, just as I can never make you happy. We are not meant for each other. You must see that?'

Rufus's face crumpled into an expression of child-like hurt. 'Why would you say such a cruel thing to me? Surely you don't blame me for deserting Ronan? I was faithful to Vortigern for so many years, but in return he treated me with nothing but contempt.'

'No, that's not -' Anya began, but Rufus talked over her.

'Ronan is a vain and stupid boy. I could not in all conscience demean myself by swearing loyalty to such a foolish youth. But your brother is cut from very different cloth. He has taken the throne of the Catuvellauni. He has taken Londinium. He is a fearless warrior and men are flocking to his banner. He is the future, Anya. And I am truly blessed, for he sees my strengths. To him, I am not invisible. And he has demonstrated his trust in me by promising me your hand in marriage.'

'I cannot marry you, Rufus.' There was an edge to Anya's voice now. 'I am a priestess of the sacred grove, my body belongs to the goddess.'

Rufus's eyes narrowed. 'Why are you lying to me? I know you share Silvanus's bed, without ceremony or oath.'

A jolt of alarm ran through her. How did he know that?

Was it an educated guess or did he have spies in Aquae Sulis?

'But I forgive you.' Rufus's tone was unpleasantly unctuous. 'I know you don't love Silvanus. I know you go to his bed because, as Hengist's sister, you are in a precarious position and you do what you must to survive.' He hesitated for a moment then smiled, his expression so fawning it turned Anya's stomach. 'You love *me*, don't you? You've always loved me, from the moment we first met at the gates of Calleva.'

'I don't love you, Rufus. I have never loved you. Now let me pass.'

Even as she uttered the words, she saw the hurt in his eyes twisting into something darker and more dangerous. He took another step towards her, so close now she could see blotches of colour spreading across his throat.

'I should have known!' he spat. 'How could I be so blind? You are a whore, Anya, a cruel, wanton whore.' All traces of tenderness had vanished, as if his love for her had suddenly, menacingly, transformed into hate. 'Vortigern would have called you a 'cock-teaser'. You have enjoyed toying with me, with your smiles and your kindnesses, and now you think you can just walk away from me? You Saxons are all the same. I am beginning to think your brother will never give me your hand in marriage. But I will have you, Anya. I have waited too long, and I swear I will not be denied again.'

He attempted to grab her arm but she quickly stepped out of his reach. 'Do you know the story of Baldur and the mistletoe?' she blurted, terrified now, her heart thumping violently.

He was closing in on her again, but his hands froze in mid-air. 'What did you say?' he asked, bewildered.

Anya wondered why she had thought of Baldur. She hadn't heard the story for such a long time. It was a popular

384

midwinter's-eve tale, when sprigs of mistletoe decorated the great hall, the roaring fire reflected in the bard's melancholy eyes.

'Nerthus, the goddess of the earth, gave birth to a son.' The words formed on Anya's tongue without any conscious thought, her voice melodic, floating like a gentle lullaby on the still air. 'She called him Baldur. She made all the plants, trees and animals swear they would not harm her son.'

Rufus stared at her, transfixed. He was so mesmerised, he did not notice she was slowly backing away, each step increasing the distance between them. The woodland was beginning to fade around him. There was only the sound of her voice, each lilting word as intoxicating as a caress.

'But Nerthus overlooked the mistletoe plant and Loki, the god of mischief, tricked one of the other gods to kill Baldur with a spear made from mistletoe,' Anya went on, her voice as soft as mist.

'Nerthus was so distraught that she brought winter to the world. And then, after many years had passed, the gods restored Baldur to life, and Nerthus pronounced that from that day, mistletoe should only be used to bring protection and peace to the world, not death.'

Her foot snapped a fallen branch, the brittle sound piercing the air. Rufus jolted as if he had been struck. He looked about, dazed and disorientated, and then his gaze settled on Anya.

She cursed out loud, and then she turned and ran.

'Where are you going? Stay where you are!'

Rufus was surprisingly fast. She felt his hands on her shoulders, his bony fingers digging into her flesh. And then he spun her around.

'Don't touch me!' Anya hissed, wrenching the dagger from her belt and thrusting it towards his chest.

Rufus smiled unpleasantly. 'You won't hurt me, Anya. You're a healer, not a murderer.'

Anya held her ground. 'I killed a man, one of my own kin, and I will do so again, if I must.'

'A murderer and a whore!' Rufus's teeth were bared and there was madness in his eyes. Seizing her wrist, he prized the dagger from her grasp and flung it aside.

'Bitch! Evil, deceitful bitch!' he shrieked. Clenching his fists, he began to beat her about the face, his arms flailing wildly as if possessed. Anya raised her hands, desperately attempting to fend off the blows. And then, without warning, he launched himself at her, toppling her backwards into the wet leaves. The air flew from her lungs, and her teeth rattled. He was on top of her now, breathing heavily, planting wet, frantic kisses upon her face in a terrible parody of affection.

Breathless with fear, Anya tried to ram her knee into his groin, but he was surprisingly heavy. She was trapped beneath him. Her fingers scrabbled blindly through the leaves in search of her dagger, but she couldn't find it.

Think! Think!' urged the voice inside her head. She had seen a dagger at Rufus's belt. If she could just reach it, but first, she needed a distraction.

'The goddess sees everything,' she yelled at the top of her voice. 'She will know you have dishonoured me, and she will curse you for all eternity. I warn you, Rufus, let me go!'

'Your gods mean nothing to me, Anya!' His cheeks were as mottled as lungwort, his eyes glinting feverishly. 'Don't you understand? This is not about you. This is about Vortigern! Can't you see that even though he is dead and gone, everything, every God damned thing, is still always about him!'

Rufus tore the clasp from her cloak then tugged the two saucer-shaped brooches from her gown. Gazing at her naked

386

breasts, a groan of desire escaped his lips. This was Vortigern's woman. This was the woman Vortigern had wanted above all others, wanted so much he had even married her. And now she was his.

In the brief moment his gaze lingered over her naked flesh, Anya's fingers tore at his eyes. She missed her mark, gouging his face instead. He let out a shriek of pain and raised tentative fingers to explore his torn, bloodied cheek. And in that same moment, Anya reached for the dagger at his belt, but he was too quick. Grabbing her by the wrists, he held her fast, the weight of his body forcing the air from her lungs, his knees pushing her thighs apart.

Anya couldn't move and she couldn't breathe. Horrific memories of her wedding night were crashing about her head, their sharp, jagged edges piercing her skull in starbursts of pain. She opened her mouth to scream but the sound died on her lips.

She saw the dagger blade approaching from the corner of her eye, a flash of sharp steel in the fading light. A hand grabbed Rufus's hair, jerking his head backwards. She watched the dagger blade slice across his exposed throat, left to right. It sank deeply into soft flesh and she heard a sharp crack as it splintered bone. And then, just as suddenly, the blade was gone.

There was the thinnest red line across Rufus's throat. And then, like a sycamore bud unfurling, the wound opened. At first, it was a mere trickle but it quickly became a pulsing torrent. Rufus's thick, warm blood splattered onto her face, her neck. Terrible gurgling sounds were coming from Rufus's throat, but it was the expression in his eyes that continued to haunt her, long afterwards. Interwoven with the fear and agony, he looked utterly bereft.

And then, quite suddenly, his heavy weight was gone. She rolled onto her side, taking painful, heaving gulps of air. Silvanus was dragging Rufus away by the ankles, leaving a trail of blood across the yellow leaves. Dumping his body unceremoniously in a patch of bracken, he ran back to her. Crouching at her side, he put her cloak around her bare shoulders.

'Was I too late? Did he - did he hurt you?' his voice was taut with emotion.

Anya was shaking so violently, she was having difficulty rubbing Rufus's blood from her face. 'No, he didn't hurt me.'

'Thank the gods,' Silvanus said fervently. 'Here, let me.'

Tipping the contents of his water bottle onto the corner of his cloak, he wiped her face as best he could. Then he retrieved her discarded brooches. Without comment, he carefully re-fastened her gown, replaced her cloak about her shoulders, and then cradled her against his chest as if she were a small child. They stayed like that for a long time. She took comfort in his warmth, but her limbs still shuddered, and her head pounded like a battle drum.

'That bastard won't hurt you again,' Silvanus said at last. 'You're freezing. We should get you to a fireside. Do you think you can move?'

He helped her to her feet and she swayed, nauseous and light headed. He put an arm about her shoulders to steady her, but he could not shield her from the sight of Rufus's blood-soaked body.

'What shall we do with him?' she asked, her voice small.

'We'll leave him for the wolves. He deserves no more.'

Anya hesitated. In the short time she had known Rufus, she had watched the humiliation and the rage eat away at his soul. In many ways, he was just another of Vortigern's victims.

Even in death, the high king of the Dobunni still had the power to corrupt and destroy.

'No,' she said quietly. 'I should like him to be buried with respect, and facing east, in the Christian way.'

Silvanus shook his head in disbelief. 'Your willingness to forgive is quite beyond me but, if you wish, it will be done.'

'Thank you,' she replied, putting a hand to her throbbing temple. She felt so weary and longed for sleep. But then she remembered why she had ventured into the forest alone.

'I came for the mistletoe, I cannot leave without it.' She pointed at the sphere of bright green leaves above her head. 'I can't reach it. Will you help me?'

He grabbed the branch easily, cutting the sprigs with a dagger blade still smeared with Rufus's blood. They walked back to the camp in silence, but a thousand images were blazing like shooting stars across Anya's over-wrought mind. She closed her eyes for a moment and tried to gather her wits. Silvanus had saved her life today, but perhaps the mistletoe had also played its part. Perhaps it had protected her, just as Nerthus had promised it would. And perhaps it would also protect Silvanus tomorrow, at Badon Hill.

THIRTY THREE

Tintagel, kingdom of Dumnonia

It was long past midnight. In the great hall, hounds dozed by the dying embers of the fire, and sparrows drowsed on the rafters, heads tucked under their wings. In the kitchens, mice scurried across the flagstones and over the feet of the young baker's apprentice who had chosen to sleep at the fireside, his toes pressed against the warm hearth stones.

Mairi however was wide awake, perched on the edge of the bed, her son held tightly in her arms. She was listening hard, straining to hear the faintest hint of footfall in the corridor beyond her locked door. Would he come? Had she done enough to save the life of her beloved son?

She looked down at Mordred. He was not yet a year old but already he had a fierce temper, and stubborn determination. And yet in sleep, he looked so peaceful, so innocent. He was crawling now, and trying to stand. And she yearned to stop time, to keep him a helpless babe in arms. Not only to protect him from harm, but also to hide his deformity, the tiny pink foot that turned inwards, the one blot on his otherwise achingly beautiful perfection. Why had the gods allowed such a shameful blight, for this was the child who would one day be king? She would never forget the wise woman's words. *'Many will bow down before him, just as many will remember him in the years to come.'*

Mairi kissed her son's cheek, revelling in the softness of his skin, his milky-sweet scent, and felt the familiar explosion of love tear her heart. A love so strong it had obliterated her own hopes and dreams. His will had become her will, his needs her own.

Her first reaction on hearing of Lucan's execution had been not pity or heartbreak, but rage. Rage that Mordred had been left without a father, rage that his precious life now hung in the balance. But once the rage had passed, she realised she was glad Lucan was dead, for he had proved himself to be a dangerous liability. It was up to her now. It was her responsibility to keep Mordred safe, to nurture him until he was old enough to claim the throne of Dumnonia.

She was so lost in her thoughts it was several moments before she became aware someone was unlocking the door.

'Garth, is that you?' she whispered, leaping to her feet.

'Yes, my love.'

Mairi pulled a face. *'How foolish men are,'* she thought. *'How easily won with seductive smiles, warm lips and the promise of more, much more.'*

The door opened and Garth's eager young face appeared, illuminated by lamplight. She could see exhilaration in his eyes, and fear and nervousness, and lust. He pulled her into his arms, crushing the babe between them, his lips hard and urgent against hers. She returned his kisses but her mind was already far away from this cold, claustrophobic room. And far away from Taliesin, the foul-smelling old priest who wished her son dead. Gently, she pushed Garth away.

'We cannot linger,' she said softly. 'Is everything prepared?'

He nodded earnestly. 'The ship is waiting.'

She stared briefly into his eyes, searching for any hint of treachery or betrayal, for Garth had sworn an oath of loyalty to Silvanus. But she saw nothing to give her cause for alarm. Garth was gazing at her with an expression of besotted devotion. He looked pathetic, but she smothered her revulsion and ran her free hand lightly across his cheek. On her tip toes, she leant closer to nibble his ear lobe, and heard his stifled groan of desire.

'Then lead the way, my love,' she whispered.

The corridor was cold and dark, the lamp casting long shadows that slid along the walls like wraiths rising from the underworld. Beyond the fortress, an owl cried as it hunted over the icy moors. Closer to hand, somewhere up ahead, a door opened, followed by low voices, muffled laughter. Garth quickly blew out the lamp. Mairi could feel her heart hammering against her ribs. Perhaps sensing her tension, Mordred stirred in her arms, and her heart beat faster still. Her son had a scream loud enough to wake an entire burial chamber of long dead ancestors. She rocked him back and forth and felt his sturdy limbs relax into sleep again.

She heard the door close again. Footsteps sounded, loud in the silence and brief flashes of candlelight illuminated the corridor. Mairi felt panic rising up within her. Who was it? Which way were they going? She was dizzy with fear now. Garth moved closer still, shielding her. She could feel his warm breath against her cheek, feel his firm young body pressed hard against her hip.

The footsteps faded into the distance, and relief flooded through her. In the pitch black now, they set off again, creeping along the corridor and down the spiral staircase. Terrified of falling, she ran the fingers of her free hand along the cold, damp walls and felt for the edge of every step. At the bottom of the stairs, Garth came to a halt and peered tentatively around the corner, but the great hall was deserted. Silvanus's favourite hound raised its head and watched them as they passed. Mairi eyed it disdainfully, mangy old brute. Garth opened the doors that led onto the courtyard and glanced about cautiously, but there were no guards to be seen. Mairi smiled to herself. It seemed the sleeping draught she had suggested to Garth had worked after all.

They kept to the shadows but once on the cliff path, Garth insisted on re-lighting the lamp, for the descent was treacherous enough in daylight but potentially deadly on a moonless night. Mairi glanced up at Tintagel and prayed no one was awake to notice a light bobbing down the winding track. More than once she lost her footing on the scree of loose stones, and found herself glad of Garth's steadying hand at her elbow.

Having spent months confined to her chamber, Mairi was out of breath by the time they reached the beach. Garth extinguished the lamp again but as her eyes gradually became accustomed to the darkness she realised he was dragging a small boat towards the sea. She followed him into the shallows. Icy water soaked the hem of her cloak and surged into her boots. Garth helped her clamber on board and settled her solicitously in the stern. Mairi huddled deeper inside her cloak, clutching Mordred tightly. She was shivering now, both from the bitter cold and the dawning awareness of the enormous task that lay ahead of her.

She watched Garth's brow furrow with the effort of rowing out to sea. The boat crested a wave then plunged down the other side, and Mairi fought a strong urge to vomit. Desperate for distraction, she glanced over her shoulder at Tintagel, perched on the clifftop like a mighty eagle. She thought back to the day she had arrived at the great fortress of Dumnonia. She had been just fourteen years old, come to be married to Etar's younger son, to a husband she had never met. She had spied Silvanus, handsome and tall, standing head and shoulders above the rest, and her heart had missed a beat. But then Lucan had stepped forward to greet her and he was not handsome but short and stocky, with unsightly blemishes on his cheeks. And she had been right to be disappointed, for Lucan had proved to be neither gentle nor kind.

But he had given her a son. Mairi looked down at the child in her arms. And she forgot the biting wind, and her sodden boots and numb toes. She forgot her loathing for her late husband. She forgot her jealousy of Anya, and her hatred of Silvanus. Without thinking, she opened her cloak, unclasped her brooch and offered Mordred her breast. Even in sleep, his lips latched on and he began to suckle vigorously. He had several teeth now and she gasped as he bit into her tender flesh, but she did not pull away. She revelled in his strength, in his fierce need of her. The dragging sensation as he fed filled her with exquisite ecstasy, an all-powerful sense of one-ness with the child who would be king.

She noticed Garth's gaze had fixed, spellbound, upon her exposed breast. She gave him a slow, seductive smile but then she lifted her gaze to the dark shape of the merchant ship which grew steadily closer with his every pull of the oar.

The ship that would take her to Frankia.

To the kingdom where Mordred would become a man.

THIRTY FOUR

Aquae Sulis, kingdom of the Dobunni

Anya chose to spend the night before battle in Silvanus's camp outside the city, for she still felt uneasy surrounded by stone and brick and tile. And besides, the basilica of Aquae Sulis was a place of ghosts and unsettling memories. Even in death, Vortigern's presence lingered there.

It was cold inside the hide tent and her breath misted the air. Lying quite still beneath the warm rugs, she enjoyed the blissful sensation of being wrapped in Silvanus's arms. He began to stir, drifting towards consciousness. Opening his eyes, he smiled and kissed her tenderly.

'You're still here.' He sounded both astonished and profoundly relieved.

'Of course I'm still here,' Anya smiled. 'Where else would I be?'

Suddenly, his expression darkened. 'There is still so much I want to do,' he murmured.

Anya felt her heart falter. 'You will not die today,' she whispered.

'How can you be sure of that?'

The vulnerability in his eyes was almost her undoing.

'There are some things I just know,' she replied, forcing herself to hold his gaze. She hated lying to him. She did not know how this day would end. She had been awake for much of the night and when sleep had finally found her, her nightmares of blood and slaughter had been infuriatingly vague, as always.

All except for one startlingly vivid dream which had stayed with her, when all the rest had faded into air.

'But if I do fall in battle today, if I do not return -'

'No!' Anya put her fingers to his lips. 'Don't say it, please don't say it.'

'I must say it, and you must listen. If I die today, I don't want you to waste the rest of your years in sadness or regret. Promise me you will live your life, and strive to be happy.'

Tears pricked Anya's eyes. How could she promise something she knew would be impossible?

'I am to blame for all this. You were safe in Dumnonia, living an honourable life. But now -'

'Anya, listen to me. None of this is your fault. In the watchtower room all those months ago, you told me the gods choose our path, and that no matter how hard we try, we can't fight against them. I may have been safe in Dumnonia, but my life was not honourable. Where is the honour in turning my back on my neighbours? Where is the honour in burying my head in the sand?'

Anya laid her head on his chest, took comfort in his strong heartbeat, for she felt as if her own heart was breaking.

'In Saxony, I thought I could hear the gods. I thought I knew what they wanted of me. And then I came to Britannia, and all my dreams were of war and death. And I didn't want to listen. It's taken me a long time to accept that, sometimes, war is the only way. But the reality of war is so much harder to bear than the mere idea of it. I love you so much, and yet I have brought you here, to this day.'

'And I thank you for it, Anya, because you have saved me.'

Anya looked up at him. 'Saved you from what?'

'From myself.' His fingers were tracing the contours of her face, committing her features to his memory. If he was to die today, he would carry this image of her, beautiful and flushed from sleep, into the world beyond the veil. He kissed her one last time, then he sat up and tugged his linen undershirt over his head.

Anya watched him dress for battle; breeches, leather jerkin, then a short coat of ancient mail. She felt suddenly in awe of him, this broad-shouldered warrior king. And then she watched him pick up his sword. Last night's vivid dream was edging to the front of her mind, like a man pushing his way through a crowd.

'Wait! No! Not that one!' she cried.

He came to an abrupt halt and glanced questioningly at her.

She grabbed her own sword from beside their makeshift bed and held it out to him. It felt uncomfortably heavy, as it always did. As if it had never belonged to her. As if it had been waiting for its rightful owner, through the countless, turning years.

'I meant what I said. This is yours now. Please take it.'

'I can't, Anya. Not today.' Silvanus fastened his own sword to his belt. 'This belonged to my father, and to his father before him, and this is the sword I must use to defend my kingdom. That is your sword, the sword of your ancestors.'

'It's never been mine,' Anya replied. 'I've known the truth for a long time, but I shut my mind to it. The curse of the exile is loneliness, the yearning for a home, a hearth. So when the sword came to me, I convinced myself it meant I belonged in Siluria. I wanted to believe it so badly I ignored what my heart was telling me.' She thrust the sword broadside at him. 'It will need a whetstone.'

'I don't understand.'

'It doesn't matter. What matters is that you take the sword, and fight with it today.'

He was staring at her, his hand tightly grasping the pommel of his father's sword. She could see the confusion in his eyes and she knew he deserved an explanation, such as she could give him.

'Taliesin took me to the cave of fires. I saw the sword in my dream paths, held aloft by a warrior-king, but I couldn't see his face. But since then, I've caught glimpses of him. It was you, Silvanus.'

She held out the sword again. This time, he took it. As it left her hands, she expected to feel the familiar sense of loss, but instead she felt only relief. What had Ceinwin said?

'Trust me. When the time comes, you will know.'

Silvanus drew the sword from its scabbard. 'It's certainly very beautiful.' He glanced questioningly at her. 'So you think I should fight with it today?'

'I know that you must fight with it.'

Silvanus swung the blade to and fro, deep in thought. If he put aside Etar's sword today, surely he would betray his father, his kingdom, his people? And yet, Anya had that look in her eyes again. It was more than mere determination. It was pure, absolute conviction.

'Will it bring us victory?' he asked at last.

'I don't know,' Anya replied. 'All I know is that you were meant to have the sword. Perhaps that's the only reason I came to Britannia, to make sure it found its way to you.'

'Not the only reason.' Silvanus leant over and put his lips to hers. His kiss was so tender, so full of yearning that Anya struggled to maintain her composure when they finally drew apart. She watched him remove his father's sword from his belt. He placed it reverentially on the low table beside their bed, and then he fastened Anya's sword in its place. She noticed his expression had hardened, his face set in concentration. He was mentally pulling away from her now, beginning to focus on the battle to come. Slinging his shield over his shoulder, he walked to the tent flap, paused then turned to face her again.

'I love you, Anya. I will always love you,' he said softly, and then he ducked his head, and went out into the grey dawn to face his men.

A wet cloak of mist clung to the earth, smothering the freshly ploughed fields below the slopes of Badon Hill in an eerie stillness. No birds sang, as if they understood what was soon to come. The assembled army of the Britons was morosely silent too, despite the charms of protection Anya had sprinkled at the men's feet, a potent blend of crushed basil, bay, fennel, hyssop, rosehips, vervain and mistletoe. The Britons were eyeing the hilltop grimly, for Hengist and his army steadfastly remained behind the ramparts of the old fort.

'Two commanders leading one army,' Jago said morosely. 'I do not see how this can end well, lord. It would have made more sense if Ronan had given you sole command.'

'We are fighting for his kingdom and his city. I did not expect him to hand command to me,' Silvanus replied evenly.

'But can we trust him?' Jago pressed.

In unison, Silvanus and Anya turned in their saddles, looking across the shield wall towards Ronan, magnificent in a cloak of imperial purple. 'We have no choice but to trust him,'

Silvanus replied. 'But first, we need Hengist to come down from that hilltop.'

He glanced expectantly at Anya, and her heart sank. She could almost feel the Saxon and British blood clashing through her veins, oil on water, incompatible, constantly at war. How could she ever reconcile the two? She felt weightless, as if time was compressing, spinning her backwards to her childhood in her father's hall in Saxony, then hurtling her forwards again, to the moment she had first met Silvanus. And as she looked into his eyes, so full of faith, so full of trust, her resolve hardened.

'Remember what I told you,' she said under her breath, so only he could hear. 'Call Hengist out as a coward. Humiliate him in front of his men.'

Silvanus nodded imperceptibly and then he took a deep breath and bellowed at the top of his voice, in Latin, 'Hengist, son of Athelwald! Why are you cowering up there like a frightened child, bringing dishonour upon yourself and your kin? What are you, a man or a mouse? Come down from there and face us, you coward!'

Taking Silvanus's lead, the Britons in the shield wall began to echo his taunts, mocking the Saxons' lack of courage, their diminutive genitalia, their mothers' dubious virtue.

Hours passed. The mist began to lift and a watery sun emerged, washing the sky in delicate pinks and golds. The army of the Britons grew hoarse from hurling insults up the hill, but there was still no sign of movement within the Saxon camp.

Anya glanced first at Ronan then Silvanus and saw the agonised tension mirrored in their faces. What if she had been mistaken? What if Hengist had no intention of leaving Badon hill until reinforcements arrived? She prayed the Britons would choose to retreat to Aquae Sulis. She prayed they would not be so foolhardy to attempt an uphill attack against a heavily defended hill-top.

'The gates! Look! The gates!'

Startled from her reverie, Anya followed Silvanus's gaze. Beneath the banner of the white wolf came Hengist's army, bedecked with arm rings and brooches of gold and garnets, bristling with spears and iron-rimmed shields, with fearsome battle helmets and heirloom swords. They were an awesome sight. In her mind's eye she could see Hengist and Horsa standing before Vortigern in Calleva. How proud she had been of them then, magnificent in their warriors' garb.

Adrift on a sea of painful memories, she turned to Silvanus for reassurance. But he was not looking at her. He was looking up the hill with an expression of intense frustration, for Hengist was mustering his army at the top of the slope, and thus retaining the advantage of higher ground.

The sun rose higher in the sky, burning off the last traces of mist. Beneath a cold blue sky, the Britons continued to hurl insults at the Saxons, but Hengist's army refused to budge one more inch down the hill.

Silvanus and Ronan were locked in a fierce debate.

'We must give them an incentive. It's time to engage the cavalry. Let the Dumnonii at them,' Silvanus insisted.

'No. I forbid it. We are on my soil. My cavalry should be the first into battle.'

'With respect,' Silvanus said, 'it was my cavalry that scattered Hengist's forces. Think how his men will feel when they see the red dragon charging towards them up the hill. They will remember their comrades falling, and they will remember turning and fleeing for their lives.'

Anya held her breath as Silvanus led the cavalry charge

across the muddy plough-land, over the small boundary stones at the edge of the field, and up the grassy slopes of Badon Hill. Surely his cavalrymen were riding to certain death? Surely no horseman could hope to break through the impenetrable Saxon wall of sharp spears and linden shields? She watched the Saxon front line steadying themselves for the impact of a hundred charging horsemen but at the last moment, Silvanus's cavalry wheeled right, riding not directly at the Saxon shield wall, but alongside the deadly, bristling wall of iron.

They rode fast, speed and shoulder-slung shields their only protection. On Silvanus's command, his cavalry turned in their saddles and launched a storm of spears into the densely packed Saxon shield wall. The spears flew surprisingly slowly, as if the air was resisting their malevolence but even so, it was impossible to avoid them in the crush of the Saxon shield wall. Some found shields, but many more found flesh.

Again and again, the cavalry of the Dumnonii rode along the Saxon shield wall, launching their spears into the massed ranks of the Saxons, and the grasslands churned to mud beneath their pounding hooves. It was a dangerous game, the horses unprotected, easy targets. Anya watched, sickened, as a stallion dropped to its knees, a Saxon spear embedded in its neck. The rider lurched forward in the saddle then righted himself. Moments later, the horse crashed sideways into the mud. The cavalryman leapt from the saddle, scrambling to roll clear of the animal's heavy body and thrashing hooves. The warrior was on his feet again in an instant, his sword in his hand, but he was exposed and vulnerable now.

He turned briefly, glancing at the assembled armies at the foot of the hill. His face was partially hidden beneath his helmet, and Anya couldn't see his features. Who was it? She raised a hand to shield her eyes from the low sun, analysing his physique, his bearing. It wasn't Silvanus, or Evric, or wiry Gorran or heavy-set Boult. She prayed it wasn't Jago. She could sense the man's indecision. Part of him was sorely tempted to turn tail and run, but the warrior within him turned back to face the enemy.

Anya felt her heart miss a beat. What was he doing? What could he hope to achieve, one man against a shield wall, five hundred strong?

And in that same moment, the spear pierced the cavalryman's chest. Its momentum was so powerful it threw him onto his back, his arms outstretched. His helmet flew from his head, and Anya felt a rush of conflicting emotions: relief it wasn't Jago, then pity for the unknown warrior.

Silvanus's cavalrymen were beginning to tire. Mistakes were made. Horses stumbled, and more men fell. But still Silvanus and Evric continued to lead charge after charge up the hill, as dying men and horses screamed in the slippery, bloodied mud.

Anya knew it was only a matter of time before a Saxon spear brought Silvanus down, only a matter of time before she watched him die. The thought was so unbearable, so horrifying, she rode the length of the British shield wall, reining in alongside Ronan.

'This cannot go on!' She was so angry she did not even attempt to lower her voice. 'The Dumnonii are exhausted. Tell Silvanus to retreat. You must engage *your* cavalry now.'

Julianus and Petilius glanced at one another, eyebrows raised, astonished by her audacity.

'Mind your tongue, woman!' Ronan snapped. 'You have no authority to issue orders here. And you would do well to remember we are a Christian kingdom. If you utter one more word about pagan gods, or throw one more sprig of mistletoe at my men, I'll have you strung up.' Turning his back on her dismissively, he removed the water bottle from his belt and took a long draught.

'Your people take great comfort from their old gods!' Anya retorted furiously. 'Tell me, where is your Christian bishop when there is need of him? He is on his knees, cowering in his empty church.' She shook her head, distraught. 'Men of Dumnonia are dying up there! They're dying for your city, for your kingdom. You can't stand by any longer. You have to engage.'

But Ronan continued to ignore her. In desperation, she grabbed a handful of his cloak.

'Ronan! You have to do something!'

'Don't touch me!' he hissed, wrenching himself from her grasp, painfully reminded of Vortigern's habit of manhandling him in front of the men. He was sorely tempted to strike Anya, but then he noticed the look in her eyes. He made no claim to understand women, but any fool could see she was in torment.

'Listen to me,' he said, more gently than he had intended. 'I swore an oath to Silvanus not to advance until his cavalry had broken the Saxon shield wall. Battles are won in the mind, not at the end of a spear. If the Saxons see Silvanus's cavalry in retreat, they will believe victory is in their grasp.'

'When the Saxons see the last cavalryman of Dumnonia fall, they will certainly believe victory is in their grasp!' Anya protested. 'For the love of the gods, Ronan, if you will not engage your cavalry, then you must order the shield wall to advance!'

Ronan's eyes were darting back and forth. She knew he was wavering, but then the shutters crashed down.

'I will not break my oath.'

Anya let out a cry of anguish and frustration. She shot a

glance at Silvanus, watched him reach down from his saddle and take another spear. He was readying his men for yet another charge. She didn't want to watch him die. Not this time. Not again. And so she kicked her heels and galloped up the hill to join him.

'What are you doing?' he asked, aghast. 'You can't be here! We're in range of the Saxon spears.'

'I am well aware of that,' she replied, scanning the Saxon lines, searching for her brother. He was not difficult to find. Bedecked with gold, and mounted on a fine warhorse, he appeared god-like, the very embodiment of his immortal ancestor. The Saxon front line was a roar of noise with men chanting and jeering and stamping their feet. Anya's mare began to fret. She shortened the reins, and scratched behind its ears. And then she straightened up, and fixed her gaze upon her brother.

'We will not retreat,' she shouted in the Saxon tongue and despite the tumult, her voice carried, clear and strong. 'How long do you intend to perch on that hill like a stupid chicken in a fowl-house? Are you afraid to face the army of the Britons? If the Valkyries choose you for Valhalla today, are you afraid the warriors of Corpse Hall will turn you away, unworthy and unsung? Or perhaps the truth of it is you are afraid of me? Afraid of your little sister? Afraid of the gifts the goddess has bestowed upon me?'

Hengist could hear every word she uttered, and so too could his men. A storm of anger swept through his veins. How dare this shamed and worthless girl attempt to humiliate him in front of his warriors? How dare she accuse him of cowardice, when he commanded an army greater than any seen on the soil of Britannia since the days of the legions? His hatred for his sister was a living creature, writhing in his gut and spewing poison into his veins. And so he did not stop to think, or weigh the odds. Defying all reason, and without hesitation, he turned to Aelfric. 'We advance! Now!'

The order was passed rapidly along the Saxon lines; short throwing spears quickly replaced with longer thrusting spears for the clash of the shield wall. Battle horns sounded and Anya watched in stunned disbelief as Hengist's army began to advance down the hill, the Saxons howling to Odin the father, to Taranis, god of the storm, to Andraste, goddess of war.

'Hold firm!' Ronan roared along the shield wall. 'Hold firm!'

Scarcely believing what he was seeing, Silvanus hastily ordered the withdrawal of his cavalry. He rode protectively close to Anya, their stirrups almost touching.

'Ride back to the city. Make haste! Be safe!' he urged.

'No. I will stay with you.'

She had stood beside Silvanus on countless battlefields, in countless lifetimes, and it had rarely ended well. And now it was happening all over again. If he was to die today, she would die at his side.

Silvanus opened his mouth to object but at that moment, a Saxon battle horn sounded two short blasts, a pause, then two more. And then, to his amazement, the Saxon army came to a ragged halt no more than thirty paces from the Britons' shield wall. He turned to Anya.

'Why has he stopped? What's he doing?'

'I don't know,' she replied uneasily.

Both armies were building themselves into frenzy, the men of Dumnonia crying 'Epona! Epona', over and over again, like an echo trapped in a valley. The noise was so great it was almost impossible to hear the Druid priest who stepped forward from the Saxon ranks. He was as small and skinny as an elf, and seemingly as ancient as Badon Hill itself. His back was stooped, and thin trails of grey hair hung limply about his haggard face. Raising his bony arms, he began to fling handfuls of salt, and blood-curdling curses, towards the British shield wall.

'What does he say?' Silvanus mouthed above the din.

'He says the salt will counter my charms of protection and he says he possesses the evil eye. He says we will all die before we throw a single spear,' Anya replied, unable to hide the tremor in her voice.

'Then I am glad my men do not speak the Saxon tongue,' Silvanus replied dryly, but in truth he was afraid. The Britons did not need to speak the Saxon tongue to understand the priest was cursing them. If this was allowed to continue, their morale would quickly crumble to dust.

'Kill him!' Ronan commanded, but not one Briton raised his spear, for fear of angering the old priest's ancient gods.

Anya eyed the priest nervously. There were countless faded tattoos upon the priest's scrawny arms, one for each year since his initiation, whilst she bore just one tattoo. She was a novice, whilst his wrinkled skin proclaimed his powers to the world. But she had to find a way to silence him.

Reaching inside the pocket of her cloak, her fingers closed around Taliesin's parting gift, the precious elf shot, crafted long ago by the ancient people of Britannia. Forcing herself to look the Saxon priest squarely in the eye, she held out her closed fist. Then she unfurled her fingers to reveal the elf shot in her palm. With her gaze still fixed on the priest, she blew a gentle breath upon the tiny flint arrow-heads then threw them towards Hengist's army. They swept high into the air, borne along as if by an invisible breeze, before finally dropping close to the Saxon front line. The drum beat faltered and the Saxon foot-solders backed away from the elf-shot as if they were poisonous snakes. They muttered counter-charms under their breath and clutched the talismans that hung around their necks, the hare's feet, hag stones, and little leather bags containing the magic bones of toads.

'This is the land of the Britons,' Anya cried in her native tongue. 'It is made strong by the blood and bones of their ancestors, and watched over by their ancient gods. This is not your land, men of Saxony. You do not belong here. You will never belong here. You anger the gods of this place with your grey-ash spears.'

The men in the Saxon shield wall were utterly silent now, eyeing one another fearfully.

Anya pointed at the priest. 'And you – you have no power here, old man!'

'Pay no heed to the fallen woman,' Hengist shouted in response. 'She is an exile, cast out of the sacred grove, shamed and worthless, stripped of all her powers. Never forget brothers, that we are the sons of Odin. His blood is our blood. We are the first amongst men, and it is our birth-right to take this land. This is the day of days, warriors of Saxony! Odin the father is with us! Victory will be ours!'

At Hengist's side, Aelfric let out a mighty roar and began to chant, 'Odin! Odin! Odin!' and Hengist's household guards quickly followed his lead. Emboldened, the Saxon foot-soldiers took up the chant, thumping iron-tipped wooden spear shafts into the ground, matching the pulsing rhythm. Battle horns sounded and suddenly Hengist's army was on the move again. The drums began to beat once more, faster and faster, hypnotic in their intensity. Saxon shields parted for the old priest, swallowing him up like a spider vanishing into a crack in the wall. And then the Saxon army was running, charging towards the Britons, their war cries unearthly, no longer words but primeval howls of bloodlust. Save for Hengist, whose words Anya could hear all too clearly.

'Today I avenge my brother! Today you die, Ronan son of Vortigern! Today, your shield wall will shatter, and the warriors of Britannia will be wiped from the face of the earth!'

Silvanus grabbed the reins of Anya's mare, forcibly bringing her alongside him.

'You cannot remain on the front line! Men will die to protect you. Get behind the shield wall. If it breaks, ride hard for Selwood, and don't look back.'

Anya hesitated, unwilling to leave him, but in her heart, she knew he was right. And so she reined around, and kicked her heels.

The Saxons were barely ten yards away now.

'This is our land!' Ronan roared. 'Our God-given land. He will not allow these heathens to take it from us. God will protect us! God will give us victory!'

The shield walls met in an explosion of noise, as if Taranis the charioteer was riding in their midst, as if mountains trembled and cracked. Spears stabbed, chain mail sang and men fell. Anya felt vomit rise in her throat. The bards were lying when they spoke of the glories of battle. There was nothing glorious about this terrible savagery. There was nothing glorious in watching brave warriors cleaved, or hearing fatally wounded men crying to the heavens for their mothers.

Silvanus and his cavalry, in close formation on the left flank, were waiting to re-engage. Soon, too soon, he would be risking his life again. Ronan and Petilius were riding behind the shield wall, closing gaps, bellowing encouragement. A wind sprang up and banners tugged at their spears, as if wishing to be set free to join in the slaughter. Anya watched the red dragon of the Dumnonii, writhing and straining against its fetters and she wondered why everything that mattered had to be settled at the end of a sword, sharp from the grinding stone.

Both the Saxon and the British shield walls held firm. Men fell on both sides, but others quickly replaced them and the stalemate dragged on. Silvanus watched the carnage with a mounting sense of frustration. He was already aware of the first insidious signs of fatigue, aware of the pounding pain behind his eyes, aware of his aching limbs. He wanted to engage again, needed to engage again, before his battle fever dissipated entirely.

He glanced at Anya's sword, hanging from his belt. She believed the gods wanted him to wield it and, as unfathomable as it seemed, she also believed in him. His fingers tightened around the grip of the sword and then he drew it from its scabbard. The pattern welding ran the length of the blade, three writhing serpents melded as one in fire.

With the sword held high above his head, Silvanus engaged the cavalry of the Dumnonii once more. Julianus, in command of Ronan's cavalry, followed his lead from the right flank. Like the snapping pincers of a scorpion, the two units galloped across the field in an arc, gathering speed as they bore down upon the Saxon foot-soldiers from the rear.

The sword's newly sharpened blade caught the autumn sun and it blazed like a torch of liquid silver. The light flashed and fractured, so blinding it caught the attention of every man on the field, both Saxon and Briton alike, holding them entranced. And at that moment few doubted Silvanus, high king of the Dumnonii, had the blessing and the protection of his gods.

The Saxon shield wall split open like a ripe fruit. Banners collided and the Britons poured through. Few of the Saxon soldiers wore helmets, and skulls were cleaved, heads severed, and limbs hewn by the cavalrymen's swinging sword blades.

Like crows to carrion, Ronan's foot-soldiers swooped upon Hengist's banner, for the white wolf had stalked above the Saxon army as it rampaged through the streets of Aquae Sulis in a drunken orgy of slaughter, creating countless widows and orphans. The Britons killed the young Saxon banner bearer, and then they trampled the white wolf underfoot.

Hengist's household guards closed about him in a tight, protective knot but the Britons were in the grip of blood lust, and set upon them in a crazed frenzy of vengeance. With a mounting sense of disbelief and horror, Hengist watched his guards fall one by one. Aelfric was the last to die, wrenched from his horse, his body hacked to pieces in the mud.

And then the Britons turned to Hengist, swarming about him like furies from the underworld. He leant low in his saddle, swiping at them with his sword as if they were persistent flies. Battle fever was coursing through his veins, but a small part of him knew he could not hold them at bay for long. He told himself he was not afraid to die; he had a sword in his hand and the warriors of Valhalla would welcome him. But in his heart, he was afraid, and strangely disappointed. This was not supposed to happen. These wretches were not worthy opponents. He had always imagined that when death found him, it would be in single combat with a renowned warrior king, an heroic end worthy of an epic poem.

Strong hands were wrenching at his legs, trying to unseat him. He kicked out, felt his boot connect with bone and the soldier fell back, blood pouring from his shattered nose.

Hengist twisted and turned in his saddle, inflicting savage blows, but still they came at him. Beneath his helmet, sweat was trickling down his forehead and stinging his eyes. And so he did not see the young Briton who took his spear in both hands, and drove it deep into the neck of Hengist's stallion. The animal squealed in agony and buckled, taking Hengist down with it. He tried to struggle to his feet, but the Britons were everywhere, blotting out the light. He raised his hands above his head in a futile attempt to protect himself.

'I am the lady Anya's brother. I am the son of a king! You cannot harm me!' he screamed.

But the bloodlust was truly upon the Britons. They showed no mercy, as if Hengist was the living embodiment of the white wolf upon his banner, cornered at last in a forest thicket. Anya felt bile rise in her throat as she watched her brother die. At that moment, she forgot all the reasons why she hated him. She knew only that he was her flesh and blood, her kin, and it was her fault he was being butchered in the blood-soaked mud.

She wanted to scream to the gods for mercy, but it was too late. The battle was over and in the centuries to come, men would call it a victory, but at that moment she could see no cause for celebration. The hill of Baden was a field of blood and suffering, of dying horses and dying men. She closed her eyes, but the image of Hengist, hands raised in terror, pleading for his life, had burned itself into her conscience. She knew it would stay with her for the rest of her days.

THIRTY FIVE

The Britons stripped the Saxon corpses of their war-gear, their gold and silver, garnets and lapis lazuli, and shared them out as battle spoils. At Anya's request, they burned the Saxon dead on funeral pyres, hung about with shields, and the smoke drifted to the heavens, carrying their souls to Valhalla.

They buried the British dead in deep burial pits, some without grave goods in accordance with their Christian beliefs, others with battle armour and libations, in deference to their ancient gods. Anya stood at Silvanus's side as the pits were backfilled and the pyres blazed. She prayed they would burn away the memories of hatred and war.

'Ronan and I have signed the treaty. So I won't be returning to Dumnonia just yet,' Silvanus said quietly. He looked ill at ease, apprehensive, and she felt a flicker of alarm.

'What is it? What's wrong?'

Silvanus took a deep breath, as if mustering his courage.

'Hengist is dead, but Cerdic is very much alive and gathering his forces on the south coast. And each new tide brings more warbands from Germania.'

Anya expression betrayed her dismay. She wanted time to mourn all those she had lost. Her grief still felt raw but already he was talking of armies and war again. As if sensing her distress, Silvanus clasped her hands in his. 'It was you who told me I should ride out and meet my enemies from a position of strength, not wait for them to invade my kingdom and burn my villages and carry my people into slavery.'

Anya could find no words, an internal battle raging. Her head knew Silvanus was right, but her heart felt weary and broken. She longed for respite, for Tintagel, for the windswept beach and the salty tang of the sea.

Silvanus clasped her hands tighter still. 'My scouts tell me there's an ancient hill-fort, long abandoned, some thirty miles south of here. The local tribespeople call it Cadbury. They say you can see for miles in all directions from the summit. It's the perfect base to establish a garrison. From there, my cavalry can ride out and meet any army that dares to push into the west.'

Anya felt a scream building inside her again, a scream of self-pity, frustration and anger. Silvanus was looking nervous and uncomfortable, and she sensed he was plucking up the courage to say more.

'Will you come with me to Cadbury?' he asked at last.

Anya stared at him, open mouthed. What exactly was he asking her to do? To make a home on the top of an abandoned hill-fort? To stand at his side as he attempted to hold back the advancing Saxon tide?

It was an impossible task. And she wanted none of it. She wanted to return to Tintagel, to walk on the beach with him, to sit beside him in the great hall, to share his bed, each and every night. She wanted peace. A home, a hearth, a family. Instead he was talking of bases, and garrisons and endless war. Was this what it had all been leading to? Was this truly what the goddess wanted?

Silvanus seemed to read her mind. 'It won't be forever, a

few months at most. I'm as keen to return to Tintagel as my men. Once we have built the fortress at Cadbury, I will send most of them home. I plan to garrison it by roster, and no man will be obliged to serve more than one month per year.' He was watching her closely. 'Say something, Anya,' he pleaded.

She was about to tell him she couldn't leave the wounded men in the place of healing, but then she saw the expression in his eyes. It was so full of compassion, of love, that her despair and anxiety vanished into air like the drifting smoke from the funeral pyres.

She glanced at her sword, fastened to Silvanus's belt. It belonged to him now. It was meant to be at his side.

Just as she was also meant to be at his side.

'Yes, of course I will come with you,' she replied. 'Where else would I go?'

Despite the aromas of lavender and juniper, the place of healing still reeked of a butcher's block. Anya moved from patient to patient, her thoughts conflicted. So many badly wounded men. Maud would look after them, but nevertheless, she felt guilty walking away.

'So, you are abandoning me?' Ronan's voice boomed across the dining chamber.

Anya spun around. He looked so like his father, the same thin mouth curled into a belligerent sneer, the same arrogant stance. Not for the first time, she wondered if she should have simply left him to die.

He gestured for her to join him. 'I want to talk to you.'

Anya stood up, wiped her hands and followed him into the council chamber. She remembered her first impressions of this room, all those months ago. A fire had been lit at its centre, and the air had been thick with wood smoke. Vortigern had stared at her like a starving man laying eyes on a joint of roasted beef, and she had felt as if her life was over. A cold shiver ran down her spine. She yearned to leave Aquae Sulis now. The place was as haunted as Samhain Eve.

Ronan sat down on the raised dais, drumming his fingers on the chair arms. 'So, tell me, what does Silvanus have that I don't?' he asked lightly.

'You don't really want me to answer that, do you?' Anya asked wearily. 'It's not important anyway, because you don't want me. You've never wanted me.'

'Would it have made a difference if I had?'

'No.'

Ronan laughed. 'Do you know, you're the first pretty girl I've not wanted to take to my bed.'

'I can't decide if that's a compliment or an insult,' Anya said drily.

'Neither. It's a statement of fact. Sit down.'

But Anya remained where she was. The Roman chairs with their flaking paintwork reminded her of Vortigern. Everything in the basilica reminded her of Vortigern.

'I won't bite,' Ronan said mockingly.

'Vortigern is gone,' she told herself. *'He cannot hurt you anymore.'*

She climbed the steps and sat down, straightening her gown, a nervous gesture.

Ronan glanced briefly at her then threw up his arms in frustration.

'It's ironic, isn't it, that on parchment, I am the most powerful king in Britannia, but in reality, I am surrounded by enemies who would see me dead. I call for aid, and no-one comes but Silvanus, the man who made a cuckold of my father.'

'Are you expecting me to feel sorry for you?' Anya asked coldly. 'Thanks to your father's legacy, you hold dominion over half this island. Tribute pours into your coffers. But your father chose to rule with a big stick rather than a silver tongue. And Rufus taxed your client-kingdoms until your people starved. There's no wonder you face rebellion -' suddenly aware of the dangerous look in Ronan's eyes, she broke off in mid-sentence.

'I did not ask for a lecture on king-ship, Anya.'

'I am just saying that your father is gone. Rufus is gone. This is your time now.'

'If only it was that easy. I am my father's son.'

'You can be whoever you choose to be,' Anya replied. 'Gather good men around you, men you can trust. Their counsel will ease the burden.'

Ronan bristled. What did Anya know of such matters, this strange Saxon girl whose loyalty he had always questioned? He studied her for a long moment. What had Silvanus said at the council of war?

'We should pay heed to Anya's counsel. Do not forget she is the daughter of a high king.'

Unsettled, he spoke more harshly than he intended. 'You gave it to him. You gave that sword to Silvanus. Why?'

'Because he was meant to have it. The sword has found its rightful owner.'

Ronan stared at her. What was that supposed to mean? What, in God's name, was she implying?

But Anya was on her feet again. 'I must take my leave.'

Ronan frowned. He wanted to hate Anya. He felt it was his duty to hate her, but instead he found himself saying, 'may God keep you and Silvanus safe. I may have need of your counsel in the days ahead.'

417

Astonished, Anya's eyes widened, and then her face lit up into a broad smile. On the face of it, his words meant little, but they held the possibility of so much. Perhaps he would find a way to crawl out from Vortigern's shadow after all.

'May the goddess watch over you,' she replied, then leant closer and whispered in his ear. 'Do something for me. Maud is a good girl. She has the makings of a fine healer. Swear to me you will treat her with respect?'

Ronan's eyes were alight with mischief. 'Are you asking me to marry a slave girl?'

'That won't be necessary,' Anya replied briskly. 'Just leave her alone.'

Suddenly, Ronan's demeanour altered, all playfulness gone. Anya glanced over her shoulder, following his gaze. Silvanus was standing in the doorway, watching them, his hand on the pommel of the sword.

She straightened up, all formality now. 'Good-bye Ronan. Until me meet again.'

'Goodbye, Anya.'

She rose from her chair, climbed down the steps and went to join Silvanus. She did not look back.

They walked across the basilica hall side by side. Neither of them spoke, each lost in their own thoughts. The bronze doors that led to the forum were open and as Anya stepped outside her nostrils were assaulted by the acrid stench of burnt timber and funeral pyres.

A stable boy held out the reins of Silvanus's stallion and Anya's piebald mare.

'You haven't asked what Ronan and I were talking about,' Anya said quietly as they mounted up.

'It wasn't my concern,' Silvanus replied. 'And besides, I trust you, Anya. I trust you with my life.'

They travelled south-west along the old Roman road, through a landscape of low-lying marshes, of willows and quiet streams, of fish traps and beaver dams, and isolated villages huddled behind ramparts of swaying reeds. At noon on the second day, they caught sight of Cadbury hill-fort. It dominated the far horizon, rising high above the surrounding flatlands. As they drew closer, Silvanus sent scouts ahead, and they returned with confirmation that the hilltop was deserted save for a herd of grazing cattle.

The light was fading as the army began to wind its way through the maze of fortified ramparts and ditches. Massive earth slides, long since covered by wild grass, slowed their progress. The horses picked their way; the wagons groaned and grounded over the uneven earth. Anya stared at the high ramparts and thought of the men who had toiled to build them as a last refuge against the invincible might of the Roman legions. And she shuddered as she imagined the burning palisades, and the scenes of carnage that followed.

The grazing cattle moved away as the army approached, unnerved by so many people disturbing their quiet hilltop. Anya dismounted and stretched her aching limbs. The cold air tasted clean and sweet after the stench of a disease-ridden city, and the view was breath-taking. To the west, the sun was setting. To the north, a low-lying basin of marshland shimmered and glinted like glass. Glastonbury Tor rose from its midst, ethereal and aloof.

She had heard it said that Christian monks had built a monastery on its high summit. They boasted of guarding a rare, secret treasure, but she wondered if discretion might not have been the better part of valour. How long would it be before a Saxon warband came to relieve them of their precious hoard?

419

Silvanus and Anya spent the first night at Cadbury in a tent at the very summit of the hill. Silvanus dropped the tent flap, and knelt to remove his heavy leather cuirass. He flung it into the far corner of the tent, and rubbed his aching shoulders, glad to be rid of its weight. Next, he pulled off his linen undershirt, and tossed it carelessly behind him. Anya hugged her knees to her chin, and smiled.

'I am glad I amuse you,' Silvanus said wryly.

'Are you always so untidy?'

'Always,' he replied.

Dragging the bucket of water towards him, he began to wash, splashing water liberally about the tent. Anya found it impossible to take her eyes from his honed warrior physique. He dried himself with his discarded shirt, and then moved to extinguish the lamp, but Anya shook her head.

'I want to see you.'

Silvanus grinned but blew the lamp out anyway.

'Why did you do that?' she asked curiously.

'Do you want my men to watch me make love to you?'

Anya giggled, imagining the lamplight casting their intimate shadows in sharp relief against the hide.

'It's good to hear you laugh.' Silvanus drew her closer, his lips finding hers in the darkness, and she returned his kisses, her fingers lightly tracing the contours of his body. The heat built between them and the world beyond the confines of the hide tent faded, and was gone.

Much later, as they lay wrapped in each other's arms, Silvanus said, 'I wish I had more to offer you than a tent on a hilltop. But I will build a hall on this very spot, to mark our first night here.'

'I have everything I need,' Anya replied. 'At last, I have found the place where I belong.'

'You belong here?' he asked, surprised. 'At Cadbury?'

'Here, there, anywhere you are. It's taken me a long time, but I finally understand now. My home isn't a place. It isn't a kingdom or a fortress or a village. My home is you.'

Cadbury was transformed from sleepy pastureland to an imposing fort within a matter of weeks. Once the local villagers realised the king of Dumnonia had not come to slaughter them but to protect them, they were more than willing to offer their services. They cut down trees, scythed the long grass and nettles, and provided cows, chickens, goats, and sacks of grain.

Silvanus's men worked day and night. They built a wooden walkway with a palisade around the entire perimeter, twelve thousand paces all told. They used stone rubble and masonry from an abandoned villa nearby to reinforce the ramparts and they built wooden gate-towers at the two original entrances. And finally, they built a huge hall, twenty-one paces by twelve, at the very summit of the hill-top, over the exact spot where Silvanus and Anya had spent their first night at Cadbury. There were many carpenters amongst the ranks of the Dumnonii, and the hall was fine craftsmanship, with a jointed timber framework and a high thatched roof, supported by twenty oak posts.

They built a place of healing, a great hall in miniature, sweet-scented with freshly hewn oak. Taliesin's medicine box was empty, but even in winter the countryside had much to offer. Anya picked shiny hips and haws from the hedgerows and the last remaining berries from the elder trees. At the fields' edges she found dandelion leaves, sticky cleavers, couch grass and the winged seeds of the ash. Soon, the place of healing became a warm and ordered refuge, aromatic with the

421

aromas of simmering infusions. And it was not long before word spread that a healer had come to Cadbury.

Word also spread that the banner of the red dragon flew over the hill, the banner of Silvanus of Dumnonia who had defeated a mighty Saxon army at Badon. In the weeks that followed, men travelled great distances to Cadbury, all ready to pledge their allegiance to Silvanus, all ready to fight at his side. And the settlement grew loud with the clash of the blacksmith's hammer, the din of sword practice, the bellowing of cattle and the bleating of goats, with women's laughter and the sounds of children playing.

On the shortest day of the year, when the sun was at its weakest and could easily be overthrown, Anya ordered a great fire to be lit on the hilltop, to ward off the powers of darkness. A bull was slaughtered and she offered its blood to the goddess and as the night wore on, the entire community gathered about the fire, and feasted on its flesh.

Anya stood beside Silvanus, their fingers entwined. Sparks were flying high into the night sky. They reminded her of shooting stars, shining so brightly one moment then passing into darkness the next. She felt unexpected tears prick her eyes. Tomorrow they were returning to Tintagel. Surely a cause for celebration, so why were her emotions so raw and volatile of late?

One moment she felt contented, for there was such joy to be had in falling asleep in Silvanus's arms each night. But sometimes, when she least expected it, she would be filled with melancholy. Nor was their much respite in sleep, for her dreams had become nightmares, not only of things to come, but of things passed, of roads not taken, and lives not saved.

And then there was Mairi. Anya remembered the day word had reached Cadbury of her escape. Silvanus's expression had darkened, his entire body visibly tensing with barely suppressed anger. He had ordered everyone out of the hall, and then he had turned to Anya and said fiercely:

'You told me I should have put her to death and you were right, as always.'

Anya pushed the memory aside, for gradually, imperceptibly, dawn was rimming the far hills with a filigree of finest gold. The people of Cadbury Hill let out a cheer to celebrate the waxing sun, and the distant promise of spring.

Anya breathed a deep sigh of relief. The threat of Ragnarok, the danger of the world sinking into perpetual darkness, had passed for another year, but her heart still felt unbearably heavy.

'So many men died at Badon Hill,' she said quietly. 'So many fathers, brothers and sons lie in the death-pits.'

'But their sacrifice was not in vain,' Silvanus replied. 'Our victory has brought us great renown. Men join us every day, and our alliance with Ronan can only make us stronger.'

'But will he help us, or will he make things worse?' Anya asked. 'We need unity, not civil war.'

'You chose to save his life, Anya. You saw the good in him.'

But Anya was remembering Ronan's words. *If only it were that easy. I am my father's son.*

'There's no end to it, is there?' she said wearily. 'As soon as winter is passed, Cerdic will march again.'

'And we will be ready for him,' Silvanus replied. 'We will ride out and meet him, and we will defeat him, just as we will defeat any Saxon warband that dares march this far west.'

He wrapped his arms around her and drew her close. 'But tomorrow, we return to Tintagel, to burn the Yule log, and decorate the hall. It's too quiet here. I've missed the sound of

423

the sea, the endlessly pounding waves. And I've missed my old friend Taliesin, for all his grumblings.'

Anya smiled, but sadness still clung to her. War loomed, only months away. Perhaps she was naïve to yearn for a solution that did not involve bloodshed. Perhaps she was foolish to hope for a time when the Saxon newcomers might live peaceably alongside the people of Britannia.

A time when a British farmer might take a Saxon for a wife, or a Saxon warlord might choose a British bride. From those first tentative steps, might a new people emerge? A new, united people?

It was just a whisper of course, a half-formed hope, a dream. But perhaps she had already taken the first, tiny step, by falling in love with Silvanus.

He kissed the top of her head, then he raised his cup and addressed the crowds gathered about the fire.

'Let us drink to Dumnonia,' he shouted in his native tongue. 'Let us drink to our kingdom at the edge of the world!'

And then he switched to Latin. 'And let us drink to Britannia. May the goddess protect her!'

'To Dumnonia!' 'To Britannia!' cried the people of Cadbury.

'And let us remember absent friends,' Silvanus added and the hilltop fell silent, save for the roar and crackle of the fire.

Anya took a mouthful of barley beer, a gift from the settlement at the foot of Cadbury Hill. She thought of Rhys and her kin from the village in the shadow of the mountain. She thought of Eown, taken from her too soon, and Emma, her beloved sister who had viewed life in her own unique way. And then she thought of Elsbet, and Horsa and the kindness in his eyes.

At last, Evric broke the silence by proclaiming:

'I have another toast - to Epona!'

He raised his cup to Anya and as he sang, the Dumnonii joined with him, their voices carrying across the still marshes.

There will be chaos and destruction at the world end.

But a second earth shall arise.

And Epona shall come, from the depths of the green sea.

And she will bring hope and new life to this new, golden earth.'

Anya felt Silvanus take her hand again, and they shared a secret smile.

With the grace of the goddess, at least part of the prophecy might be fulfilled - for Anya was with child.

Authors Note

In the fifth century, Britain was balanced on the cusp of a new age. The Roman military and bureaucratic machine had gradually withdrawn, taking with them their manpower and craftsmen. Archaeology shows that whilst life continued in the cities for some time, a lack of central government made for a hand to mouth existence at best. Archaeological evidence also hints that tribal identities remained strong throughout the occupation, and quickly reasserted themselves to form warring, political units after the Roman withdrawal.

So, how much effect did the earliest Saxon invaders actually have on Britain? Gildas, writing in the sixth century, is under no illusions about their devastating impact. The title of his work, 'On the Ruin and Conquest of Britain' says it all. He tells us a 'proud tyrant foolishly invited the ferocious Saxons into the island like wolves into the fold, to beat back the peoples of the North.' Writing more than a century later, the Venerable Bede named the tyrant as Vortigern and the first two Saxon commanders as Hengist and Horsa.

These accounts are some of Britain's earliest surviving written records, although many modern historians point out that Gildas and Bede each had their own political agenda and are therefore unreliable sources. Some also argue the story of Hengist and Horsa is most likely an ancient foundation legend, and that the Saxon newcomers were relatively few in number and integrated peacefully. In the same vein, it has been suggested that Saxon grave goods do not necessarily signify Germanic descent, but could represent the local British population choosing to emulate the lifestyle and fashions of their new neighbours.

So, were the Saxons peaceful migrants or warring invaders?

As with the later Viking era, they were probably a bit of both, with a period of bloody conquest gradually giving way to settlement. New, distinctively Saxon settlements appear across England from the late fifth century onwards. Built of wood, turf and thatch, they often feature large, rectangular, aisled halls, and smaller sunken floored structures.

Interestingly, very few 'British' words are now part of the English language. The Britons passed on their names for rivers, forests, hills and Roman cities, but the invaders gave new names to their own settlements. In fact, many of our most common words, and swear words, have their roots in the variations of the West Germanic tongue spoken by the newcomers.

This novel is set at the very beginning of 'The Dark Ages' and it's true to say the picture grew considerably more complicated as time progressed. We talk about Saxons or Anglo-Saxons, but fifth and sixth century Britain experienced incursions from not only Saxon and Anglian but also Jutish, Frisian and Frankish warbands. Intriguingly, the modern local dialects in both Angeln and Frisia bear a startling resemblance to the English we speak today.

Cornwall, Wales and Scotland largely escaped direct Roman influence during the occupation. As a result, the Iron Age continued uninterrupted for centuries, which is why Anya finds herself in a Roman basilica in Aquae Sulis, and an Iron Age round-house in Siluria. Similarly, the Germanic invaders did not push into the island's 'fringes', and consequently these regions have retained their Brittonic languages and culture.

Although Christianity was adopted as the official religion of the Roman Empire in the fourth century AD, many rural Britons probably still clung the old gods. Indeed, Britain seems to have quickly reverted to paganism after the Roman withdrawal. Christianity had to be slowly reintroduced, beginning in 600 AD with the Gregorian Mission led by Augustine.

The character of Silvanus is based on the idea of King Arthur as a fifth century warrior, rather than the later medieval stories of knights in shining armour. Arthur is mentioned in several early manuscripts. The Welsh monk Nennius, writing in about 800 AD, tells us Arthur fought twelve battles against the Saxon invaders in the fifth century, culminating in the Battle of Badon.

The early Welsh poem 'Y Gododdin', praises the warrior Gwawrddur with these lines: 'He fed black ravens on the rampart of the fortress, though he was no Arthur.' The tenth century 'Welsh Annals' also link Arthur to the Battle of Badon. Modern historians who are unwilling to accept Arthur as a historical figure, usually claim these references are later interpolations.

Most of the places mentioned in this book can be visited today. The Roman city of Calleva Atrebatum (Silchester, Hampshire) now lies under farmland but its town walls are some of the best preserved in Britain and it also has an excellent amphitheatre.

Tintagel in Cornwall is as spectacular now as it was then. According to legend, it was the birthplace of King Arthur. Intriguingly, archaeologists have uncovered evidence for a high status fortress there in the fifth century, the period when a historical Arthur would have been fighting the Saxon invaders.

A great hall with associated smaller structures stood on the cliff top and finds included luxury goods: amphorae, pottery and fine glassware from the Mediterranean and Byzantine world. Tintagel may appear isolated today but in the fifth century its location put it at the centre of an affluent, international trade network which used sea routes as we would use motorways today.

The pretty hill-fort of Cadbury in Somerset has been affectionately called Cadbury-Camelot by the locals for centuries. Excavation has shown the entire hilltop was refortified in the fifth century and a large aisled hall was built at its summit, much as I have described in The Saxon Plague.

You can still visit the baths at Aquae Sulis (modern day Bath, Somerset) where the water still steams, and tastes just as foul as it ever did.

In York, there are the remains of a Roman bath house in St Helen's Square, and the multangular tower in the Museum Gardens once guarded the Roman legionary fortress (the smaller stones in the lower half of the tower are Roman, the upper half was reconstructed in the medieval period). In this novel, Horsa sits atop York's amphitheatre, dreaming of Elsbet. As an important Roman city, York would definitely have had an amphitheatre but, to date, no trace of it has been found.

I have not yet found the village of Anya's Welsh kin either. But I imagine it must be there, in some bleak, isolated valley, deep in the heart of the black mountains. If you ever come across it, please do let me know.